MEDICAL
Pulse-racing passion

Her Secret Valentine's Baby
JC Harroway

Breaking The Nurse's No-Dating Rule
Janice Lynn

MILLS & BOON

HER SECRET VALENTINE'S BABY
© 2024 by JC Harroway
Philippine Copyright 2024
Australian Copyright 2024
New Zealand Copyright 2024

First Published 2024
First Australian Paperback Edition 2024
ISBN 978 1 867 29956 1

BREAKING THE NURSE'S NO-DATING RULE
© 2024 by Janice Lynn
Philippine Copyright 2024
Australian Copyright 2024
New Zealand Copyright 2024

First Published 2024
First Australian Paperback Edition 2024
ISBN 978 1 867 29956 1

MIX
Paper | Supporting
responsible forestry
FSC® C001695

Published by
Harlequin Mills & Boon
An imprint of Harlequin Enterprises (Australia) Pty Limited
(ABN 47 001 180 918), a subsidiary of HarperCollins
Publishers Australia Pty Limited
(ABN 36 009 913 517)
Level 19, 201 Elizabeth Street
SYDNEY NSW 2000 AUSTRALIA

Cover art used by arrangement with Harlequin Books S.A.. All rights reserved.

Printed and bound in Australia by McPherson's Printing Group

Her Secret Valentine's Baby

JC Harroway

MILLS & BOON

Lifelong romance addict **JC Harroway** took a break from her career as a junior doctor to raise a family and found her calling as a Harlequin author instead. She now lives in New Zealand and finds that writing feeds her very real obsession with happy endings and the endorphin rush they create. You can follow her at jcharroway.com and on Facebook, Twitter and Instagram.

Dear Reader,

I hope you enjoy this Valentine's Day medical story. I loved flinging betrayed Sadie and tortured Roman into an Anti-Valentine's Party at the start of the book. They were both so smug, both certain that they wanted nothing to do with love. Of course, it's not over until the final chapter, and everyone deserves a second chance. Fortunately for Roman and Sadie, Valentine's Day happens every year…

Enjoy!

Love,

JC xx

DEDICATION

To my smart, beautiful and kind daughter.
Thanks for the office and the hugs xx

CHAPTER ONE

Valentine's Day

DR SADIE BARNES was in no mood for the party filling Vienna's Danube Hotel bar. She almost turned tail. Just her luck to encounter a group of rowdy singletons on her first Valentine's Day alone for six years.

She needed wine, stat.

Ducking her head, she bypassed the loved-up gathering and headed for the bar, where she intended to order the largest glass of white possible in her stilted German. Somewhere back in London, her ex was celebrating lovers' day with his shiny new, pregnant fiancée, the woman he'd cheated on Sadie with.

On any other day, she'd have headed straight upstairs to her room, especially after a long day of lectures and networking at the Progress in Paediatrics medical conference at the hospital across the road. Instead, she placed her order with the bartender and took a seat far away from the party, wearily sagging into the barstool.

Why was it, when you'd been horribly betrayed and humiliated, your heart thrashed to pieces, so easy to believe that every other person on the planet was blissfully in love?

Realising that she had veered into a cynical and self-indulgent wallow, Sadie thanked the bartender for her glass of wine. *'Vielen dank.'*

He smiled what might have been a flirtatious smile.

Sadie looked away, took a huge gulp of Sauvignon Blanc, no longer able to trust her instincts where men were concerned after Mark's broken promises. Better to focus her energy on work, on today's highly informative symposium, on returning to London tomorrow refreshed and professionally reinvigorated, this nauseating, love-drenched day over for another year.

If only the Valentine's revellers would let her forget.

The bar resounded with a series of loud bangs as multiple confetti cannons were discharged into the air. Sadie jumped, her hand flying to her chest as hundreds of pink and red paper hearts fluttered down on the cheering crowd.

She hadn't realised that she'd actually released the groan of irritation aloud until the man next to her at the bar spoke.

'That's two sighs in the space of a minute,' he said, causing Sadie to notice him for the first time where he'd been previously obscured by a pillar, as if he too wanted to distance himself from the party.

'But don't worry,' he continued in excellent but accented English. 'Hopefully, that's as raucous as they'll get.'

'I hope so.' Sadie nodded, carefully observing her fellow party pooper from behind her wine glass.

Broad-chested, dark-haired and with kind blue eyes, he was undeniably the kind of man any woman with a pulse would notice. But she'd been so wrapped up in her private pity-fest, she'd been blind to the hottie skulking with her in the corner.

'It wouldn't normally bother me,' Sadie said with a third sigh, 'but I came in to be alone, for a quiet drink.'

A drink to help her forget that there wouldn't be a red envelope on her doormat when she returned to her flat. Mark had always ostentatiously marked the romance of Valentine's Day year after year—a dozen red roses, surprise trips to Paris, candlelit dinners… But his grand declarations and overt shows of affection had been a baseless charade, as if Sadie had been a place keeper, a stand-in until someone better had come along.

'Me too.' The stranger's sexy mouth kicked up with a hint of a conspiratorial smile that turned him from good-looking to drop-dead gorgeous.

He raised his glass in solidarity and settled back behind the pillar, making it obvious that he had no intention of hitting on Sadie.

Deflated, she took a second look.

Maybe because he was so clearly uninterested in flirting, maybe because her loneliness was heightened by the rowdy celebration, maybe because she was so utterly done with relationships after Mark's hurtful betrayal, Sadie found herself eager to prolong the harmless conversation.

'Instead,' she said, drawing his attention once more, 'we find ourselves in the middle of a Valentine's party. There should be a law against that kind of thing.'

Matching her smile for smile, the handsome stranger this time eyed her with definite interest.

'Anti-Valentine's party,' he corrected, pointing to a heart-festooned poster behind the bar, which clearly advertised the event.

She dragged her stare from his intense eye contact to ponder the poster, which was written in German way beyond her translational skills.

'What's an Anti-Valentine's party?' she asked, intrigued. 'Ordering a drink is about the limit of my capabilities. As you can probably tell, I'm not a local.'

'Me neither,' he said, sliding his stool to her side of the pillar so they could talk without a barrier. 'I'm Czech, but I also speak German, so allow me to translate.'

Sadie nodded, mesmerised by his deep-voiced, accented English. Now she was faced with the close-up of his strong jaw darkened with stubble, the ghost of a smile on his distracting lips and his blue eyes dancing with humour, the tension in her body that she hadn't been aware of melted away.

'It says "Anti-Valentine's Party Rules".' He leaned sideways to read the poster, wafting Sadie with his delicious spicy aftershave.

The sexy Czech was around ten years older than her thirty-two, his smile deepening the crinkles at the corners of his eyes, which were framed by a dignified scatter of grey hair at his temples.

Fascinated that for the first time since her break-up seven months ago, Sadie could imagine herself flirting with this man, she took another gulp of wine to hide her body's unexpected swoon and nodded for him to continue the translation.

'"Rule number one,"' Blue Eyes said. '"You must be single."'

Shrugging one broad shoulder in a way that said it was pretty self-explanatory, he paused, waiting expectantly for Sadie's answer.

Was he flirting with her?

'Tick,' she said, emphasising her unavailability by drawing the symbol in the air with a nervous chuckle.

The man helping her to forget that her ex was as shallow as a puddle copied her gesture with a playful smile that left Sadie scoping out evidence of a wedding ring on his hand, only to be pleasantly exhilarated by its absence.

Was she flirting with *him*?

Even more shocking was how the idea fizzed pleasantly through her veins.

Why shouldn't she flirt with a smart, attractive single man? Just because her ex had cast her aside despite his grand protestations and empty promises, didn't mean that Sadie couldn't once more enjoy feeling desired.

'"Rule number two,"' her companion continued, leaning closer as he read so Sadie was aware of his body heat, a thrill of excitement waking up her nervous system. '"You aren't looking for a relationship."'

'So far so good,' Sadie said as she and her mystery man ticked the air in unison, their stares colliding and holding so tingles ping-ponged around inside her belly.

He *was* flirting with her.

Thrills of delight snaked down her spine. Just because Mark had thrown her away didn't make her worthless. Yes, she had her…issues, ones that Mark had denied were a problem when they'd first met, but she could still attract a man if she so chose. The right man, of course, one who shared her new philosophy on avoiding commitment.

'What about rule number three?' she asked, her smile gaining confidence.

This was the longest rule of the three and Sadie waited with bated breath, now fully invested in the idea of this stupid party given that this sexy and unexpected man obviously shared her relationship aversion.

But was it any wonder that she would lap up the attention of a kind and handsome stranger after being so callously discarded by a man who'd claimed to love her? Perhaps it was time she had a fling to put her ex's rejection and her decimated instincts well and truly in the past.

'"Rule number three,"' he continued. '"No…" How do you say…?' He waved his hand, spoke a few words in what Sadie assumed was Czech, as if he was struggling with the exact translation.

Sadie foolishly watched his lips as they mouthed the German words, torturing herself by calculating the two hundred and eighteen days it had been since she'd been kissed.

Long, lonely days filled with self-doubt that, because of her fertility issues, no one would ever want her again.

Having figured it out, he said, '"No hook-ups…unless you are prepared to risk being lured to the dark side of red roses, broken hearts and shattered expectations when the phone stays silent…" Or something along those lines.'

'Oh…' A stab of disappointment jabbed at her ribs. Even though she agreed with the sentiment, Sadie couldn't bring herself to make a tick this time, keeping her fingers wrapped around the stem of her wine glass.

'Well, thanks for the translation,' she said, studying the liquid left in the glass, hoping to hide her crestfallen expression that they wouldn't be taking their fun flirtation to the next level.

'It turns out that this *is* my kind of party after all, but I think I'll give it a miss anyway…' she prattled on, not daring to look his way. That last rule had dumped a bucket of iced water on her fantasy of hooking up with this like-minded stranger.

Except now that the idea was out there, it was stuck in her mind like a deep splinter.

'I just came in for a drink after a long day.' She waved her hand at her near empty glass of wine. 'I'm leaving Vienna in the morning…so a party probably isn't a good idea.'

She always over-talked when she was nervous, and he was the first man in a long time to make her nervous.

'But what about you?' She finally braved eye contact. 'Tempted to join the other cynics and commitment-phobes?'

To stop her mouth making more unnecessary words, she gulped her drink, trying to forget how, for a few minutes, while they'd flirted and learned how much they had in common when it came to love and relationships and the dreaded Valentine's Day, this compelling man had made her feel attractive again, whole, hopeful that she'd be okay, even if it was alone.

His stare lingered, sending shivers of anticipation down her limbs.

His answer, when it came, was delivered with quiet intensity that left Sadie in no doubt of his sincerity.

'I can't be lured to the dark side,' he stated flatly, cryptically. 'All that love and relationship stuff is for people hoping to find *the one* and start a family. That's not me.'

He shrugged, the slight hunch to his broad shoulders, the flicker of sadness in his blue eyes telling her that they might have much more in common than either of them had realised when they struck up this conversation.

Sadie froze as his frown-pinched gaze traced her face, pausing at her mouth in a disconcerting way. Was he, like Sadie, gutted about rule number three? Had he, too, been considering a one-night stand with a stranger to banish the loneliness?

'Me neither,' she whispered, fighting the absurd urge to reach out and touch his arm, to comfort and be comforted, certain that they each had painful reasons for being alone tonight.

A different kind of tension sparked between them, an awareness, recognition, a breathless moment of possibility.

Galvanised by memories of her ex's excuses and lies, by the hurtful truth of his betrayal, which had damaged the self-acceptance she'd worked hard for following her diagnosis of infertility in her twenties, Sadie bravely raised her glass.

'Well, cheers to us and down with Valentine's Day,' she said.

Just because she couldn't be a mother, didn't diminish her as a woman. This sexy stranger had helped her to cement that conclusion tonight. She had a good life, a career she loved, her family and friends.

With an unflinching gaze, he touched his glass to hers. 'To us.'

Holding his stare while they each took a sip, Sadie searched for relief that their flirtation would go no further, only to be pleasantly frustrated.

She didn't know his name. She hadn't been

looking to meet him and would most likely never see him again. Only she sensed an affinity with this intriguing man. And something in his eyes told her he felt it too.

'Well, it was lovely to meet a like-minded romance sceptic,' she finally said, noticing that the party had all but disbanded, the staff clearing away glasses and sweeping up paper hearts from the floor.

Almost reluctantly, she slid from her stool and held out her hand for him to shake, forcing herself to walk away. As much as she found this stranger wildly attractive, as much as she'd resolved to move on, she hadn't slept with anyone but her ex in six and a half years.

But maybe she should.

Mark was in London with his pregnant fiancée, most certainly *not* thinking about Sadie tonight.

Her stranger stood too, taking her hand so her stomach flipped at his warm and confident touch. 'It's been an unexpected pleasure—the best Anti-Valentine's Valentine's Day I've had in years.'

Sadie laughed, beyond flattered.

Although he smiled warmly, he regarded her as he had done all evening—with self-assured interest and a quiet calm she found so appealing after Mark's effusive but empty promises.

'Good luck staying single,' she said, her heart hammering so hard he would surely hear it.

'You too.' He leaned in and kissed her cheek in that European way, the soft brush of his lips agonisingly brief, the scrape of his stubbled jaw thrilling, the warmth of his body enticing her to admit how comfortable she felt with him, how similar they were, how easy it would be to surrender to this unexpected and fierce attraction.

Her hand was still clasped in his, neither of them pulling away as they faced each other. Vulnerable but safe. Strangers but somehow also allies against the folly of love.

Sadie stared into his blue eyes, the word goodbye trapped in her throat. Her resolve wavered back and forth. Was there an old condom in the bottom of her wash bag? Was she wearing the tattiest underwear she owned? Could they keep tonight anonymous and regret-free?

'Although I was thinking…' she said, emboldened by the fact neither of them had moved away, by the fascination and heat in his stare, 'that for a couple of committed singletons like us, we're probably safe to break rule three.'

'Definitely safe,' he said, his irises darkening by a few shades to denim blue. 'If you're sure…?'

His fingers gripped her hand a little tighter, his index finger swiping the pulse point on her inner wrist in hypnotic circles that almost buck-led Sadie's knees with desire.

If that simple touch could ignite her libido so dramatically, how would things be between them when the clothes came off?

She couldn't wait to find out.

'Who needs Valentine's, right?' she whispered, still holding his hand as they headed for the hotel lifts.

'Not us,' he said as the lift doors closed.

He pulled her into his arms, cupping her face with one hand. 'You're beautiful.' Tugging her hair loose from its ponytail so he could tangle his hands there, he tilted up her face.

Sadie feared she might pass out. But then his lips crashed to hers in a desperate rush.

She moaned into their kiss, parted her lips, and welcomed the thrust of his tongue, glad that she'd trusted this particular instinct. Had she ever felt this instantly attracted to someone? So power-fully turned on?

She became aware of movement—the lift as-cending, or her knees finally buckling, or the earth shifting on its axis like a romantic cliche. But then her fingers were tangled in his hair to direct his kiss deeper. Her back was somehow against the wall of the lift and his thigh was pressed between her parted legs while his hand cupped her breast through her blouse, toying the nipple into a taut peak.

This wasn't about romance. It was need, pure and simple. His and hers in flawless harmony.

The lift doors opened.

Flames chased them down the hall.

Sadie hurriedly fumbled with the electronic key card while he nuzzled kisses along her neck and gripped her hips from behind, his erection pressed to the small of her back.

With her groan of relief, the door gave way and they tumbled inside the room.

There was no time to activate the lights as they discarded their shoes and kissed their way over to the bed. No time for Sadie to worry about the state of her underwear as they frantically stripped off, kissed and touched as much of each other's bodies as they could. And no need to worry about protection as he reached for his wallet before covering her naked body with his on the bed.

'I hate Valentine's Day,' she panted out as he took one nipple into his mouth and sucked, sliding his hand between her legs.

This was so much better than she'd imagined, everything about him, from his ripped naked form and impressive arousal to the way he instinctively seemed to know how to set her body alight with his touch, perfect.

'Worst day ever,' he agreed, pressing a trail

of hot kisses down her ribs and stomach before settling between her legs to pleasure her with his mouth.

Except two condoms, four orgasms and one goodbye kiss later, Sadie knew without a shadow of a doubt that it was one Valentine's Day she would never forget.

CHAPTER TWO

Eleven months later...

SLIGHTLY OUT OF breath from rushing to be on time for her first day back at work, Sadie paused at Sunshine Ward's reception desk, greeting staff she hadn't seen for the four months she'd been away on maternity leave.

'Pictures, please,' Sister Samuels, or Sammy as she preferred to be called, demanded with a smile, holding out her hand until Sadie obliged by unlocking and then handing over her phone.

While Sammy and a small cluster of other nurses oohed and ahhed at baby photos, Sadie tried to stave off the pangs of heartache and guilt for leaving her two-month-old daughter, Milly, the tiny miracle that had turned her world upside down in the best way imaginable.

Sadie itched to grab her phone back. She'd only been back at work for five minutes, and already she wanted to call her twin sister, Grace, who was a qualified nanny, and check up on the baby. But there was no one she trusted more than her twin. They'd shared a uterus, for goodness' sake.

'She's adorable,' Sammy said, handing back Sadie's phone before answering the ward phone, while handing over the keys to the drug cupboard to another of the paediatric nurses, multitasking like a pro.

Praying that Milly would be fine—after all, Grace had more or less moved in with them the minute Milly was born, and Sadie had expressed enough breast milk to feed an army of babies—she turned her mind to work.

It was the usual hectic Monday morning at London Children's Hospital.

While Sadie waited for Sammy to end her phone call so they could begin a ward round together, she settled at a free computer terminal, logged on and opened her work emails.

Unsurprisingly, her inbox was chock-a-block. Filtering out the staff memos and hospital newsletters, she worked her way through what was left, mentally prioritising the list, and postponing anything non-urgent until later in the day.

One email marked 'Urgent' caught her attention. She clicked on it, groaning when the attachment downloaded—a red heart-festooned poster advertising the hospital's Valentine's Day Fund-raising Auction, which was being held in three weeks' time.

Distractedly, Sadie scanned the adjoining message:

...welcome back...you have been allocated a role as one of the auctioneers on the night... here's the list of donations/auctions...

Sadie sighed—clearly, in her absence, she'd been given a job no one else wanted. What with caring for baby Milly and returning to work, the hyped-up hullabaloo of Valentine's Day wasn't even on her radar. She was a single mum and a part-time paediatric registrar at the UK's busiest children's hospital. The last thing she needed was the added work of this romantic nonsense.

Not to mention the reminder of last Valentine's...

A hot flush crept up her neck as flashes of erotic memories popped behind her eyes. That man had seriously rocked her world. And talk about fertile...

'I'm sorry you got lumbered with auctioneer.' Sammy spoke over Sadie's shoulder. 'We drew straws for jobs.' Sammy winced.

Sadie waved off the older woman's explanation, relieved to have something else to think about other than a pair of intense blue eyes, voracious lips, a night of unbridled pleasure that had resulted in her precious baby.

'It's okay. It's for a good cause, right?' Distractedly, Sadie scanned the list of auctions, which among other things boasted a couples skydive and a week's break in Tuscany.

Impatient to begin her review of the current inpatients on the ward, Sadie logged out of her emails. While she wanted the hospital fundraiser to be a success, she wouldn't be wasting too much of her precious time on other people's love lives.

Now, more than ever, she had different priorities: her daughter.

Sammy grabbed one of the ward tablets from the charging station, telling Sadie, to her relief, she was ready to begin the ward round.

Except her reprieve was short-lived; it seemed the Valentine's fundraiser was the hot topic of conversation.

'If we can raise enough money,' Sammy continued as they headed for the far end of the ward, 'the proceeds will fund a new state-of-the-art sensory playroom and a much-needed makeover of the family room.'

'That's great.' Sadie smiled, torn between wanting to help and justifying anything that took her away from her time with Milly. There was no denying that the fundraiser was very much needed. Play was an important part of a child's healthy recovery and the family room served multiple purposes from a place for parents to relax to the venue where some families heard the worst news imaginable.

But her precious daughter was a miracle she'd long ago stopped hoping for after she'd been diagnosed with primary ovarian insufficiency in her twenties, a diagnosis Mark had claimed hadn't mattered. Until it had. Until he'd cheated and conceived with another woman.

But then, just when she'd finally put his betrayal behind her, Sadie had met a mysterious Czech stranger in a Viennese bar.

'Besides,' Sammy said, pausing at the whiteboard, which listed the current inpatients by name and designated consultant, the place where all ward rounds began, 'as an auctioneer, you'll have the inside details on the auctions before everyone else.'

Sammy winked, knowingly.

'Oh, I won't be bidding on any of the prizes.' Sadie flushed. 'I've just had a baby.'

No one except Grace knew anything about Milly's paternity and Sadie intended to keep it that way.

'I have no use for a couple's massage,' Sadie scoffed, nervous under Sammy's keen scrutiny, 'or a romantic dinner for two, unless there's baby food on the menu.'

'I know,' said Sammy, briskly wiping the names of those patients discharged overnight from the whiteboard and updating the number of free beds available for the day's new admissions, 'but you're successful, attractive and single.'

Sammy phrased the word as a question, still fishing for a clue about Milly's father, ever the romantic at heart.

'You should never say never,' Sammy concluded, turning away from the whiteboard.

'Nope.' Sadie shook her head, adamant. Dating was still the last thing on her mind. That amazing night with her mystery man changed nothing. Abiding by the rules of the Anti-Valentine's party, they'd shared a few hours of passion and then parted ways without even sharing their names.

It had been perfect.

Now Sadie had moved on from her ex's betrayal and moved on from that anonymous night, her life taking a wonderful new direction. And if she occasionally, that was daily, wondered about the man who'd donated his blue eyes to her beloved daughter, she quickly set such pointless curiosity aside, too embarrassed to admit to anyone but her sister that she'd had a one-night stand with a man she couldn't even begin to track down to let him know he was a father.

'I have everything I need in my baby girl and my job, thank you very much.' Unlike with a romantic relationship, when it came to motherhood, Sadie didn't have to worry about trust or rejection. Milly's love was unconditional. So there was no father on the scene—Sadie could focus on being everything Milly needed.

'Not even tempted by the main prize,' Sammy pushed, 'the one you'll be auctioning, the one everyone is furiously saving up to win?'

At Sadie's blank expression, the senior nurse elaborated, making dramatic finger quotes. '"A date with an eligible doctor".'

'No, thank you. Definitely not.' Sadie snorted, wheeling the laptop trolley into the first six-bed bay of patients.

She'd take warm baby snuggles and sick stains on her shirt over being let down by a man any day. Not that she in any way blamed her Czech lover for impregnating her, in fact she would always be grateful to the man for the most wondrous of gifts. And at least this way, alone, she didn't have the distraction of a relationship, the worry that she was being lied to, cheated on or unfavourably compared to another woman.

'Who on earth did you find to volunteer for that, anyway?' Sadie asked, smirking. 'The poor guy will be eaten alive. I hope someone has thought about security on the night, because it's going to be carnage.'

Paediatrics attracted a certain kind of doctor, and a hot single man who was good with children was sure to set both ovaries and hearts aflutter.

Sammy flashed her ruthlessly persuasive smile. 'Let's just say that he was coerced rather than volunteered. But Dr Ježek, our new locum surgeon, was happy to have his arm twisted for a good cause.'

Sadie rolled her eyes at the nurse's Machiavellian tactics, already feeling a little sorry for the poor, unsuspecting guy, who was clearly a good sport and might not be aware exactly what he'd signed up for.

'You might change your mind about bidding on that auction when you see him.' Sammy winked and fanned her face, girlishly.

'Not interested.' Sadie drew to a halt at the foot of the first bed, determined to remain the only single woman in a fifty-mile radius of the hospital to stay immune to the kind of man who would volunteer to have women fighting over him, outbidding each other for a date.

'Right, let's start the ward round,' she said, bringing up the notes of the first patient on her list. The sooner she started work, the sooner the day would fly by so she could rush home to Milly.

Sadie and Sammy had reviewed three patients and marked two of them for discharge when the ward alarm sounded. Leaving everything, Sadie rushed to the emergency, adrenaline coursing through her veins, with Sammy hot on her heels.

They entered the bay where the curtains had been drawn around the bed. The nurse caring for the bed's occupant looked up gratefully, her expression alarmed.

'This is Abigail Swift—Abby—six years old,' the nurse said, lowering the head of the bed while she spoke. 'She's one day post-op for laparoscopic repair of intestinal intussusception.'

Sadie took Abby's rapid pulse, noting that she was conscious, but groggy, her colour a worrying shade of grey.

'Blood pressure has been on the low side overnight,' Abby's nurse continued, 'but it just dropped further while we were mobilising Abby. There was a brief loss of consciousness.'

While Sadie spoke to Abby, introducing herself and reassuring the little girl, noting the sweat on her brow, someone turned up a dial on the wall, adjusting the oxygen supply through Abby's mask.

While Sadie placed a hand on Abby's abdomen, Sammy increased the rate of the intravenous infusion. Sadie checked the cardiac monitor, seeing that the girl's heart was in a normal rhythm but she was tachycardic and hypotensive, an indication that she was in shock and was most likely bleeding internally.

'Let's get some more IV fluids.' Sadie reached for an IV cannula and inserted it into Abby's free arm. 'And an urgent cross match for blood transfusion, please.'

She drew a sample of blood for the lab, worried that Abby might have a serious post-operative complication and that she might crash again at any minute. Sammy began infusing the additional intravenous fluids through the new cannula, squeezing the IV bag to speed things along. They needed to get Abby's blood pressure up. Fast.

'Has the surgeon been called?' Sadie asked, relieved to see Sammy's brisk nod of confirmation. 'Great. Phone X-ray, warn them we might need an urgent scan. And find Abby's parents.'

'They just went to the canteen,' the nurse said, soothing a now tearful Abby.

Bleeding was a post-op complication in any operation. Abby would most likely need to return to Theatre to stop the haemorrhage, which might have been slowly grumbling along overnight.

While Sadie labelled the blood tube for the

lab, the curtains around the bed parted to admit a newcomer.

Noting that Abby's blood pressure had improved slightly, Sadie turned to face the surgeon, ready to bring him up to speed.

Instead the floor dropped from under her feet.

It was him. Gorgeous guy from Vienna. The man she'd spent the night with eleven months ago.

Dressed in navy scrubs, his handsome face and the blue eyes he'd passed on to their daughter shrouded in concern, he skidded to a halt across the bed from Sadie.

Their eyes locked for a split second. Awareness she might have imagined zapping across the space, as if their bodies recognised each other, even as their minds played catch-up.

'What's the situation?' he asked, already focussed on their patient, as if Sadie was just any other paediatrician.

Herself jolted into action—there would be time later to discover what he was doing in *her* hospital—Sadie briefly outlined Abby's immediate medical history and the current state of the emergency. In equal parts stunned and elated to see him again, Sadie had no idea how she managed to sound so normal when her own pulse raced dangerously high.

In contrast, the surgeon took charge of the situation in that same calm, confident manner she'd found so attractive that night in Vienna.

As the frantic activity around Abby's bed continued while they all tried to stabilise the girl, Sadie wondered if she'd imagined the moment of shock in his eyes. But focussing on their patient helped Sadie's brain to compute his surreal presence.

He was a doctor. It made sense. She'd met him at a bar close to the hospital.

'Call the lab and get cross-matched blood sent around to Theatre,' he said to Sammy, while he quickly examined Abby's abdomen. 'Now, please.'

'Do you want an urgent scan?' Sadie asked, pulling her phone from her pocket to call the X-ray department.

'No time,' he said, glancing at Sadie's name badge, before unlocking the wheels on his side of Abby's bed. 'I'll scan in Theatre.'

Still acting as if he had no recollection of Sadie at all, no recollection that they'd shared what had been, for Sadie, a life-changing night, he manoeuvred the bed from the bay. 'I'll take her there myself.'

He turned to Sammy. 'Send her parents down to Theatre.' Without a backward glance, he steered Abby's bed from the ward, towards the lifts, leaving as quickly as he'd arrived.

Sadie stood frozen in the centre of the ward, trying to catch her breath as she watched his retreat. Her adrenaline faded, leaving only confusion in its wake. The man she'd thought she would never see again, the man who'd unknowingly fathered their beautiful little girl and literally turned Sadie's world upside down, was here, in London.

Why?

Had he followed her here having somehow discovered her identity?

No, he didn't seem to recognise her at all. He'd probably wiped Sadie and that night from his memory. He clearly hadn't obsessed about her in the same way she'd endlessly wondered about him during the nine months of her pregnancy. And since Milly had arrived, she saw his face every time she looked at their baby daughter.

Sadie's blood ran cold on that last thought. Was he here to confront Sadie because he somehow knew about Milly?

No—those were thoughts of a mind in panic. There would be a perfectly logical explanation for his appearance. As soon as Abby's emergency surgery was over, Sadie would find him and tell him that he'd fathered a daughter.

His words from that night in Vienna returned. *'All that love and relationship stuff is for peo-*

*ple hoping to find the one and start a family.
That's not me...'*

What would he say when she told him about
their baby? Would he be angry? Blame Sadie for
getting pregnant? Would he want nothing to do
with his beautiful infant daughter?

Until she could confront him, Sadie was left to
ruminate on her questions with only a sick feeling of dread for company.

Aware of someone joining her, she swallowed down the paranoia gripping her throat.
She glanced at Sister Samuels, who had returned
to her usual efficient and unflappable self after
the emergency, where Sadie felt as if she'd entered a bizarre parallel universe.

'So,' Sammy said with sly grin as the regular
ward activity resumed around them, 'now that
you've met Dr Ježek, our "eligible doctor", do
you think you might change your mind, bid on
that auction to date him after all? I told you he
was gorgeous.'

Sadie's stomach, already in a tight knot after
that frustratingly brief and surreal reunion, took
another painful twist.

'I don't think so,' she mumbled, trailing after
a chuckling Sammy to resume their ward round,
cold realisation dawning.

Her baby daddy was not only here in London,
a paediatric surgeon working in Sadie's hospital,

he was also about to discover that he'd fathered a little girl during their one passionate night together. And to top everything off, the man who'd assured her that he was unerringly single and couldn't be swayed was the newest hospital hottie, and it was Sadie's job to auction him off for a date with the highest bidder.

She massaged her temples, a headache brewing.

Surely her first day back couldn't get any worse.

CHAPTER THREE

As soon as Roman finished operating on his young patient, Abby, he headed back to Sunshine Ward in search of the woman he'd all but accepted he would never see again.

His mind reeled. She hadn't acknowledged him in any way. Did she want to pretend that he didn't exist?

Fortunately, his shock at seeing her again and the emergency unfolding had precluded conversation earlier. Abby's surgery had given him some breathing space, time to sift through his shambolic thoughts now that his mystery woman had a name.

He'd read her name tag: *Dr Sadie Barnes*.

Sadie. It suited her—playful and sophisticated.

His blood stirred at the idea of a repeat of that unforgettable night, but even if she had given him a second thought after they'd kissed goodbye in Vienna, it didn't mean that he could allow himself to pick up where they'd left off. He was still the same broken man she'd met then. He'd come to London to work, nothing more. One locum position in a series of locum positions that was his life now.

In his eagerness to get this situation—them working in the same hospital for the next month—back under his control, he quickened his pace, his rubber-soled theatre shoes squeaking along the corridor. On entering the ward, he spied Sadie at a computer station.

Despite the warnings he'd recited since they'd come face to face earlier—she'd already spent far too much time in his head since that night—he took a second to enjoy the vision. She was deep in concentration, her profile accentuated by her tied-back dark hair the colour of treacle. She looked good. Better than his well-flexed memories recalled.

The jolt of attraction he'd experienced earlier but had been forced to ignore shocked him anew, as if she'd defibrillated his dormant libido the way she had that night they'd met. Two lonely strangers who'd abandoned the search for love, but were still human, still alive, still capable of connection and passion.

When it came to relationships, nothing had changed for Roman. But a part of him couldn't help the surge of gut-churning excitement as he crossed the ward. He hadn't known it back then, but she would become the first woman since his wife and son had been killed to spark in him a restless kind of energy.

If he'd known her name the next morning, when he'd almost immediately regretted their 'no names, no strings' agreement, he might have been tempted to call, to try and see her again. Of course, the anonymous nature of their night together had heightened the mystery. But just because their careers were another thing they had in common alongside inflammable chemistry and a desire to stay single, the zero-temptation arrangement had been for the best.

'Dr Barnes,' he said, interrupting her study of a chest X-ray on the monitor screen, hoping that a few moments of conversation would break the spell she'd held over him these past eleven months and he could finally put his unprecedented fascination with this woman into perspective.

'Oh!' Sadie startled, her hand flying to her chest where her blouse dipped enticingly between her breasts. 'You made me jump. I...wasn't expecting you.'

Her cheeks flamed and she laughed nervously, flashing him that hesitant smile he'd found so utterly appealing the night they'd flirted their way into bed. She glanced down as if she had no idea how beautiful she was, another trait that, for Roman, fuelled his intrigue.

'I thought you'd still be in Theatre,' she continued, 'but here you are, so soon. Good. Great. I hoped we could talk.'

So she had recognised him. Had been expecting him. And now that he was here, he made her nervous.

This interesting news trampled all over his good intentions to stay immune. And that mouth... How many times had he relived her kisses, her cries, her satisfied smile?

'Sorry to startle you,' he said, still wildly attracted to Sadie Barnes. 'I was hoping we could introduce ourselves properly.'

Earlier when their eyes had met, he'd had to snatch his gaze away. The memories slamming into him had been so visceral, he'd feared his feelings would be obvious to all of their colleagues. Now, struck again by serious Vienna flashbacks, he held out his hand, his palm once more tingling in anticipation. 'Roman Ježek.'

Despite touching her throat in a way that told him their mutual attraction was as fierce as ever, Sadie glanced at his hand as if it might be a live snake. Then she gave it a brief but decisive shake, clearing her throat. 'Sadie Barnes. But you already know my name.'

Beyond the flare of arousal, there was something defensive in her eyes, as if by indulging his natural curiosity, in finally learning the name of his secret lover, he'd broken their one-night rule. But he'd bet his last euro that she'd wondered about him, too. If she'd known his name that night, she'd have cried it out often enough.

'I read your name tag.' He shrugged, unperturbed. 'Since we're colleagues, it made sense to be on first-name terms.'

He opened his mouth to ask how she'd been since they parted that night, but Sadie beat him to it.

'What are you doing in London?' she asked, her chin raised in challenge, her composure obviously recovered enough for her to erect a defensive wall. 'How did you...find me?'

Her aloof tone grated on his eardrums, her accusatory stare tensing his shoulders.

Rather than return to him, her eyes darted around the ward as if she was ashamed to be seen with a man with whom she'd had casual sex, as if she hoped to keep their connection a sordid secret.

Well, Roman was a gentleman; her secret was safe.

'Find you...?' Why was she being so...uptight? Did she think he'd purposefully hunted her down? Deliberately invaded her work environment like some sort of stalker? Would she prefer if he ignored her now, pretend that he hadn't recognised her? Even if he was into such game-playing, he'd spent the best part of a year trying to master his curiosity for this woman, trying to forget about their night of intense pleasure and honest expectations, a night Sadie clearly regretted.

'How on earth would I find you when, until two hours ago, I hadn't even known your name?' He'd only known the sound of her soft groans when he been inside her and the places to kiss to push her over the edge.

'Right…good point.' She nodded, momentarily appeased. 'Sorry, that came out wrong.'

He concealed a sigh, the excited gallop of his pulse puttering out as disappointment bloomed in its place. 'I would have thought it's obvious what I'm doing here. I work here as a locum pae-diatric surgeon.'

He wasn't about to pounce on her at work.

Admittedly, when he'd first moved to London, he'd occasionally fantasised that he might see the Englishwoman he couldn't forget on the Tube, or in a supermarket. But he'd never once imagined that they would wind up being work colleagues. But despite the way she kept checking him out, her gaze roaming his body, she *did* want to pre-tend that they were strangers, not a couple who shared intense sexual chemistry and knew each other's bodies to an intimate degree.

'I see.' She nodded and looked away. 'Of course. Yes. Right. A locum... Temporary... Good to meet you, Dr Ježek.'

But her weird attitude and regret of their night together—a night that, for him, had been rare and unforgettable—would easily crush his temptation to pick up where they'd left off—problem solved.

Grief had changed him. He felt certain he was no longer capable of a relationship, let alone love. A good thing, then, that, unlike last year when they'd seemed to share more than their cynicism for Valentine's Day, any relationship with Sadie, even a friendly one, now seemed fraught with the complications for which he had no time.

Reining in his enthusiasm, Roman changed the subject. 'I've just finished operating on Abby Swift. Would you like an update?'

He indicated the vacant ward office, pulling professional seniority to help him ignore the involuntary reactions of his body, which, despite his own reservations and Sadie's hot-and-cold reception, was still inordinately pleased to see her again.

'Of course,' Sadie said after a moment's hesitation. 'Good idea. Lots to talk about.'

She hurried into the office as if flustered, pacing as far away from him as the confines of the small room would allow.

Roman gently closed the door, keen now that they had some privacy to reassure Sadie that he hadn't pursued her all the way to London in order to declare he'd fallen madly in love or to propose marriage.

She turned to face him and their eyes locked. A crackle of electricity seemed to spark between them in the silence.

Roman's heart thudded. This was bad. A part of him had known it would be this way if he was ever to see her again. Chemistry as hot as theirs was hard to ignore. And despite her nerves, her embarrassment, she felt it too.

She blinked and a switch seemed to flip. 'So I understand there was some post-op bleeding,' she stated, her tone distant where a moment ago she'd looked as if she might tear off his scrubs and ravish him on the desk. A not unpleasant prospect.

'I saw the results of the scan,' she continued, her hands twisting together. 'Abby was lucky. That could have been much more serious.'

She really was nervous.

Roman concealed his frustration and confusion, feeling as if he'd missed the punchline to a joke. 'Yes—a vascular clip had worked loose. The second surgery went well. Abby is now stable after a unit of blood and should be back on the ward shortly.'

'That's good.' Sadie couldn't quite meet his stare, her arms crossed over her waist, her distraction and evasiveness becoming more pronounced as if he were an uninvited guest at a party that she had to evict.

Obviously she wasn't interested in any sort of personal conversation.

But why so uncomfortable? Was it just the sexual tension or something else?

This Sadie was nothing like the chilled and playful woman he'd met in Vienna. At this rate he wouldn't need to curb his attraction, to keep her at arm's length the way he'd kept everyone since his life had imploded four years ago when a car crash had taken the lives of his wife and son.

She would do the work for him.

Perhaps staying strangers back in Vienna had been serendipity, an escape from becoming ensnared in whatever was going on here.

Except they still needed to find a way to work together.

'Look, Sadie, I know it's a bit awkward,' he said, shoving aside his attraction, 'me turning up like this at your workplace, but, I assure you, it's just a coincidence.'

He paused, hopeful that she might relax, but

if anything being alone with him in this tiny office was making her more nervous.

'Coincidence…' she mumbled and began pacing again. 'It's crazy. What are the chances…?'

He nodded. 'I know, I was shocked to see you this morning. Pleased too. I thought I'd never see you again.'

He smiled his most benign smile while Sadie looked on warily, frowning as if he'd slipped into his native Czech and expected her to understand.

Now that they were away from prying eyes on the ward, it was time to clear the air, reassure her that he was the same man she'd met in Vienna.

'So, how have you been since we last saw each other?' he pressed on, finally acknowledging their one-night stand.

To his alarm, she paled further at his innocent question.

'Good, thank you,' she said a little too briskly. 'I'm very good, you know, busy. Work, life, the usual. Busy, busy, busy.'

She touched the edge of the desk, tapped her index finger there impatiently, as if he was holding her up and she couldn't wait to get away.

Well, he was hearing the message. She might still fancy him, but she wasn't interested in another hook-up.

'I won't keep you,' he said, himself still frustratingly tangled in the threads of their sexual chemistry, but determined to shake off all pretence now he knew where he stood with this changed woman. 'I just thought, seeing as we need to work together, we should, you know, swap a few polite pleasantries. Maybe dispense with the awkwardness. Put the sex behind us.'

The growing horror of her expression gave him no satisfaction.

She squawked out a strangled laugh, her eyes darting to the door at his back. 'Yes, we do need to work together. That's a good point. We're colleagues.'

Except he couldn't bring himself to just…walk away and ignore her as if they'd never been intimate.

Confused that they were now so obviously out of sync, when the night they'd met they'd effortlessly clicked, he ploughed on. 'I was going to ask you if you fancied grabbing a drink one evening after work, but I can sense that you'd rather forget all about that night and pretend it never happened.'

It was as if London Sadie was an entirely different person.

He'd never been one to play games, another reason he'd avoided becoming romantically involved with anyone after losing Karolina. He'd tried to make that clear in Vienna, and he'd thought, wrongly now it seemed, that Sadie was the same. But she was acting evasive, playing her cards very close to her chest.

'A drink…' Sadie blushed, looked down at her feet, chewed ferociously at her lip. 'Oh…um… That was kind of you… A drink…'

Kind of him…? Roman barely held in his snort of disbelief. 'Yes, you know, they sell them in bars and café's as social lubricants.'

'Hmm… I was actually going to suggest the same thing,' she continued, now meeting his eye, 'and then I found out that you're the hospital's "eligible doctor".' She made finger quotes. 'So, you know, a drink probably isn't the best idea…' She waved her hand vaguely. 'And as we've just established, I'm a registrar and you're a consultant, so we probably shouldn't, you know, socialise or tongues will start wagging.'

Was she filling the awkward silence? Waffling out of nervousness? Surely she would soon run out of excuses.

'And I work late most nights,' she rushed on, 'as I'm sure do you, with all of your operating and stuff, so that doesn't leave a lot of time for a drink, anyway…'

Roman tuned out, marvelling that she had barely paused for breath, her vocalised stream of consciousness obviously a nervous gesture and, to Roman's ears, one big let-down.

Her cheeks were growing pinker by the second. 'And my sister is staying with me at the moment, off and on, and—'

He held up his hand, stopping her mid-flow. 'Don't worry. You don't need to add that you're busy watching paint dry. I get it. You're really not interested in clearing the air, or being friendly.'

She flicked her ponytail over her shoulder. 'I—'

'Look,' he interrupted what would likely be another raft of excuses, 'just to reassure you, I didn't stalk you for eleven months, nor did I seek out a job here just so I could swear undying love.'

She snorted, her expression horrified, as if she had no understanding that he was joking.

'Yes, I thought we had a good time in Vienna,' he continued, 'at least it seemed that way to me, unless you were faking it. And given that we've seen each other naked and now have to work together until I leave in a few weeks, I hoped we could be mature and respectful, even friends.' He shrugged, knowing that the chemistry would pose a big barrier to that. 'But you don't have to make excuses. A *no* is sufficient. I'm a grown-up. I assure you, I'll be fine.'

He stepped back, giving her more space and preparing to draw a line under this puzzling reunion. Roman shook his head, defeated.

Where had that passionate woman gone? They almost hadn't made it inside her Vienna hotel room, their heated kisses spilling over from the lift into the deserted corridor while they'd fumbled with the room's lock. She'd been as insatiable for him as he'd been for her. They'd had sex not once, but twice.

But where that unguarded part of Roman only she had managed to sneak past had seen this chance meeting as a gift, an opportunity to once more explore the undeniable chemistry they'd discovered in Vienna, for Sadie, one night had obviously been enough.

'Hold on,' she said, frowning, jabbing a finger in his direction. 'A: I faked nothing and B: Don't try and make me out to be the bad guy here. You're the one who volunteered to date a woman for the Valentine's fundraiser.'

At his gobsmacked confusion, she clarified.

'*I'm* the person who's been chosen to auction you off like a prize stud. What happened to *Mr I'm Not Looking for a Relationship*? If what you told me in Vienna is true, don't you think you're misleading all those potential bidders who think they stand a chance with you? Not to mention that you're happy to be the fundraiser's eligible poster boy and then inviting me out for a drink. That wasn't the man I met in Vienna, unless your whole "not looking for love" thing was a charade. Who's fake now, huh?'

Roman frowned, trying to decipher if she was mad that he'd tricked her, jealous that he was expected to take the auction winner out to dinner, or indifferent beyond ensuring that the auction was accurately represented.

'*You're* accusing *me* of lying?' he said, stunned. He'd been honest that night. He wasn't the man for someone looking for a relationship, not even a casual one. 'Because if you want to talk about deceptions, I can't even believe that you're the same woman I met then.'

They faced each other, breaths gusting in mutual outrage. Any trace of the common ground they'd shared that night seemed long gone.

'Look.' He sighed, scrubbing a hand through his hair. 'I didn't lie to you in Vienna, and, yes, I did volunteer for the auction.'

Allow himself to be coerced, more like. He hadn't wanted to participate in the stupid fundraiser at all. But the formidable Sister Samuels wouldn't take no for an answer. And the part of him still wondering about his mysterious Valentine's lover had needed to forget about her, to accept that he was never going to see her again. Volunteering for a good cause had seemed like a painless way to close that chapter, once and for all.

But she needn't worry. He'd meant what he'd said last Valentine's Day. Love, romance, relationships were mostly for people looking for commitment and family in their future, and Roman had already found and lost more than many people experienced in a lifetime.

'Exactly,' she said triumphantly, aiming her index finger at the centre of his chest as if her point were spectacularly proved.

Recalling the lengths he'd gone to to make Sadie understand he was unavailable in Vienna and realising it now looked as if he were actively seeking a partner, he rushed to offer reassurance. 'It's just a fundraiser for a good cause. I'm not interested in relationships, the whole "marriage and kids" thing, I can assure you. Everything I said to you that night still stands.'

He was still the loner she'd met at an Anti-Valentine's party, still trying to outrun his grief and loneliness. Still trying to forget that he'd taken his once full and happy life for granted until it was destroyed by a drunk driver one rainy night.

Maybe if she realised that he was the same person she'd slept with because they were both safe from emotional entanglement, she could relax. He wanted a casual drink, the odd polite hello, not a lifelong commitment. Maybe then, they could get back to the light-hearted vibe of their first conversation, because this one wasn't going at all the way he'd planned.

Sadie seemed lost for words, so he continued, 'I'm simply going along with "a date"—' now it was his turn to make finger quotes '—to help raise funds for the hospital.'

Making polite conversation over a one-off dinner was one thing, but he wasn't the man of anyone's dreams. 'I'm not even going to be in London that long. I'll be leaving in a few weeks for my next locum position in Ireland. The entire reason I locum is because I'm not interested in putting down any roots. What's that expression? A rolling stone gathers no moss.'

Rather than look appeased, Sadie seemed to turn a shade paler, swallowing as if her throat was dry. 'No roots… Good. That's good news. Excellent.'

Her mouth formed a bright, clearly fake smile and she brushed a speck from her blouse. 'Because I'm not sure it's a good look for the hospital's eligible doctor to go gadding about with other women when a date with you is the fundraiser's most anticipated auction. The current family room and playroom are in desperate need of a makeover,' she added primly, 'and I want to help make the auction a big success and bring in as much money as possible…'

She was doing it again, barely pausing for

breath. One vague excuse after another. He mentally scratched his head at her evasiveness. He'd never met anyone so hard to pin down to a straight answer. Emotionally, this Sadie gave nothing away.

'No one is going to bid for a date with you,' she continued, as if flustered by the idea, 'if they see you out and about with every single woman you can lay your hands on. And on that note, you'll probably need to try and be a little more charming on the night of the auction, perhaps don't lead with the whole "anti-commitment" speech thing.' More finger quotes. 'We don't want to dissuade the bidders...'

Finally, she ran out of steam. She raised her chin defiantly, her pretty eyes flashing.

'What on earth is gadding?' he said, his lips twitching, certain that he'd never done it but intrigued anew by her jealousy. There was still a part of her that didn't want to see him take out another woman.

More mixed messages.

Just then her pager sounded. She checked the screen, her body visibly sagging as if she was relieved to have a reason to get away from him at last.

'I'm afraid you'll have to figure that out on your own,' she said, moving past him and reaching for the door handle. 'I have a patient to discharge, so you'll have to excuse me.'

Had they resolved a single thing?

'Of course.' Roman stepped aside, struggling to reconcile the dismissal and confusion with their obviously mutual and ongoing chemistry.

Some women he'd had casual sex with became clingy, as if they hoped they could change him, even though he was always as honest as he'd been with Sadie. His commitment avoidance wasn't a lifestyle choice; it was self-preservation for a man who'd lost everything he'd loved.

But *this* woman was acting as if she wanted nothing more than to return to being strangers.

She tugged at the handle with force, clearly hoping to make a grand exit so that he knew exactly where he stood.

Except the door didn't budge.

She tugged again, a soft grunt of frustration leaving her lips.

Roman hid a smile. Despite their ridiculous disagreement, which for the life of him he couldn't even decide what it had been about, she intrigued him, even when she was upset.

Flustered, Sadie gripped the door handle with both hands, her knuckles white as if escape had become a matter of life or death. She blew wisps of hair from her eyes as she jiggled the handle with enough force to yank the fixing screws from the wood.

She was so close, he could detect her perfume. It brought a fleeting vision of him spinning her around, pressing her back against the door and kissing her thoroughly until this confusing interlude, her blowing hot and cold, made sense.

Not that he would ever do such a thing.

She'd made it clear: they were done.

So much for the fantasies that had crept under his guard, fantasies where they'd gone for that drink, continued to discover how much more they had in common beyond rampant attraction and resumed their casual fling for the weeks he had left in London.

'Allow me to try,' he said, when she continued to battle fruitlessly with the door.

'Fine,' she said with a huff, relinquishing the handle and stepping aside.

But the room's large desk prevented her moving too far.

He gripped the cool metal door handle, aware that they now shared a bubble of close personal space. He waited, poised for the absurdity of their unnecessary confrontation and them being trapped in an office together to trigger the laughter that had once come so easily and spontaneously while they'd flirted.

He looked down and she looked up, their eyes clashing.

Every erotic memory from that night came rushing back.

Her scent triggered olfactory reminders of how he'd left her room that night with her perfume lingering on his skin.

Her lips parted on a barely audible gasp, her breath gusting as they stared, locked together in the charged moment of stalemate. She blinked up at him, breathing hard.

Roman glanced at her mouth, recalled that first heady taste of their kiss.

His invitation to a drink hovered on his lips once more.

No; it was over.

The handle gave way under his hand, the door swinging gently open without a hitch.

He deflated, the moment gone. 'After you.'

'Thank you,' she said, averting her stare, hurrying onto the ward.

Roman stared at her retreat, the restlessness back.

Yes, she'd been the only woman to worm her way inside his mind and set up camp since his wife, but they were destined to be nothing more to each other than polite strangers who worked together.

He'd allowed himself a brief reprieve from his

solitude that night in her arms, but now he'd have to ignore the sparks and steer clear of her for a few weeks. The Sadie of his daydreams and the Sadie of reality were two completely different women. Neither of them wanted anything to do with him, and that should suit him just fine.

CHAPTER FOUR

LATER THAT AFTERNOON, Sadie flashed her hospital security tag at the theatre receptionist, her stomach a tight ball of nerves and nausea.

How had she managed to botch her interaction with Roman so spectacularly? Before she'd discovered from Sammy that her mystery lover was the hospital hottie being auctioned for a date, everything had been so clear in her head.

Her plan had been simple: express surprise that he was in London, suggest a meeting outside work so they could talk in private and then casually inform him that their night of passion had created a miracle little girl with his blue eyes and Sadie's smile.

Easy.

In her fantasy version of the conversation, he would have expressed delight at the news and understanding that she'd had no way of contacting him after their no-strings hook-up. They might have laughed at the foolishness of sleeping with an anonymous stranger and praised their good luck that fate had once more thrown them together. Roman would see how much Sadie loved Milly, certainly enough for two parents, and they would work together for a few weeks and then part as friends when he left London.

Only nothing about the conversation on Sunshine Ward had worked out the way Sadie had planned. Firstly, she'd been terrified that Sammy or some other keen-eyed nurse would see them together, put two and two together and figure out that he was Milly's father, before she'd had a chance to tell him. Then she'd been struck tongue-tied by the claustrophobic closeness of him in that tiny office, his imposing height and muscular strength reminding her how hard he'd clung to her as he'd groaned into her neck when they'd been intimate. While she'd been dealing with the roar of renewed attraction—he was impossibly and unfairly even hotter than eleven months earlier—and the unexpected shafts of jealousy that she had to fix him up with some other woman, she'd become horribly flustered, dithering and mumbling her way through a list of excuses the length of her arm.

Initially, she'd been hurt when she'd assumed he'd lied to her about wanting to stay single in Vienna. Then he'd made it glaringly clear that he still wasn't interested in a family, even clarifying the ground rules while inviting her for a drink as if he expected that they could pick up where they'd left off physically.

Great casual sex? Yes!

A relationship...a family? No way!

He was a loner. A rolling stone. The fact that she still fancied him was irrelevant.

No wonder she'd utterly fumbled her calm and rational plan to tell him her big, life-changing news. News that might ruin any chance of the amicable working relationship he suggested. She'd over-talked, weighed down by the pressure of what she had to confess, of finding the right time, and saying the right things so he understood that, when it came to raising their daughter, she required nothing from him, neither emotionally nor financially. She just needed him to know of Milly's existence.

Resolved to pull herself together and carry out her mission, properly this time, she pushed through the double doors in search of the theatre staff room. She hoped to catch him between surgeries, and before she headed home to Milly. No matter how much or little he wanted to be part of his daughter's life, he deserved to know that he was a father.

As she rounded the staffroom doorway, distracted by the enormity of what she needed to confess, and wary of his possible reactions given their disastrous meeting earlier, she smacked head first into an impressive wall of maleness.

The breath whooshed from her lungs.

Firm hands gripped her upper arms.

Awash in the heady scent of subtly sexy after-shave, Sadie looked up, meeting the piercing blue gaze of the man himself.

Roman Ježek. She couldn't get used to how sensual his name sounded.

'Sorry,' she mumbled, determined to ignore how hot he looked in his scrubs by keeping her eyes on his this time.

Except her reason for being there dissolved in the face of how horribly attracted to him she still found herself. All she could recall was that he'd wanted to take her out for a drink and how, for a thrilling, irrational second, he'd looked as if he might kiss her when she'd struggled to open the office door.

No, those thoughts were banned.

Expecting some short retort, she glanced at his mouth, which was compressed with annoyance. Big mistake. He was close enough to kiss. He was a phenomenal kisser. She hadn't been kissed by anyone since him, that restrained and tender goodbye kiss they'd shared the fodder for all of her fantasies these past eleven months.

'Are you okay?' he asked, ducking his head

to peer into her face with his intuitive-seeming concern.

She nodded as her heart banged against her ribs so hard he must be able to feel it, given she was plastered to his hard chest the way she'd been when they were naked and lost in baby-making passion.

Why didn't he push her away? Why couldn't she find the strength to move?

'Fine... I'm fine,' she muttered, not trusting herself to say anything more sophisticated in case she blurted out the truth about their baby in an emotion-fuelled rush.

But it wasn't fair for him to find out that he was a father in a busy corridor outside a crowded staff room when he still had to spend the afternoon operating.

'I... I came to find you,' she said, wincing at how pathetic she sounded.

With Roman once more up close, irrelevant and pointless memories of Roman the lover blasted her body like mini electric shocks. The way he'd held her face when he'd kissed her lips. The intensity of his passion, as if he hadn't been intimate with anyone in a long time. The split second of regret she'd noticed in his eyes when he'd kissed her goodbye.

While their baby had grown inside her, she'd imagined scenarios like this, where they somehow met once more, their chemistry still off the charts.

Except Sadie knew from experience how reality crushed dreams. And she had bigger problems than erasing Roman Ježek from her erotic fantasies. Like how, flustered earlier, she'd offended him, as good as accusing him of stalking, and now needed to apologise. Like how, despite the way he'd looked at her when he'd asked her how she'd been, she had to set him up on a date with some other horny woman. Like how a man with his gifts—handsome, intelligent, confident, willing to play the prize stud in a Valentine's Day auction—most likely had a string of casual conquests littered across Europe.

And don't forget darling Milly...

'Why *did* you come to find me?' he asked, finally releasing her from his grip and folding his arms across his broad chest. 'I thought we said everything we needed to say earlier.'

Why was she here...?

Oh, yes!

'We did say...a lot, but I need to ask you something.'

There was so much more to say. But now that the time had come to apologise, to invite him for that drink *he'd* suggested and subtly slip into conversation that, against all odds, they'd created a life together, her mind had gone blank.

'I'm listening,' he said.

What was it about this man that turned her brain to mush and her body to molten need?

Stepping back, she mentally reprimanded her foolish libido. No matter what fantasies she'd harboured of a repeat performance of Vienna—the best sex of her life—Roman was a self-confessed commitment-phobe who would likely scarper abroad as quickly as his theatre shoes could carry him once she told him about Milly.

'I'm not interested in relationships, the whole "marriage and kids" thing... I'm not interested in putting down any roots...'

Determined that this time there would be no nervous verbal diarrhoea, she cleared her throat, her composure ragged. 'I've thought about it, and I think your idea of meeting for a drink is a good one.'

She sagged with relief, her message successfully delivered.

'Really?' he said, his expression sceptical, all trace of this morning's even-tempered and friendly Roman gone.

She hadn't planned for his refusal.

Before she could explain, utter one word of her apology, a nurse left the staffroom, squeezing past Sadie and Roman, who were still partly obscuring the doorway, shoving them once more almost chest to chest.

'What about your busy schedule and your list of excuses, and the fact that I'm to be auctioned off like a prize bull?' he said seemingly completely unfazed by their proximity, where she was struggling to forget how it had felt to be naked and crushed in his arms.

Sadie winced, looked away from the sexy peek of dark chest hair at the V-neck of his scrubs, regretting that her earlier dithering had armed him with ammunition to mount a counter-attack.

'I did make excuses,' she said, wishing she could just blurt out her announcement and then run. But this busy hospital corridor wasn't the right environment for the serious conversation required. Although she was struggling to come up with an appropriate venue to tell someone they'd unknowingly fathered a child...

Her flat was packed to the rafters with baby paraphernalia. She couldn't just invite herself to his place. It would have to be a café or a pub.

'I'm sorry about that,' she added, stepping aside so they no longer obstructed the doorway. 'I was just a little thrown by seeing you at my hospital, appearing like a genie from a lamp, looking...' she waved her hand in his general direction '...heart-attack gorgeous in scrubs.'

He leaned one shoulder against the wall in a relaxed slouch, a smile playing around his mouth. 'Gorgeous, eh?'

Sadie flushed and his stare softened slightly, although Sadie might have imagined his empathy, because he continued, 'But you think it's inappropriate for us to socialise, so why your sudden change of heart?'

Despite his justified objections—she had made him sweat earlier—he infuriatingly tilted his head in that distracting way she remembered from Vienna when he'd been playful and flirtatious and seductive, the look in his eyes doing things to her body she'd thought were impossible after the physical ordeals of pregnancy and birth and the fatigue of new motherhood.

Sadie chewed her lip, wishing that she'd prepared better for both his up-close hotness and his understandable resistance.

'You said it yourself.' She shrugged, hoping he couldn't sense her desperation. 'We're colleagues.'

Sadie wasn't ready to be completely honest and vulnerable with this cool and aloof version of Roman. It would be hard enough to tell him that they'd made a baby together.

Instead she smiled sweetly. 'It makes sense for us to clear the air, after...you know.'

She whispered the last two words, heat scalding her neck. She didn't want to talk about the amazing sex where they could be overheard by other hospital staff. She didn't even want to think about the amazing sex given there was now no chance of a repeat. But all she could think about was the amazing sex and how it would be criminal to waste the opportunity to see if it was just as good a second time.

The seconds ticked while he watched her with narrowed eyes.

The longer they stood here arguing, the greater the risk that she would be spotted by someone she knew, someone who might ask after the baby.

His baby!

The last thing she wanted was for him to find out about their daughter inadvertently.

'So, are you in or out?' She backed up towards the exit, trying to keep the emotional maelstrom taking place inside from her expression. She was close to begging, fearful of his eventual reaction and desperate to escape his magnetism, which only seemed to be growing stronger the more time they spent together.

Her rampant hormones were torturous. And her tingling breasts told her that she needed to get home to feed Milly.

Roman held up his hands in supplication, stepping closer so they wouldn't be overheard.

'Look, Sadie, I'm a simple man. I'm just here to do my job for the next three and a half weeks, and then I'll be moving on. I don't want to get involved in anything…complicated. I thought you understood that in Vienna.'

Sadie forced the frozen smile to remain on her face, aware that what he wanted—no strings, no ties, no roots—was irrelevant. A child was the ultimate in complications. He might be the same man she'd met in Vienna with the same priorities, but for Sadie, everything had changed since then, for the better.

But his reminder of his footloose and fancy-free attitude mocked her for the idiotic fantasies she'd indulged since seeing him again. Her hope that they might once more become temporary lovers, or find an amicable way to co-parent, shredded like sodden paper. She should have known not to trust her instincts when it came to men. Mark's cruel betrayal had taught her that valuable lesson.

A dull throb pounded at her temples.

'So you need to make up your mind,' he continued, his arms crossed, 'to be sure of what you want. Because I'm not into playing games.'

'I am sure,' Sadie said, growing increasingly frantic inside. If she'd agreed to go for a drink when *he'd* issued the invitation, she wouldn't need to grovel now. 'I just want us to talk, in private, away from the hospital.'

This was ridiculous. She was practically begging him to meet her for a purely platonic drink, when in reality she still wanted to tear his clothes off and could do no such thing.

The universe clearly hated her...

Still he made her suffer, his expression unconvinced. 'I'll be honest—you seem like a completely different woman from the one I met in Vienna. Evasive, hard to pin down, uncertain of what you want...'

Sadie gaped, horrified that he saw her most telling traits so clearly. But she *was* different. She was a mother now. To *his* daughter.

'I'm the same person, just a year older and wiser.' She hadn't lied to him that night, either. Yes, their chemistry fried her brain, but she wasn't looking for a relationship either.

He frowned. 'Earlier on the ward,' he said in that low, calm voice that was starting to irk her, 'I sensed some...what's the word in English...?' He glanced at the ceiling while he searched his vocabulary then clicked his fingers as he found the right word. 'Hostility from you.'

Sadie's jaw dropped. 'Hostility?'

He nodded, inflaming her further. 'I thought we could behave like adults, but one minute you're dismissing my invitation, the next changing your mind.'

'I was not being hostile. I think the word you actually mean is "circumspection". I was being respectful of our working relationship.'

But of course, she had dismissed him, out of fear and nerves and sheer panic, everything all at once conspiring to throw her into a state where all she'd been able to offer were blabbered excuses.

He stared, his lips twitching with amusement. 'I'll look up the meaning of that one while I'm also looking up "gadding".'

Sadie tried to stay aloof with him, but the absurdity of their bickering finally registered and she laughed it off with a shake of her head.

When she looked up he was smiling.

'So, will you meet me for a drink or not?' she asked, dragging in a shuddering breath, because this Roman was the man she'd flirted with in Vienna. A straight-up, say-it-like-it-is, intelligent and funny guy who would surely react positively to the news that he had a daughter.

Wouldn't he…?

But what if, for him, Milly wasn't wanted, even though for Sadie their daughter was a treasured miracle?

Well, if that was the case, it would be his loss. His disappearance from their lives would even be convenient, given that Sadie couldn't seem to switch off her attraction to the exasperating man.

He inched closer, his smile fading. 'How could I refuse such a romantic invitation?'

He looked up from staring at her mouth and their eyes met.

Sadie held her breath, trapped in his magnetic

force field the way she'd been when she'd lost her battle with the stubborn office door earlier.

'Thank you.' With trembling fingers, she took a piece of paper from her pocket and thrust it his way. 'Here's my number. There's a bar not far from here. I won't be at work tomorrow, so text me what night works for you.'

With a nod and an inscrutable look, he slid the piece of paper into the breast pocket of his scrubs.

Just then, a surgical technician appeared and interrupted them so they moved apart, once more at a respectable distance.

'We're ready for you, Doc,' the man said to Roman.

'I'll text you,' he said to Sadie, the intense and searching look he shot her before walking away setting off another cascade of hormones that left her weak-kneed and emotionally drained.

She waited until he was out of sight before she sagged against the wall, exhausted, all her adrenaline used up. This infatuation was bad. Worse than she'd expected. Because no matter how rampant their persistent chemistry, she needed to see him as a colleague, and a co-parent and nothing more. No lusting, no kissing and, categorically, no more amazing sex.

CHAPTER FIVE

THE FOLLOWING EVENING, Roman stood as Sadie walked into the small, intimate bar not far from the hospital. His nerves buzzed with excitement. She looked sensational in black jeans and a red top, with silver hoops in her ears.

Brushing a hand down the front of his freshly pressed shirt, he stepped forward to greet her, reminding himself that this wasn't a date even if they had dressed up for each other. Except his eyes moved over her figure, reacquainting themselves with her pert breasts, her slim waist and the tantalising curve of her hips.

He released a silent groan of frustration, relieved when she spied him, her smile that hesitant one he found so intriguing. Her approving gaze gave him a similar once-over as she walked his way.

It was still there, the undeniable chemistry that had driven them from strangers to lovers.

'Hi. You look gorgeous,' he said, using the

term she'd applied to him yesterday, outside the theatre staff room.

He pressed a kiss to her cheek, catching the scent of her shampoo, briefly closing his eyes against the flood of erotic memories he would need to crush, and fast.

'Thank you,' she said as he pulled out her chair before taking the seat opposite. A hint of wariness lingered in her expression; like him, she was nervous. 'Thanks for coming.'

'No problem.' He'd made a decision on the way to the bar: he intended to explain to Sadie why he didn't date beyond casually, why he needed to keep constantly moving, why he could never be truly *eligible*.

His story wouldn't be pretty, but would hopefully put Sadie's mind at ease once and for all, manage expectations between them so they could focus on being friendly colleagues.

Colleagues who needed a fire extinguisher to douse the flames of their chemistry.

The waiter appeared and took their drinks order and then left again.

For a moment, they faced each other in silence across the table for two near the window that Roman had chosen for privacy. It was as if this drink represented a fresh start, and neither of them wanted to put a foot wrong after yesterday's misunderstandings.

'I'm sorry—'

'I wanted to apologise—'

They spoke over each other and then laughed, the tension easing.

'After you,' he said, resting his forearms on the table and watching her across the flickering flame of a candle in a jar.

'I wanted to apologise for yesterday,' she said, glancing down. 'I was totally thrown by seeing you again, especially at work.'

Roman nodded, entranced by the way she toyed with her hair, which tonight was an exhilarating tumble of soft waves he wanted to cup to his face and inhale.

'Me too. I understand and I'm glad we're being honest. If only we'd talked about our jobs that night in Vienna. I was a locum at the hospital.'

Sadie smiled, rolling her eyes at their foolishness. 'And I'd attended the Progress in Paediatrics conference that day.'

Roman relaxed. The easy-going, animated Sadie was back, and the sight of her laced his blood with endorphins.

But he couldn't allow the sparkle in her eyes when she smiled to distract him from his purpose. 'Listen, Sadie, I feel like I owe you an explanation—I wasn't entirely open with you that day we met.'

Sadie waved her hand, began shaking her head

as if to shut down his apology, but he needed to lay all his cards on the table so they could move on as colleagues. The sexual attraction would fade and, if it didn't, the physical distance of his next locum position in Ireland would finally cure his obsession.

'Please let me say this,' he pleaded.

She stilled, her stare wary once more.

'I don't tell everyone I meet my whole story,' he said, dragging in a shuddering breath, steeling himself as he always needed to in order to speak about his loss, 'but with you, I think it's relevant and I want you to know.'

Stricken, she flushed. 'Roman, you don't owe me any explanations. In fact, I have something—'

He held up his hand, cutting her off. 'I want to explain. Please let me. Hopefully you'll understand me a little better.'

'Okay,' she said in a small voice.

The waiter returned with their drinks, the pause giving Roman a few seconds to prepare. No matter how painful to relive, he hoped his confession would finally settle any awkwardness between him and Sadie. She would see that he was the same man she met in Vienna, that he wasn't romantically pursuing her or anyone else.

That he would always be content to spend Valentine's Days alone.

'I was married once,' he said when the waiter

had walked away. He braced for the familiar dull ache in his chest, which varied in intensity depending on how occupied he kept his mind, but never fully disappeared and likely never would.

'Oh...okay,' Sadie said, subdued, glancing down at the flickering candle in the centre of their table.

'My wife died four years ago,' Roman added, keen to have his part of the conversation over with, as if spewing out the words would lessen their devastating impact.

She looked up. 'I'm so sorry,' she whispered, horror and compassion in her stare.

Roman shook his head, trying to recall the last time he'd opened up to someone. 'Since then, I've been a bit of a loner—the man you met that night where we were both avoiding Valentine's Day.'

Her hand covered his on the table between them, instinctively offering comfort.

His body jolted at her touch, the jarring juxtaposition between grief and arousal.

'I wanted to explain,' he continued, relieved to see she understood, 'how I might be game for a one-off dinner date to raise money for a good cause that helps sick children, but I'm not, and never will be, relationship material.'

She started blinking, her frown deepening. 'You're grieving,' she said as if to herself, moisture shining in her eyes. 'Really, you don't have to explain further.'

She looked crestfallen, more devastated than he'd expected. Sadie certainly wore her heart on her sleeve. He'd seen glimpses of her compassion for her patients on the ward, where she was a favourite with the kids. But to have that compassion directed his way left him unsettled, a return of the restless energy he'd experienced the night they met.

'I know, but there's more.' He rubbed a hand over his clean-shaven jaw, sucking in another fortifying breath, confiding in her easy.

'Okay.' Sadie nodded, her eyes round with trepidation.

Roman forced out the words a big part of him still struggled to believe could be true. 'I also had a six-year-old son. He was with my wife in the car the night of the accident. They died together.'

Shock drained the colour from Sadie's face, one hand squeezing his and her other hand coming up to cover her mouth. 'Oh, my goodness. I'm so sorry, Roman. I don't even know what to say.' Tears filled her eyes. She looked bereft.

Roman turned his hand over under hers, palm to palm, the gesture natural after their other intimacies. 'No need to say anything.'

He smiled a sad smile, not bothering to hide

his feelings from this empathetic woman with whom he'd found a surprising connection.

But now she knew his darkest moment.

As she stared into his eyes, Sadie swallowed, visibly struggling to regain her composure.

'I just wanted to be straight up with you,' he continued, 'to avoid any more misunderstandings. Of course, you're more than a work colleague, although we're putting our physical relationship behind us.'

She looked away, but not before he witnessed her disappointment.

He too felt the stomach-sinking emptiness. He would struggle to ignore their chemistry. Aside from fierce attraction, he liked and respected Sadie. Opening up to her felt good, brought them closer.

'So now you know; I'm not a stalker or a liar or a player. Why we had so much in common last year, wanting nothing to do with Valentine's Day.' He smiled, worried that his news seemed to have hit Sadie hard.

That she was so affected by his story touched him, but now he wanted to lighten the mood.

'Of course, I feel the same this year, but what can I say…? I found it very hard to say no to Sammy about the auction. She twisted my arm the first day I arrived.'

'Yes…that does explain…everything.' She'd

turned pale, seemed agitated, shifting in her chair and tugging at the neck of her sweater.

'We don't have to talk about it if you'd rather not, but how do you even begin to deal with something like that?' she asked, her voice a bewildered whisper.

'Staying away from the memories of my family life in Prague helps,' he admitted. 'That's why locum work suits me. I keep moving, keep my life simple—work, sleep, repeat.'

'A rolling stone,' she said, frowning, glancing down at their still-clasped hands.

As if self-conscious that they'd comforted each other in a moment of vulnerability, she slid her hand from his and took a shaky sip of her drink.

'Thanks for listening,' he said, hoping to draw a line under the subject while trying not to focus on how cold his hand was without her touch. 'I hope now we can work together for the next few weeks without any...awkwardness.'

Who knew, maybe they could even be friends? Although how he was going to switch off his attraction to her, he had no clue.

She nodded, forcing a smile that didn't reach her eyes, sat up straighter. 'Absolutely. That's what I want, too. Good. Great.'

She didn't sound certain. She sounded distant again.

'I'm sorry. My turn to do the listening,' he said,

recalling how she'd invited him for this drink. 'I interrupted you earlier. You wanted to talk about something?'

He smiled, encouragingly.

She gave a nervous laugh and couldn't meet his eyes.

His stomach sank. It made no sense. He'd been honest. Cleared the air. Sadie's bouts of evasiveness brought out his need for control. He'd deliberately kept his life simple these past four years—a coping mechanism. But now he wondered if, physical compatibility aside, he and Sadie would ever again be on the same wavelength.

Sadie's heart was beating so fast she feared she might pass out, collapse face first onto the candle and singe her hair. But after Roman's tragic revelation, even that humiliating scenario would be preferable to confessing the real reason she'd invited him there tonight.

How could she tell him about Milly when her news would surely heighten the grief she saw so clearly in his tortured eyes?

He'd lost the people he'd loved the most. Her chest ached from watching him paste on a brave face. She couldn't cause him any more pain. Sadie's revelation should be joyous and optimistic, not shrouded in the understandably heartbreaking sadness of this moment.

But would there ever be an appropriate time to break the news that he was already a father again, when he had such compelling reasons to avoid being in that vulnerable position?

Offering him what felt like a watery smile, Sadie trawled her stunned mind for a substitute topic of conversation.

'I...um...actually wanted to ask you some background questions,' she said, frantically improvising by taking out her phone. 'You know, for the fundraiser. I have to write up a biography for your auction, something to get the bidding started. Is that okay?'

The fundraiser. It seemed so trivial now.

'Of course.' Roman shrugged in that laid-back way of his, levelling his unwavering gaze on Sadie.

She blinked away the sting of tears, still haunted by Roman's grief and by what it meant for his relationship with his daughter.

Ever since he'd strode onto Sunshine Ward, Sadie had indulged fantasies of the kind of father he'd make, the kind of relationship he'd have with their baby. Only, considering what she'd just learned, there was no guarantee that he'd want anything to do with Milly and, worse, a part of Sadie would understand why.

How devastating to lose your only child and your partner in the same tragic event. As a new mother, Sadie could only imagine the heartache he'd endured, every parent's worst nightmare. He hadn't blithely sworn off relationships and family to enjoy his life free of responsibilities, as she'd assumed. He'd closed himself off to emotional entanglements as a defence mechanism.

That she definitely understood.

Focussed on her phone, Sadie opened the notes app. 'So what made you choose a career in Paediatrics?' she asked, pretending to read from a list of prepared questions.

The way he was looking at her, as if his intense stare might be able to read all her secrets, was not only terrifying, it was also leaving her hot and bothered.

How could she possibly be any more attracted to this man?

Except he'd opened up to her, trusted her with his deepest wound. Her hormones were running amok.

'My uncle is a surgeon in the Czech Republic,' he said with fondness in his eyes. 'Growing up, I knew that I wanted to help people. While I was training to be a surgeon I completed a post in paediatric surgery and I loved it.'

His expression became animated. It took a special kind of person to work with sick children.

But there must be moments when his work reminded him of his own son. It showed his already impressive dedication and compassion in a whole new and utterly appealing light.

'I like the variety of the work,' he continued, the spark in his eyes mesmerising, 'which is much like the old adult general surgical position that is now becoming obsolete as sub-specialisation grows.'

Sadie nodded, making brief notes on her phone, while every word he spoke embedded in her memory and set her nervous system aflutter. His commitment to paediatrics was seriously compelling and a massive turn-on.

No matter how hard she hoped, their chemistry wasn't going to just evaporate.

If only there were a way to move past it so she could focus on introducing Roman to Milly. If only it were as simple as resuming a casual fling to get each other out of their systems. But how could she allow herself to embrace the passion she felt simmering below the surface when she still needed to tell him her big secret?

She was trapped in limbo, wanting him but needing to stay objective.

'And the locum work also provides plenty of variety,' she said, unsurprised now that he needed to outrun such painful memories by keeping on the move.

The idea of him leaving London, of never seeing him again, hollowed out her stomach for both herself and Milly. Sadie and Grace had a close relationship with both their parents. She'd wanted the same for Milly.

But Roman had no intention of putting down family roots again, and she couldn't blame him.

'Until four years ago,' he continued speaking while Sadie tried to come to terms with the flood of her emotions, 'I'd never considered leaving Prague. I was lucky.' The haunted look returned to his stare, and Sadie wished she'd been more careful with her questions.

'I had it all,' he said. 'A job I loved. A loving relationship. A family...'

Then his world had collapsed, a devastating loss from which he might never heal. No wonder he wasn't looking for love; he'd already found it, was as emotionally unavailable as it came.

A crack split her heart. Her beloved baby might never get the chance to know this good man. His rejection of her precious Milly would sting, no matter how much Sadie understood Roman's motivation.

Painful memories flashed in her head—her devastating diagnosis, the years of yearning for a child, Mark lobbing blows, one after the other. *It's over. I've found someone else. She's pregnant.*

'What about you?' he asked, blind to Sadie's inner turmoil and feelings of inadequacy, which were shaking her like a rag doll. 'Did you always want to work with children?'

Sadie looked away, terrified that he'd see the knowledge of his daughter lurking in her eyes. A part of her, that maternal instinct, wanted to fight for Milly, to stand up and say, *I feel your pain, but you have a beautiful daughter who deserves to have a father.*

'Not really. I always wanted to be a doctor.' Sadie cleared her throat, torn between understanding for Roman's defence mechanisms, and heartache for their innocent baby, who to Sadie had been only a source of extreme joy.

Except it was too late; Milly was already here.

'I never really thought much about children,' she continued, lured by Roman's honesty to lower the guard she'd had in place since her fertility issues and Mark's cruel betrayal had left her doubting she'd ever again be good enough for a relationship, 'until I was told that I might never be able to have any of my own.'

Now it was his turn to be shocked, his turn to take *her* hand.

They really needed to stop touching each other.

'Then children became all I could think about,' she said in a rush, her history of infertility all tangled up with her omissions about their miracle daughter.

Offering Roman a sad, ironic laugh, she relived the years spent managing the pain of her diagnosis by refusing to think about the uncertainty of her future. And she'd been doing great at self-acceptance, at living each day as it came, right up to the moment when her ex had changed his mind about wanting children of his own, cheated and made Sadie feel worthless for something out of her control.

Although hadn't a part of her always known his grand declarations and big dreams and promises had been too good to be true?

Roman frowned, squeezing her fingers. 'I'm sorry to hear that, Sadie.'

Realising that she'd shared a deeply personal detail with a man she was desperately trying to keep at arm's length, emotionally, she batted away his concern. 'It's fine.'

Because of Roman, because of that night in Vienna, she no longer deserved his empathy. She'd been beyond lucky. She'd been gifted Milly. But as tonight proved, living in the moment worked, because the future was horribly uncertain.

'After that,' she rushed on, trying not to think how she was withholding one key piece of information, 'I was drawn to paediatrics. Like you I sidestepped into it and found a rewarding career that I love.'

'Is that why you're single? The infertility?' he asked, his voice soft, his thumb stroking the palm of her hand in the hypnotic way that loosened Sadie's tongue.

'Kind of,' she said, glad that she could at least be honest about one thing. 'The night I met you was my first Valentine's Day as a single woman in six years.'

He nodded, urging her to continue, his stare reminding her of the way he'd looked at her that night.

'My ex denied that my infertility bothered him for the whole time we were together,' she continued. 'I'd told him about my diagnosis of POI, primary ovarian insufficiency on our first date. I thought I'd come to terms with it, accepted that I would never have children, but I had a career I loved and a great partner. But his promises were lies. He changed his mind, cheated on me and left.'

Her smile felt brittle, but she forced herself to hold Roman's stare. She didn't want his pity. She'd toughened up since then, learned not to take people at face value. If that meant she sometimes expected the worst, that was a small price to pay for her protection.

'I'm sorry you were so badly betrayed.' Roman's eyes turned dark and stormy with repressed emotion. 'He obviously didn't deserve you.'

They stared at each other, their hands still clasped, the fragments of their pain scattered all around them like confetti. She hardly knew this man, but they'd shared so much: passion, secrets, the miraculous creation of a life.

Pressure built in Sadie's chest.

The words *Don't feel too sorry for me because I had your daughter* strained the back of her throat, clamouring to be set free.

Instead she whispered, 'So what now?'

Her fingers were still entwined with his, a reminder of the burning heat of his touch all over her body. A sensible woman would move, but she couldn't seem to make her hand obey.

How was it possible to feel so close to someone she'd known a matter of days? But as she'd learned from her years spent with Mark, time alone was no guarantee of intimacy.

'Now we've laid everything out in the open, I was going to suggest that we be friends,' he admitted, still stroking her palm in a way that was far from friendly while the heat in his stare sent darts of arousal pooling in her pelvis.

Except she *hadn't* told him everything. She was holding back the most important fact.

'But I think we should acknowledge our ongoing chemistry,' he said, staring into her eyes as if she fascinated him, as if he couldn't look away, as if some lonely, broken part of him recognised the same in Sadie, 'which kind of complicates things.'

'It does,' she agreed, the rush of blood to her head dizzying.

His eyes blazed at her admission. 'I can't deny that when I saw you at the hospital I envisaged us getting to know each other better while I'm in London, perhaps going out on a few casual dates, because now you understand why I'm not interested in dating anyone seriously.'

Because he was still grieving, still in love with his wife.

Sadie nodded, her head woolly with guilt and confusion, her heart aching with dashed hope and irrational disappointment. 'I totally understand.'

Except she wished it could be different, for Milly's sake, and perhaps for her own, too.

Then another thought occurred. The auction!

'Listen, I'd be happy to talk to Sammy, to persuade her to find someone else to volunteer to be our eligible doctor. You shouldn't feel coerced or uncomfortable. After all, it's just a silly fundraiser and not important in the grand scheme of things.'

'Look at you, protecting my honour.' He smiled and Sadie's heart skipped a beat.

He shook his head. 'But I said I would do it, and I'm a man of my word. Believe it or not, I allowed myself to be coerced because I was trying to forget about this amazing woman I met in Vienna.'

He'd been thinking about her all this time? Struggled, just like her, to forget about their night together? Dumbfounded, Sadie blinked, ensnared by the desire she saw in his eyes, by the memories of how good they'd been together, physically, by the certainty that they would still rock each other's world.

But now that she knew him better, she felt as if she could tell him anything. Just not about Milly. Not tonight.

'You were a balm to the soul I didn't know I needed that night,' he went on, 'so thank you.' He raised her fingers to his lips and kissed them like an old-fashioned hero.

'You made me feel desirable again that night, so thank you, too.' Sadie all but combusted as the sexy half-smile tugged at his mouth.

Did he too feel this deepening connection that left Sadie bewildered, because, no matter how strong, it could only ever be temporary? It might even be non-existent once she'd told him about Milly.

As if answering her unasked question, his stare dipped to her mouth.

Only the knowledge of Milly waiting at home stopped Sadie from leaning in for a kiss.

'I think I should go,' she said, slipping her hand from the comfort of his as prickles of guilt and confusion made her itchy under her sweater.

Their situation was indeed complicated. She needed to focus on finding the right moment to tell him about his daughter and on preparing herself for his likely reaction. Indulging in their chemistry now would only make things worse.

She reached for her phone and ordered a ride, eager to get away from him to clear her thoughts. She needed to forget about how good it would be to kiss him again so that the next time they met, she'd be ready to break her news.

Roman nodded, a brief flicker of disappointment in his stare.

'Can I walk you home, make sure you're safe?' he asked as they headed for the bar where he paid for their drinks.

Sadie saw that his offer wasn't a line. Roman wasn't that kind of man. But Milly was at home with Grace and prolonging his company meant prolonging the torture of wanting something she couldn't have.

Flustered by the conflicting desires tugging her off balance, she waved her phone. 'I've just ordered a ride, actually, but thanks.'

She needed to be careful. For all their sakes.

She couldn't allow her feelings for him, her attraction and compassion to cloud her judgement.

'Okay. Do you mind if I wait with you?' he asked, holding the door open.

'Of course not.'

As they waited outside, Sadie returned to the one light topic of conversation that felt safe. 'I was thinking… Do you own a tux? It might add an elegance to the auction. Get pulses racing and loosen up the wallets of the bidders a little, although your scrubs would also do the job, just fine.'

The idea of other women drooling over Roman gave her chills she had no right to feel. Just because they'd spent one night as lovers a year ago didn't make him her property.

'I can hire a tux. But you like the surgeon look, huh?' He smiled, knowingly, his eyes full of playful sparkle. 'I think the word you used was *gorgeous*.'

She rolled her eyes, laughing, but it was pointless denying their chemistry. 'Chocolate cake is gorgeous, that doesn't mean it's a good idea to indulge.'

He stepped close, ducked his head and whispered, 'Except once you've indulged, you know how good it will taste next time…'

Sadie shuddered with excitement and longing. He was right. Once wasn't enough.

Before she could make a mistake and kiss him again, a car pulled up at the kerb.

Sadie checked the registration. 'That's my ride.' Relief flooded her system.

Roman cast the driver an assessing once-over, resting his hand on her waist. 'Share your journey with me, so I'll know when you get home safely.'

'I will.' Sadie nodded, touched by his concern and horribly turned on. Now that it was time to part, she didn't want to leave him after the emotional roller coaster of their evening, after everything he'd shared.

'Will you be okay, you know…after our talk?' She hated the idea of him being alone with his grief and his pain, and his memories, when she had their beautiful baby girl to cuddle.

'I will. Goodnight, Sadie.' He swooped down and pressed a swift kiss to her cheek as he'd done when he'd greeted her earlier.

She froze, poised for it to last too long, for it to turn into something heated. She could so easily raise her face to his until their lips connected. His strong arms would encircle her, his hand between her shoulder blades. Their lips would lock with passion while their bodies met once more from mouth to thigh…

It would feel so good. Better, perhaps, than the last time when they'd been total strangers.

But their situation was more complex now. This time there would be no walking away un-scathed. She cared about Roman. How could she not? He was Milly's father. A kind and honourable and broken man.

Wary of undoing the fragile emotional ties they'd woven in the bar, she stepped back.

It was only their daughter, waiting at home for her last feed, that gave her the strength to hurry into the waiting car.

Later that night, still horribly conflicted, she hugged a sleeping Milly, who was warm and safe and replete after her feed. The baby's downy hair tickled Sadie's lips as she pressed a kiss to their daughter's forehead.

'I was wrong about your father,' she whis-pered, thinking about the final text he'd sent shortly after she'd arrived home.

Thanks for letting me know you're safe and thanks for listening.

'He's complex. Hurting. I just hope that when he finally meets you, you bring him as much joy as you've brought me.'

Her final thought just before she fell asleep was that she was in an impossible position. She couldn't fall back into bed with him, no matter how much she wanted to. But until she found the perfect moment, she couldn't tell him the news she hoped would be welcome. She had no idea what to do next, but she'd have to do it soon, before her options became even more limited.

CHAPTER SIX

TWO DAYS LATER, in the early hours of the morning, Sadie sat at the bedside of eight-year-old Josh, her stare obsessively drawn to the monitor recording his oxygen saturation levels, pulse and respiratory rate. The young boy, who was also one of Roman's patients, had been admitted a week ago for an urgent splenectomy following injuries sustained in a car crash. He'd lost a lot of blood, requiring a transfusion, and had spent several days post-op on ICU.

He'd already been through so much, and today, at the start of Sadie's night shift, Josh had spiked a fever. Sadie had diagnosed his latest setback—a post-op chest infection that required close monitoring.

She shifted in the hard plastic chair, looking down at the sleeping boy. The unease making her extra watchful tonight was all tangled up with her constant thoughts of Roman, who'd lost a son around this boy's age. Ever since he'd bravely shared his story with her, she hadn't been able to get Roman off her mind.

Roman's team had been on call, the ward busy as usual, so they'd only seen each other from a distance a few times, shared a nod of greeting and a secret look. Sadie had even texted him 'Thinking of you' messages.

But as the days passed, the urge to track him down and blurt out her secret grew stronger.

Before she could wonder for the millionth time just how she would utter the words *You have a daughter*, the curtains around Josh's bed swished aside and Roman appeared, as if he'd heard his name whisper through her mind.

His brief smile for Sadie lit her up inside.

'How is he doing?' he asked, glancing at the monitors, his concern for their patient mirroring her own.

She rose and joined him at the foot of the bed, close but not touching, the air between them charged with electricity.

'He's stable at the moment,' she said in a hushed voice, some of the tension leaving her now that Roman was here to share Josh's care. 'I've started broad spectrum IV antibiotics and made an urgent referral for physiotherapy for the morning. Hopefully we can get on top of the infection.'

The last thing anyone wanted was to see Josh back in ICU.

'Let's talk in the office,' Roman said, touching her arm and leading the way just as Josh's nurse arrived to repeat his observations and note them on his bedside chart.

'I encouraged his parents to grab a hot drink and some toast in the family room,' Sadie said as they entered the small ward office. She'd left Josh's chest film displayed on the monitor, and Roman paused to examine the X-ray.

'The consolidation is subtle; good spotting,' Roman said, flicking her an impressed smile that, despite her concern for this patient, did silly things to her already elevated pulse.

Sadie nodded, unable to shake her unease, probably because, she couldn't help but draw parallels between Josh and Roman's son.

Looking at him now, knowing that Milly shared his blue eyes, she wondered what Roman's boy had been like. Had he looked like his father? Would baby Milly remind Roman of her half-brother? And how could he possibly feel joy for his daughter, having lost his son in such a sudden and senseless way?

'You're worried,' he stated, his stare full of understanding and compassion, because they shared a profession that often took an emotional toll.

The stakes seemed higher in paediatrics than

adult medicine. Some young patients faced more hurdles than others for no rhyme or reason. Being objective was a big part of their job.

'A little,' she admitted with a small sigh. 'We managed to get a sputum sample for the lab before we started the antibiotics.'

Maybe because she was now a mother, or maybe because she knew what Roman had been through, Sadie couldn't help but see every case through the eyes of a parent.

'Hopefully we'll be able to target the correct pathogen with our treatment.' Sadie shrugged, looking away from Roman's probing stare because she could read him so easily now that she understood his past.

Could he read her in the same way? Could he see that, in addition to her patients, Sadie was worried for them: her, Milly and Roman?

'Then you're doing everything you can,' he said, stepping closer to rest a hand on her shoulder. 'Tell me what else is bothering you.'

Of course he would intuitively sense Sadie's hesitation in Josh's case. He was a good doctor, and he had personal experience of how suddenly things could go wrong.

'I don't know.' Sadie glanced at her feet because she was hiding something life-changing from him.

Admitting that she was worried for this patient

felt like admitting that she was worried for the future she tried to avoid examining.

'Sometimes it's hard to stay detached...' she said.

From work... From him... From wanting impossible things...

She'd perfected living in the moment, but, in light of Roman's tragic past, she couldn't help but wonder if they'd be able to find a way to make their complex and emotionally charged situation work. She didn't want any of them to be hurt, but of course she couldn't voice any of that.

'Sometimes a patient just gets to you.' Roman tilted his head, understanding in his eyes. 'We're only human.'

That he understood her professional concerns so well left her irrationally close to tears.

'Things always feel more serious in the middle of the night.' He slid his hand down the length of her arm and took her hand. 'I'll check in with you both again when the sun's up. Fresh perspective.'

Sadie nodded, grateful for his support, basking in the heat of his illicit touch that she'd grown to expect in just these few short days. Desperation to unburden herself fully rose up in her chest. But the more time that passed, the harder it was to find the right moment to tell him about their baby.

It was three a.m. Roman would be on his way back to Theatre. He needed to work. She couldn't be selfish, just because her secret weighed more and more heavily.

'How are *you* doing since we talked the other night?' She clung to his hand. 'I haven't been able to stop thinking about you. Worrying. Our work must be triggering sometimes.'

She'd watched him on the ward these past few days, her respect for him growing, alongside her desire. His calm manner never failed to put both patients and parents at ease, just as he'd reassured Sadie tonight. He always seemed to be the last surgeon to go home and the first one there in the morning. Even now, he'd obviously come up to the ward in between surgeries to check on the sickest of his patients.

Seriously attractive dedication.

'You don't have to worry about me.' He smiled a heartbreaking little half-smile, squeezing her fingers so a thrill zapped up her arm. 'I've developed coping strategies over the years, some of which probably aren't too healthy—you might have noticed I'm a bit of a workaholic.'

Sadie's heart fought its way into her throat as they stared at each other. If only they were anywhere but at work. She would hold him, be there for him the way he was there for her tonight, show him that he wasn't alone.

Except he chose to be alone. That was how he coped.

Her stomach fell, her feelings redundant.

As if deciding he could trust her with his most honest response, Roman sobered. 'Besides, I'm more scared to forget than to remember.'

The huge lump in her throat made breathing hard. 'Scared to forget your family?'

Her voice was an awed whisper that he trusted her with such a deeply private admission. But it also brough fresh waves of guilt that she was carrying such a monumental secret.

Roman gave a curt nod, his eyes tortured. 'My son in particular. I had many more years of memories with Karolina.'

'I'm sorry.' She gripped his hand tighter, aware that she should let them both go back to work. 'Do you mind me asking—what was your son's name?'

'I don't mind. His name was Mikolas.' His eyes shone with love for his little boy. 'We called him Miko.'

'Miko.' Sadie said, blinking away the burn of tears. 'I like that.'

The name painted a picture of an energetic little boy, with a contagious giggle and Roman's cheeky smile. Surely a man with Roman's capacity for love and commitment would, in time, welcome Milly into his heart?

They stood in silence, sad smiles fading. The tension in the room shifted.

'You have a big heart, Sadie.' He cupped her cheek and swiped his thumb over her cheekbone, his touch a brand, sharpening her awareness of every inch of him.

Sadie's stare latched onto the intricate depths of his irises. 'So do you,' she whispered.

'Basic job requirement.' He shrugged, the light-hearted comment most likely offered as a lifeline, an escape from the moment of intimacy into which they'd somehow stumbled.

But Sadie was right where she wanted to be.

'It makes you a good doctor,' he continued, his stare moving over her face, 'one who relates easily to people. But also makes you vulnerable to compassion fatigue. Look after yourself, okay?'

Sadie nodded, overwhelmed that he cared. She *was* tired, but her fatigue came from fighting this chemistry every time they spoke. She was tired of second-guessing her feelings. Sometimes, you had to follow your instincts, even when they'd been brought into question by your past mistakes.

Vienna hadn't been a mistake.

Surely one more kiss wouldn't be either.

She closed the gap, her heartbeat pulsing in her fingertips, clanging in her ears, like a roar.

Roman's expression shifted from conflicted to surrender.

He gripped her face in both hands, their lips connecting.

Desperation clawed at Sadie. Hot. Urgent. Crazed.

She tugged his neck and parted her lips, matching the passion of his kiss. Zero hesitation.

It *was* as good as before. Better.

Sadie closed her eyes as his arms gripped her so tightly, she couldn't breathe. But she didn't want to breathe in case she came to her senses. In case Roman came to his.

They were kissing. At work.

Outside the room, the ward was quiet, most of the patients asleep while the night staff made silent rounds. But they'd left the door ajar. Anyone could walk in. Not that Sadie could bring herself to stop.

Roman slid his hands around her waist. She gripped his bunched shoulders, tunnelled her fingers into his hair as she inched them towards the desk, resting her butt on the edge. She tangled her tongue with his, needing to condense everything she wanted, everything she needed into this moment of madness.

Soon she'd stop. Any second now.

Roman grunted, pressing his body between her parted thighs, snatching kiss after kiss in a frantic rush that told Sadie he'd struggled with wanting her every inch as much as she'd fought her desire for him.

Gifting herself one last minute of bliss, Sadie kissed him back, finally admitting that, for her, this had been inevitable from the moment he'd walked onto her ward. It didn't matter that it could only be temporary. Sadie was an expert at living in the moment.

Except there was one thing that *did* matter: Milly. Roman's daughter, the baby they'd made the last time they'd allowed their passion to override all else. A baby he knew nothing about.

With a sickening lurch of her stomach, she tore her mouth away.

'We can't do this.' She panted, guilt a scald creeping over her skin.

It took monumental effort to shove at his shoulders, but she succeeded, standing and moving away.

'Of course,' he said, his expression dazed and confused and then contrite.

He glanced at the door behind him and scrubbed a hand over his face. 'I'm sorry. I wasn't thinking.'

Sadie shook her head violently. If only their problems were simply an ill-judged smooch in the workplace. But they had bigger issues, and, perfect timing or not, Sadie could delay no longer, her secret pressing down on her like a lead straightjacket.

She gripped his arm, willing him to show the same caring and compassionate side that emerged for his patients and colleagues. The time had come to tell him. Even if it ruined the connection they shared. Even if her news was devastating. Even if he reacted with anger and accusation and wanted nothing to do with darling Milly, it was time Roman knew about his daughter.

Breathing hard, Roman's head spun like a case of vertigo after being so violently ripped back to his senses.

'No, I'm sorry.' Sadie gripped his arm, shook her head again, a deep frown creasing her brow and tugging down her kiss-swollen lips.

She was so beautiful. That she'd leaned on him for reassurance tonight, confided her clinical concerns for their patient, shown concern for Roman and even asked about Miko had finally pushed him to breaking point.

He wanted her.

He knew it was wrong to indulge at work, but he'd also recalled how right it had felt to kiss her the first time.

'Roman, we need to talk.' Her hand fell away, the new resolve in her tone the bucket of cold water to the face he needed.

He nodded, grappling with his breathlessness. 'That was really unprofessional of me, Sadie. I shouldn't have touched you. I'm sorry.'

What had he been thinking kissing a junior colleague at work? But from the moment she'd smiled at his son's name, he'd known he couldn't fight their chemistry any longer.

Even now, with shame nipping at his heels, he wanted her still.

'No.' She frowned, staring with what looked like fear in her eyes. 'I wanted to kiss you. It's not that, it's just—' She broke off, nervously licking the soft lips that had a second ago melded to his with the passion he remembered. 'I need to tell you something.'

When she looked up the determination on her face made his heated blood run cold.

'Okay.' Trying to get his heart rate under control, Roman stepped back, away from the temptation of Sadie. 'What is it?'

Reminding him of that first confusing day when they'd talked in this very office, Sadie paced to the desk and then faced him once more.

'I should have told you before.' She wrung her hands. 'I planned to tell you. I almost did. So many times. I just…couldn't seem to find the right moment.'

She twisted her mouth as if in anguish. 'And

I know now isn't ideal…because it's the middle of the night and we both have work to do…but I have to tell you, because we kissed and—'

This time he struggled to find her nervous rambling cute. 'What's wrong? Tell me now,' he ordered, his mind going to dark places. 'Please, Sadie.'

Trepidation was a tight fist around his heart. Memories slayed him; that terrible night four years ago when he'd stood in a dark hospital corridor while some poor young emergency doctor had given him the news no person ever wanted to hear.

'Please don't be angry.' Sadie swallowed, her stare imploring. 'I didn't want to hurt you…'

Hurt him? What had she done?

'Just tell me what's wrong.' Roman's pulse leaped, pumping trickles of adrenaline around his blood. His imagination was running wild. 'Are you ill? About to emigrate? Have you met someone else?'

Sadie shook her head. 'Nothing's wrong. Everything is fine. It's just—' She looked down at her hands and Roman wanted to tear at his hair in frustration.

The seconds pulsed through him like electric shocks. He had to draw on every scrap of patience he possessed to wait for her to say the upsetting words she was holding back.

Finally, her shoulders sagged, her eyes locked to his. 'I had a baby,' she said, expelling the announcement on a rush of air.

Roman took a few seconds to catch up, ninety per cent of his brain still stuck on how fantastic it had been to have her back in his arms and the other ten per cent braced for her announcement of bad news.

'Oh... That's wonderful. Amazing. Congratulations.' He took her hands, overjoyed that the fertility issues she'd confessed to him had been overcome. 'But that's happy news, isn't it?'

She didn't look happy. She looked nauseated as she offered a feeble nod. 'It's wonderful.'

Relief pooled in his veins. She wasn't sick, just a mother.

'So are you seeing someone?' He winced, thinking about their incendiary kiss, about how he might have been utterly carried away if they hadn't been at work. 'You should have told me. I would never have kissed you if I'd known.'

Now that the shock had worn off, hollowness rushed in. She *was* seeing someone. He had no right to kiss her, no prior claim. She deserved to be happy, deserved so much more than Roman had to give.

'I'm not seeing anyone,' she said flatly, desperation in her eyes. 'You don't understand...'

'Then explain it to me.' He was trying to follow, but she wasn't making much sense. She was doing that evasive thing again...

'I haven't slept with anyone since you. Since Vienna.'

Roman frowned, the lust fog in his brain finally clearing as if he'd just broken the surface of the water after a deep-sea dive.

His stunned gasp sounded in his head.

Sadie had given birth to *his* baby.

Sadie nodded, seeing that his understanding had finally dawned. 'We um...made a baby last Valentine's.'

A baby...? Roman's first thought turned his blood to ice. 'Did something happen? To the baby?'

It must have been the worst thing imaginable. Why else would she keep this a secret from him all this time?

Sadie frowned, gripping his hands tight so his focus sharpened on her mouth. 'Nothing happened. Nothing's wrong. She's beautiful. A healthy two-month-old.'

'What...?' The floor tilted under Roman's feet. He reached out to steady himself on the edge of the desk. This couldn't be happening.

He had a baby. Another child. A two-month old.

'We used protection,' he muttered, blindly

scrambling for the first idiotic thought to enter his head. But he was deliberately careful. He'd never wanted to be a father again.

'You said you couldn't have children.' If he'd been able to think, he might not have chosen such accusatory statements, but he had no thoughts that made sense. This must be some sort of joke.

Sadie nodded, her sympathetic stare and her hand clutching his all the confirmation he required that her words were true. 'I know. She's a tiny little miracle. Her name is Milly.'

Milly... He swallowed, his throat full of sawdust.

Stunned, Roman shook his head. 'No... I can't... No...'

A baby...? A miracle baby. A baby he knew nothing about.

'Why didn't you tell me sooner?' Staring at Sadie, he tried to deflect the emotions pounding him like blows from a heavyweight boxer.

He welcomed the pain; he'd lived with it so long. Fresh guilt sliced through him, like slashes from a scalpel. Miko was his baby. He loved Miko.

'I'm sorry,' Sadie said, her eyes brimming with tears. 'I know it's a shock for you. I wanted to break the news better than this.'

Nausea gripped him, disbelief rendering him speechless.

He closed his eyes, but that didn't help, because all he could see was his beloved son as a two-month-old. How could he possibly be a father again when he was so...broken? How could he be what a child needed when he'd spent so long alone, shutting down his need for other people? How would he love another child when his heart was full with Karolina and Miko?

'If I'd had any way of contacting you during the past eleven months,' Sadie continued with her explanation, 'I would have told you as soon as I found out I was pregnant. And when you showed up here, I was so shocked that I couldn't find the words. I never intended to keep it from you. I planned to tell you that first day. But then I was still attracted to you and I'd just found out that you were our eligible doctor and the moment passed. After that, I just couldn't seem to find the right time.'

He opened his eyes. The fear lacing his blood was as fresh as the moment he'd received a bad-news call from the hospital four years ago.

'Is she okay?' he gritted out, some innate protective instinct in him needing confirmation, even though he didn't know this child. His child.

'She's fine. Perfect,' Sadie rushed to reassure him as her tears spilled over, landing on her cheeks. 'I'm so sorry you had to find out this way.'

'So am I...' Still dazed by the mind-bending news, Roman looked away. He was in survival mode, his empathy for Sadie's anguish missing in action while he tried to process the news he'd never thought he'd experience again.

'I called the hotel in Vienna, when I was pregnant,' Sadie added. 'But even if I'd known your name, they have a policy to protect guests' privacy.'

She glanced down at her twisting hands. 'I planned to tell you that night at the bar, but then you shared your past with me and I was scared that my news would upset you even more.'

Just then, his pager emitted its silence-shattering tone. Roman scrubbed his hand through his hair and cancelled it, mumbling, 'I need to go back to Theatre.'

'Of course.' Sadie collected herself, swiping the tears from her cheeks. Perhaps sensing how overwhelmed he felt, she reached for his hand. 'Roman, don't worry; I don't expect anything from you. I know you're leaving London soon. I know you didn't want another child.'

She meant what he'd said in Vienna about marriage and kids. What he'd reiterated on several occasions since seeing her again. Of course he hadn't wanted another child. He never again wanted to experience the pain of loving and losing.

Only Sadie's miracle had intervened. His daughter was here anyway.

Numb, he stared at her hand on his, shattered anew by Sadie's blotchy face and haunted eyes. Her confession had taken its toll on them both.

She dropped his hand. 'I know how you feel about it and it's okay,' she whispered.

'Do you know how I feel?' he said, shaking his head.

A child changed everything. Right now, he didn't even know which way was up. 'Because I can't even begin to verbalise my feelings.'

She nodded, a frown of concern on her face as she watched him inch towards the door. 'That's fine, too.'

Her teeth snagged her bottom lip, catching Roman's gaze.

It seemed like hours since they'd kissed. Another lifetime.

If only the constant pull of their chemistry were his most pressing consideration. Now there were bigger issues to contemplate. Now Sadie and he weren't simply past lovers, reunited, they were parents. Now there was a tiny baby called Milly.

Overwhelmed by his conflicting emotions, he rushed back to Theatre, choked by fear and grief.

Was he capable of being a father again? Could he love another child? Would a new baby diminish his precious memories of Miko even further? And could he bear to find out?

CHAPTER SEVEN

Two days later, a distracted Sadie headed to the paediatric multidisciplinary meeting, or MDM: a once-weekly team discussion where professionals from different specialities reviewed patients' diagnoses, care and treatment options.

As she sneaked quietly into the room where the MDM was already under way her heart raced at the possibility that Roman might be there. She hadn't seen him since that fateful night they'd kissed and she'd told him about Milly. Guilt for the way it had eventually unfolded had stopped her from reaching out to him; he obviously needed space to think.

The room was in darkness while a radiologist explained the MRI scan findings displayed on a large projector screen. Sadie took a seat near the back and scanned the occupied seats for a glimpse of Roman.

He sat in the front row, next to the two paediatric oncologists, his handsome profile highlighted by the glow from the screen. Her heart rate accelerated with longing; they'd been growing so close. Now everything was uncertain.

Sadie sat still, trying not to draw attention to herself.

Part of her had been relieved by his absence on the ward these past two days. If he'd appeared while Sadie was there, she might have had to face his understandable hurt that she'd kept her news a secret, or, worse, witness again his pain and confusion. It had been hard enough to watch the first time around, when all that lovely desire following their kiss had been slashed and shredded by guilt.

Who could blame him for his hesitance to embrace Milly? Sadie had given him a lot to process and he was still grieving for his family. But the impatience to know where she and Milly stood, one way or another, was a constant itch under her skin.

In allowing him space to work through the knowledge that he was once more a father, Sadie had essentially been shut out, forced to ponder the future and fill in the blanks, to contemplate the dreaded *what ifs*.

What if, because of his past loss, he was incapable of loving Milly? What if he was too broken to even welcome their baby into his life? What if, when he left London, she never saw him again and their darling and innocent daughter grew up never knowing her intelligent and caring father?

While she would understand his reasons, his rejection of their precious daughter would still be devastating.

Sadie had never considered herself a coward, but right now, she wasn't certain which was worse: knowing those answers or her current state of ignorance.

Sick to her stomach with fear and longing, Sadie startled as the room lights came on while, around her, the case discussion continued.

'So we're looking at a stage two nephroblastoma,' Roman said, his deep and confident voice jangling Sadie's nerves. 'Would you want to give neoadjuvant chemo in this case?' he asked the medical oncologist at his side. 'Or is everyone happy for me to go in and operate?'

How could he sound so…normal, when Sadie felt as though she'd been sleep-walking through her life?

With his question hanging in the air, he cast his eyes around the room for corroboration from the assembled team.

His stare landed on Sadie.

She froze, her breath catching in her throat as their eyes locked for a split second before he turned away to resume the discussion.

Sadie swallowed, her mouth dry. How could she still want him so violently when they had monumental issues to discuss and try to overcome? How could she crave his touch, his kiss, the way he'd opened up to her emotionally, when he'd so obviously withdrawn to lick his wounds?

Fear was her constant companion. Fear that she'd hurt Roman, irreparably. That she'd ruined any chance of them being a parenting team. That he'd want nothing to do with her, or beloved Milly.

With a treatment plan in place for Roman's nephroblastoma patient, the discussion continued to other cases on the list. Sadie tried her best to focus on the clinical deliberation taking place, but her gaze returned to the back of Roman's head, time and again, as if willing him to be okay, willing him to let her back in.

As the meeting wrapped up, Sadie stood and made a beeline for the exit, her stomach on the floor with defeat. How could she have forgotten her own resolve to live for the moment? She and Milly were fine as they were. They'd be fine whatever Roman decided. Milly's happiness and stability were all that truly mattered.

'Dr Barnes, a word, please.' Roman's voice halted her in her tracks.

Sadie paused, ducking into in a doorway to

avoid the flow of foot traffic leaving the MDM, her nerves now completely shredded.

Today, Roman was wearing a navy-blue suit, as if deliberately taunting her with his out-of-reach hotness. Her stare caressed the crisp tailoring moulded to his broad shoulders and trim waist. The shirt and tie gave him a sophisticated look that almost buckled Sadie's knees. It wasn't fair that he looked so good.

Swallowing the lump of lust and trepidation in her throat, she searched his stare for some clue of how he was feeling on the inside, spying fatigue around his eyes.

'Thanks for waiting,' he said, his body stiff with formality, as if they were complete strangers. 'How are you?'

He slung his hands in his trouser pockets and Sadie withered a little, desperate for his touch, desperate to know things between them would be okay, desperate for the emotional closeness they'd shared when he'd been comfortable enough in her to confide his deepest pain.

She genuinely cared that he might be suffering.

'I'm fine, Dr Ježek. How are you?' Sadie stepped deeper into the alcove, aware that the MDM room was still emptying of their colleagues, not the optimal venue for a private conversation.

How could they act so…distant when they'd

made a Valentine's Day baby together? The last time they'd worked together, they'd all but ripped off each other's clothes and had sex on the desk. No matter what else was going on between them, for Sadie, the attraction was as strong as ever.

Except she had no idea how he was feeling.

Glancing over his shoulder to ensure they were alone, Roman stepped closer. Catching her totally unawares, he reached for her hand. 'Listen, I wanted to apologise.'

His voice was low, husky with emotion.

'Please, you haven't done anything wrong. There's no need to apologise.' Excited and confused by his touch, Sadie used all her strength to slip her hand from his.

There was no point indulging her attraction when their connection was now so fragile. Emotionally, things between them seemed to have gone a few steps backwards. Now that he was close, she saw the turmoil in his eyes, the dark smudges beneath as if he hadn't been sleeping.

Her news had clearly left him tormented.

The lump returned to her throat, her heart aching for this honourable but wounded man, her spirit crushed for darling, innocent Milly.

'There is,' he said, his stare stony as if he was holding his emotions in check. 'Last time we spoke I was…overwhelmed. I reacted badly.'

He held her stare, his hand reaching for hers

again before he thought better of it and dropped his arm to his side. 'I came across as accusing, and that wasn't my intention.'

'I understood. It was a shock for you.' Compassion rose up in Sadie like a surging wave. Of course he'd be overwhelmed. She'd had nine months to come to terms with the fact that they'd made a baby.

She couldn't be angry with him; it might be easier if she could.

'I feel horribly guilty about that night, if it's any consolation. Kissing you at work,' she whispered, 'and then dropping that bombshell...'

She should have found a way to tell him sooner, somewhere private.

His stare softened, the ghost of his playful smile tugging his lips. 'There's no need to feel guilty.' A shrug, a sparkle in his eyes. 'And I too must hold my hand up and take responsibility for the kiss.' He glanced at her mouth, sending sparks along her nerves. 'Not my finest decision, so, again, I apologise.'

Flames engulfed Sadie's body, even as she agonised over his meaning. Did he regret kissing her? Or just regret kissing her at work? But what did it matter when they had bigger issues to resolve, when he seemed a million miles away?

Peering over his shoulder, confirming that they were still alone, Sadie braved another question.

'I don't want to rush you—I've been giving you breathing space—but have you had any thoughts on what you want to do?'

She held her breath, watched doubt flit over his expression, her stomach swooping with disappointment. She could absolutely raise Milly alone. But she wanted Milly and Roman to have a relationship, as long as it was a mutually positive thing.

He sighed, glancing up at the ceiling, as if the weight of the world rested on his shoulders, telling Sadie everything she needed to know.

'I've had too many thoughts to count.' He faced her, his stare sincere. 'This news has brought up a lot of feelings I thought I'd already dealt with. I'm questioning everything. I wish I could give you answers, but you might need to give me a little more time. Is that okay?'

Sadie swallowed, crushed anew for unsuspecting Milly and heartsore for broken Roman. 'Of course. I respect your honesty and I understand.'

It was true. He'd been through so much loss. Given his circumstances, it would be hard for Sadie to trust less considered or profuse reactions. If he couldn't commit to knowing his daughter, it might be better for them never to meet.

'I'm grateful, actually,' she said, 'that you

aren't rushing to make promises that you might not be ready to keep.'

Except she couldn't help the tiny flicker of hope that one day he would embrace their beautiful daughter into his life.

Sensing her disappointment, he reached for her hand once more, his gaze pleading, tearing her heart to shreds. 'I wish it were just simple joy that I was feeling. Ordinarily, that's what your news would deserve. It's what I long to feel.'

Sadie nodded, too choked to speak, too comforted by his touch. She wished she could throw her arms around him.

'But I'm all over the place, Sadie. My grief has resurfaced. I don't know which way is up. And until I've worked through some of these feelings, it wouldn't be fair to you or to Milly to rush into anything.'

Sadie blinked up at him, her eyes smarting as she dragged in a deep breath for courage. He was so wonderful, so different from her ex. 'You're right, and I appreciate that, believe me.'

Roman's cautious but honest response was way better than the kind of grand declaration Mark would have made but then failed to deliver upon. This way, Sadie was no worse off for having told Roman about Milly, her and the baby's day-to-day routine unchanged.

Except waiting, seeing him at work, wanting him despite it all, was its own brand of torture.

'Where is she now?' he asked on a whisper, his stare stormy with repressed emotions. 'What happens to Milly while you're at work?'

Even while he processed the life-changing news while also dealing with renewed grief, he was thinking about the daughter they'd made.

Her heart lurched, reaching for him. 'She's at home, with my sister. Grace is a trained nanny. There's no one I trust more.'

She wanted him to know that his daughter was safe and cared for, even if he wasn't, and might never be, ready to be her father.

He nodded, appeased, but his jaw clenched as if he was holding back further questions.

'Would you like to see a picture of her?' Sadie asked, emboldened by the fact that he clearly cared, but braced for his answer. 'It's okay if you want to say no.'

She didn't want to rush him, but he was hurting, not indifferent.

How awful that, for Roman, Sadie's miracle gift, her precious adored baby, brought such heart-rending conflict of emotion. On the one hand, he was understandably curious and on the other, overwhelmed by grief and doubt.

He nodded, visibly swallowing as if he couldn't trust himself to speak.

Her stomach twisting with apprehension, Sadie took her phone from her pocket and brought up a recent baby photo: Milly asleep like an angel, her tiny fingers curled into a chubby fist.

Roman took the device, his hand trembling and his stare haunted.

She'd never seen him uncertain of anything.

His eyes scoured the image, one hand covering his mouth as if to hold in a primal sound. Of anguish or joy or both, Sadie couldn't tell.

'You can't see from that photo,' she said, her own voice scratchy with empathy and grief for her dreams for Milly, 'but she has your eyes. As soon as she was born, she looked up at me and I recognised them.'

'Just like Miko,' he whispered, his tortured stare glued to the phone.

Sadie's pulse pounded in her temples, hope blooming; surely his reaction to the sight of his daughter was promising?

Just then, Sadie's phone rang, its piercing trill breaking the moment of strange and stilted intimacy.

Roman handed the device back and scrubbed a hand over his haggard face.

Sadie spoke to the nurse from Sunshine Ward, glancing Roman's way with concern when she heard the news.

'It's Josh,' she said, work temporarily resetting her priorities. 'He's gone off. Saturations dropping. Tachypnoea. Cyanosis. I need to go.'

Milly and Roman's relationship would have to wait.

'I'll come with you.'

They started running, side by side, making it to the ward within minutes. When they arrived at his bedside, Josh was breathing rapidly, his lips blue despite the oxygen mask covering his nose and mouth.

Sadie placed her stethoscope in her ears and listened to the boy's chest while Roman checked the latest chest X-ray and blood test results and spoke to Josh's nurse.

'Reduced breath sounds on the right,' Sadie informed Roman, who placed his hand on the boy's chest, before listening for breath sounds with his own stethoscope.

'He has subcutaneous emphysema,' he said, inviting Sadie to palpate Josh's chest, their eyes meeting in the kind of silent communication that had become second nature.

Pneumothorax was a complication of pneumonia, and in Josh's case it seemed that the air was leaking, not only into his chest cavity, causing a partial collapse of the lung, but it was also leaking into the skin and subcutaneous tissues over his ribs.

Was Roman, like her, thinking about Miko?

But for a cruel twist of fate, Roman's son could have ended up in Josh's position, surviving the car crash, hospitalised with complications. But, of course, Roman's son was likely never far from his thoughts. He was probably acutely aware of the parallels.

'Let's wheel Josh into the treatment room,' Roman said, telling Sadie that he intended to stick around and help out. 'We need a portable chest X-ray asap, please,' he added to Sammy, who'd appeared to assess the commotion.

The treatment for pneumothorax was a chest drain. Sadie had done the urgent procedure many times. While Josh's parents were called for their verbal consent, the radiographer arrived to take the chest X-ray that would confirm their diagnosis.

Working with their hunch, Roman and Sadie prepared the equipment they'd need in order to insert a chest drain to alleviate Josh's symptoms.

'You insert the drain, I'll assist,' Roman said, his concern for their patient evident.

'Thank you,' Sadie said, grateful for his ongoing professional support. They stared at each other for a second, as if aware of the other's thoughts.

They might not have the future all figured out—that was how Sadie preferred it—but when it came to their work, they could set their personal issues aside. At the hospital, they had the one thing that mattered: trust.

Roman flashed her a sad but reassuring smile and handed her some gloves.

The digital X-ray confirmed their diagnosis of pneumothorax. While Roman administered a light intravenous sedative to keep Josh calm through the minimally invasive procedure, Sadie swabbed Josh's skin and injected local anaesthetic between his ribs.

Sadie glanced at Roman for the all-clear to proceed.

'Slow and steady,' he said, giving her a nod of encouragement that she lapped up. He was senior, a surgeon. He could have easily commandeered the situation and taken over the procedure or walked off the ward and left her to it. But by staying to assist, he'd shown Sadie that he trusted her to care for their patient.

She couldn't ask for more.

With the procedure complete, the chest drain sited to suck escaped air from the chest cavity so the lung could reinflate, Roman and Sadie left a sleepy Josh to the care of his nurse and his parents.

'You did well,' Roman said as they washed their hands before heading to the ward office where Sadie would type up the incident in Josh's hospital notes.

'Thanks for your help—I've never done it with a surgeon before.' Realising what she'd said, she covered her face in her hands. 'Sorry. That came out wrong.'

But her faux pas had broken the earlier tension.

Roman grinned, the playful flare of heat lingering in his eyes. 'Don't worry, I know what you meant.'

And just like that, many of the doubts that had plagued her these past few days evaporated. At the hospital, they made a good team. Surely with patience and caution and the honesty they'd always shared, they'd get through this. Yes, he needed time to come to terms with the news of Milly's existence, but maybe he also needed... encouragement.

Closing the office door, she stepped close, resting her hand on his arm. They couldn't seem to stop touching each other.

'I've been thinking,' she said, 'and there's absolutely no pressure either way, because I meant what I said about giving you space, but...would you like to meet her? Milly, I mean?'

Tension tugged at the corners of his mouth.

'My sister brings her to the café across the road most lunchtimes,' Sadie rushed on, 'so I can feed her while I grab a sandwich. You'd be very welcome to join us. But if you think it's too soon or a bad idea, that's okay. I just thought...you know...

with us being here and her being right across the street… Actually, I don't know what I thought. You're right; it's overwhelming…'

Catching her off guard, Roman rested the tip of his index finger on her top lip, silencing her. 'Please, no more nervous chatter.'

His hesitant smile turned indulgent in that way that told her he found her amusing. 'I get the idea of what you're saying.'

The burn of his finger against her lips turned her insides to jelly.

'What time will you be there?' he asked non-committally, his hand falling to his side, so Sadie missed his touch all over again.

'One p.m., emergencies notwithstanding of course.'

'I won't make any promises,' he said, reaching for the door handle at his back.

'Okay,' Sadie whispered, both grateful that he wouldn't let her down and disappointed that Milly might go another day without meeting her kind and compassionate father.

Before he left the room, he cast her one final glance, laced with confusion, haunted by pain.

Sadie exhaled her held breath, her hand resting over her pounding heart. His concession was a small step in the right direction, one with which she could live. Now she just needed to set aside the way he made her feel every time they touched, which, despite everything else going on, seemed to be something of an addiction.

CHAPTER EIGHT

ROMAN GLANCED THROUGH the café window, his throat constricted with fear. The place was busy with lunchtime diners, but, attuned to Sadie as he was, he spotted her easily at a table near the back, sitting with a woman who was obviously her identical twin, a buggy between them, facing away so there was no sign of Milly.

He watched Sadie chat to her sister for a few minutes, her stare falling to her phone often. She was clearly waiting for him, apprehensive that he might change his mind about meeting his daughter.

Compassion for Sadie surged through his chest. This situation wasn't easy for either of them. Not only had she felt forced to keep her secret, when their baby must have brought her so much joy, given her fertility issues, but she was also giving him time, because she knew about his past and understood how he must be feeling…torn.

Entranced and curious, fearful and desolate all at once.

Drawn to meet his daughter, as he'd been almost from the first instant he'd known of her existence, Roman entered the café. The minute Sadie had put the idea of today's introduction in his head, he'd struggled to think about anything else. Meeting Milly would of course jeopardise the emotional status quo he'd inhabited since he'd lost Karolina and Miko. But it was too late.

He couldn't pretend that his baby didn't exist, and he could no longer stay away. He needed to see her, just once. Then he could make sense of his conflicted thoughts, make a plan, move forward from the numb void he'd inhabited these past few days.

Roman ordered tea he likely wouldn't be able to drink and headed for Sadie's table.

The two women looked up.

'Grace, this is Roman Ježek,' Sadie said, her voice wary but her eyes alight with a spark of excitement he'd come to depend upon whenever their eyes met. 'Grace is my sister, obviously. The one I told you about,' she added for Roman.

'Hello,' Roman said, smiling at the woman, so much like Sadie, who cared for their daughter while her parents worked.

'Nice to meet you.' Grace stood, nudging the buggy in Sadie's direction and reaching for her bag. 'I'll leave you two alone. I…um…need to make a phone call.'

Grace discreetly melted away.

Roman stared at the hood of the buggy, the feeling that he'd forgotten to do something vital clawing at his insides. Pressure built in his head. He'd imagined this moment a million times since Sadie had informed him of his daughter's existence, but now that it was here, now that he was about to see his baby in the flesh, he feared his legs would buckle.

'Why don't you sit down?' Sadie suggested, attuned somehow to his inner turmoil.

Roman folded himself robotically into the chair, feeling brittle, as one false move would shatter him into a million mismatched shards.

Sadie reached across the table and took his hand. He clung tight.

'Do you want to see her?' Sadie asked, her smile soft with sympathy and understanding.

'Yes,' he said, a catch to his voice that threatened to reveal the cascade of conflicted emotions pouring through him.

Fear because he'd spent the past four long years shoring up his emotions to protect himself from further pain, and might not be able to open himself up once more. Longing to see his child so intense, he had to curl his hands into fists to stop himself from whirling the buggy around. And guilt. Not only because, as broken as he was, he couldn't be the kind of father that his baby deserved, but also because welcoming a new baby into his heart felt like a betrayal of Miko, somehow.

As if in knowing his daughter, he might forget his son.

'She fell asleep after I fed her,' Sadie explained as she wheeled the buggy to face him so the baby came into view.

Time stopped.

She slept with her fists curled beside her face, her delicate eyelashes crescents on her cherubic cheeks.

Ever since Sadie had told him about Milly, Roman had been terrified to make another human connection, one he knew from tragic experience would have the power to tear him apart emotionally. Except fate had other ideas, taking out of his hands his decision to never again put himself in such a vulnerable position as loving another human being. The universe had given them Milly.

'Isn't she beautiful?' Sadie said, her eyes on the baby, her expression brimming with maternal love that flooded his body with relief.

He remembered Karolina looking at Miko that way.

Roman nodded, mutely, unable to take his

burning eyes off his tiny daughter, who looked just like Miko at the same age—same wispy soft dark hair, same cute little nose, same dimpled chin.

'She looks like her brother,' he choked out, his chest lanced with fresh grief as he recalled his beloved son at Milly's age. Miko would have been ten now, a perfect big brother, a fun and responsible role model. 'But she also looks like you.'

When he met Sadie's stare, gratitude and confusion fighting for control of his pulse, there were tears in her beautiful eyes. He cupped her cheek, wiping one away with his thumb.

He needed to stop touching Sadie, his feelings for her only complicating an already fraught situation. But touching her made him feel better, reminded him of their growing emotional connection before the baby bombshell. Reminded him that, even in pain as they'd both been the night they met, their connection had produced something unique and magical.

'I'm sorry, Roman,' she said, blinking. 'If this is too much, that's fine, honestly. I can't imagine what you must be feeling, but I do understand how hard this is for you.'

Roman swallowed, touched by Sadie's maturity and empathy. She could have reacted so differently.

'But I want you to know that, for me...' she put her hand on her chest, over her heart '... Milly is everything. She's a miracle I never thought I would have the chance to experience. She's deeply, deeply loved and always will be.'

She was letting him know that he was free of parental responsibility, if he wanted to continue his rolling-stone lifestyle. Except her impassioned assurances left him restless once more. He still didn't know what he wanted, but none of the scenarios he'd imagined these past few days felt right.

'I want to provide for Milly, financially,' he said, clearing his tight throat. He'd reached that decision almost immediately, his sense of responsibility the one certainty that came easily and painlessly.

Sadie frowned, as if the idea had never once occurred to her. 'That isn't necessary. As you know, I have a secure job, so she will want for nothing.'

Roman compressed his mouth, picking up on Sadie's slightly defensive tone of voice. 'It's necessary to me to share the responsibility. We made her together, after all.'

Walking away without providing for the daughter they'd made had never once crossed his mind.

'Okay...' Sadie nodded warily. 'If you want.'

There was that nebulous word again, want.

'Life isn't always about having what you want, is it?' he said, glancing at the baby. They both understood that. But financial support was the one practical thing he could do immediately, without ripping open the scabs on his battle-scarred heart.

Roman turned over his phone, keeping an eye on the time. The screen lit up and Sadie saw the background image.

'Is that Miko?' she asked, her curiosity natural after the things they'd shared.

Roman nodded, despite the stab of pain he always experienced on seeing his favourite photo of Karolina and Miko, unlocking his phone and passing it over.

'Karolina had just tickled Miko when I captured that shot,' he said, watching Sadie stare at the phone, her eyes wide, a soft smile playing on her lips. Of course he was biased, but his son's laughter and joy would surely make anyone smile.

'He looked like a mini version of you,' she whispered in awe, 'but with his mother's fair hair.'

'It was dark when he was a baby, just like Milly.' Roman glanced once more at his sleeping daughter, emotions slamming into him.

Could he do this again? Be the kind of father this tiny innocent girl deserved? What if he tried and failed, let her down the way he'd failed Miko? But could he seriously walk away from his daughter, when he was already in love with her, just knowing that she existed?

Sadie handed back the phone and he checked the time with a wince.

'I need to go. I'm due in clinic.'

'Of course. Will you…be okay?'

Roman nodded automatically, still too awed by the turn of events and overwhelmed by his conflicted feelings to describe himself as *okay*. Would he ever be okay again now that there was Milly? Parenthood brought responsibility. Fears for a child's safety and well-being.

He pocketed his phone, the image of Miko's smile fresh in his mind. Of course the joys of being a parent, the uncontrollable love, outweighed the fears and doubts tenfold.

'I'll call you,' he said, standing and resting his hand on Sadie's shoulder. 'I know we need to talk, but I'm on call tonight.'

He wished he could offer some sort of reassurance beyond financial aid.

Sadie nodded, squeezed his fingers. 'When you're ready, I'll be here.'

The trouble was, his greatest fear of all was, that he might never be ready to be the kind of father that Milly deserved. He'd been there once before and a big part of him believed that he'd somehow failed his son, Miko.

He was a doctor, the boy's father. He should have been there for him in his moment of greatest need. It was irrational, but that didn't make it less visceral or devastating. Until he'd reconciled that part of his grief, until he had some clarity on the correct course, he wouldn't fail anyone else.

The following evening, Sadie was about to leave the emergency department after admitting her final patient of the day, a seven-year-old with suspected appendicitis, when an A and E nurse called her to assess a newly arrived emergency.

'Nine-month-old with possible foreign body ingestion in Resus,' the nurse said, handing Sadie the ambulance summary.

Sadie hurried into the resuscitation room, where the most serious cases presenting to the emergency department were assessed. Choking was one of the hazards designed to terrify all parents, so Sadie's heart went out to the concerned pair as she introduced herself.

Sam, the baby, was grizzling and drooling, a distinct high-pitched sound, known as stridor, coming from his throat on every inhaled breath.

'I think there may be an object stuck in Sam's throat,' she explained after taking a brief history from the parents, who hadn't seen the baby swallow anything.

Sadie reached for her stethoscope and listened to the boy's lungs and looked inside his mouth.

'It could be lodged either at the top of his trachea or his oesophagus, the tube to his stomach.' She kept her voice even, while urgency pounded through her blood.

'Most swallowed objects pass through the gut without intervention,' she continued, 'but I don't think this one is going to pass on its own. It's stuck there, and is affecting Sam's breathing. So I'm going to run some tests.'

While the worried parents tried to soothe Sam, Sadie ordered an urgent chest X-ray and paged the on-call surgical registrar. If the object wasn't removed quickly, it could cause tissue damage and, in return, scarring, leaving baby Sam with lifelong complications.

'I'm going to ask my surgical colleagues to take a look at Sam,' she explained to the parents, her mind turning to Milly, who was only a few months younger than this baby. 'It may be that he requires a small procedure under sedation to look into the throat and remove whatever is lodged there.'

Sam's parents appeared understandably horrified. Sadie left them with the ED nurse, who was trying with infinite patience to encourage Sam to wear an oxygen nasal cannula.

She was examining the chest X-ray when Roman walked in.

'What have we got?' he asked, shooting her that smile that shot her pulse through the roof.

He paused beside her, peering over her shoulder at the screen, the hint of his cologne tickling her senses. Unfair memories bombarded her: the scent of his skin, the delirious passion of his kisses, the feel of his body moving inside hers.

Her entire body reacted with goosebumps; she was so pleased to see him.

'Ah, foreign object?' he said, as if completely unmoved by Sadie's proximity, whereas she was engulfed in flames at his casual closeness. 'Some sort of plastic block, I'd guess.'

'That's what I was thinking,' she agreed, leaning away for self-preservation. 'Shouldn't you have left by now? You were on call last night.'

She noted the fatigue around his eyes, the dishevelled mop of his hair, his crumpled scrubs. Was he hiding out from his personal life at work? He'd once admitted workaholic tendencies. But what did that mean for Milly and their...situation? Perhaps he hadn't given it any thought.

'I was about to head out,' he said, 'but my registrar is busy, so I said I'd come down and see what's going on.' He pinned her with his eye contact. 'Thanks for caring.'

'Any time,' Sadie said, flustered because there seemed to be a new resolve about him tonight, and it was crazy sexy.

'Come on. Let's sort out this baby.' Without further discussion, he ducked through the curtains where Sam and his parents sat, with Sadie on his heels.

The baby really didn't want to wear the nasal oxygen cannula, constantly grabbing at his face to pull it away. He took one look at Roman, the newest arrival in a long line of scary strangers, and burst into pitiful tears.

Taking the slight in his stride, Roman introduced himself to Sam's concerned parents. 'My name is Dr Ježek. Dr Barnes has correctly identified a foreign object stuck in Sam's throat.'

Without missing a beat, he handed a fractious Sam his phone and the baby instantly calmed, distracted by the lit-up screen.

Sadie sighed with longing. He was so good at his job. He was such a natural with kids and on the parents' wavelength. For what must have been the thousandth time since they'd reconnected, she imagined what kind of father he would make to their baby girl, if only he could overcome his grief.

But he might never be ready for more and she would have to be okay with that.

'We need to get whatever it is out before it can cause any damage, okay?' Roman asked with the kind of calm assurance that was instantly soothing.

The parents nodded in unison.

Glancing at Sadie to include her in the process, he went on. 'We'll just give Sam a light sedation. Through here.' He indicated the butterfly IV Sadie had already inserted into the baby's arm. 'Dr Barnes and I will then place an endoscope, a small telescope-like tube, into Sam's throat and, fingers crossed, we can grab hold of whatever it is and pull it out. Any questions?'

The couple shook their heads, appearing awed and relieved by Roman's command of the situation.

Sadie exhaled, trying to settle the admiring flutter in her chest. The way he referenced Sadie, including her in the decision-making process, put them once more on the same team.

While Roman asked Sam's dad to sign the consent for the procedure, Sadie injected the IV with a mild dose of sedative.

'You're welcome to stay with Sam if you want,' Sadie said to the grown-ups as the baby lolled drowsily in his father's arms, 'but he'll be asleep and won't really know if you're here. You might find the procedure distressing to watch, so if you prefer to wait in the family room, one of us will come and get you as soon as it's over.'

Agreeing, they laid Sam on the bed, where the nurse adjusted his nasal oxygen cannula and attached a pulse oximeter to monitor his blood oxygen saturations.

With the parents departed, Roman stepped close and cast Sadie a discreet look. 'Any psychosocial concerns?' he asked, pulling on gloves and preparing the endoscope.

It was a sad fact of the job, but paediatricians and those working with children had to constantly be aware of neglect or non-accidental injury in the children they treated.

Sadie shook her head. 'He has an older brother,' she said, donning her own gloves. 'Sam most likely got hold of a stray toy left on the floor.'

For a moment they stared at each other, silently communicating understanding and compassion because they too were parents. Or perhaps that was just in Sadie's head. Wishful thinking.

'Okay. Let's do this,' he said, lightly touching Sadie's arm and directing her to stand at his side so they could both see the screen where the digital images from the endoscope would be displayed.

With a mouthpiece inserted, Roman passed

the flexible tube into Sam's throat, while Sadie closely monitored the baby's breathing.

'There it is,' Roman said, indicating the image on the screen, relief in the glance he flicked Sadie. 'Just at the top of the oesophagus.'

'You're right. It is a plastic block.'

'Right, let's test my fishing skills,' Roman said, extending the tiny forceps at the end of the endoscope to grasp hold of the piece of plastic.

It took several attempts, but when Roman managed to snare the object, Sadie exhaled in relief.

'I know,' he said, flicking her a conspiratorial smile that made her feel as if she'd known him for years, not weeks. 'For a minute there I thought I might need to take this little guy to Theatre. No one wants that.'

With the object retrieved and the endoscope withdrawn, Roman peeled off his gloves and addressed one of the nurses. 'Can you please let Mum and Dad know that everything went smoothly? We'll just admit Sam for observation tonight.'

He looked down at the peacefully sleeping baby, who was breathing easy now that the obstruction had been removed.

Sadie watched in wonder as Roman reached out and gently stroked the baby's head, murmuring something in Czech.

Sadie froze, mesmerised by the telling gesture.

Roman might be a busy surgeon, a breed known for their arrogance, but he truly cared about his patients and their families.

He looked up and their eyes locked.

Sadie's heartbeat whooshed in her ears. He was so competent and compelling. So intelligent and supportive. Every time they worked together she felt their connection growing stronger. At the hospital, they trusted each other and there was a big part of Sadie that craved the same connection in their personal lives, where nothing was certain.

He eyed her sheepishly. 'What?' he asked, tossing his balled-up gloves in the nearby bin.

'Nothing,' Sadie said, fighting the urge to fling herself into his arms and tell him how wonderful he was, beg him to want her with the same all-encompassing desire.

'Are you heading home now?' he asked as they finished up the paperwork on Sam's admission. 'I hoped we could talk.'

His stare carried that vulnerability she wanted to soothe away.

'Yes. I'm done for the day.' Nervous tension coiled in Sadie's belly as they left the emergency department side by side. She didn't want to talk. She wanted to quiet all the doubts in her head with the mind-numbing passion they shared.

'You won't be surprised to hear that I've been

thinking,' he started, holding open a door for Sadie to pass through as they headed for the staff locker rooms. 'And I've decided that I need to try and be a part of Milly's life.'

Sadie's step faltered, her heart leaping in her chest as if she'd just walked into a brick wall. 'Roman, you don't have to rush into any decisions. There's absolutely no pressure from my end.'

It was only yesterday that he'd met Milly in person. Why had he changed his mind so quickly when, in the café, he'd been so hesitant and cautious?

'I know there's no pressure from you,' he said, scanning his security pass to unlock the doors to the changing rooms, 'but this comes from in here.' He pressed his balled-up hand to the centre of his chest, his voice impassioned.

The doors closed behind them, he stepped close and gripped her arms above the elbows. 'I see babies every day at work, even in passing around the hospital, and all I can do is think about my baby, Milly.'

His stare searched Sadie's, imploring. 'I'm walking around feeling like something's not right, as if I've left the oven on at home or forgotten to take my passport to the airport, or I'm missing a surgical clamp in Theatre and the patient is already back on the ward.'

Sadie swallowed, empathy an ache in her chest. 'I can understand that.'

Of course she could. If the situation were reversed, if she had a daughter she'd never met, she wouldn't be able to stay away for one day. But their situations were different. For Roman, Milly's existence also represented painful reminders.

Except his sudden change of heart left fear trickling through her veins.

'Take Sam, for example,' he rushed on. 'Back there, I couldn't stop imagining how I'd feel if it was Milly who needed an operation or emergency treatment. You must sometimes feel that too?'

She nodded, mutely, because she'd been thinking exactly that. But Roman had been through the worst thing any parent could experience. He might never be ready to be fully open. She didn't want hasty promises she'd struggle to trust.

As if reading her mind, he continued. 'I'm still not making any big promises,' he said with heart-rending sincerity, 'but the past few days have shown me that I need to meet my daughter properly, to try and get to know her, and somehow make up for the time I've already missed.'

As if he sensed the chills of doubt that crept up Sadie's spine, he reached for her hand, his touch adding to her confusion. 'What do you think?'

Sadie swallowed the lump of fear in her throat.

How could she deny him anything when she agreed? When she felt closer to him with each passing day? When Milly deserved a father?

Except she'd been so wrong about Mark that she still struggled to trust her instincts.

She hated future-gazing and she didn't want to start now. But surely if they were careful, if she could keep a lid on her desires for him, they could take things slowly and apply the same trust to their personal lives as they practised at work.

Desperately trying to ignore the flicker of excitement in his eyes, she brought her hands up and gripped his arms. 'I think we should take things slowly.'

She would never keep Roman from his daughter, but this about-face left her...unsettled. 'After all, you're going to Ireland in a couple of weeks.'

A small frown pinched his brows.

But it was a good reminder for them both to proceed with caution. No matter how close she felt towards him, he was still leaving London. Trusting him with the most precious thing in her world, Milly, meant trusting her instincts and taking a giant leap of faith, something that had gone badly for her in the past.

'Of course, I want you and Milly to know each other,' Sadie said, taking that leap for her daughter's sake. And for Roman. 'So if you're sure you're ready...'

Tugging her into his arms, Roman kissed the top of her head. 'Thank you. I agree; we'll take it one day at a time.'

Sadie nodded against his chest as he continued to hold her, turned on by his touch, conflicted by his gratitude and restraint. Her head felt full of cotton wool, the longing for it to work warring with her maternal protective urges for her darling baby.

And something darker—the demands of her own tangled needs.

But with so much else going on, that would have to be the last thing on her mind.

'That being said—' he pulled back, his stare vulnerable '—how would you feel about an outing tomorrow, just the three of us? Perhaps we could take Milly to the zoo?'

He looked so hopeful, so exposed, Sadie nodded, her smile feeble. 'That sounds nice.'

His delighted expression burned Sadie's eyes. How could she deny him when she'd always hoped that he'd want to be a part of Milly's life? But how would she spend time with him away from work and keep him at arm's length, emotionally and physically, so she could follow her own edict and take things one day at a time?

CHAPTER NINE

THEY'D ARRANGED TO meet just inside the main entrance of the zoo, near the aquarium. The minute Roman spied Sadie pushing Milly's buggy, he breathed a relieved sigh, his heart pounding with excitement.

He had no idea how today would unfold, but it was time to come to terms with the fact that he and Sadie had made a beautiful baby together.

He couldn't stay away any longer.

He walked towards them, his stare greedily taking in Milly, who was awake, wearing a tiny woollen hat and covered in a blanket. Awestruck by her big blue eyes, he dragged in a lungful of chilly air, braced against the waves of feelings almost knocking him off his feet.

Shocking him the most was the instant love, some visceral protective part of him springing to life. But it wasn't strong enough to completely dispel the trickle of fear tightening his gut or the hot stabs of guilt between his ribs.

'Have you been waiting long?' Sadie asked, breathless, pausing to scrutinise his expression in that caring way of hers.

'Not long,' Roman lied, leaning in to press a kiss to her cold cheek, without hesitation now that they were away from the hospital. He'd arrived way too early, nerves and anticipation shrinking the walls of his one-bedroom flat in the hospital accommodation complex.

He took Sadie's hand and gazed down at the baby, his stare compulsively drawn to his daughter. 'Thanks for agreeing to this.'

Sadie smiled, squeezed his hand, enabling him to draw a decent breath. 'How are you doing? Big day.'

'I'm nervous,' Roman admitted, ashamed, but wanting to be honest.

She nodded in agreement, her beautiful eyes soft with compassion. 'We'll take it slow, together.'

Touched that this amazing woman understood him so well, he held out the small gift he'd brought. 'This is for Milly. Open it later— It's cold out here.'

Sadie took the gift and tucked it into her bag as Roman held open the door to the aquarium exhibits. 'Let's go look at some fish.'

Once inside the aquarium building, Sadie parked up the buggy and unstrapped Milly, removing her hat. Static electricity raised her fine downy hair so it stood on end. Sadie laughed and Milly smiled, oblivious to what was funny.

Roman's heart jolted as if he'd been electrocuted.

Watching Sadie smile at their daughter, seeing her unbridled love and joy and awe for the baby they'd made together... A beautiful moment of maternal love he would try to hold onto for ever. A moment like a thousand others he'd lived with Karolina and Miko.

His chest ached as he remembered the good times, his euphoria tainted with guilt and grief because he'd had these chances before.

As Sadie wandered the three-hundred-and-sixty-degree tank filled with coral and colourful tropical fish, holding Milly up to the glass to point out the brightly contrasted creatures, Roman trailed along, watching their breathtaking interactions with wonder.

Did he deserve a second shot at being a father when there was a part of him, an irrational, primitive part, that felt somehow responsible for the deaths of his family? He'd spent years torturing himself with unanswerable questions. What if he'd been driving the car that night instead of being at work? What if he'd been with them, able to help in a medical capacity? What if they'd all stayed home, safe and sound?

How had he imagined he would be able to keep his emotions in check today, one glimpse of his daughter's smile leaving him raw and exposed?

Shoving those thoughts aside—it wasn't fair to Milly—Roman watched his daughter jerk her arms and legs with excitement, her gaze following the movements of the fish swimming past.

Sadie smiled and pointed and made fish faces, her animation contagious, glancing over at him to include him in the moment.

A wild storm of longing and admiration spun inside him like a hurricane. Being around his daughter was wonderful and heart-wrenching. Watching Sadie mother their child made him want her even more. He already knew that she was good with children from work. But this was different.

This was *their* child.

Clearing his dry throat, Roman clung to a distraction. 'What have you told people about Milly's father?'

Sadie stiffened, her delighted smile for Milly fading. 'Umm…not much. My sister knows about you, obviously,' she said, apologetically. 'But no one at work knows, if that's what you're worried about.'

Roman shrugged, some deeply rooted primal imperative demanding the world knew that he'd fathered this beautiful baby. 'I'm not worried, just curious.'

How he and Sadie met was their business. They weren't a couple. And she clearly didn't want anyone at work to know that he was Milly's father.

'Have *you* told anyone?' Sadie asked warily.

Roman nodded. 'Just my parents and my brothers and sister.'

'How many siblings do you have?'

'Five. I come from a big family.'

'Five?' Sadie said, her eyes wide with shock.

He smiled, changing the subject because, one day, he'd like Milly to meet her Czech family, but they'd agreed to take each day at a time. 'And the baby is thriving? Growing, eating, sleeping?'

His hands itched to hold Milly, the bonding instinct primal.

Sadie smiled up at him, the baby happy in her arms. 'She's perfect and doing everything she should be doing.'

Roman swallowed the lump in his throat; she was perfect.

'Would you like to hold her?' Sadie asked, her expression relaxed and encouraging.

'Yes,' he said, instinctively, holding out his arms. His heart pounded, but he needed to feel the baby's weight in his arms, to feel her tiny heartbeat and know that she was real.

His daughter.

Sadie handed over Milly with a bright smile that told the baby she was safe with this stranger.

Roman gripped the precious bundle, dipping his head to catch the warm baby scent of her. He tried to commit it to memory, his eyes closing on a wave of primitive feelings: innate recognition, fierce protective instincts, a surge of love.

'It's okay,' Sadie said, talking to Milly in a reassuring voice, her arm coming around his back, enclosing the three of them in a bubble of intimacy.

For an unguarded moment, Roman saw a flash of what might have been, imagined the three of them as a family. But he'd already had that.

A frisson of panic slithered down his spine.

Was he capable of being a proper father again? The idea of loving another child laced his blood with fear that he'd forget Miko. But now that he'd met her, held her, recognised her, the doubt that he might be too broken to love his innocent daughter didn't bear thinking about. With each passing day since he'd discovered her existence, the urgency to know her, to ensure she was safe and happy, to protect and care for her had taken over.

'*Poklad...*' he whispered, pressing a soft kiss to the top of Milly's head.

'What does that mean?' Sadie asked, resting

her head on his arm, as if she understood he needed her close.

'I called her *treasure*. It's a Czech term of endearment.' His gaze was drawn to Sadie's soft smile, her embrace slotting a piece of him back into place.

'She is precious.' Sadie nodded, staring deep into his eyes.

This woman had brought his broken spirit solace, first in Vienna, when their night of passion had reminded him that he was capable of feeling something positive and light-hearted, and again when she'd turned his world upside down with news of his daughter.

'Thank you,' he whispered, trying to untangle his gratitude from the other feelings he had for Sadie.

'Why are you thanking me?' she said, her eyes swimming with emotion and flickers of desire he was so relieved to see.

'For making such a beautiful baby,' he said in a low voice, thick with reverence. 'For giving me time to come to terms with the news. For sharing her with me.'

His voice broke on the last word.

Sadie gripped his waist tighter. 'You're welcome. I'm sorry that you missed out on her first two months.'

He cast her a sad smile. 'Time I missed because I made a stupid decision to seduce a sexy stranger without getting her name and number.'

Sadie stared, her body warm against his. It would be so easy, almost second nature to cup her face close for a kiss. Part of him was desperate to explore their chemistry, their growing connection, the rest of him certain they should set that aside and focus all their energy on Milly.

'She seduced you too,' Sadie whispered, clearly battling a similar dilemma.

Then something amazing happened. Milly smiled, first at Sadie, waving her little fist, and then up at Roman.

He gasped, something inside him cracking open, letting in a shaft of light.

He had no idea if he'd be able to do fatherhood a second time, but he wouldn't waste the amazing chance he'd been given to be a member of this little family. Milly deserved a father willing to make a fresh start. She deserved to have as much stability and love and opportunity as he'd lavished on Miko.

The question was, could he put down the roots he'd avoided for so long when he was so out of practice? And what would those roots represent for him and Sadie? Constant temptation or the foundations of something neither of them expected?

* * *

Roman placed a tray on the table and took the seat next to Sadie in the zoo's Forest Café. 'I brought you water as well as tea. Nursing mothers need to stay hydrated, as you know.'

'Thank you.' Sadie swallowed the lump the size of a rock in her throat, high from the emotions of the day.

Spending time with Roman away from work was terrifyingly easy, their connection back on track.

After a few hesitant moments, he'd embraced Milly with wonder and tenderness that had been hard to watch. Holding her as if she was precious, staring at her funny baby faces and nonsensical gurgles with awe, whispering to her in Czech.

How could Sadie be expected to stay immune to such exhilarating moments of father and daughter bonding? To stay immune to Roman the doting father?

Milly finished her feed, and unlike a few weeks ago, when she would usually fall asleep afterwards, now she was more intent on taking in all the new sights and sounds.

'You drink and I'll get her wind up,' Roman said, reaching for the muslin square Sadie kept handy for milky burps.

Telling herself she was simply awash with love hormones from nursing their daughter, Sadie handed the baby over, braced once more for the sight of Roman holding Milly, staring down at her with that breathtaking smile on his face.

'I'm hogging her, aren't I?' he said, unapologetically cuddling her close.

His eagerness made Sadie's eyes smart. 'It's okay; she's waited a long time to meet you.'

Considering that a few days ago she'd been scared Roman would disown their daughter, his reaction to being properly introduced to their daughter had squashed many of Sadie's doubts—her concern for Roman's grieving process and her fear of introducing her precious Milly to a stranger.

They stared at each other over the daughter they'd made together. Just as they'd been doing all morning, feelings rushed Sadie, wave after wave of desire for this wonderful man, a new level of contentment, stronger than anything she'd experienced before. Every time he'd looked at her today, she'd seen admiration, as if he saw Sadie in a whole new light. A woman with whom he'd created a life.

Heady stuff for someone already turned on by his hand-holding, moved by his small acts of thoughtfulness, and overcome by the way he seemed to have welcomed her beloved Milly into his heart.

Was this how it felt when children brought couples closer?

Except she and Roman weren't a couple and never would be.

Roman would always be in love with another woman, and Sadie had trust issues and insecurities. He came from a big family and Milly was likely to be Sadie's only child. He moved around to avoid the pain of losing his family, and, after years of yearning but accepting that she might never have a baby, Sadie couldn't bear to think of sharing Milly in some complex custody arrangement. But realistically, if Roman intended to stay in his daughter's life, that was exactly what awaited the three of them.

Unless his itchy feet, the lure of that rolling-stone lifestyle of his, would eventually outweigh his desire to change nappies.

In an attempt to distract her from the panic hijacking her pulse, Sadie retrieved the gift from Milly's nappy bag. 'Can I open this now?'

She didn't want to consider what *the future* entailed for them now that Roman wanted to be a part of Milly's life.

'Of course.' He looked up from winding Milly, turning his adoring expression on Sadie with a smile.

She couldn't get carried away by one successful outing. It was early days. Plenty of time for

Roman to change his mind about wanting Milly in his life.

Inside the wrapping was a charming wooden pull-along toy in the shape of a duck. The minute the baby saw the bright yellow beak she grasped for it.

'Wooden toys are traditional in the Czech Republic,' Roman explained, sliding closer to Sadie so their thighs touched. 'I know she won't use it for a while, but I wanted her to have something from the oldest toy shop in Prague.'

'It's beautiful,' Sadie whispered, the flicker of pain dimming his eyes telling her that he'd probably shopped there for Miko, too. 'She'll treasure it.'

'She's amazing, Sadie,' he said, stroking the soft curls at the nape of Milly's neck.

'I know,' she managed to choke out, the sight of this sexy, competent and intelligent man as a gentle and nurturing father almost too much for her poor weak and hormone-ridden body to endure.

Spending time as a family, while wonderful for Milly and Roman, was messing with Sadie's head. She didn't want to be hurt.

'I've been thinking,' she said. 'I know you didn't have a say in naming Milly, so if you want to add a middle name, perhaps something Czech, we can officially alter her birth certificate.'

'I'd like that.' His smile of gratitude spurred her on.

'Also, I wonder if you could send me a picture of Miko. I'd like to put a framed photo in Milly's room, so I can tell her about her big brother as she grows.'

'Of course.' His stare filled with stormy emotions as he reached out and cupped her face, his thumb gliding along her cheekbone. 'You're a special person, Sadie, and a wonderful mother.'

His eyes bored into hers, shutting out the people around them. 'I know we're taking one day at a time, but I hoped you might one day bring Milly to Prague. My family would love to meet her.'

'Of course... I hadn't thought of that, but of course they want to meet her...'

Fear fizzed in her veins. Roman wanted to proudly introduce his daughter to the Czech side of her family. Maybe when she was older, the visits wouldn't include Sadie at all.

The idea of Roman and Milly spending time without her pinched at Sadie's stomach. But she'd need to get used to that. The future held shared custody, separate holidays and Christmas Days and birthdays where they'd need to find some fair way of sharing their daughter.

No wonder she was reluctant to think too far ahead. The future was horribly uncertain.

'The idea unsettles you,' he said, his stare full of understanding. 'You've been used to having Milly all to yourself.'

Sadie shook her head. 'It's not that. I just don't like planning too far ahead. Life is...unpredictable, as you know, and I try to live in the moment rather than freak myself out with scary what ifs.'

When she'd first met Mark, he'd seemed too wonderful to be true. And as it had turned out, she'd been right.

'Okay,' he said, not pushing, but taking her hand.

Sadie squirmed, forcing herself to open up because Roman deserved more of an explanation. 'It's a habit that began when I received my infertility diagnosis, but my ex, Mark, was a very demonstrative person, always making grand romantic gestures, or voicing big plans for our future as a couple. *"When we get married, we can go to Bali for our honeymoon..." "If we buy this two-bedroom flat in Islington, in three years we'll be able to afford to upgrade to a bigger home in Hampstead..." "When we retire, we could move to Spain..."'*

She glanced away from the compassion in Roman's eyes, way out of her comfort zone.

'Over the years we were together, he drew me into his dreams, made me believe that our future was out there waiting for us, full of hope and optimism even though I was unlikely to ever have my greatest wish: a baby of my own.'

Roman tensed at her side, his face slashed with a harsh frown.

'He'd said that we'd be happy even if it was just the two of us, and I believed him, felt lucky to have such a wonderful partner in my life, someone who accepted me just the way I am. Then one day,' she said, taking comfort from his touch, 'he came home from work and told me he was leaving me, just like that. While we'd been making plans to get engaged, to have a spring wedding and that honeymoon in Bali, he'd also been making plans with another woman. A woman from work he'd been sleeping with for three months. A woman he'd got pregnant. She was giving him the one thing I couldn't, so he chose her over me.'

'I'm sorry that you were so badly let down,' Roman said, his stare searching hers.

'I'm not the only person to have ever been cheated on,' Sadie said, a little numb and a whole lot uncertain how her instincts had been so wrong where Mark was concerned. 'And I was mostly angry that he used me as a place holder until someone better came along. That, when it came to the crunch, he'd lied: my infertility *did* matter.'

'People cheat for many complex reasons,' Roman said, defensive on her behalf. 'It was about him, not you.'

'I know.' Sadie shrugged. But she had allowed herself to be sucked into Mark's dreams, the pretty promises and the pictures they'd painted. 'I was long over him the night we met in Vienna. I'm well shot of a shallow person who would lie and cheat.'

But her ability to trust her judgement still felt bruised, some small part of her deep inside still doubting that she'd ever be good enough for another relationship.

Roman tilted his head in that way of his, seeing her too clearly. 'You deserve so much more than a man like that. You're kind and caring and funny and smart. You deserve someone who—'

As if he'd had an unpleasant thought, he broke off abruptly.

Was he jealous of this fictional future man? Did he hate the idea of someone else helping to raise their daughter? Or was it simply that he'd been about to admit aloud that the man she deserved could never be him.

Fortunately, Milly started to grizzle, rubbing at her eyes and giving Sadie a legitimate reason to shy away from the moment of vulnerability.

'Oh—it's nap time. We should probably go.' Sadie wrestled Milly into her coat and hat, and Roman tucked her into the buggy, covering her with a blanket.

By the time they'd walked to the Camden

Town Tube station, the baby was fast asleep. As they were headed in different directions, Sadie paused inside to say goodbye.

'Thank you for today, Sadie,' Roman said, glancing down at a sleeping Milly. 'I know we still have a lot to figure out, but I appreciate your patience with me.'

He looked frozen, as if he couldn't bring himself to walk away from his baby, now that they'd met.

Sadie blinked, her eyes stinging. 'We don't have to figure everything out. One day at a time, remember.'

Roman nodded, hesitating as if he had more to say.

'Will you be okay?' she asked, her chest aching with compassion.

He nodded once, decisive. But he didn't move, only scoured her face for what felt like hours, returning time and again to her mouth.

She was reminded of that first day, when they'd been stuck in the ward office together, the lock jammed. Part of her had been desperate to flee and the other part unable to move, waiting for his kiss. Except she knew him so much better now, the sexual tension between them fierce and unrelenting now that they had the most important thing in the world in common: a child.

Only it was because of that child that they needed to be, oh, so careful.

Perhaps deciding that he could delay no longer, Roman cast one last look at the baby and swooped close, gripping Sadie's arm and pressing a swift kiss to her cheek.

There was a split second where time seemed suspended. Sadie considered turning her head so their lips would connect. But their chemistry was too strong. She wanted him too badly. If she kissed him now, she'd invite him home. They'd end up in bed.

But it had been an emotional day, for both of them.

Stepping back, she retreated to safety. 'I'll see you tomorrow, at work.'

Scanning her travel card, she pushed the buggy through the accessible barrier, without looking back, her heart and her stomach a knotted mess.

It would be so easy to allow her desire for Roman to rule her head. They were grown adults each with valid reasons for keeping their attraction in check. It was exhilarating to believe that neither of them would allow anything to get in the way of what was best for their baby. That they could indulge their physical connection without consequence.

Except Milly was living proof that repercussions could sneak up on you.

CHAPTER TEN

'SO THE GOOD news is that you're doing so well,' Roman told Josh, resting a hand on the boy's shoulder, 'that we can take out the chest drain and make you more comfortable.'

Josh gave a hesitant smile, his eyes bright with excitement, a sign that he was clearly on the mend, and Roman glanced at Sadie for confirmation.

'We can remove it this morning.' Sadie nodded, making a note in Josh's file while Roman answered a couple of questions from his parents.

Roman forced himself to look away.

Ever since the trip to the zoo two days ago, he hadn't been able to stop thinking about Sadie and Milly. Sadie's devotion to their adorable daughter had boosted his attraction to her tenfold. Motherhood brought out new and rousing aspects of her personality. He lived for the glimpses of her at work. Craved her texts and the pictures she sent of her and Milly together. Even now, with her standing right next to him, he missed their connection.

But just because they were parents who shared potent chemistry, didn't mean a relationship between him and Sadie should be full steam ahead. As it was, he was reeling from a crash refresher course on how to be a father.

His daughter... He'd so easily fallen in love with his baby; he'd had little choice. Milly gave him a reason to open his eyes in the morning, already an undeniable and permanent piece of his heart.

After the accident, he'd embraced his solitary existence. But he hadn't realised how much he'd missed simple everyday things. Family things. Outings. But now that there was Milly to consider, the things he'd lived without seemed important once more. His world had opened up. All the things he wanted to show Milly. All things they could do together. All the moments he would cherish and never take for granted leaving him full of restless excitement he hadn't felt for many years.

And it was all down to Sadie, the woman who had given their daughter life, a passionate, caring woman who'd been badly hurt.

Could the three of them be a family, his second? Was he capable of being the father he needed to be while also trying to build a relationship? Would Sadie even want that after her past experiences?

Because if it all went wrong, he could lose everything.

'Can I leave you to remove the drain?' he asked as they left Josh's bedside, wishing they were anywhere else but at work.

The more time he spent with Sadie, the harder it was becoming to separate the instant love he felt for Milly from the admiration, respect and gratitude he felt for Sadie.

And lust, don't forget lust.

But that didn't mean he was ready to risk his heart in a romantic way.

'Of course. I'll see to it.' She looked up at him, questions in her beautiful eyes.

She wanted to know if he was okay after meeting Milly. Could he explain the disorientating collision of his painful past and this unexpected present he'd experienced meeting his baby girl. How mesmerised he'd been by the maternal love he saw between Sadie and Milly because he'd witnessed the same between Karolina and Miko. How holding Milly, inhaling her scent and touching her baby soft skin, somehow made his memories of Miko more vivid. How Sadie's thoughtfulness when she'd asked for a picture of his son had almost undone him.

'I miss her,' he whispered, knowing that Sadie would understand who he meant. 'Is she okay?'

The ward was busy; they had no privacy, and he needed to go to Theatre. Only he couldn't bring himself to walk away.

'She's good.' Sadie's smile lit her eyes with tenderness. 'Why don't you come over after work? We can chat about the auction while we bath her together. You can read a bedtime story.'

Pain lanced his chest, bittersweet. 'I'd love that.'

How many bath or story times had he shared with Miko? Not enough. He wouldn't take the opportunity to participate in such a simple everyday moment with his daughter for granted. But the restlessness he'd felt since he'd learned of Milly's existence, bloomed anew.

If he was struggling to go a couple of days without seeing Milly, how would he endure weeks or even months apart? His next locum position in Ireland loomed. How could he contemplate moving away when he'd only just begun to know his daughter? How could he miss another second of her precious life?

'You're hesitant,' Sadie remarked with a frown.

He wanted to tell her all his fears and reservations, but he didn't want to scare her after the things she'd told him about her past. Sadie had understandable trust issues and he couldn't make her any promises while he was figuring out how he could be everything he needed to be: doctor, father, lover.

It was better to make a plan, find a way he could be in his daughter's life first, take one day at a time.

The need to have his uncertainties mapped out beat at him anew. He wanted to know Sadie's views on him having regular visitation or even shared custody of Milly. He needed to voice his thoughts on relocating permanently to London to watch his daughter grow up. He hated the idea of Milly being shipped overseas for her school holidays to visit Roman wherever he was working, and he wanted to know how Sadie saw co-parenting working for them.

Only now wasn't the time to thrash out the details.

More pressing was exactly how he would spend more time with his daughter and not want Sadie.

But acting on those desires could undo the fragile ties of their tiny new family.

'Only because it's hard to be around you and not be…distracted.' His gaze sought the temptation of her lips. She needed to understand that their furious chemistry hadn't gone away. If anything, it was stronger.

'Oh.' She flushed, smiled. 'Do you want to risk it?'

He nodded, wishing he could touch her, wondering for the millionth time why he was fighting his attraction so hard. 'I think we should talk about it. Later? I need to go.'

'I'll text you my address.'

Because he could delay no longer, he turned to leave, his hand deliberately brushing hers at her side. It wasn't the contact he craved, but it would need to sustain him for the rest of the day.

As he walked to the operating suites, he dragged in a deep breath. For a man who, until now, had been content to live out of a suitcase, this evening, spending time with his girls, shone like a beacon of golden light he wanted to run towards.

Except every moment he spent with Sadie was a lesson in temptation.

Roman sighed as he scanned himself into the theatre changing rooms. Never in his life had he needed to be more in control of his feelings, which were a confusing mash-up of past and present, grief and joy. Of his new relationship with his daughter, which would prioritise her security and happiness. Of his attraction to a woman who, because they'd created a life together, had overnight gone from temporary lover to a significant and permanent person in his life.

Determined to find that control so that no one—not him, or Sadie or, most importantly, Milly—got hurt, Roman pulled on his scrubs and prepared for a long day.

Milly jerked her arms and legs excitedly, squealing and splashing Roman in the face with bathwater. He laughed, smiling down at their beautiful daughter with delight in his eyes.

'Good shot, Milly,' Sadie said, reaching for a towel to dab at Roman's dripping face. 'She normally soaks me, so I'm glad that you're here.'

'I needed a soaking after a long day,' he said, reaching for some suds and playfully dabbing them on the end of Sadie's nose when she continued to giggle at his expense. 'And I'm glad I'm here too.'

Sadie shuddered with desire; there was nothing playful about the heat in Roman's eyes. She wiped her nose, taking a second to hide behind the towel while she struggled with the arousal leaving her breathless.

'Are we ready to come out?' Sadie asked Milly, splashing her belly with water to make her smile.

She lifted the baby out and handed her to Roman, who was waiting with a warm, fluffy towel to wrap her up. They dried and dressed Milly together, smiling at her funny facial expressions and the triumphant gurgling sounds she made when she managed to grab a handful of Sadie's long hair.

'I've been thinking,' Roman said, his expression falling serious as Sadie buttoned up Milly's sleep suit. 'I'd like Milly to call me Tatínek if that's okay. It's Czech for Daddy.'

Sadie froze, trying to downplay the significance of the moment. The last time he was called that, it would have been by Miko.

'Of course it's okay.' Sadie picked Milly up, looping her other arm around his waist, holding him to let him know that she understood the importance of his request. 'Tatínek it is.'

Choked by the conflicted emotion flitting across his face at her use of the Czech word, Sadie settled on the sofa with Roman at her side.

Roman read Milly's favourite story and then sang a song in Czech.

'An old Czech folk song my grandfather sang to me, that I used to sing to Miko,' he explained, watching Milly latch on for her final feed.

'Do you ever miss home?' Sadie asked, scared to know but also aware that Roman's heritage was Milly's heritage.

He shrugged, entwined his fingers with hers in a gesture that now felt second nature. 'Sometimes,' he said in a quiet voice. 'But I think home isn't a place, a town or a city. It's in here.' He pressed his fist to his chest.

Sadie's own heart thumped at his intensity, at how much she wanted to hold him and chase away the shadows in his eyes. At the fever-pitch of how badly she craved their intimacy.

'That's why I can travel around as a locum and still carry Karolina and Miko with me wherever I go,' he added.

Sadie pressed her lips together, desperate to know if he also planned to carry Milly in his heart when he left for Ireland. But she couldn't bear to ask, because thinking about the future meant admitting that Roman might want Milly in his life, but that didn't mean he wanted a romantic relationship with Sadie.

The future was full of all the important days of Milly's life that Sadie would miss while Roman and Milly and eventually some new woman in Roman's life were together. No matter how much she fantasised that she and Roman might one day be a proper couple, reality intervened.

The minute he'd said he came from a big family, a part of her hope had shrivelled to dust. Roman had probably wanted a large family of his own before tragedy struck. But now that he had Milly, there would be nothing to stop him from filling his heart with the love of more children. With the right woman, of course.

And that wasn't Sadie.

'Mind if I put her down?' Roman asked, taking the baby, who'd fallen asleep after her feed.

'Go for it.' Sadie pasted on a brave face, and flopped back against the sofa cushions as he left the room.

She'd never in a million years have imagined that the commitment-shy man she'd met the night they'd conceived would be such a hands-on, caring and dedicated father. But now that she knew the real Roman, she couldn't have asked for a better *tatínek* for her treasured daughter.

It was a serious aphrodisiac, not that she needed one where Roman was concerned.

He was making it so hard for her to ignore what a special man he was, to hold him at arm's length physically so she could keep her emotional distance from their deepening connection. They spent so much time together that the casual touches, comforting embraces and heated looks were becoming increasingly hard to fight.

But maybe she didn't need to fight so hard. Maybe she could sleep with him, one more time, knowing that by keeping things physical she could trust him not to hurt her.

'She didn't stir,' he said as he rejoined Sadie, looking slightly tired and rumpled, his hair mussed, in a thoroughly arousing way, as if he'd run his fingers through it.

He sat, stretched his arm out along the back of the sofa behind Sadie.

'Thank you,' she said, her eyes locked with his, her throat tight.

'What for?' A small frown pinched his brows together as he regarded her with quiet intensity.

'For being you. For embracing Milly the way you have.' His obvious adoration of their baby combined with his extreme hotness left Sadie dangerously off-kilter. 'I'm so glad you found a space in your heart for our little miracle.'

'How could I not? She's delightful. I'm head over heels.' His expression turned serious but his fingers found the back of her neck, stroking. 'Although don't thank me yet. I think I've forgotten how to do fatherhood. I'll probably get it wrong at some point.'

Sadie shook her head, her body melting at the hypnotic rhythm of his touch. 'I think it's naturally coming back to you. Milly will help you remember.'

'She already is.' He nodded, holding her eye contact so she saw the love for their daughter shining there. 'She's a wonderful blessing, for both of us. Getting to know Milly, reliving all these beautiful everyday moments, is somehow making me also feel closer to Miko.'

Of course every joyful moment he shared with their daughter must remind him of similar mo-

ments he'd had with his son. That loving Milly
was somehow easing his pain shifted something
deep inside Sadie's chest, her bruised heart trying to beat to a new, hopeful rhythm.

Sadie stilled, that same heart thudding. Tonight, they'd bonded deeper over their daughter,
but they were also two adults insanely attracted
to each other.

'You wanted to talk about the auction?' he said.

'Did I…?' Idiot. Why would she want to bring
up the topic of him dating another woman?

Why hadn't she given in to temptation and
kissed him as soon as he sat down? They could
be naked by now.

'I need to work on your bio,' she said. 'I might
need to ask you a few more questions.' She
sounded half-hearted at best.

His fingers sliding up to her hairline and then
down to the bumps of her vertebrae were driving her crazy. But it stopped her thinking about
him on a date with another woman. It stopped
her thinking that after the Valentine's fundraiser
he'd be moving on to his next locum position.

'You know everything important about me already, Sadie.' His voice was low, seductive, luring her in.

But he was right. She did know the most important things about this man. She knew that he

cared about people, including her. She knew that he kept his word. She knew she wanted him.

She'd never stopped wanting him.

'But I want you to know this, too.' As if he saw her deepest fears in her eyes, he cupped her face. 'I know you've been hurt in the past. But I'll do everything in my power to do right by you and Milly.'

Choked by the depth of feeling in his admission, by his vulnerability and the way he included her in his new family, Sadie groaned. 'Roman...'

She was desperate now, his touch lighting up every cell in her body.

She rested her forehead against his. 'We should stop.' It emerged a feeble whisper.

His fingers curled into her hair at the nape of her neck, his breath coming hard. 'I know... I know.'

'I want you.' Her hands found his waist, fisting his T-shirt.

Their breath mingled.

He pulled back, his hands sliding to her shoulders, fingers digging as he fought some epic internal battle. 'Kick me out.'

Sadie shook her head, her heart rate dizzyingly high. 'We just need to be careful.'

He nodded, something in his eyes shifting.

Sadie instinctively knew that he understood

everything she'd left unsaid. That he'd be true to his word. That they would put Milly first.

Roman was different. She could trust him with her body, knowing that, with the exception of their daughter's happiness, their priorities hadn't changed since their first night together. It would just be sex. Amazing, wonderful sex.

Reaching the limit of their endurance together, they pounced. Their lips met in a rush. Eager. Days of longing rendering Sadie wild with desire.

Roman scooped his strong arm around her waist with a groan, hauled her close, chest to chest. Sadie gripped his neck, tunnelled her fingers in his glorious hair, returned his kisses with all her pent-up passion.

Yes, they were parents, but they were also humans. They had their own needs. And right now nothing mattered more than this connection.

'I thought you'd never kiss me,' she panted, straddling Roman's lap.

'I never stopped wanting to,' he said, gripping her hips and tilting his head back against the cushions so Sadie could lean over him, press kisses to his jaw, his neck, his lips, in a thorough exploration. Every sigh and moan swallowed. Every taste savoured.

'You are so sexy.' His hands slid beneath her top, along her ribs, cupping her breasts through her bra. 'Are you sure about this?'

'Absolutely.' She rocked her hips on his lap, grinding his erection between her legs, where she wanted him.

Despite the fact that since they were last intimate she now had stretch marks, Roman made her feel sexy. Wanted. And, oh, how she wanted him in return.

'You've just had a baby,' he said, his thumbs stroking her nipples. 'I don't want to hurt you.'

'You won't.' Sadie collapsed against him, her tongue duelling with his to counter the pleasure he was wreaking with his touch.

He popped the clasp on her bra and raised her top, exposing her breasts with a groan. 'I've thought about this so many times.' He raised her breast and laved her nipple. 'I thought I'd go mad for wanting you.'

'Me too.' Sadie removed her top and tossed it aside, moaning, as his mouth sought her other breast. 'Although we need to be more careful with the condoms, this time…just in case I've become the most fertile woman on the planet.'

Tugging off his shirt, she pressed kisses over his bare chest, goosebumps rising as his chest hair brushed her nipples.

'I'm always careful, but don't worry; this time you've got my number.' He winked, standing up with Sadie in his arms.

Sadie wrapped her arms around his neck,

burying her face there while he strode to her bedroom. As he laid her down on the bed and stood back to admire her partial nakedness, she feared that she might not survive another night as Roman's lover.

Because, aside from his irreparably broken heart, everything else about Roman was dangerously wonderful.

CHAPTER ELEVEN

ROMAN STARED DOWN at Sadie, his breath gusting, the promise he'd made to her still spiralling through his mind. He'd meant it: he'd never hurt Sadie, nor risk hurting Milly. He would always strive to put his new family first. That this amazing, beautiful woman had been so badly let down in the past brought all of his protective urges to the fore.

Plans he'd been mulling over ever since he'd known about Milly solidified. He wasn't sure exactly how yet, but he wanted to be around to help to raise his child, whether or not he and Sadie were romantically involved.

He loved his daughter. He never wanted to miss another bath time.

But tonight was about him and Sadie. And she was right; they would need to be careful. This time, there was more at stake.

'Come here.' Sadie took his hands, drawing him close.

Roman leaned over her and pressed a kiss to her lips, determined to go slow and wring every drop of pleasure from the night. Desire urged him to kiss a path along her neck, pausing when she sighed.

'I want you to know,' he said, kissing her collarbones and the tops of her breasts, 'that because of you, for the first time in years, I feel hopeful.'

Her pupils dilated, her breaths coming faster as she gazed up at him, her stare pleading. 'Roman...'

She tugged the belt loops of his jeans, her hands skimming his ribs, back and shoulders.

But he wanted her to know that she'd turned his life around. 'I haven't slept with anyone else since that night in Vienna.'

For the intervening months, he hadn't questioned why, but now, with her scent on his skin, with her beauty softened by the dim glow of lamplight, with nothing but Sadie in his head, he realised that subconsciously he'd been waiting for someone...extraordinary, like Sadie.

Her eyes widened in surprise.

'I couldn't get you off my mind. It was as if fate had some important reason to draw me back to you.' He stripped off her jeans, skimming his hands up her legs as he lay at her side.

And fate had been right. No matter what the future held for him and Sadie, they would always stay connected.

'I want to make you feel good.' He traced her ribs, cupped her breast, swiped at the nipple with his thumb, watching her reactions. 'Are your breasts tender?' he asked, noticing her shiver.

'No.' She turned to face him, wrapped her arms around his neck, pressing her lips to his. 'Don't treat me like I'm fragile. I want you.'

'I want you too.' It scared him how much; they were so in tune. They'd figure everything else out.

'These need to come off,' Sadie said, her hands working at the buttons of his jeans. Obviously the time for talking was over.

He smiled against her lips, brushing her hair back from her flushed face. 'All in good time.'

She pressed her mouth over his chest while her hands roamed his back, making it hard for him to cling to his sense of control. Roman closed his eyes, momentarily lost in the intensity of her touch, the brush of her nipples, the thud of her heart alongside his, the scrape of her fingernails against his skin.

Unlike the last time they were intimate, now they were so close. For him, it was more than lust and gratitude. More than their shared views and values. More than the way she intuitively understood him. They'd bonded. Over their pasts, over their work, over their daughter.

A deep connection he would always cherish.

Drawing her lips back to his, he kissed her, his thumbs toying with her nipples until they stood erect and she whimpered in pleasure.

'I don't want to hurt you,' he said, 'so tell me to stop if anything is uncomfortable.' He kissed a path down the warm fragrant skin of her neck, across her chest, over her breasts. Embracing the chemistry they'd each fought for so long, he tongued her nipples one by one, smiled when she twisted his hair in her hands, groaned when she stroked him through his jeans.

He moved lower, kissing her stomach, the place where she'd carried their child, running his tongue over her skin, lower and lower, sliding off her underwear so he could kiss and tongue between her legs.

She gasped, holding his head, telling him all he needed to know with her pleasure-glazed eyes. He lingered, lost in their uncomplicated passion, the high of making her feel as good as she made him, spreading her thighs so he could lick her until she was clawing at his shoulders and crying out his name.

Wound too tight to wait any longer, he removed the last of his clothes, grabbed a condom from his wallet and covered himself, his fingers trembling with repressed need.

'Why did we wait so long?' she whispered as

his body covered hers, their legs entwined, hands roaming feverishly.

He gazed into the depth of her eyes. 'I have no idea.'

Holding her in his arms felt so right. Their passion seemed second nature. Their trust mutual after everything else they'd shared.

But he couldn't wait any longer. He covered her body with his, kissing her deep. She clung to him, her hands around his neck, her legs encircling his hips, her kisses growing frantic. 'Roman...'

His name was a plea on her lips and he finally relented, giving them what they both craved, pushing slowly inside her and then holding still but for the crazy beating of his heart.

'Are you okay?' he asked, panting, using every scrap of his willpower not to move.

'Yes. Don't stop.' She shifted under him, restless, needy, and he scrunched his eyes closed, seeing flashes of light, so intense was the pleasure.

He kissed her, swallowing up her mewls and moans as he gently thrust inside her, revelling in her hard-won trust and their strong emotional bond, which intensified his desire.

This time was so much better. He knew this woman. Her smile raised his spirits. Her sense of humour left him light-hearted. Her passion matched his, consuming him until she was all he could think about.

'Sadie...' he groaned as they held each other tight, the tempo building, each of them chasing the finish line.

Her nails dug into his skin as she gripped him tight. He pulled back from kissing her, stared into her beautiful eyes, now glazed with arousal. Their stares locked.

Despite everything, his own reticence, the promises he'd made, Sadie's warnings, something inside him reached out to her. He had no idea if could ever again love, but the new hopeful part of him she'd awoken wanted things: this deep emotional connection, the passion that left him speechless, a relationship with a woman who understood him and asked nothing of him that he couldn't give.

Now, moving inside her, he'd never felt more convinced that he was ready to try and open himself up to a new relationship.

With Sadie.

When Sadie shattered, crying out his name, his own climax tingled at the base of his spine, as if her pleasure was inexorably linked with his own. He groaned, staring down at her, and for a few blissful and heady seconds anything seemed possible while they were together like this.

As if she felt it too, Sadie gripped his face, holding his eyes to hers.

All his needs and wants coalesced. He was a flesh and blood man, yes, but since meeting Sadie, he had dreams and aspirations, hopes for the future. A future that included this beautiful, caring woman.

His orgasm tore at him. He buried his face against her neck, dragging in her scent, holding her so tight, she felt a part of him.

Having fought this physical release for so long, Roman already wanted Sadie again. Their bond was addictive. Sadie was balm to his body and soul. One he wasn't sure he could do without.

They held each other, catching their breath, kissing, laughing, the release of a year's worth of tension euphoric.

'Please tell me you can stay the night.' Sadie sighed, curling her body against his, her head resting over his thumping heart.

Roman stroked his fingers through her hair. He wanted that. Except he also wanted more.

Having Sadie in his arms while their daughter slept peacefully in the other room made the gaping holes in his life more evident, their edges sharper, their depths vast lonely spaces. He wanted to plan with her, to figure out a way they could be a family, know if Sadie felt the same way about him.

Did she see a future for the two of them? Or was she still too scared to look?

'I can stay the night, if you think it won't confuse Milly.' His hand caressed her shoulder as he pressed his lips to her forehead. He couldn't stop touching her.

'She's not even three months old.' Sadie smiled up at him. 'She's not going to remember seeing you in the morning and even if she could, you're her father.'

'Good point.' He drew her face up to his and kissed her lips.

He was Milly's father. He needed to be there for his girl. And he wanted to be there for Sadie too. No one could replace Karolina and Miko in his heart. But just as he'd found a new and limitless source of love for his daughter, perhaps there could also be space for another relationship. With Sadie.

'I know you have doubts,' Sadie said, staring up at him, 'but I hope you know that you're a great father.'

He hummed non-committally. 'Right now, all I can think about is how to be everything I need to be. How to do everything in my power to ensure that our girl is safe and happy.'

'Our girl,' Sadie whispered. 'I like that.'

He gripped her tighter, worried that he'd never let her go. 'I understand your fears for the future.'

Sadie stiffened, but Roman continued, needing some concession that they would have this necessary conversation. 'But promise me we'll talk about a plan for sharing the parental responsibilities some time. I know you've been hurt in the past. But I never thought I'd have a second chance at a family, and I never want to let anyone down again.'

Sadie raised her head from his chest, from the thump of his heart. 'What do you mean? You don't blame yourself for the accident, do you? Because it wasn't your fault.'

'Intellectually, I know I wasn't responsible,' he said, stroking her back. 'I didn't cause the accident. But there's a part of me that feels like I let my family down because I wasn't driving that day. I'll never know if I might have been able to avoid the collision, if I'd been behind the wheel instead of at work.'

'I'm so sorry,' she said, pressing her lips to his, her kiss a perfect distraction from his pain. 'I promise we'll talk about a shared custody arrangement,' she said, her stare glittering with fear and uncertainty, 'if you promise me one thing in return.'

'Anything.' He nodded, resolved to tread so carefully, to give Sadie the reassurance she needed. He didn't want to hurt her. If he rushed her, she'd withdraw, so damaged was her trust.

But could he be everything *he* needed to be, could he keep Milly safe and happy and be the things Sadie needed also? Perhaps living day to day was the right plan.

'Promise you won't over-promise.' She blinked, her stare so vulnerable, he wished he could kiss away all her fears. 'This has all happened so quickly. And people change their minds. As you said, it's Milly's happiness that's most important.'

So she *was* still scared for the future. She didn't see them as a couple, only as parents with some depressing amicably shared custody situation. And she was right. He couldn't promise more. Yes, he hoped they might be able to build on this intense chemistry and have a relationship, but he wasn't ready to fully risk his heart until he knew he could always be there for Milly.

Because Sadie's caution made sense: if it all went wrong, he could lose everything.

'I promise,' he said, her hesitation inflaming his own fears that he could be what both Milly and Sadie needed.

Satisfied with his word, she straddled him, kissed him, luring him back to the one certainty between them: their desire.

Roman closed his eyes and surrendered to his physical hunger.

Sadie didn't want to get hurt again and he

didn't want to be the one to let her down. Nor did he want to fail Milly, the way he'd failed Miko.

But caution and sense were no substitute for the passion that made him feel alive. Could Sadie's craving for him match his for her? Could she ever trust him, or was that a foolish illusion?

Did she expect any connection between the two of them to fail, and what if she was right?

His last thought, before his head filled with only Sadie once more, was now that his heart was inexorably linked with his little girl, the one thing he couldn't do was mess up this second chance at a family or risk losing another person he loved.

CHAPTER TWELVE

So how was last night?

GRACE'S TEXT CAME through the minute Sadie left the Tube station and emerged on the wintry street a short walk from the hospital. Roman had left at the crack of dawn and her sister had spent the night at her boyfriend's place. There had been no time for more than a few words as Sadie had handed over a fractious Milly to her sister and rushed to work, relief nipping at her heels.

What was there to say?

Her night with Roman had been wonderful.

After their promises to each other, they'd made love again with the same desperation as the time before, as if both aware that their moments together, just Roman and Sadie, were limited.

But of course they were.

No matter how hard she tried to live in the moment, to savour every one of his kisses, to lavish in the way he made her feel cherished and store the amazing things he'd said to memory, harsh and uncertain reality was about to intrude.

Because her feelings seemed to have a life of their own. What if she allowed them free rein, allowed her guard to fall, opened herself up to a committed relationship with Roman, and he decided that she wasn't what he wanted after all? What if he changed his mind?

Images of a possible future flashed in her head like scenes from a horror movie. If Roman and Sadie didn't work out, what would happen to Milly? Would their daughter lose her wonderful father, or would Sadie be forced to see Roman every time they handed over Milly, be reminded over and over that, while he cherished the child they'd made, for him, Sadie wasn't good enough?

Was having him for herself worth the risk of losing everything, including her peace of mind?

She was terrified by her bone-deep fears, and the last thing she'd wanted was to discuss Roman with her twin. Sadie might as well be made of glass, her every emotion on display to her perceptive sister.

Hoping a few well-placed emojis would appease Grace, she fired off a reply.

Good. He adores Milly, but then what's not to love?

And it was true. Roman loved their daughter. That didn't mean he had feelings for Sadie. He was in love with Karolina. And even if he could one day develop feelings for Sadie, she would always be second best. Could she live with that knowledge, that feeling of soul-destroying inadequacy, again?

With Roman as comparison, she now wondered how she'd ever failed to see through her ex. Roman had been right. She deserved better.

But there was one man for whom any woman, including Sadie, would never be enough: Roman.

Besides, she still had to get through the Valentine's Day auction. She still had to fix him up on a date with another woman, and he still planned to leave for Ireland afterwards. And she'd promised to discuss the future of Milly's custody...

Fighting the nauseated roll of her stomach, Sadie walked swiftly across the hospital car park to the rear staff entrance. Desperate to work as a distraction, she removed her scarf and coat and headed upstairs to Sunshine Ward.

As she arrived on the ward, she'd barely had a chance to glance at the patients on her list when Roman appeared at her side, looking drop-dead gorgeous dressed in one of his immaculate suits.

Her heart galloped with longing, mocking every word of denial she'd just spouted in her head.

'You're here early,' Sadie said, desperate to

kiss him hello the way they'd kissed goodbye a few hours ago.

'I slept incredibly well, Dr Barnes. I feel... rejuvenated,' he said, replacing the ward tablet into the charging station on the desk. Apart from the knowing look in his eyes, his manner was all business.

Sadie breathed through her hot flush, her body recalling every second of pleasure they'd shared.

'I wanted to check on Josh's progress, before my clinic,' he continued, his voice the professional one he used at work.

Sadie nodded, the surge of excitement shunting her heart rate trickling away. What had she expected? That he'd march onto the ward this morning declaring not only his paternity of Milly but also that he couldn't live without Sadie?

That was the ridiculous kind of stunt Mark would pull. Roman was twice the man.

Of course he wasn't on the ward to see her.

'And I've just admitted a six-year-old with a fractured clavicle and abdominal contusion following a road collision,' he continued, indicating the bay he'd come from. Roman's expression turned stony, so Sadie immediately knew that, of course, he was thinking of his family, of Karolina and Miko.

Sadie paused, desperate to reach out to him, missing the way that same voice had whispered her name as he'd moved inside her. 'Are you okay?'

But they weren't a couple.

Only, like Josh the presentation of this new patient was a little close to home for Roman.

He nodded, brushing aside her concern, so Sadie deflated. 'There's a small haematoma around the liver consistent with a seat-belt injury, but no signs of ongoing haemorrhage. I've prescribed IV analgesia, which the nurses are administering at the moment.'

Recalling how, last night, he'd confessed his fears that he'd let his family down, Sadie welcomed the reminder that Roman was still grieving for his wife and son. That no matter how close they'd seemed last night, he was still alone by choice.

It wasn't usual for consultants to perform everyday tasks, admitting patients and prescribing. But Roman liked to work, his self-prescribed antidote to his grieving process.

'Thank you,' she muttered, busying herself with some routine paperwork, disappointment twisting her insides.

While she'd spent last night agonising over every touch, every kiss and whisper, wondering if he might one day, if she waited around long enough, be ready for a relationship, Roman was still content to be the same workaholic loner planning to locum his way through his life. He couldn't help but love Milly, but that didn't mean he wanted Sadie.

As if proving her point, he lowered his voice. 'How's our girl this morning?'

Shoving aside depressing images of future Roman dropping in to see their daughter in between locum positions, or sending for her when she was old enough to travel overseas, Sadie forced her eyes to his. 'She's fine, a little bit grizzly. I think she's teething.'

She kept her voice low not to be overheard. As far as everyone at work knew, Roman was just the hottie surgeon with whom they could win a date.

'I've been thinking,' he said in the same quiet conspiratorial voice. 'I think you're right about the auction. Is it too late to pull out? I might have a friend who'll stand in for me.'

Sadie swallowed, her throat aching. He couldn't face dating anyone. He wasn't ready to put himself out there, not even for a good cause.

She was a fool to think he might one day be ready for more with her.

'I'm sure it will be fine,' she said, her vague hopes withering. 'I'll talk to Sammy.'

But of course he couldn't go through with the charade when he was still grieving for his wife, still in love with her, still dreading Valentine's Day.

'Is everything okay?' he asked, eyeing her with wariness that told her they were once more out of sync.

They might have been discussing a case or the cold snap in the weather for all the warmth between them.

'Fine. It's going to be a busy day, that's all.'

There was no chance of privacy and they each had jobs to do. He was on call that night and Sadie couldn't wait to get home to Milly, to cuddle away all her doubts.

Just then, the emergency alarm sounded.

A flurry of panicked activity surrounded the bedside of the boy Roman had just admitted.

Sadie rushed over, Roman following.

The little boy was struggling to catch a breath, his chest wheezing and his skin almost translucently pale and covered with a fine sheen of perspiration.

'He just went off,' his nurse explained. 'I'd just started the analgesia and was taking his observations when he stopped responding.'

While a concerned Roman placed an oxygen mask over his face, Sadie checked the boy's responsiveness and took his pulse, which was a weak and rapid flutter.

'Have we got a blood-pressure reading?'

Roman asked, glancing at Sadie, his stare almost frantic.

'Hypotensive. Eighty-five over fifty,' the nurse said.

'Could be anaphylaxis,' Sadie said, reaching for the IV to switch off the drip that was administering the painkiller that Roman had prescribed earlier that morning.

She shot him a reassuring look; she knew him so well now, understood how he would blame himself.

But he was focussed on the patient.

He turned to Sammy, who'd also arrived, wheeling in the emergency crash trolley. 'Can we have intramuscular adrenaline now, please?' Roman said, nodding to Sadie to insert a second IV cannula.

'Get rid of that drip and start some intravenous saline,' he ordered, his voice strained with self-reproach.

'Any documented allergies?' Sadie asked, both Roman and the boy's nurse shaking their heads.

Because she knew him so well, Sadie saw the guilt in Roman's expression.

An allergic reaction to a drug could be life-threatening.

But it wasn't his fault. Hopefully, there would be time to comfort him in private later.

'Call the next of kin, please,' Sadie instructed the nurse.

The nurse ducked out of the bay to call the boy's parents.

Instead of leaving Sadie to manage the emergency, as other busy consultants might do, Roman stayed, administering the adrenaline, jabbing the needle into the boy's leg muscles.

Sadie winced as the boy cried, but being responsive to pain in a shock situation was a good indicator that they'd treated the anaphylaxis in time.

'Saturations are ninety-three per cent.' Sadie met Roman's stare, trying to offer him reassurance.

For now the emergency was contained. Stopping the offending drug infusion had been the first treatment, and hopefully the adrenaline would work quickly to dampen the body's violent immune response to a foreign agent.

They faced each other for a few tense seconds, waiting, silently communicating their concerns in their stares.

Within seconds of the adrenaline injection being administered, the wheezing eased and the boy's colour improved. His heart rate slowed to a hundred and twenty beats per minute and his blood pressure rose.

Sadie shot Roman a hesitant smile. Despite

the uncertainties for the future, she and Roman were still a team when it mattered.

Everyone around the bed relaxed a fraction.

'It's okay, Tom.' Roman spoke to the frightened and tearful boy, resting his hand on Tom's shoulder. 'Your body didn't like the medicine we gave it but you're going to be okay. I'm sorry that I had to give you that nasty injection in the leg, but Mummy and Daddy are on their way to give you a hug.'

While Sammy and Tom's nurse soothed the boy, Roman and Sadie spoke away from the bedside.

'I'll keep an eye on him,' Sadie said, wanting more than anything to touch Roman and soothe those worry lines from around his eyes. But he still wasn't hers to comfort.

'Thank you,' he said, distracted, a helpless look haunting his eyes. 'I asked about allergies,' he muttered as if to himself. 'I checked with his mother.'

'Of course you did.' Sadie stared up at him, willing him to be gentle with himself. 'A case of an undocumented allergy could happen to anyone.'

Roman glanced back at Tom, concern still etched over his face.

Of course, if he lived with the guilt that he might have been able to help his beloved wife and cherished son if only he'd been with them that day, a caring doctor like Roman would sometimes struggle to stay impartial and not be triggered by the cases he saw.

Roman's pager sounded and he winced. 'That's clinic. I need to go.' He shot her a preoccupied smile that didn't quite reach his eyes. 'It's going to be one of those days. You're sure you're okay here?'

'Of course.' Sadie pasted on that brave face. 'I'll text you an update on Tom's progress.'

As he walked away Sadie sagged in defeat.

Their work was often demanding. But today, rather than pull together, they seemed to be drifting apart. How were they expected to discuss the big issues, like the custody of their daughter, when they seemed so distant once more?

Roman wasn't obligated to share his deepest fears with her, but it was obvious that, no matter what they'd shared, his family were clearly never far from his mind.

She'd always known it, but some secret part of her had hoped that their relationship might help him come to terms with his loss.

As she set about her morning duties, a busy morning making the night before, the closeness she'd imagined, feel like a distant dream, she clung to the timely reminder that the only part of Roman available was the part she'd had from the start.

They'd enjoyed one more night together before reality dawned, but she wouldn't torture herself with doubt-fuelled maybes. She needed to start weaning herself off, to check the lock on her heart and move forward, putting their baby first.

Because no matter what the future held, she wouldn't be second best again. Not even for Roman.

CHAPTER THIRTEEN

IN THE EARLY hours of the following morning, Roman swished opened the bedside curtains of his newest patient—a thirteen-year-old boy with suspected torsion of the testis—and headed for the nearest computer terminal to order an urgent ultrasound scan.

Accident and Emergency was surprisingly quiet. There were no urgent, on-call surgeries requiring his attention, but Roman knew he wouldn't be able to sleep a wink. Better to keep busy with work than to toss and turn the night away thinking around and around in circles about his situation with Sadie.

Not that she was very far from his thoughts no matter how he tried to occupy his mind. Today they had seemed to go two steps back in their emotional journey. She'd been evasive on the ward earlier, when all he'd wanted to do was get her alone and tell her about the plans brewing in his head, plans she probably wasn't ready to hear.

Roman pressed send on the scan request and sighed.

Every time he and Sadie inched closer to some sort of discussion of the future that might settle the worst of his anxieties for Milly's well-being, Sadie backed off. She wasn't keen on the idea of Milly visiting Prague. She hadn't told anyone that he was Milly's father. She wasn't even interested that, because of his feelings for Sadie, he felt increasingly uncomfortable about going ahead with the auction.

When it came to their relationship and future for them as a family, she was like a wisp of smoke, vague and elusive, slipping further through his fingers.

How could he confess all of his ideas and dreams and hopes, when each sliver of her trust gained cost him the slamming-up of another of her barriers? How could he broach the subject of them having a proper relationship, when she wasn't even curious about his plans to leave London? He understood her fear. He was scared too. But as long as they trusted each other, they could make anything work...

Except not knowing how Sadie felt was driving him crazy. Perhaps he'd given her enough time...

He was just about to select the next surgical patient waiting to be seen when he saw Sadie rush into the ED clutching a wrapped-up Milly in her arms.

His blood ran cold.

His body lurched in their direction, feet skidding to a halt inside the resus room where they'd been ushered by a nurse.

'What's wrong?' he said, concern for his daughter trumping social niceties.

Milly was flushed and fractious, restless in Sadie's arms.

'She's fine.' Sadie shot him a reassuring look, but he saw her worry.

Roman dismissed Sadie's assurance, his eyes scouring the baby for signs of what was wrong. 'If she's *fine*, you wouldn't have brought her to hospital in the middle of the night.'

'I thought she was teething,' Sadie said, taking a seat and undressing Milly on her lap so one of the ED doctors—a young guy who appeared to be barely out of medical school—could examine a grizzling Milly.

'But Grace said she's had a cold today, sniffling, a mild temperature. Nothing alarming,' Sadie explained to the young doctor as if she was completely unaware of the panic building inside Roman's chest.

Roman moved to stand at Sadie's side, his hand resting on her shoulder for comfort, although he couldn't be certain which of them needed it more.

'She spiked a fever tonight at bedtime,' Sadie continued and Roman winced, wishing she'd called him, 'and wouldn't settle with paracetamol. I tried sponging her down with tepid water, but her temperature stayed high.'

He felt Sadie stiffen and steeled himself. 'She had a convulsion about thirty minutes ago.'

Every bone in Roman's body threatened to collapse. His hands itched to reach for his darling Milly, who was alert but grumbling pitifully, the sound designed to tug at his heart and urge him into action to protect his daughter.

'Has she had a seizure before?' the junior doctor asked, glancing at Roman and taking in the surgical scrubs and his hospital security tag.

'No,' Sadie and Roman said together. Roman checked Milly's bare torso and limbs, noting the absence of a rash.

Because the ED doctor was now frowning at Roman, trying to figure out his role, Roman educated him.

'I'm Milly's father,' he said, loud enough for his voice to carry so the entire ED might hear. 'I'm a consultant paediatric surgeon at this hospital, and her mother works here as a paediatric registrar.'

How could Sadie be so calm? Why wasn't she barking orders and ordering tests?

The guy nodded and returned his attention to

Milly, performing an examination of her neurological system.

Sadie glanced at Roman, her stare accusing, as if he was losing it. Well, newsflash, he was close. This was his baby in distress. She'd had a seizure.

'How long did the seizure last?' the doctor asked.

'Not more than a minute,' Sadie said, apologetically, while he tried to examine a crying Milly while her doctor parents looked on.

But Roman didn't care about treading on toes when it came to his daughter's safety. He and Sadie were senior specialists. They had more combined experience than this youngster. He was moments away from snatching Milly up and assessing her himself.

As if she sensed his restlessness, Sadie rested her hand on his and continued giving a history. 'It appeared to be a generalised seizure, with symmetrical tonic-clonic jerking of her limbs and momentary loss of consciousness.'

Roman winced, berating himself for not being there. How could he have been so...preoccupied with his feelings for Sadie when there were more important things to worry about? How could he have let Milly down when he'd made her a promise in his heart? How would he survive if anything terrible happened...?

'Post-ictal drowsiness lasted five minutes,'

Sadie said, flicking a cautious glance at Roman, as if she could tell he was worried sick, 'but she was rousable throughout.'

Because he was so far beyond worry, Roman's frantic mind helpfully provided a list of worst-case scenarios, serious life-threatening infections that might be responsible for Milly's temperature, most of which he couldn't bear to contemplate. But his medical training wouldn't allow him to wallow in ignorance.

Febrile convulsions were common in infants and young children. This one, Milly's first, sounded simple in nature. As long as there was no recurrence in the next twenty-four hours, the prognosis for this being an isolated event was good.

But this was *his* daughter. He wanted every test ordered, every serious infection ruled out. Every consultant in the hospital awoken to come and tend to his sick little girl.

'Any history of epilepsy in the family?' The doctor looked at both Roman and Sadie, who shook their heads.

'And no history of head trauma?' he asked.

'No,' Sadie confirmed.

Roman paced while the guy, to his credit, performed a thorough examination, including looking inside Milly's ears. No mean feat given that she was now wailing and writhing in Sadie's lap.

The minute he'd finished, Roman took the baby and rocked her gently. She was flushed and cross, hot to the touch, her temperature still reading thirty-nine degrees.

'I think you should order some tests,' Roman said. 'A lumbar puncture is indicated in an infant under six months of age with a first seizure.'

As if she wanted to distance herself from Milly's neurotic father, Sadie said nothing, eyeing him warily. But Roman knew the statistics. Despite the lack of clinical signs—neck stiffness, photophobia, a rash—they needed to exclude meningitis as a cause of Milly's fever.

'I... I...' the young doctor stuttered, his stare darting between Roman and Sadie.

'Roman...' Sadie rose and stood at his side, cooing to Milly and slipping her arm around his waist. 'Let him do his job.'

He stared, pleading through every pore of his body. Couldn't she feel the tension in him, the fear and explosive impotence building inside him like contained steam that brought to mind every horrific outcome of a missed diagnosis?

He couldn't lose his daughter.

'We will perform a lumbar puncture,' the doctor said, his voice impressively calm, to his credit standing up to Roman's unyielding authority. 'But she also has a middle ear infection on the left, which as you know is enough to trigger a febrile convulsion. The eardrum has actually perforated, which will ease the pain that was most likely the cause of her being difficult to settle tonight.'

Roman breathed for the first time since Sadie and Milly had walked into the ED, but it was still only ten per cent of his usual lung capacity.

'With your consent,' the doctor continued, addressing them both, 'I'll start Milly on some antibiotics, which should help to tackle the fever.'

'Thank you,' Sadie said, while Roman pressed his lips to Milly's soft and downy head, shushing her gently while he tried to rein in the urge to wake the entire hospital.

Within minutes, they were moved from Resus to a regular bay with a stretcher and two hard plastic chairs. Sadie sat and tried to nurse Milly, who drank intermittently, clearly wanting the comfort of her mother's breast, but also lacking much of an appetite.

Still wound tight, Roman paced the small space, coming to a halt when a nurse appeared with a syringe of pink liquid that she gently squeezed into Milly's mouth.

Milly cried and fussed for endless minutes as if she couldn't get comfortable. Roman silently prayed for his daughter's relief, vowing never again to minimise the concerns of his patients' parents.

As he looked at Milly, another promise solidified. No matter the status of his and Sadie's relationship, he would be there for Milly, every day
of her life. He'd fight her corner while she was
too young to do it for herself and dry her tears.
Even if it killed him, he'd be the father she deserved.

Everything else, even his feelings, paled into
insignificance.

'Don't you need to get back to work?' Sadie
asked eventually once Milly had fallen into a
restless sleep.

'No. I'm a consultant,' Roman said, fighting
the urge to wrap his daughter up in cotton wool
from head to toe. 'My registrar is here somewhere.' He waved his hand dismissively, wondering anew at Sadie's appearance of calm.

Wearing just a nappy, his tiny daughter was
curled up on the soft white sheet, her skin almost
translucently pale.

He couldn't even adjust the blanket to cover
her given they were trying to bring down her
fever. How would he protect her from the world,
from the scraped knees and the mean words in
the playground? From disappointment and heartache?

'I think they should admit her for tests,' he
added, helplessness still crawling over his skin
like nettle rash.

Sadie looked at him as if he'd grown a second head, but her voice was soft when she spoke. 'It's only an ear infection. There's no need to over-react.'

'Overreact...?' Couldn't she tell how he clung to his fear, his terror, with all his might? If he freed everything he was feeling inside for all to see, she would understand his current levels of restraint.

'How can you be so calm?' he asked, jealous now of Sadie's ability to live in the moment and not plot out every worst-case scenario like a mind map of doom.

'Please sit down,' she said, her voice tinged with sympathy, her stare soft.

But could she truly see the depth of his fear for Milly? Did she know him well enough after everything they'd been through to understand how tonight had, not only triggered his grief over Miko, but also inflamed his insecurities that he could ever be a good enough father to keep his baby safe?

Because every second that he delayed the big discussion he and Sadie needed to have was a second where he wasn't fully a part of his daughter's life.

And he needed to be.

'I'm worried too,' Sadie said, taking his hand again when he folded himself stiffly into the spare chair. 'And I understand where your mind is going.'

He swallowed. He couldn't lose another person he loved. It would destroy him.

He'd never wanted to be this vulnerable again, but darling Milly had found a way to come into their lives, and from the second he'd known her he'd been powerless against the flood of paternal love that had swept him off his feet.

'But look—she's quiet now, sleeping like a baby,' Sadie said, in her soothing doctor's voice, because Roman had opened up to her, exposed his grief, shown her his broken pieces.

She wrapped her arms around him and held him tight. 'I brought her in to be checked over, but we both know that febrile convulsions affect one in twenty children. The chances of another seizure fall as her temperature drops. And hopefully this will never happen again.'

When she eased back to observe him, Roman scrubbed a hand over his face, feeling a hundred years old. 'You're right. But she's not leaving here until she's seen the paediatric team on call. You and I are too close to be objective. I want an impartial expert opinion.'

Sadie nodded. 'I agree.'

They fell into a tense silence, holding hands while they watched their daughter breathe in and breathe out.

For Roman, there was no longer any debate. He needed to live near his daughter. Regardless of their romantic aspirations, he and Sadie were Milly's parents, the three of them a family.

They always would be.

But the time had come to discuss the future because, more than anything else, he unapologetically needed to keep his loved ones safe.

CHAPTER FOURTEEN

TO ROMAN'S RELIEF, by the time Milly's lab results were back, the all-clear from the point of view of a more serious infection, she was almost back to her smiling, gurgling self. But while he'd watched her sleep fitfully, pacing her room while Sadie dozed in the chair, he'd come to some big decisions.

'I'm taking some sick days to stay home with her,' Roman said while they waited for the discharge papers to be signed. He couldn't wait to have Milly out of the hospital, as if just by being there she was at risk of a relapse.

'There's no need,' Sadie said, once more eyeing him as if he'd grown a second head. 'I have the next two days off. I'll be home with her.'

'I want to be there.' He cuddled Milly close, whispering Czech endearments, while he fought for the threads of his composure. 'I'm her father.'

'I know that,' she said, her voice tinged with

resentment. 'The whole hospital knows now after your announcement in the ED last night.'

Roman winced, remorse a hot rush through his veins. 'I'm genuinely sorry if that upset you, but I'm proud that this beautiful baby is mine. Last night was terrifying. It made me realise a few things.'

He'd given Sadie as much time as he could to come to terms with the fact that he was going to be a permanent fixture in Milly's life. The minute she'd told him that they'd made a baby together, he'd been brainstorming possible solutions, knowing that there was really only one answer that worked: him living where Milly lived.

Where Sadie lived, too. Because he had feelings for her. Feelings that he wanted to explore as they continued their relationship. Feelings he'd only ever had for one other woman.

Time for them to talk.

Sadie stood, holding her arms out for the baby. 'I was scared, too. But the worst-case scenario didn't happen.' She took a deep breath, clearly searching for patience. 'Let's just both go home, have a shower, try to get some sleep. Everything will sort itself out.'

Frustration gripped him; he needed to make her understand his point of view, because if he didn't do something definitive to safeguard his family, fear would tear him apart.

'I know you don't want to discuss it, Sadie, but I had a lot of time to think last night, and the moment has come for us to face facts.'

Fear clouded Sadie's tired eyes. 'What facts do you mean?'

They were both exhausted. Except as he'd watched the sun dawn over London from Milly's hospital room, he'd found the clarity that had eluded him since Sadie had come back into his life.

He no longer wanted the lonely life he'd tolerated before. He needed to find a way to make them work as a family. And he wanted him and Sadie to try and have a relationship. Except voicing all of that would scare her away.

Roman hesitated, reached for Sadie's hand. 'I'll be honest, when you first told me about Milly, I was terrified that I wouldn't be able to love her the way I should as her father. I spent so long shutting myself down, you see.'

Sadie nodded, her eyes glistening with emotion.

'But loving Milly happened so naturally,' he continued, his voice tight, 'and it helped me to remember more of the happy everyday moments I had with Miko.'

Sadie stared in silence so he carried on. 'Last night, while I watched our girl sleep, everything became crystal-clear. I need to live where she lives. It's the only option that makes sense. The only option I can tolerate. I'm moving to London.'

Holding Milly like a shield, Sadie paced across the room. 'We said we'd take it one day at a time. You can't just drop that bombshell and expect me to agree. You're being irrational, making big decisions when you're clearly emotional after yesterday…'

Roman tensed, his body chilled with apprehension. 'I thought you'd be happy. I'm not breaking my promise to you. We will take one day at a time, but we can do it together, not apart.'

'We can't discuss this now,' she said, dismissively, as if she'd never once given the future for them a thought.

Unlike that night at her place when they'd seemed to be on the same page emotionally and physically, when the possibility of a relationship had been a tangible thing, now he had no idea what Sadie wanted. But it was clear she continued to think only a few days ahead.

'Milly is sick,' she continued making excuses, 'and we have the fundraiser to get through and then you'll be leaving for Ireland. We can talk about everything else when you get back.'

'I don't care about the fundraiser. I told you I'll find someone else to take my place.' Nothing mattered but the three of them building on what they'd found. The three of them being together as a family.

Why couldn't she see that?

She looked down, pale and sombre. 'You're right; you shouldn't feel forced to date someone when you're not ready. I'll talk to Sammy, explain that you felt coerced, that because of your past, what you've been through, you were always going to be the wrong person...'

She thought he wanted to pull out because he was still in love with Karolina. He would always love his wife, but she wasn't the only reason he couldn't stomach the Valentine's charade. The main reason was Sadie.

Except where he was laying himself bare, she was still holding back, keeping her emotions safe, showing him that she trusted him with their daughter but not with her own heart.

Was she really so blind to his feelings? Had he alone experienced their growing closeness, so powerful that being intimate with her again had robbed him of breath?

Perhaps she was just scared that things were moving too fast.

'Sadie.' He stepped close and cupped her face, willing her to see him, to listen while he opened up deeply buried wounded parts of himself that he'd never expected to again see the light of day. 'I don't care about the auction because I don't want to date another woman, even for a good cause. I only want to date you.'

She gasped, a spark of the passion he'd been hoping to see flaring bright in her eyes.

'Tell me I'm not alone in wanting that? Be honest,' he continued, his throat raw with everything he left unsaid. 'Tell me what *you* want.'

She turned her face away but not before he saw a flash of longing in her expression. 'I'm not sure what I want is relevant. I'm a mother. I have to put Milly first.'

'What does that mean?' Fear twisted his gut. That was exactly what he was trying to do: put Milly first. That didn't mean he couldn't also pursue a relationship with Sadie. But was that relationship one-sided? Was Sadie still living in the moment that she clung to so ferociously, still classifying them as a casual fling, something she expected to fizzle out any day now?

'It means that whatever is going on with us is meaningless compared to what we want for our daughter.'

She looked up, meeting his stare, acting as if they'd made the same argument, but from Roman's point of view they were speaking a different language. Right from day one she'd expected nothing from their connection, and not even these past couple of incredible weeks, working together, spending time as a family, making love and opening up to each other, had changed her view.

To Sadie, Roman was doomed to let her down, the one thing he vowed never to do. She expected them to fail. She saw no future for the two of them beyond their roles as parents, because she still didn't trust him enough. She wasn't even willing to give them a try.

'So everything we've been through together,' he said, 'everything we've shared, was meaningless to you?'

Had he allowed himself to get carried away in their relationship? Maybe because a part of his heart would always be broken, the part that beat for Karolina, he'd failed to inspire Sadie's absolute trust.

Maybe it was his fault that they were so emotionally discordant because she believed he couldn't be the man she needed.

But he was at least willing to try.

She flushed with shame. 'I'm not saying that. I just don't think we should be making any life-changing decisions right now.'

'I disagree,' he said with all the passion he felt for this woman. 'We only get one life and I don't want to waste another second of mine being away from Milly when I could be there for her, a proper father to the best of my abilities.'

Tears filled Sadie's eyes as she stared. 'You

are her father. I'd never stand in the way of your relationship.'

The unspoken *but* echoed around the room.

'Okay, well, if you won't tell me what you want, I'll put myself out there first: I want you, too, Sadie. I want us to try and have a proper relationship. I'm happy to go at your pace, because I understand you're scared to be hurt, but I want you to trust me. I want us to be a family. You, me and Milly.'

Pain twisted her features as tears slid down her cheeks. 'I do trust you...' she said in a broken whisper. 'But if you want my honest answer, tell me one thing first. Before Karolina and Miko died, did you want more children?'

Roman frowned, jolted by the shift of topic. Then he realised where this was going. Despite creating their beautiful daughter, Sadie still saw herself as somehow defective because of her fertility problems and the way she'd been let down by her ex.

'Yes. We talked about it,' he said, defeated, wanting to be transparent even though the truth would hurt her. 'In fact, we were trying for another child when she was killed.'

Sadie's face paled. She nodded, as if he'd handed her the winning argument on a plate. 'Thank you for being honest.'

He rushed to her, took her in his arms, kissed

her forehead and whispered, 'I'm sorry to hurt you. But I want to be honest. We've always had that, haven't we? But I'm a different man now from the one I was with Karolina.'

He could never be the same after what had happened to his family, but that didn't make him and his feelings for Sadie any less. 'I'm ready to try again,' he continued. 'With you, if you want the same thing.'

She sniffed, slipping on a brave mask as she looked up at him with resolve. 'It's okay for you to want something that isn't me, Roman. You come from a big family, you wanted more children and you deserve to be happy. But I promised myself that I would never accept second place again. And for a man who already loves another woman, a man who dreams of another child, I'm a bad risk.'

'I don't care about having more children.' He gripped her shoulders, willing her to hear his truth. 'What matters is that I treasure Milly, take nothing for granted and never let her down.'

'I agree,' Sadie said, now eerily calm. 'That's what I've been trying to tell you. We both need to be there for our daughter and if we don't focus our attention there, we could mess that up for her.'

'But what about what we want for ourselves?'

he whispered, losing his grip on Sadie. Or perhaps he'd never had her in the first place.

Her eyes shone with tears. 'I stopped asking myself what I wanted in my twenties, when I had my infertility diagnosis. What I want—' she rested her hand on his chest '—doesn't matter, because I can't ever be what *you* need.'

Her fingers curled into his scrub top as if she might hold on and never let go. 'Milly was my miracle, Roman, but I can't give you more children. You say it doesn't matter now, but it might come to matter. It might matter very much one day.'

'I'm not that man, Sadie. I won't let you down.'

She shook her head, dismissing his promise. 'I know you'd never intentionally hurt me. But you've already been through so much loss. I couldn't bear to be the reason for your heartache if one day you decided you wanted another child more than you wanted me. Nor could I survive one day seeing in your eyes that I wasn't quite good enough. Can you blame me for holding something back to protect myself from that knowledge?'

Roman opened his mouth to argue, his jaw slack.

His stomach lurched with the familiar taste of defeat. After everything they'd been through, after everything they'd shared, she was choosing to protect herself from rejection that might never come, where he was exposing his battered and bruised heart and handing it to her on a platter.

She trusted him, but not enough.

'So that's it?' he asked, hoping with all his heart that she'd relent, that she'd throw her arms around his neck and trust her heart in his hands. 'That's all you're willing to risk?'

She tilted her chin, determined. 'Yes. Now I'm taking Milly home. When you return from Ireland, we can talk again, figure out a way to parent Milly together, but I think it's best if we put her first.'

Defeated, Roman nodded and stepped back. This was all she was willing to give. If he pushed her for more, he might lose everything: Sadie, what little trust they'd built up to now and, most devastating, Milly.

As if Sadie's fear were contagious, it gripped his throat, choking him. As choices went, he had no choice. He'd been there once before, so he knew with absolute certainty that he wouldn't survive losing another person he loved.

CHAPTER FIFTEEN

*Dr Roman Ježek, consultant paediatric
surgeon from Prague...*

WAS A WONDERFUL MAN, lover and father, and
she'd thrown him away...

Disgusted, Sadie deleted her sixth attempt to
write Roman's bio for the Valentine's Day auction that night, her finger stabbing angrily at the
delete key. But the only person she had to be
angry with was herself.

Taking her eyes off the accusing blank page
before her, Sadie glanced over the top of her laptop to where Grace was playing with Milly, her
heart a tender ache in her chest. Grace wheeled
the wooden duck toy from Roman through
Milly's line of vision. The baby, now fully recovered from the ear infection that had led to
Sadie's soul-destroying showdown with Roman,
squealed with excitement.

Sadie sighed, fixated on Roman's simple gift

and what it had represented. Their first outing together as a family, a day of blossoming love between father and daughter, hope for the future.

Of course, that unbreakable bond still stretched ahead of Milly and Roman. Sadie had no doubt that they would always have a wonderful relationship, be a close family. Roman wouldn't let Milly down.

But that bright future awaiting Roman and Milly wouldn't include Sadie. She'd messed up, thrown his dreams for the three of them as a family back in his face, breaking her own heart in the process.

No wonder she couldn't compose a single word.

'Shouldn't you be working on his bio instead of watching Milly's tummy time?' Grace said, scooping Milly into her lap so the baby too faced Sadie, as if with accusation.

Sadie rested her head in her hand. The trouble was, every time she tried to summarise Roman Ježek into an appealing few lines of type, his handsome face swam before her eyes on the screen. All the wonderful things he'd said at the hospital that day returning to haunt her.

He wanted to date her. He wanted them to try and have a relationship. He wanted the three of them to be a family.

Sadie stared with stinging eyes, not bothering to plead ignorance about who *he* was. She'd never been able to hide anything from Grace. It was a twin thing.

'Why don't you just ask him for his CV? That would be a start at least,' Grace said, spinning the cheerful yellow wheels of the pull-along duck.

Although Sadie hadn't seen Roman since that terrible day, she'd spoken to him every evening on the phone. Grace didn't know about the fat silent tears of anguish that had fallen down Sadie's face for the entire duration of last night's three-minute phone call, where they'd talked about Milly's improving health, her impending childhood immunisations, about the fact that she seemed to be teething.

But not about them. Because there was no them.

Roman had accepted that Sadie had given all she could give, and she'd run scared, pushing away his wonderful offer. After what he'd been through, it had been easy to convince him that it was best to focus on being parents together, that neither of them could risk losing what they had, the way she'd convinced herself.

Except she'd spent every hour since certain that, by taking the safest option, she'd made the biggest mistake of her life.

'Why don't you just write that you're cancelling his auction because you're in love with him?'

Grace said, standing and ambling over to Sadie with Milly in her arms.

Rather than deny the accusation, Sadie bit her lip to contain the crushing pain in her chest.

'Sometimes love isn't enough,' Sadie said, reaching for the baby for comfort.

Of course she loved Roman. Desperately. Now that she'd sabotaged their relationship, it was clear. How could she not fall for such an amazing man? But just like her wants, her love, too, was irrelevant.

'It's enough that he's committed to Milly,' she continued as Grace plopped down on the nearby sofa. 'He adores her. I can't let anything get in the way of that.'

Only, Roman wasn't the kind of man to act or speak rashly. Yes, he'd been scared for Milly. That didn't mean his declarations weren't well considered and genuine. It must have been agonising for him, after everything he'd been through, to bravely put himself out there and fight for her and Milly, for the three of them as a family. Especially when Sadie had clung to her fear that she wasn't good enough for Roman, that he loved Milly, but could never love Sadie.

'Including the fact that he might love you too?' Grace didn't believe in sugar coating.

Sadie shook her head, refusing to consider the

possibility. 'He loves Milly. He wants us to be a sort of family. But he doesn't love me.'

Roman loved Karolina and Miko and Milly. His devotion to their daughter was enough for Sadie.

'He's been through so much, he deserves happiness,' she continued, cuddling Milly close for comfort. 'What if he wants more children and I can't give them to him…?'

Except what if Roman did have strong feelings for her? What if that was enough? What if she'd allowed fear to overwhelm her just because Mark had made her feel inadequate over her fertility issues? Wasn't having any part of Roman better than having no part at all?

'You hate *what ifs*,' Grace pointed out.

Nauseated, Sadie closed the laptop. She should have given Roman a chance instead of shutting him down. She should have embraced what *she* wanted and gone after it. She should have kept her promise and discussed the future. So what if it was uncertain? Wasn't that its very definition? If Roman didn't care about having more children, Sadie should believe her own hype to live in the moment and trust his word.

Was it too late?

'You're right, I do.' Excitement pounded through her veins. She should tell Roman how she felt about him and just take one day at a time.

To hope that they could make a relationship work and, one day, he might love her the way she loved him. The opposite, embracing her fear, seeing him all the time because of Milly, never knowing how her future might have looked different if only she'd been honest and brave, didn't bear thinking about.

Handing Milly back to Grace, Sadie headed for the shower. 'I need to get ready for the fundraiser.'

'You haven't finished his bio,' Grace called, playing peekaboo with Milly from behind a cushion.

'I'll make something up.'

She knew all the important things about Roman by heart. She knew he was the best man she'd ever met. She knew his heartfelt declarations meant more than a million flashy red roses. She knew, as he'd tried to promise, that he'd never intentionally let her down. And she knew the depth of her love for him.

As she stepped under the spray of water, she closed her eyes, praying that what she knew would be enough.

Valentine's Day evening, Soho's Thames Gallery was decked out with tables and a stage for the much-anticipated hospital fundraiser, lights dimmed and atmosphere abuzz, most of the hospital staff and their families dolled up in black tie.

Roman waited in the shadows at one side of the stage, his stomach knotted with dread. He'd arrived late after collecting his Czech friend, Xaver, from the station. His old surgical colleague from Prague was now working in Oxford and had agreed to be auctioned in Roman's place. Roman had considered going through the motions himself, but his feelings for Sadie wouldn't allow it, even though they weren't reciprocated.

Now all he wanted to do was see Sadie. Maybe it wasn't too late to tell her how he felt. Maybe there was something to salvage. Maybe he'd given up too easily, lured off course by the argument of ensuring Milly's happiness.

But this wasn't about their daughter; it was about them, him and Sadie.

Braced for the agony ripping through his chest, Roman watched Sadie approach the microphone from the other side of the stage.

She looked stunning in a black gown with a beaded bodice, her hair sexily tousled, silver earrings sparkling in her ears. Roman curled his fingers into fists, fighting the urge to stride on stage and kiss her until she changed her mind about them and gave him a chance.

The background music stopped, and she gripped the microphone, nervously clearing her throat.

'Ladies and gentlemen. I hope you're all enjoying the evening.' She paused for the round of applause, her stare scanning the spacious room as if she was looking for Roman.

He'd texted her that he would be there, that he was working on a plan. He would wait until she announced him and then join her on stage with Xaver, declaring the last-minute substitution.

'The next auction,' she said, her voice tremulous, 'is the highlight you've all been waiting for: A date with an eligible doctor.'

The room erupted with cheers and whoops.

'I know you've all been looking forward to this one.' Sadie's smile turned feeble as she glanced down at the sheet of paper in her hand. 'But thing is, I've…um… I've messed up.'

Roman's heart thumped erratically. He ached to march on stage and wrap her in his arms, to tell her that she didn't need to go through with this, because he was in love with her. Except she didn't even want to discuss them having a relationship, let alone their feelings.

Sadie scrunched up the sheet of paper and glanced down at her feet. The audience fell silent, waiting.

Roman stepped forward, ready to show himself, to let her know that the auction could go ahead, but some instinct held him back.

Sadie raised her chin, addressing the crowd

with determination. 'You see, Dr Roman Ježek had kindly volunteered for this auction, but he's not here tonight.'

Before the groans of disappointment could drown her out, she rushed on. 'It's really not his fault. It's mine, but I've already said that... You see, I met Dr Ježek a year ago, funnily enough at another Valentine's Day event. And, well...we had a relationship. And a daughter, in fact. Milly, although that's by the by—'

She was rambling the way she did when she was nervous. Roman froze, his breath stalling. He wanted to hear where this was going.

'And anyway,' she continued, her hands twisting the paper, 'neither of us had been looking for a relationship and Dr Ježek signed up for this fundraiser in good faith, because he is a wonderful man and a brilliant doctor and an amazing father.'

She stopped abruptly, swallowing as if choked.

Unable to stand still a moment longer, Roman stepped forward, only to have his path blocked by the formidable Sister Samuels, who held out her arm like a barrier. He almost didn't recognise her out of uniform, she looked so glamorous. But he recognised her no-nonsense expression and stayed where he was.

'And the thing is,' Sadie said, her voice small, 'he wanted us to be a proper family, for me and him to have a real relationship, and I want that more than anything.'

She held her hand to her chest. 'But I got scared, you see, and I wouldn't listen to his dreams for the future when he tried to tell me about them. And now he's going to go to Ireland when I really want him to stay here, not just for Milly's sake, but for me. Because, the thing is...' she sighed '... I've fallen in love with him and I didn't tell him that, and now he's not here... And I might not get the chance now...'

She loved him?

Roman's heart climbed into his throat.

'But the final thing I wanted to say is this—' She faced the audience defiantly. 'Even if he were here tonight, this auction couldn't possibly go ahead. Because *I* want to date him. I want us to be a couple. I want us to be a family: me, him and Milly. And if he was here, that's what I'd say, so...'

Finally running out of steam, she glanced to the other organisers, who appeared either gob-smacked by the turn of events or on the verge of tears at Sadie's heartfelt speech.

Stunned, Roman itched to go to her. He needed to look into her eyes to see if what she'd said was true. He needed to tell her that he loved her too. That they'd work everything else out, together.

Sadie stood tall, gripping the mic and pasting

on a bright smile. 'We'll just move on to the next auction: a couples skydiving adventure.'

Without waiting for the crowd's reaction, Sadie hurried from the stage and Sammy dropped her arm.

Roman took off running.

CHAPTER SIXTEEN

CLOSE TO TEARS, Sadie left the stage, shaking her head at the other organisers as she hurried past. If she stopped to talk, she'd break down. She couldn't believe Roman hadn't shown up for his auction. Obviously she'd hurt him too much. Perhaps he'd already left for Ireland.

She'd missed her chance.

Biting back a sob of despair, Sadie left the backstage area as the auctions continued and exited the gallery into a dark staff corridor, the roar of pain in her head drowning out everything but her own words of recrimination.

He'd offered her a chance for them to be a family, offered her almost everything she wanted, and, instead of grabbing it with both hands, she'd succumbed to her cowardice and now she'd lost the man she loved.

Now that he was gone, she could see their relationship with alarming clarity. He'd shown her that he cared through his actions, he'd made her feel safe and cherished and desired. He'd been honest, and trustworthy and dependable, and she'd retreated, closed off, stayed safe.

Someone gripped her arm, spinning her around.

Roman was there, dressed for the auction.

Sadie gasped, clutching her crumpled ball of paper to her chest. 'You made it?'

He looked gorgeous, the tux suiting his colouring, his blue eyes bright.

He gripped her upper arms, his thumbs gliding over her skin as if he couldn't bear to keep his hands to himself. 'Sorry I was late. I had to meet a friend at the station.'

He cupped her face, holding her stare captive. 'That was some grand declaration you just made. I thought you hated those?'

His eyes burned into hers, the intensity breathtaking.

Sadie gripped his arms, worried if she didn't hold onto him, he'd disappear. 'You heard that?'

He'd been there all along? Her brain couldn't compute why he was there, but her heart leaped at the sight of him.

He nodded, his smile indulgent. 'Every amazing word.'

She smiled, eyes stinging with unshed tears, her legs jelly. 'Well, I used to hate them, but then I met this man who showed me that sometimes you just have to be honest and say what you want. That some risks are worth taking.'

Before she could utter another word, Roman backed her up against the wall. Their eyes locked for a split second and then his lips descended, covering hers in a crushing kiss.

With euphoria spiking her blood, Sadie clung to his waist as she kissed him back. All of the pining and heartache of the past few days left her in a rush. He was there. If she held on tight, he'd have to stay.

When they parted for air, both panting, Roman rested his forehead against hers. 'Sorry. I sensed another one of your nervous rambles and I've missed kissing you.'

'Me too.' She rested her head on his chest, felt the pound of his heart against her cheek. 'I'm so sorry, Roman. I'm sorry that I pushed you away. I was scared. I doubted my instincts, because they'd steered me wrong in the past.' She looked up at him. 'But you helped me to see that the last time I'd tried to have a relationship, I'd still been grieving my diagnosis, grieving for that part of myself I assumed was out of reach. I ignored the warning signs that he wasn't the man for me because I was grateful that someone wanted me even though I was broken.'

Now was her chance to tell him that she loved him, that she'd been stupid, that she wanted any sort of relationship he was ready for. 'I meant what I said out there. I love you, and I'll take any part of you I can have. I know what I want now. I want you. I want us. I want the three of us to be a family.'

He stared, fiercely, his eyes darting over her face, as if he was scared to trust what she said. 'You really love me?' he asked, his expression tortured.

'Yes. How could I not? You're kind of wonderful. I think I fell in love with you when you opened the office door that time I was stuck. I was just too stupid to recognise my feelings.'

He kissed her again, pressing her against the wall.

This time when he pulled back, he appeared resolved. 'Sadie, it's time to talk about the future.'

Sadie nodded, raising her chin. 'I know, and I'm ready to lay myself open emotionally, to plan with you, to be the strong, unflinching woman you need.'

'Sadie,' he groaned, taking her hands and raising them to his lips, kissing her fingertips. 'You always were. I've fallen in love with you, too. Can't you see that?'

Sadie froze, spellbound. He loved her? Could it be true?

'I should have told you that before,' he rushed on, 'but I was scared too. I'm a risk for you, because you've been let down before and because I'll always carry a scar in here.'

He pressed a fist to his chest, over his heart.

'It doesn't matter,' she croaked, dizzy with the love she felt for him in return, but he placed his thumb gently over her lips.

'You know that I will always love Karolina and Miko,' he said, sombre. 'That's a lot for any woman to take on. But if you can trust me, I'll show you every day that there's room in here—' he grasped her hand and pressed it to his chest '—to love you and Milly, too. And I love you both, just as much.'

At his wonderful words, Sadie allowed the tears of joy to fall.

Roman cupped her cheeks, swiping them with his thumbs. 'You asked me not to over-promise. But this is a promise I can keep: I love you. You've given me a second chance to be a dad, showed that I deserved a second chance to fall in love, and if you allow me to be a part of your life, yours and Milly's, I promise to show you every day that you can trust me to love you for ever.'

'Roman, I do trust you,' Sadie whispered, her throat thick and hot. 'Let's go home.'

They took a taxi, kissing in the back seat, touching each other in reverent silence.

Milly was at her grandparents' for the night, with Grace, so the minute the door closed, they kissed some more, tugging at each other's clothes as they headed for the bedroom.

'How can I have missed you so much in two days?' he said, kissing a path down her neck, across her chest, sucking first one nipple and then the other.

Sadie tangled her hands in his hair, whispering, 'I love you. I missed you too.'

Roman pressed another fierce kiss to her lips, holding her close. 'Sadie...loving you, loving our daughter, has brought the unscarred parts of my heart back to life.'

He entwined his fingers with hers, his stare searing her soul. 'I want you to wake up every day of our future and believe that, by being at your side, I'm exactly where I want to be. That I choose you. I choose us.'

'I will.' She nodded, reaching for his lips with hers, committing his promises to memory.

In the end, with the right person, believing in dreams was easy.

Pressing her hand to his chest, she rolled him over, straddling his hips so she could pepper his face, his neck, his chest with kisses.

Sadie stared into his beautiful blue eyes, getting lost and finding home. 'When you look at me, when we're alone, just staring, I feel loved for the person I am.'

'You are loved,' he said, drawing her back for another kiss. 'How long have we got?' he asked, curling his fingers through her hair as she pressed a path of kisses down his abdomen.

'Milly will be home at nine, so until then, you're mine.'

Things were just getting hot when he tugged her to a stop.

'Wait.' He drew her into his arms and rolled them, so he was once more on top.

With breath-stealing tenderness, he pressed his lips to hers. 'Happy Valentine's Day.' His voice was low with desire, love shining in his eyes.

Sadie shuddered, everything she felt for this man welling up inside her chest. 'Happy Valentine's Day.'

'I didn't get you a card, or flowers,' he said, pressing kisses of apology along her jaw and down the side of her neck.

Sadie cupped his face, staring deep into his eyes. 'I don't want those things.'

Now that she'd been brave enough to build a future with Roman, all the red roses and heart-shaped cards in the world meant nothing. She had something more important and precious: a family, a man she loved, who loved her in return.

'You are the best Valentine I could ask for,' she said, closing her eyes as he groaned and rained kisses on her face, losing herself in the love they'd found together, love that would always be enough.

EPILOGUE

Fourteen months later

LAUGHING, ROMAN SNAPPED A photo of Milly with his phone. His girl was covered in a fine dusting of icing sugar, squealing excitedly as she brandished a wooden spoon in the air like a flag. Blobs of chocolate icing hit the kitchen bench, the tiled floor and even Milly's blonde head.

'Oh-oh…' Roman said, scooping Milly up and transporting her to the sink where he managed to de-bulk the worst of the cake ingredients from his daughter while she unsuspectingly slashed the wooden spoon through the stream of warm water.

'Tatínek is going to be in trouble with Mummy. Unless we can clean up all of this mess before she gets out of the bath.'

Roman cherished every second with his girls, the ordinary and extraordinary. They enabled him to reflect on how lucky he was to have the love he'd found with his two families, strengthened his vow never to take any moment for granted.

'Clean what up?' Sadie said from the hallway as she entered the decimated kitchen, her smile, as always, brightening his day.

'Just a little baking detritus,' Roman said, placing their toddler on her own two feet so he could wrap his arm around Sadie's waist and kiss her as thoroughly as possible while keeping one eye on Milly.

With a toddler awake and exploring, couple moments were rare. But in the year or so they'd been together, and with the help of Grace and both sets of grandparents, they'd somehow managed to carve out a little grown-up time among all the wonderfully normal everyday family moments.

'What did you bake?' Sadie said a little breathlessly, her eyes scanning the cluttered counter where he'd used every single bowl and utensil they owned.

'A cake!' Roman once more picked up Milly and, with a flourish, whisked off the tea towel covering their creation. 'Ta-da.'

Sadie chuckled, covering her mouth with her hand as she tried to hide her laughter.

'What?' Roman said, admiring the lopsided and partially burned cake. 'So you think it's funny, huh?'

Impatient, he'd put the butter-cream icing on too soon while the cake had still been warm and it was starting to melt, but hopefully it would still taste good.

Slinging his arm around Sadie's shoulder, he drew her close, calculating the hours until Milly's bedtime when he and Sadie could be alone.

'Well, I mean, it's not that funny,' Sadie said, reaching up to kiss Milly's floury cheek. 'It has a certain charm... I mean...if you like burned cake that is, which fortunately I do, so that's good.'

'Oh-oh.' Roman rounded his eyes at Milly. 'Mummy's doing the nervous-chatter thing.'

Because he couldn't be this close to Sadie and not kiss her, he snagged her lips, brushing them with his in a tease, a promise of more to come.

'What are we celebrating?' Sadie asked breathlessly, staring up at him with the passion that was never far away when they were together.

'Nothing in particular,' he said, dipping his finger in the icing and dabbing it first on Milly's nose and then on Sadie's, the sound of their laughter squeezing another drop of love from his heart. 'Just a celebration of us three, and how lucky we are to have each other.'

Sadie sobered, her shining eyes dipping to his mouth just before she gripped his face and kissed him again, this time winding her arms around his neck and pressing her body to his restlessly.

'I love you,' she said, the look she shot him full of heat and promise.

'I love you too,' he said, scooping his arm around her waist, so she couldn't escape, 'which is why I think you should marry me.'

He ignored Sadie's shocked gasp and turned to Milly. 'You think Mummy should marry me too, don't you?'

Milly garbled something unintelligible, waving her wooden spoon in agreement.

'See,' he said, facing Sadie once more. 'She agrees.'

Placing Milly on the floor, he got down on one knee and took Sadie's hand. 'Sadie, it's time to promise we'll be together for ever…you, me and Milly. Will you marry me?'

Laughing through her tears, Sadie kneeled on the floor in front of him, throwing her arms around his shoulders. 'Yes, I will.'

She kissed him, hugged Milly and then kissed him again.

There was flour on the floor, a cupboard spilling out pots and pans. Not the most romantic setting for a proposal, but, for Roman, it was perfect. And he'd make it up to Sadie later, when they were alone.

Roman gripped Sadie's waist and pulled her close, holding both his girls. 'I'd say that was something worth celebrating, wouldn't you?'

Sadie rested her head on his shoulder with a contented sigh. 'Absolutely. Every day with you is worth celebrating.'

* * * * *

Breaking The Nurse's No-Dating Rule

Janice Lynn

MILLS & BOON

USA TODAY and *Wall Street Journal* bestselling author **Janice Lynn** has a master's in nursing from Vanderbilt University and works as a nurse practitioner in a family practice. She lives in the southern United States with her Prince Charming, their children, their Maltese named Halo and a lot of unnamed dust bunnies that have moved in after she started her writing career. Readers can visit Janice via her website at janicelynn.net.

Visit the Author Profile page
at millsandboon.com.au for more titles.

**Janice won the National Readers' Choice Award
for her first book,
*The Doctor's Pregnancy Bombshell.***

Dear Reader,

Nurse Julia Simmons is one of the most complicated heroines I've written. She is working hard to overcome past mistakes. To do that, she has life rules to keep herself on track to becoming the person she wants to be. Unfortunately, the hospital's new pulmonologist, Dr. Boone Riddle, tempts her to toss aside the rules she lives by. She won't give in, which means he'll have to wait. She doesn't believe he will, and if he does, her heart's in trouble because she's already on the verge of falling.

Boone doesn't understand why Julia insists on their being just friends until after she completes her master's in nursing program. If waiting six months for their first date is what he has to do, then so be it. She's worth waiting for. But when he discovers her past is similar to one that has already cost him someone he loved, dare he risk such loss again? Or has his heart already decided for him?

I hope you enjoy their story. If you'd like, feel free to reach out to me at janicemarielynn@gmail.com. Take care and much love.

Janice

DEDICATION

To those who don't allow past mistakes to
forever define who they are

CHAPTER ONE

"HOW DO YOU stay so cheerful all the time? I've never seen you without a smile on your face. That can't be easy when you're surrounded by seriously injured and ill patients."

Intensive care nurse Julia Simmons smiled at her seventy-year-old patient's husband and wondered what the man would say if she told him the truth, that she strove to be a bright light in the hope that the darkness lurking deep within her never found its way out again. Yeah, that was way too heavy for an early Monday morning.

"I doubt anyone is cheerful all the time, but I do my best to choose happiness each day." She even had *Choose to be happy* listed in her Rules for Life Success notebook. Glancing toward the man's unconscious wife, her heart gave a painful squeeze. Irene Burch's viral pneumonia had sent her into respiratory failure, and she'd nearly died. Requiring life support to oxygenate her body, she seemed improved, but still might die. Working in the ICU meant knowing your patients were more likely to pass away than survive, but Julia did everything she could to increase their odds. "Some days are easier than others."

Taking a deep breath, the man nodded. "I know you're right. The past few days haven't been easy, but we've much to be thankful for. Irene is still with me and is improved some from when she was admitted earlier this week. Will Dr. Richards be by this morning to check on her?"

Cheeks hot, Julia averted her gaze at the mention of the hospital's newest pulmonologist. Had she thought Mr. Burch was going to see something in her eyes that she didn't want seen? That choosing happiness was all too easy when Dr. Boone Richards made his hospital rounds?

"Dr. Richards usually stops by the ICU prior to going to his office and then again after he finishes with his last appointment of the day." And sometimes in between when a patient had an issue. Not that she kept tabs.

Ugh. There went her cheeks bursting into flames again.

She finished checking her patient, assured Mr. Burch that she'd be close if anything changed, and stepped out of her patient's room. The moment she did, she scanned Knoxville General's intensive care unit. Boone was nearby. Exactly how she knew didn't make logical sense, but her awareness of when he was near happened too frequently to be coincidence. She figured it went back to some innate survival skill of sensing imminent danger. Despite how giddy being near him made her, she wasn't oblivious to the perils of getting too close.

Six feet tall, athletically built, quick-witted, and with the most appealing grin she'd ever seen, Boone was D-A-N-G-E-R. Not that she had a chance with him even if she did date—which she didn't. Boone was gorgeous and successful and the kind of guy that women like her admired from afar, but knew they didn't have a chance with in the real world. Plus, there was the beautiful orthopedic surgeon he had been dating since long before they'd came to Knoxville. She'd heard rumors they weren't together anymore, but she'd learned long ago not to pay much heed to gossip.

Spotting him, she bit her lower lip, watching him laugh at something a coworker said at the nurse station. Heavens, from the top of his shiny brown locks to the tips of his tennis shoes, he looked as if he starred on a television show rather than working as the highly skilled physician she knew him to be. Yeah, girls with pasts like hers didn't date men like Boone Richards, but even if they did, Julia had other plans for her life. No doubt he and the orthopedic surgeon made the perfect power couple and dazzled everyone who saw them together—if they were still a couple.

Boone's gaze shifted, pinning her with baby blues that had featured in more fantasies than she cared to admit. Immediately, he grinned, and a lot of thumps and bumps clanged around in her chest. Excusing himself from chatting with a respiratory therapist, he came to where Julia lingered at the hand sanitizer dispenser outside Mrs. Burch's room.

"Good morning, Julia. How's our lady holding up today?"

Despite how her blood raced through her vessels and made her a little light-headed, she met his gaze. "Becky was on shift last night. She reported that Irene remained stable. I cleared her airways with a suction catheter a few minutes ago and was pleased with her vitals. I believe she's improved some this morning."

"Great. I know you've just been in there, but will you round with me while I examine her?"

"Of course." It wasn't as if she'd refuse that request from any of the physicians she worked with, but Julia had major respect for Boone and enjoyed patient care with him. He was a great doctor. The best. She loved observing him with his patients and their families. Someday when she'd earned her master's and worked as a nurse practitioner, she imagined that she'd use him as a role model for the type of care she wanted to provide—professional, kind, and truly concerned for others.

"See, I said I'd be back soon," she told Mr. Burch when she reentered the ICU bay. "Look who I brought with me."

"Dr. Richards," the man greeted Boone, reaching out to shake his hand. Boone did so, then disinfected his hands prior to examining Irene.

After he'd checked her and answered her husband's questions the best he could, he dictated a few chart notes via his phone, then turned to Julia. "As you heard, I agree with you that Irene has improved some this morning. I'm decreasing her sedation in the hope that we can get her awake and wean her off the ventilator. Respiratory therapy should be by later this morning, and we'll start decreasing her ventilation settings."

Assessing the rise and fall of her patient's chest created by the lifesaving machine, Julia nodded. "I'll check regularly and keep you posted."

"Thanks."

"Use the call button if you need anything," she reminded Mr. Burch, then followed Boone from the room.

Rather than head toward the nurse station, he paused, chatting with her a few moments as they often did to discuss their favorites on a singing competition reality show they both enjoyed. Julia usually multitasked while exercising or house-cleaning, but she made a point to keep up with the show just so they could argue the merits of their favorites.

"The young girl from Kentucky whose father was a coal miner is going to win the whole thing," she assured him despite his claim that a male contestant would take final prize.

"So you keep telling me." One side of his mouth hiked up. Then he asked, "Are you going to the hospital Christmas party in a few weeks? I hear the hospital does a really great job putting the event together."

"They really do," she agreed. "Unless I'm needed here, I plan to go."

From the end of the fall term to the start of the spring semester, Julia got to breathe a little while not having classes, studying, and homework.

"That's great." His smile suggested it really was. "Are you bringing a plus-one?"

"No. At last year's, I was the plus-one for Stephanie and her boyfriend Derek." She laughed at the memory. Her bestie and coworker had insisted Julia join them as their designated driver and had made sure Julia didn't felt like a third wheel.

Boone's eyes sparkled like sunshine hitting the bluest sea. "Do you want to?"

Hello! She'd thought he was just chitchatting… Was he asking what she thought he was asking? Surely not. There was that whole out-of-her-league thing and the orthopedic surgeon he might or might not still be dating. Her heart pounded so hard it beat the air from her lungs, and she fought to keep from steadying herself by holding on to the wall. Did Boone want her to be his date, or was he trying to set her up with a friend? Or to just go with her as friends? In any case, no matter how insanely her heart raced, she shook her head.

"No plus-one for me. I don't date."

The sparkle in his eyes dimmed a little. "You don't date? As in, at all?"

She shrugged.

"Any particular reason why you don't date?"

She had dated once upon a time without thought or apparent care if the guy was a total loser—and she'd been with some doozies. After she'd straightened up her life, she'd bent her Rules for Life Success and dated a man she'd thought truly cared for her, even exposing her most shameful secrets to him. Of course, he'd never looked at her the same, teaching her a valuable lesson.

Wisely, she'd vowed to never stray again from the rules that had worked well for her thus far. Who had the time or energy to date, anyway?

She had other life priorities that didn't include squandering precious time on relationships that never lasted. Just look at how Clay had left her despite his promises to love her forever.

Then there were her mother's many relationships prior to her passing. Her father wasn't any better. His most recent wedding had been his number four, and the last Julia had heard, they weren't living together. Yeah, dating didn't fit into her life plan. Maybe after she graduated from school in May, but not until after she'd checked that off her list.

"My reasons are really not any of your business, Dr. Richards." Perhaps it was thoughts of Clay that had raised her hackles and put the haughtiness in her voice.

Boone studied her a moment, probably wondering why she'd gone so tense. But rather than questioning her further, he brandished one of those smiles that made her think it might be okay to toss aside her rules and just bask in his attention for however long it lasted. The man was seriously more tempting than the tastiest chocolate when she was on a diet. Good thing she'd just been thinking of Clay, so she had a fresh reminder of the devastating blows delivered by caring for someone who couldn't love you back.

"Fair enough," Boone conceded. "But if you

change your mind about dating, I'm free the night of the Christmas party."

He was asking for himself.

Not that it mattered, but the idea he was asking for himself rather than someone else seemed surreal. Surely he meant as just friends?

"You're free that night so you want me to change my mind about dating and then ask you to be my date?"

He pretended to consider, then gave another lopsided grin. "Not exactly what I meant, but that works. I promise not to play hard to get."

Still shocked that he wanted to go to the Christmas party with her, even as friends, Julia dug deep for the fortitude to look him straight in the eye. "I wouldn't hold my breath if I were you."

"I don't have to hold my breath to feel breathless around you, Julia."

His admission stunned her, and her head spun. Self-preservation kicked in, and panic filled her. What was Boone doing? She needed to keep her eyes on the prize. The prize was not a date with the hospital's most gorgeous doctor. She'd secretly crushed on him but had never dreamed he'd share her interest. Well, she had dreamed, but that's all it had been. A silly, secret fantasy. "Don't you have a girlfriend?"

He shook his head. "Surely you know that we

wouldn't be having this conversation if I had a girlfriend. I'm single."

The rumors had been true. He and the orthopedic surgeon were no longer a couple.

"Good for you." She fought to cover her astonishment that he was interested in a date with her. Not that she hadn't caught him watching her more than once. She had. She'd figured it was because he'd noticed the way her brain turned to mush when he was near.

She was flattered, stunned, but she wouldn't waver. She had rules that were working for her, and she was sticking to them. She recalled much too well that ignoring her own rules had led to having her heart broken. She enjoyed her work relationship with Boone, and even her private fantasies, but that's all they could ever be.

She needed distance from him, physical and emotional. "If you'll excuse me, Dr. Richards, I'm going to log my new notes on Mrs. Burch. Have a good day."

He didn't follow her to the nurse station, but she felt his gaze boring into her with each step she took. She ordered her feet to keep moving one step in front of the other—*Don't fall...don't break into a run*—partially because she didn't trust them to move away from Boone rather than toward him. He'd just asked her to go to the hospital Christmas party *with him*.

He'd said she took away his breath. Oh, heavens. Her insides were shaking at his dreamlike comment. Did he feel how attracted she was to him and assume she'd be an easy distraction while he was in between girlfriends? She didn't want to think poorly of him, but maybe it would be better if she did. Anything to put up a wall between them.

"Your cheeks are red," Stephanie pointed out when Julia reached the nurse station. "Wouldn't have anything to do with our favorite hunky doctor you were just talking to and who is still looking your way, would it?"

"No." She fought the urge to glance toward Boone.

"Yeah, I don't believe you." Stephanie laughed, then asked, "What were you talking about that's got you so red-faced? It's rare I see you flustered."

"Our patient."

"Mrs. Burch is what's got you all twitterpated?" Stephanie eyed her suspiciously. "Is everything okay?"

"She's stable, and I'm not whatever that word is."

"Girl, you are so off-kilter. I'd give my right eye to have been a fly on the wall and hear what Dr. Richards said to you. There's that rumor going around that he and Dr. Cunningham are no longer an item."

"You know better than to believe rumors." Julia shrugged as if she couldn't care less. She shouldn't. Whether Boone was available did not matter. Julia wasn't available. She'd keep it to herself that Boone had mentioned going to the Christmas party. She knew what Stephanie would tell her to do. Her friend thought she worked too much and needed to let loose, that it was long past time for her to be over the past and Clay. There were some things her friend couldn't fully understand. Julia knew, though. Letting loose was why she now had to buckle down so strictly.

"Most of the time I'd agree with that." Stephanie propped her elbows on the desk. "But on this occasion, I'm inclined to think it's true. Too bad if not, because I was hoping that you two had finally admitted what everyone already knows."

Rubbing her finger over the small tattoo on her left wrist, Julia gulped. "What's that?"

Stephanie wagged her perfectly sculpted brows. "That the air sizzles when you two are in the same room."

Others could feel it? Her cheeks burned, but glancing toward Stephanie, she snorted as if her friend was way off base. "That's your own man-crazy, happy-in-love-so-everyone-else-must-be-too, fried brain you're hearing sizzling. I wish you the best. Derek is a great guy. However, in my experience, relationships don't last."

"Derek's and mine will last." Stephanie informed her with full-on sass. "But you keep telling yourself every guy is like Clay so that you can hide behind those walls you erected when he left. They aren't. Dr. Richards is a great guy. If he's single, you should invite him to dinner or something." She stuck her finger up in the air. "Sizzle. Sizzle."

Sizzling air around Boone or not, she wouldn't admit to there being anything more than professional admiration in the way she felt about Boone. Not to her friend. Nothing good could come from doing so. She was happy, healthy, and on course. The last thing she needed was a refresher course in Heartbreak 101.

Later that week, Dr. Boone Richards smiled at the petite brunette wearing a bright pink scrub top with colorful dancing cats on it. He was starting to blame her more and more for his discontent in life. Which wasn't fair to Julia. He had a great life, the career he'd always wanted, and he could have moved on to the next step in his personal life with Olivia. Instead, a few weeks back, he'd ended the five-year relationship that had led him to Knoxville. Olivia hadn't taken the breakup well. She'd been expecting an engagement ring, not a goodbye.

The reality was they should have ended it years ago but had grown so comfortable in their seemingly "perfect" life that they'd overlooked a really big thing they were missing. They weren't in love. No matter how much he'd tried, he'd been unable to picture himself growing old with her. As soon as he'd admitted that truth to himself, he'd set her free. Set them both free.

After that, things that should have been obvious all along gained clarity. Things like Julia Simmons and how much he looked forward to seeing her when he consulted in the intensive care unit. How he hoped she'd be the nurse taking care of his patients, so he'd have reason to directly interact with her because he enjoyed their chats and her cheerful enthusiasm in all she did.

Not that there had been enjoyable chats or cheerful enthusiasm that week. He'd ruined everything because she'd not met his gaze since his Christmas party invite, instead quickly disappearing whenever he came to the unit. Her avoidance was driving him crazy, but he could only blame himself. He hadn't asked a woman on a first date in five years and had majorly botched his attempt.

"Dr. Richards." She averted her gaze, staring at the med cart drawer she'd just closed. "Mrs.

Burch has done well with the decreased pressures on her ventilator. Do you intend to completely remove her ventilation tube today?"

Look at me, he silently demanded. *Let me see your eyes to know if I've completely misread what I thought was mutual attraction.*

"Call me Boone, but yes, unless something has changed with her exam or vitals, then I will take her off the vent."

"Her family will be glad to hear that. Now that she's awake and wanting to communicate with them, she seems motivated to come off. As far as the other—" her long lashes swept down over pink cheeks "—that's not appropriate."

He raked his hands through his hair. "Lots of our coworkers call me Boone. There's no reason you can't do the same."

"You worked hard to earn your title. Be proud. It's not a problem for me to use your title when addressing you."

Perhaps not for her. For him, it was. Of course he was professional when they were together, but he was also a man interested in her as a woman. But she was obviously not a woman interested in him as a man. If only her eyes didn't say otherwise. Was that why she refused to meet his gaze? Because she didn't want him to see whatever shone there? Regardless, what her eyes were saying didn't matter when she verbalized a lack of interest. He had no choice but to accept her words.

"If you insist." Frustrating, but he forced a smile. "Let's go extubate Mrs. Burch."

The seventy-year-old woman was awake when he and Julia entered her room. Her husband stood beside her bed. The love the man had for his wife was obvious as he held her hand. That's what he wanted, Boone thought. A love that lasted a lifetime, through ups and downs, like the Burches had, like what his parents had. He'd not been wrong to end things with Olivia, but perhaps what he sought didn't exist for him.

"Good morning again, Irene," Julia said, flashing the warmest smile at their patient, who gave a thumbs-up as she was unable to verbalize with the ventilation tube in place. Julia then gave the woman's husband an equally bright smile. "Harry," she addressed him. "I missed you when I was here earlier."

"I went downstairs for a coffee."

"I told you I'd bring you anything you needed," Julia reminded him.

"You also told me to stretch my legs and not just sit as it wasn't good for me." The man smiled fondly at her. That Julia made the extra effort to know her patients was just one of the many reasons Boone preferred her being assigned to his patients. She genuinely cared and it showed.

"Morning," he greeted them, chatting a few seconds, then listening to the woman's chest to make sure there were no surprises prior to taking her off the machine that helped her breathe. When he was satisfied with her examination, he looked her directly in the eyes. "As you know, we've been doing spontaneous breathing trials as we wean down how much the mechanical ventilator is doing over the past few days. There's always a risk that you might have to be intubated again, but the things we watch for that let us know you're ready to come off the ventilator—heart rate, blood pressure, labs, cough strength, oxygenation and so forth—indicate that you should do fine."

Mrs. Burch gave another thumbs-up.

"What you do today is very important. Julia will be encouraging you to use your incentive spirometer to continue to strengthen your lungs and help keep them clear of secretions. Breathing deeply is vital. Your respiratory therapist will be by, as well, to work with you. Breathing without the machine is going to leave you feeling short of breath at first. Just know that's normal and focus on taking those big, deep breaths. You've got this."

Julia suctioned Mrs. Burch's lungs, removing excess secretions that naturally formed with mechanical ventilation, then stood on the opposite side of the bed from Boone, ready with a wash-cloth and to further suction the lungs as needed after he'd pulled the tube.

Boone focused on their patient, talking her through what he was doing as he could see the fear in her eyes. "You'll likely have a sore throat for a few days. That's normal and should pass," he said as he removed the tube. Mrs. Burch gagged. Julia stood at the ready to clear her airways. Fortunately, her gag morphed into a noisy cough.

"Coughing is important," he stressed. "Cough as needed as it's your body's way of clearing sputum."

When he felt confident that Mrs. Burch was stable, he removed his personal protection equipment and tossed it into the appropriate disposal bin. "I'll be back this evening to check on you." Then to Julia, he said, "Call or message me if there are any changes."

"Yes, sir, Dr. Richards," she answered without glancing up from her patient, whom she encouraged to take a deep breath through her nose and to blow out slowly through her mouth, trying to get her to fully expand her lungs.

Boone inwardly sighed at her formality with him and the immediate contrasting warmth with which she addressed Mrs. Burch. Prior to his botched date attempt, she'd showered him with her smiles and warmth. Now she wouldn't even look directly at him. He didn't like this new cold shoulder treatment and needed to find a way to correct it. Maybe with time and patience, she'd want more. A guy could hope.

But even if she didn't want to date him, they could still be friends, because he missed her smiles and quick wit.

"Julia, I need to clear the air."

Tired from the long day, Julia eyed the man who'd jogged to catch up on her way toward the elevator that would take her to the hospital's ground floor. She let out a long sigh. Hadn't Boone done enough damage to her peace of mind already that week? She just wanted to go home, take a hot shower, eat something, and snuggle with her cat, Honey, while studying her class notes for her upcoming fall term final exams. Only one more semester to go to have her master's in nursing. She had this.

"I owe you an apology," Boone continued, and when she tried to stop him, he said, "Hear me out, please."

Curiosity getting the best of her, she slowed her pace. "Okay."

"When I asked you about the Christmas party earlier this week, I never meant to make you feel uncomfortable or pressured. Neither was my asking you to call me Boone."

"I know." That he was making the effort to say so made her like him all the more, which was not the goal. She didn't want to like Boone more. She liked him too much already.

"You've avoided me since I asked you to the party, and earlier today felt awkward, when you didn't want to call me Boone."

Yes, she had done that, and her response to the idea of calling him Boone had been very awkward. She'd always been aware of him, but thinking about anything other than him had been almost impossible since he'd asked about the Christmas party. Being so distracted the week prior to that semester's final examinations wasn't a good thing.

"I don't like the change to our interactions but do accept that it's my own fault. I'm sorry."

"Apology accepted." An apology of her own was on the tip of her tongue. Only, how did she apologize for doing the right thing? As flattered as she was by his invite, things would never work between them. Even if by some miracle he was serious, she knew they were too different. She was saving them both a lot of wasted time.

"I didn't think that my attraction to you was one-sided." He gave her a self-derisive grin. "But now that you're giving me a wide berth, I've realized I strained our friendship and our professional relationship." He gave her a look that could only be described as completely sincere. "I never intended that. You're an amazing person and nurse. I wouldn't purposely give you a reason to not want to take care of my patients or to work with me. If I offended you by showing my personal interest, I hope you'll forgive me."

There were so many things she could say. That she'd been stunned and flattered, not offended. That she knew he was a good guy, but good guys broke hearts, too. That with work, school, school clinical hours, and volunteering at the Knoxville House of Hope, she didn't have time to date. She'd vowed not to date again until after she'd graduated. Even then, she hadn't really thought she would risk doing so. After Clay, she'd imagined she'd fly through life solo.

"Tell me how I can make things right."

If ever a man had puppy-dog eyes, Boone's blue ones shone with such yearning that Julia sucked in a deep breath.

"There's no need for you to do anything to make things right beyond what you just did. We'll forget it ever happened." She wasn't admitting just how blown away she was that he was attracted to her and was making the effort to try to repair their working relationship. If things were different, she'd have been over the moon about his interest. Ha, things weren't different, and she was still over the moon. How could she not be when he'd just said he was attracted to her? Of course, he didn't know the real her, just the one she presented at the hospital, but at least that assured her she was well on her way to becoming a better person. Too bad one's past never truly went away.

"Julia?"

She glanced up, wondering if she'd made a mistake by looking into the mesmerizing blue of his eyes. She'd been avoiding doing that for fear of what he might see. She didn't fool herself that she was a good enough actress to completely hide that he wasn't wrong on his initial assessment.

"I'll try not to bother you, except regarding work. I want to get to know you better outside the hospital. I do. But I will respect that you don't feel the same."

The biggest problem with his comment was that it wasn't true. She did feel the attraction between them. The difference was that she knew the consequences of becoming involved with someone she could never truly live up to.

"If it's not too much to ask, I do have one question."

Waiting, she braced herself for whatever he might say.

"Did you answer no because you aren't interested in me? Or because I asked you to go to the hospital Christmas party and our coworkers would see us? If others knowing is what held you back, pick your pleasure. I'd take you anywhere you want to go."

Pick her pleasure. Had he really just said that? Looking at him was a pleasure. She could only imagine that touching him would be more so. *Stop it, Julia*, she scolded herself. *You don't date and if you did, you'd be a fool to get involved with someone like Boone.*

"I appreciate the offer, and certainly I wouldn't want a first date to be such a public one with my coworkers, but like I told you, I don't date."

She had to keep focused on the future. Risking that future on a man, even one as fabulous as Boone, wasn't happening.

CHAPTER TWO

THINKING IT MIGHT be best if she avoided the Christmas party altogether, Julia offered to work that night. She'd learned long ago that avoiding temptation was the best defense from giving in to things that would hurt her. Unfortunately, the nurse manager hadn't put her on the schedule. A mixture of anxiety and anticipation warred. She'd enjoyed previous celebrations with her coworkers, but she suspected she'd be on pins and needles at this year's. Maybe she should stay home with Honey.

Had Boone asked someone else to go to the party? Julia didn't plan to change her mind, but she wanted to be mentally prepared if he'd be there with someone else. Then again, for all she knew he'd gotten back together with his longtime girlfriend. Over the weeks since he'd apologized, he'd been professional, friendly enough, but definitely on guard to not overstep during their interactions.

"You're staring at the schedule awfully hard," Stephanie pointed out, coming up behind Julia to glance at the computer screen. "Oh, great! You're not working on the ninth. You want to ride with Derek and me again?"

"I'm not sure I'm going."

Stephanie frowned. "Why wouldn't you? A night to hang with the gang without the stress of worrying about our patients? You have to go."

"I really don't." Stephanie knew the highlights of Julia's past. Julia sure couldn't imagine going back to the lifestyle she'd lived during her teens, but she didn't put herself in harm's way, either. Not that the hospital Christmas party would be anything like the parties she had once frequented. Lord forbid. "I should volunteer to work while I'm in between school semesters. With clinicals, I haven't been pulled many extra hours this past semester, and I don't expect this last one to be any better. Putting back a little money over the break would be great."

Julia felt Boone vibes, signaling he was in the ICU.

"Hey, Dr. Richards," Stephanie greeted him, brandishing a big smile that made Julia nervous. "We were just talking about the hospital Christmas party. Are you going?"

Nervousness justified, Julia's face heated.

Boone's gaze briefly touched upon her. Then he looked toward Stephanie. "That's the plan."

Stephanie's elbow nudged Julia's shoulder. Julia ignored her friend and continued to stare at the computer monitor that had morphed into screensaver mode with the hospital's logo.

"Derek and I are picking up Julia." Stephanie gave another one of those smiles that hinted her news should mean something to him. "You'll have to look for us. We're a lot of fun, aren't we, Julia?"

Julia could feel Boone's gaze and fought looking toward him. Closing the computer screen, she pushed back her chair and stood. "I mentioned that we'd see about my going and whether I'd want a ride."

"Come on, Julia," her friend beckoned. "You'll be done with finals and will be between semesters. The timing is perfect to celebrate finishing up and to get you into the Christmas spirit."

Julia wasn't anti-Christmas, but the holiday held more disappointment than happy memories. These days, holidays meant earning double-time pay and volunteering to work to make the most of that opportunity.

"You're in school?" Boone's gaze burned into her, making Julia's face even hotter. She was very proud of what she was trying to achieve, but she wasn't one to go around talking about it, either.

"She's working on her master's," Stephanie supplied. "I'm so proud of this girl. Smart and beautiful. She's stressing about finals, but don't be fooled. She's acing her classes. She always does."

Julia gave her friend a look that said, *Thank you, but please don't do this.* A beeping noise sounded in Stephanie's pocket, and Julia was grateful for the interruption.

"Oh, that's me. Good to see you, Dr. Richards." Stephanie took off toward her patient's room.

"I didn't know you were in school." Boone sat down in a chair near hers behind the nurse station desk. He obviously wasn't going to steer clear of personal topics that day.

"Why would you?"

He sat there a moment, then ran his fingers through his hair, slightly rumpling the silky locks. "I promised I wouldn't bother you, so I won't respond by saying that I'd like to know."

Unable to keep from looking his way, she met his gaze, saw the sincerity and couldn't help but marvel. "Why?"

She wasn't sure whether she asked why he wanted to know, or why he was looking at her with genuine attraction shining in his eyes.

"It's not a secret that I'm interested in knowing more about you, Julia. I asked you to go to the Christmas party. Admittedly, that wasn't my most brilliant move. You were right that the party is too much under coworkers' eyes for a first date."

She nodded. Even if she had been interested, she'd never have agreed to being under a microscope on a first date.

"I hadn't thought that one through. We'll chalk it up to the fact that it's been a long time since I've asked anyone to go on a first date. I'm a bit rusty on dating etiquette. If I had it to do over, I'd simply have asked you to dinner somewhere nice, with good food and atmosphere, to just eat, talk, and get to know each other outside of work."

There wouldn't have been anything simple about his asking her to dinner. Just breathing near the man was complicated.

"That would definitely be a better plan if you intend to ask out another coworker."

He frowned. "I won't be asking out another coworker. I'm not interested in dating anyone else, Julia. Just you." He took a deep breath. "But I have a promise to keep, so we'll change the subject to work. Tell me about the new admit, Aaron West."

If ever there were a topic to remind her of the reasons why she needed to keep her eyes trained on the goal and not let anything or anyone deter her from her carefully plotted path to success, her next patient was it.

"Aaron is a seventeen-year-old male who over-dosed on fentanyl-laced oxycodone tablets. For-tunately, his friends…" *if you could call them that* "…had naloxone on hand, administered it, and called for emergency help immediately." Her heart squeezed as it often did on similar cases. Cases that were flashbacks from her own past. "The paramedic administered another naloxone injection upon arrival as he was barely breathing even after being hit twice already."

Boone's expression tightened. "He's lucky his friends were sober enough to save him."

She nodded. The young man had been lucky. Just as she had once been. Unfortunately, Aaron was far from out of the woods.

"Is he responding to stimuli?"

"No. Earlier during visitation, his mother thought he moved his fingers in response to her talking to him, but there was no change in his monitor readings to indicate that it was anything more than a coincidence. His Glasgow Coma Score is seven."

"Such a waste." Shaking his head, Boone sighed. "Let's check him, and then we'll let his parents visit again."

She followed him into the ICU room. Seeing so many tubes and wires exiting her patients never failed to humble Julia and make her thankful for modern medicine. As critical as the young man was, at least he had hope of getting a second chance to make better life choices. She prayed that he would recover and do just that.

"I've looked over his notes but didn't see a history of a previous hospitalization. Is he a repeater?"

That Boone had to ask was a sad testament to how frequently the intensive care unit did have repeat overdose patients.

"No. According to the girl who called for an ambulance, he'd drunk on a few occasions but didn't do drugs. She feels confident that he only took one pill."

"That's all it takes if that pill is laced with enough fentanyl." Boone made a frustrated noise. "These pill mills put such garbage out that a single tablet can be lethal. The kid probably had no idea what he was risking. Many don't even realize some dealers lace their goods to get people hooked specifically to their product. Hopefully, Aaron will live to learn from his mistake and not suffer any long-term consequences."

Julia had been traveling the same destructive path at his age. It had taken lying right where the young man lay, a wonderful nurse, and a rehabilitation program to wake her up to the risks she'd taken. She'd been one of the lucky ones who had gotten that second chance and had done her best not to waste that precious opportunity.

"Hopefully."

That Aaron had survived the night was a blessing, but he was critical. If he survived, the next worry would be that he hadn't suffered any permanent damage from his overdose.

Boone examined him, then sighed.

"It doesn't look good, does it?" She couldn't help but ask. She usually didn't, especially not in the patient's room as one never knew what a patient was aware of, regardless of what monitors showed. But Aaron's mother weeping over him that morning had gotten to her, and Julia had been saying extra prayers all day that the young man pulled through.

Boone shook his head. "Keep it to not more than two visitors simultaneously, but let his family spend as much time with him as they wish so long as they aren't disruptive to his care or the unit. If they become a problem, then go back to standard protocol."

Grateful that he was approving the extended visitation, she nodded. With one last heartfelt glance toward the young man whose pale chest rose and fell thanks to his life support, she followed Boone from the room. "I'll talk to his parents and let them know."

He paused, pressing the sanitizer dispenser. "Those are tough, aren't they?"

Watching him rub his hands together with the disinfectant, Julia blinked. All their patients were tough. In most cases, each one was a life that impacted many others. Did he ask the question because he'd heard something about her past? Or was he just making conversation and she was being paranoid? Boone knowing just how many mistakes and poor choices she'd once made, well, the thought made her feel raw and exposed.

"I had someone close get messed up with drugs," he continued, a faraway expression on his face. "She was a star athlete, good grades, beautiful. Her entire life ahead of her just waiting to be lived. She lost everything to her drug habit." He shook his head as if to clear a memory. "I've never understood how someone could mess up their life over getting high."

"Getting high is rarely the true reason people overdose." His misconception was a common one. Doing drugs was about so much more than getting high. Depression, anxiety, peer pressure, poor life circumstances, the list went on. That Boone's comment irritated her so much didn't make sense. Maybe it was because she expected him to know better. She suspected he did know better and had just been musing out loud while frustrated by his memories. She also suspected that she was being overly sensitive because it was him, and she was grasping at any reason to like him less.

His gaze flickered to her. "I certainly don't believe that kid meant to overdose."

Julia didn't believe the young man had meant to, either. He'd given in to peer pressure and been very unlucky that he'd gotten a pill laced with enough fentanyl to overwhelm his naive system.

"Ultimately, he alone holds the responsibility for making the choice to take the drug."

"I suppose."

He eyed her a moment. "Did I upset you just then, Julia?"

"No. Maybe. It doesn't matter," she answered, feeling flustered. She put her hands beneath the dispenser and got a large dollop of the cleansing gel, so much that the alcohol scent burned her nostrils. Trying not to sniffle, she rubbed her hands together. "My point was that you shouldn't judge others unless you've walked in their shoes."

"Agreed, and neither should you," he surprised her by saying.

Not that he wasn't right. She was judging him unfairly. Obviously, she was grasping at anything she could to put up a defensive barrier against how he affected her now that he was single and had expressed interest. She was desperately seeking character flaws.

"For the record, I appreciate your protectiveness of your patients and the wonderful care you give them and their families. It's one of the first things I noticed about you when I started at Knoxville General." His tone was gentle and hinted that there was a lot more he'd like to say. Instead, he glanced at his watch. "I'm headed to the clinic. Let me know if anything changes. Have a good day, Julia."

"Uh, yeah, you too." She bit into her lower lip, watching as he headed toward the unit's double door exit. He had her insides twisted into knots.

If she ever was going to waver from the life course she'd set for herself, Boone Richards would be the reason. But she wasn't going to, no matter how much what she saw in his eyes tempted her.

"Wow. That red dress looks fantastic on you, and those gold bell earrings are so festive with their red bows."

Feeling self-conscious, Julia smiled at her nurse manager, whom she had bumped into almost immediately upon entering the Sunsphere ballroom with Stephanie and Derek. The gold glass sphere on a high tower remained from the 1982 World's Fair. It overlooked the city and was her favorite place to attend events. It looked especially beautiful tonight, decorated with deep evergreen garlands and trees adorned with gold ribbons and ornaments. The crisp air even smelled of balsam, although Julia was certain the greenery wasn't real.

"See, I told you that you look gorgeous," Stephanie reminded her. "I've never been one who could pull off a headband and am completely jell of the one holding back all your glorious hair."

Why had Julia left her heavy curls down? For that matter, why had she paid such close attention to her appearance? *Why ask questions I don't want to know the answers to?* She wasn't fooling anyone, especially not herself, by styling her hair loosely about her shoulders rather than pulling it back in its usual tight ponytail.

"Thank you," she told Patti. "I feel a little over-the-top since I rarely wear anything beyond mascara, tinted sunscreen, and lip gloss."

"Which is fine for work, but at a Christmas party?" Patti lifted her drink glass. "Go for glam. Besides, it's fun to dress up on occasion."

"She's right. You're gorgeous, Jules. Someone is going to eat his heart out that he didn't ask you to be his date." Stephanie whispered the last bit, then gave her a one-armed hug. "Oh! There's Kevin, Rob, and Becky. I'm glad they got here early and snagged a good table close to the dance floor. You want something to drink?"

"A water would be great." Julia spotted their friends, waving as they motioned her over. She really did love the crew she worked with at Knoxville General. Julia headed toward where they sat and complimented them on how they cleaned up out of their scrubs, trying not to blush too brightly when they did the same about her new-to-her secondhand store dress. It appeared brand-new and fit perfectly. It spoke volumes that she'd gone shopping with Stephanie for a new outfit rather than wearing her go-to black dress that she usually pulled out for special occasions. Volumes she didn't want to hear because they played a beat she'd rather not give in to any more than she already had.

Her insides got a quivery sensation. She'd not spotted Boone on her way to the table, but he was obviously somewhere close. Or maybe she felt that vibe because she'd been thinking of him.

"Don't look now, but your favorite doctor is on his way over here," Stephanie teased, handing a glass of water to Julia as she slid into the chair next to hers.

Knowing Boone was headed her way had her taking a deep breath. She couldn't even argue that he wasn't her favorite doctor. He was.

"Mark my words, after he sees you tonight,"

her friend continued with a brow waggle, "he's going to want Santa to deliver you on Christmas morning. Ho-ho-ho."

Julia rolled her eyes. "You're crazy, but I love you anyway."

Stephanie grinned. "Now that he's single and knows you're single, my friend, he's not going to be able to resist asking you out."

"How does he know I'm single?" Not that she hadn't pretty much told him when she'd said she didn't date, but she'd never breathed a word of that conversation to her friend. Stephanie would have been all over a juicy morsel like that.

Her friend's painted pink lips curved. "I may have mentioned it."

Julia cringed. "You shouldn't have done that. You know I don't date."

Unfazed, Stephanie's gaze didn't waver. "Only because the right person hasn't asked."

"That's not my reason. You know my reasons. I have too much going on in my life to date Boone." Not to mention that he was way out of her dating pool league. She still didn't understand why he'd asked unless it was merely to scratch a sexual itch.

"Boone, is it?" Stephanie teased. Then, seeing Julia blush, her eyes widened. "Seriously? Is that why you look like a million bucks tonight? Because you have a secret Christmas stocking stuffing rendezvous planned with Dr. Richards? Girl, I'm thrilled for you."

"Shh," she hushed her friend, shifting in her chair to where she could see Boone. Dr. Vaughn had intercepted his path to their table and was introducing him to his wife. Boone laughed at something the intensivist said, and Julia's heart hiccupped. Wearing dark slacks, a crisp red shirt, and a green tie with a pattern she couldn't quite make out, Boone stole her breath. Not that he didn't in scrubs. He was gorgeous, but it was more than that. Perhaps the warmth of his eyes, his genuine smiles, or how he truly cared about his patients.

His gaze shifted toward her and, catching her looking at him, his brow lifted in question. No wonder. She'd told him no and yet, even if he were blind, he couldn't possibly miss how he affected her. Yeah, he wasn't the only one with questions. She had them, too. Like why was her heart flip-flopping in her chest, and why did looking at him make her a little dizzy?

After a moment, he seemed to come to some conclusion, one he obviously liked based upon his grin, which was so big that Julia gulped. Heaven help her. Heat radiated from her insides to her immediately clammy skin. Ugh. She needed to keep her eyes anywhere but toward him. Glancing back at her friend, she saw

Stephanie's grin was almost as big as Boone's had been.

"Admit it. You like him."

"There's no denying that Dr. Richards is an attractive man." *Understatement of the year.* "What's not to like? He's smart, funny, kind, and a seemingly decent human being. But he's also the hospital's star pulmonologist who just got out of a long-term relationship with a gorgeous orthopedic surgeon. For all we know, they got into a tiff and will work things out."

"Maybe, but I don't think so." Taking a sip of her drink, Stephanie considered her. "He's asked you out, hasn't he? Say what you want, but I've seen how he lights up when he spots you and vice versa. He wants you, Julia, and I'm convinced the feeling is mutual."

Julia hesitated too long.

"You, my friend, are crazy. Every single woman at the hospital is all agog since he's become Knoxville's most eligible bachelor. You've been holding out on me. Not only has he asked you on a date, but you obviously shot the poor man down despite the fact that the air threatens to ignite when you two are near each other. We need to get your head examined." Stephanie's expression grew dramatically concerned. She glanced toward where Boone still talked with Dr. and Mrs. Vaughn as she asked, "Is there a doctor in the house? Doctor? Doctor? My friend needs medical attention. Maybe some mouth-to-mouth to get oxygen to her brain."

Julia grabbed her friend's hand, lowering it to the table. "My head is just fine, but I'm worried about yours." It was all Julia's other body parts that were the problem. "Let's not talk about Boone," she urged as, catching her gaze again, he excused himself and joined them.

Standing opposite her side of the table, he chatted with their coworkers, who greeted him heartily before he was able to say something directly to Julia. No wonder they were happy to see him. He was a friendly, likable guy. His baby blues met hers, and desire flickered there. She couldn't label it any other way. That he appreciated her dress-up efforts was obvious. Try as she might, she couldn't help but be flattered by that look, by the smile that slid onto his face, by his interest. If only she believed his interest wouldn't vaporize if he had a glimmer of what lay beneath her carefully constructed shiny surface. Still, the way he looked at her warmed her insides, boosting a feminine confidence that had long ago been diminished.

"Red is your color," he complimented her when he moved to stand near her and Stephanie, "but then, I've never seen you wear anything that didn't look great."

Unable to hold that sparkly blue gaze, she glanced across the glitzy room that was becoming more and more crowded. "Thank you. You clean up nicely yourself."

Oops. Had she just said that out loud? Stephanie's snicker warned she had. Cheeks warm, Julia pretended a fascination with the handful of couples sashaying on the dance floor. The hospital had hired a great local band who played a mix of country and pop. Julia loved to dance, but rarely went out. She appreciated that she'd be able to have fun with her friends tonight.

"Derek wants to grab food from those scrumptious-appearing buffet tables before it gets too crowded in here. You want to go with?" Stephanie gave Julia an out if she wanted one. Knowing her friend probably wanted to question her further, Julia shook her head, then wondered if facing her friend's inquiry might be preferable to remaining with Boone.

"Thanks, but I'm good." Her stomach was way too nervous to put food into the mix of flip-flops, anyway.

"Oh, I do. I'm starved." Becky popped up from across the table. "Save our seats, Julia?" she asked as everyone else stood, too, leaving Julia trapped there until her coworkers returned.

When the others had gone, Boone slid into

Stephanie's chair. "I'll give her seat back when she returns," he promised. "Having fun?"

"We've not been here long, but everyone seems to be having a good time."

His brows rose. "We?"

"I rode with Stephanie and Derek."

"That's right. I recall her mentioning you were riding with them."

She took another drink. "How about you? Is there someone waiting for you to get back to her?"

Why didn't she just lift her not secondhand but splurged-on shiny red heels and stick them into her mouth? Her question was as obvious as his had been. Her stomach knotted tighter. What was wrong with her?

"I came alone as it wouldn't be fair to have brought someone when I'd rather be with you."

She sucked in a breath. He was such a great guy that she wished she could just throw caution to the wind and say she'd love to go on a date with him. But she couldn't.

"Don't clam up on me, please. That was just an honest answer to your question. You've told me you don't date, and unless you've changed your mind, then we'll just be friends."

Just be friends with the most attractive man she'd ever known when he was also attracted to her? Easy-peasy. Not.

"I—I can do that." Maybe. Goodness knew she'd done tougher things over the years, so surely she could manage keeping her relationship with Boone compartmentalized.

"I never doubted your abilities." His gaze didn't waver. "So, as friends getting to know each other at a company Christmas party, tell me more about yourself. How long have you worked for Knoxville General?"

"Since nursing school graduation." Answering his question shouldn't make her feel as if she were lowering her defenses, but where Boone was concerned, the more he knew, the more exposed she felt.

"Which was?" he prompted.

"Two years ago."

"Which makes you twenty-four?" he guessed.

"Twenty-seven," she corrected him.

His brow lifted again. "Which means you graduated from nursing school at twenty-five. What did you do prior to nursing school?"

His question was a natural one, but she couldn't prevent her muscles from tensing at what the most honest answer would be, that she had more empathy for Aaron West than most could ever understand.

"Odd jobs here and there." Which was the truth. She'd done just about every odd job she'd been able to find but had never been able to hold on to any of them until she'd gotten clean. "I waitressed, worked at convenience stores, in retail, bagged groceries." She shrugged. "Whatever I could find that paid my bills. I wasn't picky."

Intrigue flickered on his face. "You were putting yourself through school?"

The school of life.

"I did work to put myself through school." She just hadn't started her nursing education straight out of high school. "Why are you the one asking all the questions?"

"Ask anything you want."

Fine. Let him be the one to have to come up with answers. She'd much rather go on the conversation offensive than discuss her past. "When did you graduate?"

"I finished residency in May."

"Knoxville General is your first nonresident position, then?"

He nodded.

"I'd ask where you went to med school, but I recall hearing right after you started that you attended in Memphis. How about your residency? Where did you do that?"

"Philadelphia."

"Is that where you're originally from?"

"I'm from West Tennessee. That's why I chose to go to school in Memphis, so I could be close to home during undergrad and medical school. My dad and brother are both physicians who work for St. Jude's, and my mother manages a shipping company that's been in her dad's family for over a hundred years."

Not surprisingly, his background sounded quite different from Julia's. Doctors and a multi-generational business. The closest thing to a multi-generational business in her family was that as a teen she'd bussed tables at bars where her mother worked.

"You're close with your family?" she asked.

He nodded. "My mom is one of my best friends. She's tough, but fair. I can tell her anything. We chat or text most days. My dad and brother are great, too, but I am admittedly closest to Mom. I would've returned to Memphis except Oliv…" He paused, seeming to weigh how much he wanted to say. "As you know, I'd been in a relationship for several years, and we mutually decided that Knoxville better suited our immediate future."

"That sounds serious." Curiosity, not jealousy, twisted her stomach.

"It was. We met in early med school and dated for five years."

"What happened?" The question slipped out, and she started to retract it, but he shrugged.

"I'm not sure anything happened. Maybe our interests changed, or we grew apart, or perhaps it's just that we were never right to begin with.

Don't get me wrong. She's great, but continuing in our relationship when I knew we had no future seemed unfair."

"You're the one who ended the relationship?" She'd wondered, thinking maybe if he'd been dumped, that played into his interest in her as a trial run to fluff his ego back up.

He nodded. "Not quite two months ago. I didn't want to hurt her, but it was for the best when we weren't right together."

He'd been single just over a month when he'd asked her about the Christmas party.

"Five years. That's a long time to be with the wrong person." Not that Julia would know. Other than Clay, she'd never been in a relationship for more than a few weeks at a time. In the grand scheme of things, her relationship with Clay hadn't lasted so long, either, but it had been long enough to break her heart. He'd been different, a good man with morals and…and he'd found her lacking. Sometimes she wondered if she ever would be good enough when her past held so much bad. "I'm sorry it didn't work out."

Boone and Dr. Cunningham, not her and Clay.

Boone nodded. "Me, too. She's a wonderful woman, and I have no regrets about the time we spent together. But I don't want to continue in a relationship that for some time had felt like a stepping stone to where I'm supposed to be in life."

A gorgeous orthopedic surgeon who by all accounts was as brilliant as she was beautiful and who he'd just called wonderful wasn't the right woman for him, but he'd asked Julia out? Had he lost his mind? If she'd said yes, how would he have someday described a relationship with her? A pebble in his shoe on the journey to where he was supposed to be in life?

"More questions?" he prompted when she didn't immediately ask another.

"Not really." She already knew enough to understand that she and Boone came from two different worlds. Pretending otherwise would lead to heartache.

"Good, because I have another for you. When you said you don't date, was that a nice way of telling me no, or do you really not date?"

"With work and school, I don't have the time or need the distraction of dating." It's the answer she'd been giving for the past five years because it had been that long since she'd been in any type of personal relationship. Since Clay.

"Noted, but you have to eat. Surely the occasional dinner date wouldn't be a problem."

"Going on a date with someone implies that you have an interest in them, that you're willing to make spending time with them a priority. My interests and priorities are committed elsewhere."

Looking thoughtful, he eyed her. "You mean school?"

"My job and school come first. I have a life plan and find success comes more readily when I stick to it. No dating until I graduate."

"After you finish graduate school? You plan to date then?"

If she met a man who could forgive her past and keep her strong when she felt weak. If she met a man she could trust enough to reveal the horrible things she'd done, and know he wouldn't use those weaknesses against her during the normal ups and downs of a relationship. He wouldn't judge her harshly, and could see how she was working diligently not to be that person anymore.

She suspected any such man would need to have gone through something similar to truly understand, forgive, and love her. Most days she struggled to do those things herself. Mindlessly, she stroked her thumb over the tattoo on the inside of her left wrist. She was a better person than she'd once been. She was.

"Maybe."

Boone leaned back in his chair and flashed another smile. "It's good to know there's hope."

Surprised, she blinked. "I won't graduate until May."

"So, what you're saying is that I picked the wrong holiday when I asked you to the Christmas party, but you'll gladly be my date to the hospital's Memorial Day picnic?"

Her stomach somersaulted. "We discussed that a work gathering was a terrible first date."

"That's right. We did." His grin had her heart pounding. "Glad you caught that. We'll need to have gone out a few times prior to being under the work family's curious eyes." His expression grew thoughtful. "You'll have celebratory lunch plans with your family, but how about I take you to dinner on the evening of your graduation? That's usually the first Saturday in May, right?"

Celebratory lunch with her family? Her mother had passed long before her college graduation. Her father had lived out of state and hadn't chosen to attend the ceremony. She had no reason to think he'd be there when she walked the line for graduate school. What would it be like to have Boone to celebrate her successes with? No. No. No. She didn't need to let her thoughts go there. She took a sip of water to moisten her dry throat.

"That's six months away," she said.

"Time flies." He didn't seem fazed. "I'm calling dibs."

Dibs? Surely he was teasing. But although he was smiling, sincerity shone in his eyes.

"You plan to wait six months to take me on a

date? I should hold you to that," she threatened, heart pounding because she couldn't believe he was even saying such nonsense. No way would he wait for her. Not that she wanted him to. She didn't really have a plan on when she'd start dating, or even if she would. She just knew that she wouldn't while in school to avoid anything that might distract her from success.

"Good, because I intend to hold you to our graduation day date. I know I did a train wreck of a job when I asked you to this party, so let me get the next one right." He gave her one of his lopsided smiles. "Julia, will you give me the honor of taking you to dinner to celebrate earning your Master of Science in Nursing degree in May?"

Why did his question feel like so much more? As if her entire life depended upon her answer.

"You'll have long forgotten wanting to take me to dinner by then."

He shook his head. "Not a chance. My memory's good, and some things are worth waiting for."

"A date with me being one of them?"

"Definitely. Until you graduate, we'll be co-workers and friends." His eyes sparkled more brilliantly than the Christmas lights flashing across the room. "After that, we'll take one day at a time and see what happens. Deal?"

"I— Okay, one day at a time is how I live my life, anyway." There was no point in arguing with someone who was obviously certifiable. Time would prove her right, so why waste breath trying to point that out? Despite what he'd claimed, he would forget all about his impulsive invitation long before her graduation.

If only she could.

CHAPTER THREE

LEANING BACK IN his chair, Boone watched Julia laugh as she grapevined and twirled in a popular line dance with Stephanie, Becky, and a group that mostly consisted of women. Held away from her face by a wide red band, her hair fell long and luscious about her shoulders. He'd never seen her hair down because she always kept it up at the hospital, and his fingers itched to tangle in the thick silky strands to see if they were as soft as they appeared.

"I'm topping off our drinks. You want anything?" Stephanie's boyfriend, Derek, asked. Boone hadn't previously met the real estate broker who Stephanie had met when he'd sold her a house a year or so back and they'd hit it off.

He shook his head. The man couldn't deliver what Boone wanted. "I'm good. Thanks."

Rather than walking away, Derek gestured toward where Boone stared at the dance floor. "Stephanie really likes Julia, says she's been through a lot, is a great nurse and friend. For whatever it's worth, she also says that Julia likes you."

What things had Julia been through, and had she told her friend that she liked him or was Stephanie making assumptions?

"She's such a cheery little thing most of the time. I really like her, too, and have tried to set her up with a few friends over the years. She always shoots that down, saying she doesn't date."

Good to know that it truly wasn't just him.

"She's mentioned that a time or two," he admitted. He'd keep that she'd agreed to go out with him to celebrate her graduation to himself. He'd seen the distrust in her eyes when she'd said she should hold him to his dibs claim. She'd only agreed because she fully expected him to have changed his mind. He couldn't imagine that being the case. There was something different about her, something in the way he felt when he looked at her, when their eyes met, when he saw her smile, in how she was strong, and yet made him feel protective. He wanted to know more.

"We have our annual group Christmas ski trip planned to Gatlinburg over New Year's weekend. Ober Mountain's ski slopes aren't huge, and the snow is mostly machine-generated, but they're close, and we always have a great time. What could be better than good food, good friends, and fun memories, right? You're welcome to join us."

"Julia's going?"

Derek grinned. "She has the past two years, and her name is on our list. If she tried to cancel, Stephanie would drag her anyway. She says it's one of the few times Julia takes off work to do something that isn't school- or volunteer-related."

Saying yes was on the tip of his tongue. If Julia wasn't in the picture, he'd have agreed without hesitation, but what if she'd rather he not infringe upon her time with her friends? She had just agreed to go on a date with him half a year down the road, but that didn't mean she'd want him as a constant addition to her outside of work activities.

"I'll check my hospital schedule, but I'm off on New Year's." He'd planned to go home to ring in the New Year with his family. His parents always threw a humdinger of a party, but he'd be home during their more intimate Christmas celebrations. The holidays were hard on them all, but especially his mother. Sometimes he suspected that was why she threw herself into such elaborate celebrations, to distract from things she'd rather not think about. "When do you need to know by?"

"Anytime over the next week or so should be fine." Derek pulled out his phone. "Dial your number so that you'll have mine. When you know for sure, shoot me a text."

Boone did so, then handed back Derek's phone. "Thanks. I'll save it in my contacts. I visited Gatlinburg over the summer for a day hike at Mount Le Conte, but my friend and I didn't make it to Ober. The trip sounds like it will be a good time. I'll let you know."

"Sure thing, man. Now, my advice is for you to get out there and dance. Chicks love that."

Boone gave him a skeptical look. He could line dance—hey, he'd been in junior high once upon a time, and the skills he'd learned back then had seen him through his university days. But he'd stay where he was. He didn't want to end up driving away Julia by pressing too hard.

Patience was a virtue.

She glanced up, met his gaze, then misstepped, bumping into Stephanie. First apologizing to her friend, she moved back into line and didn't look his way again. Boone stayed seated, enduring Derek and the other guys' good-natured ribbing with a smile when they returned and called him out on where his attention stayed. Fortunately, they honored the bro code when the ladies rejoined them at the table and never let on that they'd been ragging him nonstop about his fascination with Julia.

A slow song came on.

Stephanie tugged on Derek's hand. "Come on, big guy. I want to dance with you."

Kevin and Becky joined the other couple on the dance floor, along with Rob and the phlebotomist who was smiling up at him with adoration, leaving Boone and Julia as the table's sole occupants. She stared straight ahead at her water glass as if she was afraid to look up.

"No pressure, feel free to say no, but would you dance with me, Julia? As friends?"

To his surprise, and maybe to her own, she nodded. Boone did a mental high-five as he stood, and they made their way to the dance floor. Unlike the other slow-dancing couples, Julia didn't melt against him, but Boone wasn't complaining. How could he when she'd placed her hands around his neck, touching him for the first time, and sending his pulse racing?

That he was so aware of her light touch, that it was the first time they'd been skin to skin, spoke volumes about how much she affected him. Or perhaps it was the zings shooting through him at their innocent touch making that so clear. Julia poured gasoline over him, then set him on fire. Did she have any idea just how much she got to him? Breathing in her soft vanilla scent had him wanting to lean close, to nuzzle into her tresses and fill his lungs with her very essence. His hands loosely at her waist had him longing to pull her flush and feel every inch of her pressed to him.

Boone swallowed the lump in his throat. "You looked like you were having fun line dancing. You're good."

She kept her gaze averted, staring at his chest. "Other than in the privacy of home, it's been last year's Christmas party since I've danced, so thank you. I didn't know some of the newer songs, but it's amazing how you just fall into step when the ones you know play."

"Like riding a bicycle. Once you've got the basics mastered, the rest just comes naturally."

Still not glancing up, she smiled. "I guess so."

They moved in silence for a few minutes, Boone enjoying having Julia in his arms and wondering how he couldn't have realized sooner just how attracted he was to her when it was so obvious. How had he worked with her for months and not acknowledged what that excitement at seeing her meant? Now that he'd touched her, there was no denying anything. At least, not for him. He wanted her and would be as patient as he needed to be.

He said, "Derek invited me to go to Gatlinburg over New Year's weekend."

She stiffened.

"I haven't given him an answer. I didn't want

to do that without talking to you first. I won't go if you don't want me to."

Her throat worked. "You don't need my permission."

"No, but showing up at your getaway with friends isn't cool without discussing it with you first to be sure you're okay with my being there."

She hesitated, seemingly thinking about what he'd said. "Why wouldn't I be okay with you being there?"

"Avoiding each other would be difficult on a trip where we are all staying in the same cabin."

"Oh. That's true." Although she kept her grip around his neck light, her arms tensed. "You want to avoid me?"

"It's more a case of the opposite. I keep promising not to push and yet, if I go, I'll struggle to stay away from you. If you don't want me there, I'll tell him I can't make it."

"I…" She repositioned her hands. "That's not fair to you. I'm an adult. We both are. If Derek invited you and you want to go, then you should go."

"It wouldn't bother you for me to be there?"

"We work together, Boone. Whether you go on this trip or not, it's not as if we aren't going to be seeing each other on a regular basis. My saying you shouldn't go would seem silly."

"Away from work is different. I don't want you to feel pressured."

"I appreciate that. You going to Gatlinburg on a group trip that you were invited to isn't you pressuring me."

But he could see her mental wheels turning, could feel the tension in the arms around his neck. Was she rubbing her thumb over the bird inked onto her left wrist? He'd noticed her doing that from time to time over the months since they'd met. "You're sure?"

"I'm not a delicate flower, Boone. You going to Gatlinburg is fine."

In some ways, Boone knew she told the truth. She was strong, and yet there was a fragility within her. A fragility that he needed to handle with care. "I'll let Derek know that I'll go."

She nodded, then with a deep breath added, "For the record, if you've met someone or gotten back together with your girlfriend, it's okay if you bring her."

"What?" Did Julia really think he might get back with Olivia? "Ex-girlfriend, Julia. We won't be getting back together."

Regardless of what happened between him and Julia, the future didn't hold anything other than the possibility of friendship with Olivia.

"Well, I didn't want you to feel awkward or as if you couldn't come if that happened. You're not the only one who doesn't want the other to feel pressured. Truly, it would be fine if you brought someone. Actually, you should."

Realizing she was serious, he sighed. "I hope you feel differently about that someday, Julia. That someday you won't be fine at the thought of my dating someone else. You'll want all my dates as your own."

Her gaze lifted to his and, looking into her big brown eyes, he wondered if maybe she hadn't been quite as serious about his bringing someone else as he'd thought. Because there was something in those honeyed depths, a yearning that called to every bit of him. A very vulnerable yearning that said she'd like to want all his dates but wouldn't dare let herself. Who had put that distrust there?

"For now, I'm going to count my blessings that the most beautiful woman here is in my arms and that I'll get to say goodbye to the old year and welcome the new with her in a few weeks— as her current friend and future graduation day date. Life is good."

Her feet stopped moving. She stared up at him with those eyes that held such wonder, with such uncertainty in what he said evident on her face, that he longed to kiss her to put all doubt to rest. But then, she gave the slightest nod. "I—yes, life is good."

Boone wanted to know what was going through that brilliant mind of hers, but as she relaxed against him, he held his questions and cherished the feel of her cheek against his chest, her fingers at his nape, and her thumbs gently brushing along his hair there. Was she even conscious she was doing that? He didn't think so.

The first Saturday in May. Yeah, he could be patient when he had to, but her graduation couldn't come fast enough. If she changed her mind between now and then and wanted a pre-graduation celebration, well, he'd be a happy man.

"What a great Christmas party!" Stephanie greeted Julia the following morning.

Glancing up from the computer screen where she'd been reviewing her nursing notes on Aaron West, Julia smiled at Stephanie. "I half expected you to call out of work today."

"Yeah, yeah, so maybe I had a little too much fun last night." Rubbing her temple, her friend sank into an empty swivel chair at the nurse station. "But admit it, the party was the best ever."

Although it was probably a mistake to do so, Julia nodded. "I had a good time."

Coming to life, Stephanie clasped her hands together. "I knew it. I wanted to jump up and down when you two were dancing."

Julia rolled her eyes. "I'm glad you didn't. That would have been all kinds of embarrassing."

"You looked so happy. Dr. Richards did, too. How many songs did y'all dance to? Five? Six? I've never seen you do more than line dance and had no idea you could swing and spin that way. Y'all looked like y'all were having a blast. Even Derek commented on it. Did Boone ask you out again?" Her friend blasted her with questions so quickly that her last sentence came out breathy. "Please tell me you said yes."

"Stephanie, I'm not going to date Boo— Dr. Richards." Because Julia wasn't counting on his being single half a year down the road. Last night it would have been impossible to miss just how many women had made a point to come over to talk to him, a few of them even asking him to dance, which he'd politely declined.

"Derek said he invited Boone to go with us to Gatlinburg."

Heat flushed Julia's cheeks. "Dr. Richards mentioned that."

Stephanie's smile was huge. "This is going to be the best trip yet. Oh, and we'll have to make sure he knows to bring a white elephant gift for our Friends-mas."

A long weekend spent with Boone away from work. As friends. She could handle being his friend—maybe. But if he was as wonderful as he'd been the night before, how would she resist the temptation in those baby blues? In his smile? It had felt wonderful to lean against him, and to pretend that she belonged in his arms and might have a happily-ever-after of her own someday. Who got that in real life?

Hands shaking, Julia logged out of her patient's chart, then stood. "I imagine Derek will let him know about the gift exchange. The more the merrier, right? I'm going to check on Aaron."

At the mention of the young man, Stephanie allowed the subject change. "His parents are just the sweetest. I ran into his dad in the elevator on my way up to the floor this morning."

"Yes, they are wonderful. You can see how much they love him. They've barely left the hospital since his admission. His mother stayed last night and is still in with him."

Julia went to the ICU room, disinfecting her hands prior to entering, and pausing just inside the doorway to take in the various tubes and lines attached to Aaron. Without them, he wouldn't survive. With them, she prayed he got strong enough to no longer need their life-extending capabilities.

While chatting with his mother, Julie checked him, making sure all lines and settings were as they should be, and recording the readings in his electronic medical record. She was still working in Aaron's room when Boone arrived. He smiled at Julia, but almost seeming nervous, he greeted the young man's mother rather than giving Julia a chance to respond. But if he had, what would she have said?

Good morning. I barely slept last night because I couldn't stop thinking about you and I really wish that wasn't the case.

Yeah, she was glad that he'd immediately focused on Mrs. West.

"Good morning, Mrs. West. How are you holding up?" He chatted with her a few minutes, then examined Aaron. "I'm decreasing Aaron's sedation today."

"And then he'll wake up?" the boy's mother asked, her face full of hope.

Boone shrugged. "I wish it was that simple. It is possible that he will awaken, but his brain may not be ready to wake up yet, and he may remain in a coma. If you recall, he wasn't conscious prior to our giving his body time to recover."

"Has it healed enough for you to decrease his medications, then? Should we wait longer? I want him to wake up, but I don't want to rush things if there's a risk it might hurt him."

"The sooner we can successfully get him off the ventilator, the better. He's reflexively moving to certain stimuli, and his EEG is indicating increased brain activity with stimuli. His progress has been slower than we'd hoped for, but I believe he's strong enough for us to start decreasing his sedation. As far as if he wakes up or how he will do—" he sighed "—that's something I can't say for sure at this point."

He answered the rest of her questions. Then he and Julia walked out of the room, pausing outside the door. "I wish I could give her better reassurances."

"You were honest." Julia rubbed her palms together with sanitizer. "I'm sure she appreciates that."

"Is her husband here? I was surprised he wasn't with her."

"He went home last night to be with their other kids. Stephanie said she rode up in the elevator with him, so he's likely in the waiting area. Some family friends had stopped by."

"I'll go talk to him." Boone paused, glancing her way. "They have two other kids, right? Both younger? It's so difficult on the entire family when something like this happens, especially at this time of year. I'm glad he went home to spend time with their other children. Hopefully, Mrs. West will soon. It would be good for them all."

Something in Boone's voice caught Julia's attention, just a nuance to his tone, but a definite inflection of emotion that made her unable to look away.

"He tried to get her to go home, but so far she's refused to leave for fear something will happen while she's gone." Julia's heart squeezed. "They live in Maryville," she continued, "so at least it's not too horrible of a drive for him to go back and forth."

"Do you have family close, Julia? It just occurred to me that although you know I'm from Memphis, I have no idea where you're originally from."

"The South."

He arched a brow. "You're purposely being vague?"

She'd found that few people ever asked her to elaborate on the answer she always gave. She should have known Boone would be one who did.

"Not really," she admitted. "We moved a lot. Pinning down one place would be difficult as none of the places we lived ever felt like home. The South is the most honest answer I could give."

"I see," he said, but she doubted he did. It was better that he didn't. No kid should grow up as she had. "Did your dad travel for work?"

"You could say that. He changed jobs frequently. My mother did, too." She reached out to the hand sanitizer, squirted another generous amount onto her palm, then rubbed her hands together more vigorously than was needed. Nothing wrong with double disinfecting, and she needed to be doing something with her hands. "My parents divorced when I was small. I lived with Mom most of the time with only the occasional visits with my dad." There were also the times she'd ended up in foster care until her mother could get herself pulled back together when child protective services had been unable to track down her father. Julia would have been better off had the state never given her back to Leah Simmons or Julia's father. She'd been happy with a few of her foster families but had never gotten to stay long enough to feel as if she belonged. Maybe she wouldn't have no matter how long she'd stayed.

"I'm sorry."

For a moment she thought she'd said her last thought out loud, but she hadn't. Still, Boone looked at her with such sympathy that she cringed and straightened her shoulders. "Lots of kids have divorced parents. It's not a big deal."

"It is when you're the kid whose parents are no longer together. I could see on your face that it wasn't easy on you."

His softly spoken comment reached inside and uncovered that mostly-by-herself kid she'd once been. She'd been four when her father had left her mother for the final time. Her home life had never been idyllic, but she hadn't known that. She'd just known that one day her father was there and then he wasn't. Her mother had gone a little crazy after he'd left. But her mother had always teetered on the edge. Julia had been seventeen when she'd died. It had only been after Julia had hit rock bottom herself that she'd begun to understand why her parents had made the choices they had. She wasn't sure she'd ever fully understand, though.

She forced a smile and hoped Boone couldn't really see beyond that facade.

"I was young and barely knew anything else. It's fine."

Her parents' divorce had been one of the easier things she'd dealt with where her parents were concerned. Fortunately, she'd buried those demons long ago.

Mostly.

Julia tried not to get too attached to her patients, but always felt vested in each one's outcome. The nature of working in the ICU meant her patients had a higher risk of not surviving, but she did all she could to will each one well.

Aaron West got to her more than most. Each day she came to work, she'd hold her breath when checking to find out how he'd fared since she'd last clocked out. He continued to improve little by little but hadn't awakened and was still dependent upon the ventilator for life-giving breath despite attempts to wean him.

"Good morning," she greeted the young man's mother on Christmas Eve morning. The woman looked as tired as she had when Julia had told her goodbye at the end of her last shift a few days previously. "Have you been home at all since I was last here?"

The woman nodded. "Geoff insisted I go home, shower, and spend some time with the other kids while he stayed with Aaron."

Julia was glad. Being at home, remembering life outside the hospital, was important for Aaron's mother's mental, emotional, and physical health. "I know your children were glad to see you."

The woman nodded. "It's just so hard to be away from Aaron. What if something happened and I wasn't here? What if he woke up and was all alone, or what if…" Her voice trailed off, and she visibly trembled. "I know I need to spend time with my other kids, too, especially with the holiday. I want to, but I need to be here. I hope they understand it isn't that I love Aaron more. It's just that he needs me more right now, you know?"

Julia hugged the woman she'd grown fond of since Aaron's admission. Oh, how she prayed for this family. "No one expects you to stay here 24/7. It's okay if you go home at night, sleep in your own bed, hug your children, but I do understand your fears about leaving Aaron's side. I've heard everything you're saying many times. What you're feeling is completely normal under the circumstances."

"Geoff wants me to go home tonight since it's Christmas Eve, for us to both be at home with our other kids. I'm so torn." The woman gave a weak, watery-eyed smile. "I don't know how you do what you do. You and all of Aaron's nurses have been so wonderful." She glanced back toward her son. "He looks better than he did during your last shift, don't you think?"

"He does. He's definitely fighting to get better. You have to stay strong so that you can help him when he does wake up. He's going to need your love and support."

The woman squeezed her son's hand. "I know."

Julia changed out his feeding bag and recorded his intake.

On her way out of the room, she ran into Boone. "Oh! Hi."

He grinned. "Hi back at you."

Awkward, she thought. Awkward. Awkward. Awkward. Because he was grinning down at her and she was smiling up at him as if…as if something was happening between them.

Nothing can happen between us.

Not just because of her vow not to date until after she'd graduated, but because she wasn't sure how she'd survive being involved with someone like Boone when it eventually ended. She didn't kid herself that it wouldn't end. Probably if she'd agreed to go out with him, he would have already lost interest. Maybe she should just…no, she shouldn't agree to go out with him. What she should do was just tell him everything, so he'd lose interest that way. Why did that thought twist her stomach into knots?

Focusing on what she should be doing, she filled him in on Aaron instead.

"I'd hoped he'd be off his ventilator long before now," Boone mused. "The longer he's on it, the harder it's going to be. We've got to get him weaning down. Is his mother with him?"

"She is."

"Poor woman. That kid never gave a thought to how many lives his taking that tainted pill would impact."

"Speaking of tainted pills— Room two has a consult for your services. The patient is a twenty-five-year-old female who overdosed during a fishbowl party last night."

Boone frowned. "Not a good way to spend the holidays. Why do people do such mindless things as dumping medications into a bowl and then blindly taking them?"

Julia could have listed the reasons, but just said, "She's a repeater and was here about ten months ago, also for an overdose."

"Two overdoses in less than a year. That doesn't bode well for her future." He sighed, then almost sounding angry, added, "You'd think she would have learned to make better choices."

"If only it was that easy."

Boone gave her an odd look, as if maybe she'd let too much of her personal emotions into her comment. His eyes shone with curiosity, but he just nodded. "Listen to us trying to solve a problem that's much bigger than us and our ICU. Thanks for the update and for being such a strong patient advocate. I'll check Aaron, and then I'll be in to examine the new admit."

Later that day, Boone held out a Christmas present toward Julia. He'd hoped to make her smile, but her frown contrasted sharply with the jolly Santa Clauses on her scrub top.

"What do you mean, this is for me?"

The past couple of weeks had been good, not back to the way things had been prior to his asking her to the Christmas party, but better. Now there was an anticipation running through him that he'd eventually know what it felt like to have

Julia look at him as more than just her friend. He'd swear she already did, so maybe his anticipation had more to do with her acceptance of what was happening between them. An acceptance that sure wasn't showing on her face currently.

Had he messed up in buying her a gift? While shopping for his family, he'd toyed with the idea of giving her a present. Once he decided, he'd put a lot of thought into figuring out what that gift would be. Although he'd have liked to shower her with presents, he'd known she'd balk if he went overboard. He'd thought himself quite clever when he'd made his purchase.

"It's Christmas Eve. We're friends. Friends give each other Christmas presents, Julia."

Not surprisingly, she clasped her hands and nervously brushed her thumb across her tattoo. "Did you buy anyone else on this unit a Christmas present?"

Patting himself on the back that he'd anticipated she wouldn't want to be singled out, he nodded. "Of course. They're my friends, too, right? Like I said, friends give each other Christmas presents."

Her brow lifted, and her big brown eyes gave him a suspicious look. "You bought them gifts? For real?"

He grinned. "For real."

"Then I guess it's okay, except I didn't get you anything, so it doesn't feel right." She eyed the present hesitantly.

"I didn't give anyone anything with the expectation of a return gift. Everyone on the unit works hard and has been great to me since I started. I wanted to show my appreciation. What better time than Christmas? Besides, haven't you ever heard that it's better to give than to receive?"

"I've heard that, but you shouldn't have done this."

Maybe, but he was glad he had, especially as curiosity shone in her eyes. He couldn't wait to see her expression when she saw what he'd given her. Would she laugh as he'd intended at the first gift? And the secret small box inside the larger one, well, although he'd meant to keep what he spent on her in line with the others' presents, it had reminded him of her, and he'd given in to temptation. After all, it was Christmas.

"You're the third person to tell me that today." He handed her the gift. "Here, take your present. No strings attached other than friendship. Giving it to you makes me happy, okay?"

Holding the gift as if it were something fragile, or perhaps as if the box contained something toxic, she cut her gaze toward him. "Three people? You should take a hint."

"I like giving presents."

"That's very kind of you, Santa."

Grinning, he gestured to the box. "This one is a little self-serving. Open it."

"Right now?" Her eyes widened, and then she shook her head. "I couldn't. I'm on the clock and should get back to work as it is."

He wouldn't risk her getting into trouble by insisting. Not that he believed she would. But she obviously didn't plan to open the present with him watching, so he sighed with exaggeration. "Okay, but you'll have to let me know what you think."

"I would have sent you a thank-you text, anyway."

That he didn't doubt. He'd be hard-pressed to name a more polite person than the pretty brunette in her red Christmas scrubs with the silly Santas smiling at him.

"I'm having visions of my family complaining because I keep checking my phone to see if you've messaged yet and I somehow missed hearing it." He grinned. "Better open it early so I don't get in trouble. Mom has a rule about our phones not being out during get-togethers, which isn't easy when there are three doctors in the family."

Her gaze lifted. "You're going to Memphis tonight?"

"I wouldn't miss being with my family on

Christmas." Her stunned look surprised him. Had she thought he wouldn't go home for the holidays? Since his sister's death, spending time with family was more important than ever. Part of him was still a little guilty that he'd miss New Year's with them. "The whole family does our best to spend major holidays together. That isn't always easy as doctors, but even during residency, my brother and I managed to be home for Christmas morning. I'm heading that way as soon as I finish here."

"Knoxville to Memphis after working all day," she mused. Genuine concern shone in her eyes. "That's what? Around a six-hour drive? Be careful."

That concern shone in her eyes pleased him more than such a simple gesture should.

"If I get sleepy, I'll call a friend to keep me awake."

"With driving from one end of the state to the other, it's going to be late by the time you arrive in Memphis. Depending upon the time, you might no longer have that person as a friend." She cleared her throat with emphasis. "Perhaps you should stop for coffee."

Boone laughed. "You have a point. Unless I get stuck in traffic. I wouldn't expect I-40 to be too bad on Christmas Eve, so I should arrive by nine. What about you? Big plans for tomorrow?"

Rather than answering, she averted her gaze, making him even more curious as to how she planned to spend her day, but also cognizant of how she'd just walled up.

"Sorry, I wasn't trying to pry—well, actually I was," he admitted, wanting to be as honest with her as he could. "If you weren't busy, I could wait to leave until you finish your shift so you could go with me to keep me awake during that tedious section of I-40 between Nashville and Memphis."

Her jaw dropped and her skin paled. He immediately regretted his offer. He wasn't sure why he'd even made it. He sure hadn't planned that one. Bringing a woman home for the holidays would certainly have livened things up. His family was still grieving his breakup with Olivia, and he'd no doubt hear all about how crazy he'd been to end the relationship. He disagreed. But if Julia would have gone, he'd have brought her with him and faced their curiosity. Gladly.

"What am I saying? Of course, you're busy. It's Christmas Day." He gestured toward the gift box again. "Enjoy that, and I hope you have a great holiday, Julia. Merry Christmas."

CHAPTER FOUR

THAT NIGHT, JULIA eyed the present Boone had given her as if the box held a rattlesnake. If not for the fact that he'd given her coworkers gifts, too, she would have refused to take the pretty package. She probably should have, anyway. But it was Christmas, and the truth was, curiosity got the better of her. She needed to know what the box held. She was even more curious about his invitation to go with him to Memphis. Had he been serious, or had that just slipped out, one of those random, casual things people say without thinking? What would he have done if she'd said yes, she'd go home with him for Christmas? How would he have explained her unexpected presence to his family?

Either way, she really did have plans. She was volunteering at the Knoxville House of Hope. The people there deserved a Christmas, too. She'd play a small role in helping to make that happen, and later that day she'd be covering a shift at the hospital.

After arriving home, she went through her normal routine: love on Honey, shower, eat, do a little cleaning in her apartment. But her insides were anything but routine. All because her gaze kept wandering to the present on her living room coffee table. What had Boone gotten her? He truly had given their coworkers thoughtful gifts. Gifts that said he knew who they were as individuals. Nothing expensive, just presents that were a testament to what a kind and observant person he was.

Just because he was nice did not mean she needed to give in to his charm, though. It was a reason why she shouldn't. Boone's upper-crust world was very different from her own lowly beginnings. Men like him didn't fall in love with women like her. Not outside of fairy tales.

Not that she wanted Boone to fall in love with her. She wasn't looking for that with any man. Not really. She liked her life, liked how she could depend upon herself, how she had picked herself up from the ashes and now was a worthwhile member of society. She wouldn't easily let anyone threaten the peace she'd worked so hard to achieve. Yet she couldn't deny that Boone did more than threaten her peace. With a mere smile, the man had her insides all shook up and tempted her to toss her Rules for Life Success notebook.

Picking up the cat brushing against her leg, she hugged the calico close and sat down on the sofa. "What do you think, Honey? Should we open this so we can quit obsessing about what's inside?"

The cat purred.

"Yeah, that's what I was thinking, too." If she opened the present tonight, then she'd be present-less on Christmas Day because she and Stephanie had already exchanged gifts, and the rest of her work crew held their Friends-mas white elephant exchange at their weekend getaway but didn't otherwise do gifts.

The cat wiggled free of her hold, but only so she could turn for Julia to stroke her back.

"Decisions. Decisions. I can open it tonight, but having something to look forward to on Christmas morning would be fun, wouldn't it?" Something that felt like it should be normal and yet was so unfamiliar to her. She couldn't recall ever opening a present on Christmas.

So instead of ripping into the shiny paper, she picked up her remote and clicked on the television. Flipping through the channels, she settled on a Christmas special she'd seen numerous times, but it was one of those shows that she could watch over and over and still enjoy. A show about hope, family, and Christmas miracles.

A little misty-eyed from the movie, Julia jumped when her phone beeped, indicating a text. Thinking it was probably Stephanie, she opened her messages.

Julia's breath caught.

"So far, so good," she read aloud, staring at the selfie of Boone sitting in his car.

His lips were stretched in a big smile that revealed his movie-star-perfect teeth. The man really was too beautiful to be real. Not that she was biased, because what reason would she have for bias? He was just a coworker and friend and future date if he truly stuck around the next six months.

She shot back her reply.

Do not text and drive!

Although judging from the background, he appeared to be parked.

I agree. I'm sitting at an electric vehicle charging station. I'm in Nashville, so about halfway home.

Halfway home. What would it feel like to have a home to travel to at the holidays? To have people anxiously awaiting your arrival and to be excited when you walked through the door, greeting you with hugs and kisses? People who called you family? She'd probably never know firsthand, but obviously, it felt good enough that Boone was willing to drive six hours for the experience.

She texted back, blaming her nostalgia on the sappy movie she was watching.

Be safe.

Will do. Did you open your present?

Tomorrow is Christmas. I'll open it then.

No need to tell him how tempted she'd been.

You're a woman of great discipline.

Then, before she could respond, he sent:

Merry Christmas Eve, Julia. I hope Santa is good to you.

What would he say if she told him that his gift was the closest thing she'd have to Santa being good to her? Ugh. How whiny and pathetic was she tonight? She was happy, had a good life, and was on track to have an even better life.

She strove to make a difference to others every single day and was blessed to have that opportunity. Life really was good.

You, too. Julia hugged her phone to her chest. Then, realizing what she was doing, she put the phone next to the present on the coffee table. She'd obviously lost her mind because no way should she allow herself to get caught up in whatever Boone was signaling with the present. She was flattered. But she knew better.

The following morning, she got ready to go to the center, fed Honey, and opened the presents she'd wrapped up for the cat, who curiously inspected what she was doing. "Catnip. Toy. Treats. Aren't you a lucky girl? Because I'm positive you weren't that good."

The cat plopped down on top of the torn paper and licked her paw.

"You're welcome." Julia laughed. Then, eyeing her present from Boone, she picked it up and gave it a gentle shake. Something small rattled inside the shirt-sized box.

"What am I doing? It's Christmas morning. Just open it already." She removed the ribbon, then carefully tore the paper and lifted the box lid.

Beneath a few layers of red and green tissue paper, she saw a wall calendar and a smaller wrapped present. The smaller box was what had rattled. Julia picked up the calendar. The funny doctor jokes on each page made her smile, as he'd probably intended. Flipping through the pages, she read one silly pun after another. When she came to May, she paused. He'd handwritten a note on the first Saturday.

Swallowing the lump in her throat, she read aloud, "Celebrate graduation with Boone."

He'd scribbled a few other notations on key dates. "Memorial Day picnic with Boone." "July Fourth fireworks with Boone." "Labor Day picnic with Boone." "Halloween party with Boone." "Thanksgiving with Boone." "Christmas with Boone."

Ah, that's what he'd meant about the gift being self-serving. He'd penciled himself into all major holidays that followed her graduation.

She eyed the smaller box. Then, a bit breathless, opened it, revealing a velvet jeweler's box inside. What had he done? With shaky hands, she lifted the lid to reveal a white-gold phoenix curved around a diamond pendant on a thin chain.

As with the gifts he'd given their coworkers, her gift had been personal, had reflected that he knew who she was, or in this case who she strove to be—a phoenix rising from the ashes of her crash-and-burn life.

With moisture prickling her eyes, she reminded herself that he was a doctor. Buying a piece of jewelry was no big deal to him. He'd obviously noticed her tattoo and thought the pendant would be something she'd like. Only, that he'd chosen something so meaningful...

Julia sniffled. No. No. No. She could not be bought. Not that the piece was an overly expensive one. At least, she didn't think so, but what did she know about jewelry? She never bought real, and this was the first piece she'd ever been given. Once upon a time she'd dreamed Clay would buy her something special, but that dream had been quickly crushed.

Part of her considered setting the necklace aside to give back to Boone, but another part won. The part that thought it was the most perfect pendant she'd ever seen and was completely wowed by his insight. She removed the necklace from its box, put it on with trembling hands, then went to the mirror to look at her reflection. The intricately cut stone encircled by the phoenix reflected the light and seemed to catch fire within the sparkly depths, perhaps a sign that her good intentions would soon do the same.

"You are in so much trouble, Julia Simmons," she warned herself. But neither the warning, nor her discomfort at his gift, was enough to wipe away the joy spreading through her. She couldn't imagine any gift that would mean more than the beautifully designed pendant.

Impulsively, she picked up her phone and took a funny-faced selfie.

I hear this used to be coal. Does that mean Santa thinks I've been bad this year?

Squeezing her eyes closed, she hit Send. What was she doing? Now she'd be a nervous wreck that she'd texted him. What if he didn't answer? Would she be the one continuously checking her phone? What was wrong with her? A well-to-do man had given her a piece of jewelry that meant nothing to him beyond that he'd noticed her tattoo. Still, she'd promised to thank him. Her message hadn't quite been that, but...

Ugh, why hadn't she just sent a simple thank-you, and been done with it? Why did she always end up doing more where Boone was concerned than she should have? What was it about him that continually pushed her so far beyond her comfort zone?

Her phone beeped, and with heavy anticipation, she looked to see what he'd written.

Perfect.

Relief filled her that he'd messaged back. The necklace did look perfect. It must feel perfect, too, because she couldn't quit touching the pendant. How could a piece of jewelry delight and terrify all at the same time?

Her phone beeped again.

The necklace isn't bad, either.

A smile spread across her face.

Ha-ha. You're a funny guy. I absolutely love it, but it was too much.

He was too much.

I am a funny guy. It wasn't too much. Did you like your calendar?

You need to return it. Someone has scribbled on several pages.

Picking up the calendar, she flipped through the pages again, pausing when her phone beeped.

You know how doctors' handwriting can be. One scribble after another.

Apparently... Thank you, Boone. Your gifts are very thoughtful.

I didn't want you to forget.

As if she could.

Besides, like I said, the calendar was as much for me as it was for you. The necklace is your gift. Although it would seem that ended up being as much for me, too.

She reread his message, trying to decipher what he meant. When she couldn't decide, she asked him.

How so?

I can't think of a better gift than seeing your face.

Julia had friends who'd been wooed in the past, but she had never been the recipient of anything beyond someone buying her a beer. She couldn't help but wonder if this was how it felt to be wooed, to have a decent man want to date you. Clay had been a decent man in many ways, but he'd never been able to get beyond her past, had never been able to see her as capable of rising above who and what she'd been. Nor had his family. No matter what she'd done, she hadn't been good enough in their eyes. Clay had cared about her, but that hadn't kept him from walking away.

Julia touched the pendant, pressing it into her

chest and wondering if the jewel would leave a mark as it burned intensely against her skin. Boone was just making conversation. He was just generalizing and being his usual complimentary self. His words didn't mean anything, and yet, they puffed her chest.

She typed back, although she wasn't sure how to respond. Did he have any idea how thoroughly he affected her?

That drive must have really gotten to you last night.

Scrolling back a few texts, she found the selfie he'd sent her the night before. Handsome, smiling, and such a good person. Seriously, he wanted to date her? Maybe she'd fallen and was dreaming it all. That was it. She'd been watching television the night before, had dozed off, and was having a dream miracle on her street.

The drive wasn't bad and was worth it to be home for Christmas.

Before she could respond another message arrived.

My mother has a breakfast feast this morning and has invited the entire Richards and Heming-

way clans for dinner tonight. The house is in lit-
eral Christmas chaos.

Visions of smiling people celebrating the holidays together danced through her head, contrasting greatly with her own Christmas memories.
He continued,

It's a good thing we're texting because you
wouldn't be able to hear me for all the background noise. I'd forgotten how loud my family is.

Clenching her phone, she took a deep breath.
Enough of this silliness. She needed to get ready
to spend the day with the only family she had
outside of work.

I've got to go, but thank you. The calendar made
me smile, and the necklace is beautiful beyond
words. You shouldn't have.

Closing her eyes, she hit Send. She knew better, but she'd be lying if she didn't admit to being
flattered. Even if only for a brief moment in time,
Boone Richards was attracted to her. If nothing
else, that was a rosy testament to the person she
painted herself to be. If only she could recolor

the past and truly soar so high no one could look down upon her.

It would help to stop getting distracted by a gorgeous man who seemed to say and do all the right things.

Stick to your rules, Julia. You have them for a reason.

Her phone beeped, and she glanced at his message.

Merry Christmas, Julia.

Merry Christmas to you, too.

Then, eyeing the cat, who had followed her into the bedroom, she sighed. "I'm in trouble, Honey. I have this next portion of my life planned out. If I'm not careful, Boone Richards is going to derail those plans, and I'm going to be left dealing with the wreckage."

She'd almost backslid when Clay dumped her. How could she risk going through that again? How would she survive if it was Boone who found her lacking when already she recognized that he affected her in ways Clay never had?

"What has you smiling so big?"

Boone glanced up from the dining table and flashed an even bigger smile at his mother. "It's

Christmas morning, and you've got all my favorite foods served. Why wouldn't I be smiling?"

"Right." His mother rolled her eyes, but her smile was genuine when she gestured to his phone, "What's her name?"

He never could get anything by her. "Whose?" he asked anyway, but with a grin.

"Whomever you were texting with. Not Olivia, I assume." She gave him the same patient look she always had when they both knew he would end up telling her what she wanted to know. He imagined that look had been perfected over the years of running the shipping business. No wonder the business had flourished under her guidance since she'd taken control after his grandfather had passed.

"You assume correctly."

"I didn't think so. As much as I liked that dear girl and know that she would have made you an ideal wife, I'll admit you have a sparkle in your eyes now that I like seeing." She took a sip of her coffee. "When will we meet this new woman in your life?"

Good question, and one that he didn't have an answer for. Just because Julia had said yes to his taking her out to celebrate her graduation, that didn't mean she'd go along with the rest of his penciled-in itinerary. He'd like to think she would since his gut instinct was that she was just as interested in him as he was in her. Well, maybe not that much, but she was interested.

"I might bring her home this summer."

His mother's eyes widened. "This summer? Good heavens. Surely you're not planning to wait that long before your next trip home? I expect you here for your birthday."

"I'm planning to come home for my birthday."

"But not to bring your new lady friend?" His mother gave him a stern look. "Are you afraid for her to meet your family?"

Boone snorted. "You know better than that. I invited her this Christmas, but she turned me down."

Obviously shocked that anyone could turn down one of her children, his mother regarded him for a long moment. "What kind of woman doesn't want to meet the family of the man she's dating?"

"Good point, but we're not dating." And he'd have been floored if Julia had said yes to going to Memphis with him. With all the walls she hid behind, she probably wouldn't come to Memphis with him next Christmas, either.

Looking more and more curious, his mother eyed him. "But you want to be dating?"

"I do. She doesn't." Or maybe she did but was just sticking to the plans she'd made for herself. He could respect that. Not that he had a choice.

"She's a nurse and working on her master's degree."

Curiosity shown on his mother's face. "She sounds like a smart girl."

"Smart, funny, beautiful. Perfect manners." He shrugged. "You'll like her."

"You obviously do." She set her coffee cup on the table and pinned him beneath her blue gaze. "She's why you broke things off with Olivia?"

He shook his head. "I broke things off with Olivia because we weren't right together."

"But you realized this after meeting this nurse? She refused to go out with you because you were involved with Olivia?"

Boone frowned. "I've known Julia since I started in Knoxville. I didn't ask her out until *after* Olivia and I weren't together anymore. I was single. Julia was single. I asked. She said no."

"Julia…" His mother let the name roll off her tongue. "Does Olivia know about her?"

"Whether or not Olivia knows no longer matters to me, Mom." He sighed. "Not that there's anything to know. Julia refuses to go out with me until she graduates. End of story. Our first date is my taking her out to celebrate the night of her graduation."

Her perfectly shaped brows lifted. "In May? But that's months from now."

He nodded. "It is, but she refuses to date me, or anyone, until she finishes school. She claims dating might distract her from her priorities."

"This woman wants you to wait around six months for her to graduate? What if she changes her mind between now and then? What if she meets someone else and you've wasted half a year waiting on a woman who isn't that interested in you? If she's that okay with waiting, she mustn't like you as much as you think. Not that I understand how any woman could resist such a wonderful young man as yourself, but I don't want to see you hurt."

Boone had considered that Julia might change her mind about going out with him, but he hadn't considered that it might be because she'd met another man. His chest squeezed at the thought of someone sweeping Julia off her feet despite the fact that Boone had called dibs. His calling dibs didn't obligate Julia in any way, but…he wanted it to.

"I suppose that could happen. If it does, I'll be disappointed, but since I can't imagine going out with anyone else—" he shrugged "—well, that wouldn't really be fair to whomever I was with, would it? I'll take my chances and wait."

His mother eyed him a moment, then smiled the slyest smile. He wondered if she'd been play-ing him with feigned shock and misunderstanding to elicit more information from him. "I look forward to meeting your Julia this summer and hope she's worth your wait."

"She is." He took a deep breath. Oh, yes, Amelia Hemingway Richards's smile was smug. "As far as this summer, we'll see. She's agreed to a single dinner date after her graduation, nothing more."

"But if you have your way, she will agree to more?"

"Definitely."

"Then, as I said, I look forward to meeting your Julia this summer."

"This is going to be the best Friends-mas getaway ever," Stephanie assured Julia from the front passenger seat of the SUV Derek drove up the steep mountain road. "And not just because it's snowing, and all around us looks like something from a holiday movie. Can you believe there are twelve of us staying at the cabin this year?"

Twelve, and all were couples except Julia and Boone. Reaching up, she touched where her necklace lay hidden beneath the neckline of her shirt. She'd made sure to wear something that covered it, but she hadn't taken it off since she'd put it on. Somehow the pendant felt as if it was as much a part of her as her tattoo.

"Did you bring the giraffe?" She changed the subject to the white elephant gift that had made a return appearance each of the past two years.

"Maybe." Stephanie laughed in a way that let Julia know her friend had. "I checked the weather, and there's real snow on the slopes, too. Yay!" With Tennessee weather, one never knew, but there were snow machines to keep the slopes operating regardless of the fluctuating winter temperatures. "We've got a great view from our cabin on Ski View Drive. I'm glad Dr. Richards didn't mind sharing a room with Cliff."

"He seemed okay with it once I assured him there were two beds," Derek added from the driver's seat, glancing briefly at Julia via the rearview mirror and grinning.

Cliff was a respiratory therapist at the hospital. Julia was sharing a room with his girlfriend, Dawn. She'd met the woman briefly at the Christmas party, and she'd been friendly enough. Cliff and Dawn had been dating a couple of months but weren't sleeping together. He'd asked if Julia would mind sharing her room if he covered half the cost. Cutting expenses was always a good thing. This last semester, she would have a lot of clinical hours, had to finish her thesis, and worried about how much she'd have to cut back her work hours. She lived low and had a decent savings account, but having been homeless at more than one point during her life, being financially secure was a big deal. She knew well how quickly things could change.

Stephanie was still chatting away when they pulled into the small parking area in front of the gorgeous mountainside cabin Derek had secured for them through his realty office. Kevin, Becky, and another couple were already there as they'd driven up earlier in the day to check in and pick up food and supplies. Julia had spent the day before baking goodies and had packed them along with Derek's cooler and more supplies in the back of his SUV.

Besides Kevin's car, there were two other vehicles already in the parking area, one of which she recognized as Boone's expensive electric car. As there was only a light dusting of snow across the top, she guessed he'd not been there for more than half an hour.

Almost as if he'd been watching for them, he appeared in the doorway just as Derek was opening the back hatch. His gaze met Julia's, and he smiled. "Hey." Then he said to Derek, "You were right about this place. The view of Mount Le Conte is spectacular. What can I carry in?"

"If you want to grab the other side of the cooler, we'll bring it to the kitchen and come back to get the rest of this stuff Stephanie insisted we needed," Derek told him.

Stephanie waved her gloved hand dismissively. "Yeah, yeah, but when you have yummy food, plus party hats and kazoos for welcoming in the new year tomorrow evening, you can thank me."

Derek waggled his brows at Stephanie. "Something like that."

Pulling her coat tighter around her, Stephanie rolled her eyes. "Men. One-track minds."

"Which you appreciate about me," Derek reminded her, handing her the suitcase that had been on top of the cooler.

Stephanie gave him an innocent look. "You think?"

"Baby, I know." He pulled the large cooler forward so he and Boone could readily grasp the handles.

As they walked off, Stephanie reached for another bag, draped the straps over her shoulder, and giggled as she glanced toward Julia. "He's right. I do appreciate that about him."

Julia reached for her own brightly patterned cloth overnight bag, a gift two years prior from Stephanie. "I'm positive I don't want to hear this."

Her friend laughed. "Someday someone is going to sweep you off your feet, Julia, and you're going to know exactly what I mean." Stephanie's grin turned sly. "Maybe even this weekend. A girl can hope."

Julia gave her a horrified look. "Promise me you aren't going to throw me and Dr. Richards together all weekend."

Stephanie shifted her overnight bag on her shoulder, then pulled up her larger suitcase's handle so she could roll it inside. "As you're the only singles, I won't have to. You'll be paired off without me doing a thing."

Bingo. Julia had known that was going to happen. She'd come anyway. What did that say?

Nothing. It meant she wasn't changing her plans with her friends just because Boone would be there, too. It meant she could be his friend. It meant... Why was her pendant burning into her chest?

"I should have begged Patti to let me work this weekend." But the truth was that she was looking forward to the trip. Obviously, she'd lost her mind.

As they made their way into the cabin, Stephanie laughed. "You working this weekend would have been a real shame. Can you think of a better way to ring out the old and bring in the new than with all of us?"

"You're forgetting how much I love my cat."

Stephanie laughed. "Honey will be just fine with Mrs. Smithfield."

Having dropped off the cooler and meeting

them at the door, Boone reached for Julia's bag. "Let me get this for you. Who's Honey?"

"My cat."

Boone took her bag, along with Stephanie's.

"You're in the room across from mine and Cliff's," he told her. "He and Dawn haven't arrived yet, so you get first choice on which bed you want. I picked the one closest to the window. The view is spectacular."

"That's sweet of you to get our bags, Dr. Richards," Stephanie exclaimed, giving Julia a knowing smile as they stepped into the cabin. "Thank you."

"Call me Boone," he reminded her. "I don't want to be called Dr. Richards all weekend."

"Do you hear that, Julia? He doesn't want to be called Dr. Richards all weekend," Stephanie practically sang as she took her bag from him.

"La-la-la… Did you say something?" Julia responded, but with a smile. "Seriously, I can finish carrying my bag to my room if you'll just point me in the right direction."

"Showing you is easier. With three stories, this place is a maze. We're upstairs from the main floor, so head toward those stairs. There are two bedrooms on that floor, one on the main, and three on the lower."

Following him, Julia nodded.

"This is you." He gestured to the doorway.

Julia stepped into the room with its wooden log walls and black bear decor. "Nice."

"Ours is similar." He placed her bag onto one of the two full-sized beds. "I'll go help Derek finish unpacking his SUV."

"I should help, too."

He shook his head. "Stay. Unpack or go warm yourself by the fire Kevin has blazing in the main room."

"I— Thank you, Boone."

At her use of his name, he grinned. "I like that."

She liked a lot about him, particularly the way he was looking at her, not sexually, although the physical tension was there between them, but with genuine affection.

"You like me showing my gratitude?"

"You saying my name," he corrected her, his smile widening.

Those eyes. That smile. Be still her rapidly beating heart. Had she majorly miscalculated this weekend? Or had she purposely not fully acknowledged how spending this time with him was going to affect her?

"Get used to it," she warned. "As the only non-couple here, we'll be paired together for every activity. I'll be 'Boone this' and 'Boone that' all weekend." She'd put up a fight at the hospital, but addressing him so formally at a gathering of friends would seem strange.

"We both know I'm good with that. However, I will ask Derek to buddy up with me if you want. I meant it when I said I didn't want my being here to make you uncomfortable."

Too late. His very existence pushed her outside her comfort zone.

His lips twitched. "I'll even do my best to not make Stephanie jealous."

"I could see how she might be," Julia teased to give herself time to process his sincerity. Stephanie would have a fit if Julia accepted his offer. She breathed in, then slowly exhaled. "I think we're adult enough that we'll be fine without you making moves on my best friend's guy."

"You think I'm adult enough?" His grin begged to differ.

"There's still time for changing my mind."

His gaze searched hers a moment. "I'm glad Derek invited me, Julia, and that you're okay with me being here."

She gave him a questioning look. "Did I say that?"

His gaze held hers, making her insides flutter like the fat snowflakes dancing outside the window. "No, but it's true, isn't it?"

Unfortunately, he was right. If something had come up and he'd canceled, she would have missed him, which didn't make sense since he never had been there in the past. How could she miss something she'd never experienced?

Including his parents' large gathering, Boone had turned down several New Year's Eve party invitations and had no regrets. Glancing around the cabin's main room at the smiling faces, there was nowhere he'd rather be.

Not completely true, he admitted, because he'd much rather be next to Julia sitting on the sofa with Stephanie and Derek. Instead he was in the kitchen chair he'd moved into the living area for their white elephant gift exchange. He'd considered placing it by the sofa but had opted for across the room instead as it put Julia directly in his line of vision.

"Who has number seven?" Stephanie looked around the room.

"That's me." Becky jumped up from the oversized chair where she'd been snuggled next to Kevin. "Hmm, do I want to take that yummy-looking cheese board from Cliff, or do I want to see what another one of these packages holds?"

Cliff hugged the gourmet cheese board gift set to his chest. "Keep your paws off my cheese."

Everyone laughed when Becky took his gift. He then opted to open another present and let out a woo-hoo at the barbecue set he unwrapped. "Nice. Who's number eight?"

"That would be me." Julia walked over to the tree and chose a gift. It was a fuzzy blanket with a black bear on it. She undid the binding and wrapped the fleece material around her shoulders. "Aww, it matches our cabin. Wearing this puts me in stealth mode."

Everyone laughed.

Kevin went next and groaned when he unwrapped Stephanie's gift. Everyone burst into laughter.

"You have to bring it back next year," Stephanie reminded him.

"No worries about that," Kevin assured her. "If I don't accidentally on purpose leave him here, this guy will be making another appearance on the mountain."

They went through the remainder of the gift-picking, and at last it was Boone's turn. As number twelve, he had his pick of taking anyone's gift or choosing the last unwrapped one. Pretending to contemplate, he eyed each gift.

"Take mine. You know you always wanted a ceramic giraffe," Kevin offered.

"I'll restrain myself," Boone told him, then moved in front of Julia. "Anyone think there's a draft in here? I feel a bit chilly."

"No!" she gasped, clasping the blanket more

tightly around herself. "You don't want this ole thing."

"I do. Hand it over." By doing so, he'd be giving her the choice of any of the gifts. He'd seen how she'd eyed the hot cocoa and mug set when Dawn had unwrapped it, and yet she'd not stolen the gift when it had been her turn. Before the weekend was over, he'd give the blanket back. That way she could have two gifts.

Sighing and faking a pout, she handed over the blanket. "I can't believe you'd take my Christmas present."

"Believe." He wrapped the blanket around himself. Julia's body heat clung to the fuzzy material, as did her vanilla scent. Instantly, visions of dancing with her at the Christmas party flashed through his mind, warming him much more than the blanket or the fire Kevin still had roaring. "Just what I always wanted."

"A bear blanket?" She shook her head, then glanced around the room. Her gaze lingered on the cocoa set that Dawn held.

"No. Don't do it," her roommate for the weekend cried.

Just when he thought Julia would take the set, she walked to the tree and picked up the last remaining package instead, ending the game with whatever was inside.

She smiled when she unwrapped a box of

chocolate-and-caramel-covered pecan candy with a department store gift card taped to the package. "This is awesome. Thank you to whoever brought this."

"That was fun." Stephanie began gathering wrapping paper and trash from the floor. Everyone pitched in and quickly had the room restored.

Derek grabbed Stephanie around the waist and pulled her in for a kiss. "You up for a game of pool? Boone, you in?"

"Come on, Julia." Stephanie wiggled free of his hold. "We'll play partners. Girls against guys. Pool's your game."

"Oh?" Boone glanced in Julia's direction. "This I want to see. Count me in."

Julia eyed the blanket still draped over his shoulders like a superhero cape. "Winner gets the blanket."

His lips twitched. "You want to strip me of my bear blankie?"

Her brown eyes sparkled with mischief. "Turnabout is fair play."

"Assuming you'll win," he teased.

"Assuming that, of course." She arched a brow. "Do we have a deal?"

"We do." Boone was pretty sure he was being suckered, but he didn't mind in the slightest. "This thing better bring me luck."

Looking pleased with his answer, she asked,

"You're going to play while wearing my blanket?"

"You think I shouldn't wear *my* blanket?"

"We'll see whose blanket," she warned, lips twitching. "Haven't you ever heard that thing about a cape being a superhero's downfall?"

"I'll take my chances. This one is *beary* lucky."

Moving next to them, Stephanie snorted. "You better hope so, because you're going to need it playing against us, right, Julia?"

A smile upon her lush lips, Julia just shrugged as she headed toward the stairs that led down to the cabin's game room. Turning at the top, eyes twinkling with a mischief he adored, she crooked her finger. "Hurry up, Boone. I want my blanket back."

Later, hot chocolate in hand, Julia went outside to sit on the covered balcony that looked out toward Mount Le Conte. Boone grabbed his jacket and followed to sit in the rocker next to hers. An outdoor heater was lit near them, blowing warm air in their direction.

"Sure would feel better if I hadn't lost my blanket," he moaned, knowing his comment would make her smile and feeling pleased when it did. He'd always admired her cheery disposition at work, but more and more he recognized the smiles that went deep compared to the surface ones. That one had been real, and he liked it.

She glanced his way. "Between the heater, hot chocolate, and my blanket, it is quite comfy. Too bad you lost this magnificent gift."

"I can tell you're heartbroken about it." He laughed. "Where did you become a pool shark?"

She hesitated a moment, then answered, "No one place. My mom waitressed at one honky-tonk after another over the years and brought me with her until I got old enough to stay on my own. By then I often wanted to go rather than stay in whatever rathole we currently called home. I'd have to stay out of sight in the back when they were busy, but during slow times I could entertain myself with pool or darts. Regulars would let me play, giving me pointers. After a while, you learn a few things."

He didn't really like the idea of a child hanging out in bars, but he understood what she meant.

Julia turned back to stare toward the mountain. She took a sip of her hot cocoa from the package Stephanie had brought, which reminded him of something he'd been wondering.

"Why didn't you pick Dawn's gift?"

She continued to stare out into the darkness. "What do you mean? I like my chocolates and gift card."

"I saw how you eyed Dawn's cocoa gift set,"

he pressed. "It's what you wanted, but you didn't take it. Why not?"

"I knew Stephanie had brought a giant box." She held up her cup as evidence, then took a sip. "It wasn't a big deal."

"The idea of the game is to take what you want, though, right?"

"It's all in fun. Besides, what I liked best was my bear blanket." She snuggled within the blanket that dragged the floor at the rocking chair's base.

"Which I took." Not that he believed she liked the blanket better than the gift set. At least, not initially. Now he was quite fond of the blanket himself.

"Then proceeded to lose back to me," she reminded him with a smile and a lift of her mug in his direction. "Poor Boone. You ended up without a gift. Since it's Christmas, I'll share my chocolates with you."

"Nice of you. I'd planned to give the blanket back anyway."

She narrowed her eyes. "You're saying you lost on purpose?"

"For the record, I never lose on purpose."

She looked relieved. "Good to know."

"But I suspect you do." His words were quiet, but he knew she'd heard them. He'd meant her to.

Turning toward him, she frowned. A breeze

caught at her hair, and the strands danced about her face. "What's that supposed to mean? That I'm a loser?"

"You're not a loser. Far from it. It's just a hunch that you put others before yourself most if not all of the time." It was a quality that she shared with Amy, with the exception of his sister's fatal flaw. On that, he could only think Amy had been selfish, as how else could she have done the things she'd done?

Julia swatted at her hair with her free hand, brushing it back to tuck behind her ears. "Obviously, that isn't true." At his doubtful look, she reminded him, "I didn't hesitate to beat you earlier, even though such a devastating loss had to hurt your male ego."

He laughed. "There is that, but that's different, isn't it?"

She'd gone back to gently rocking the chair. "If you say so."

"So, you're a pool shark. Sounds like I should avoid playing against you at darts. Anything else up your sleeve that I should know about?"

She took another sip of her hot chocolate. "Nothing that comes to mind."

"What about skiing? Are you going to show me up tomorrow with your traversing?"

She laughed. "I'm not sure what traversing is, but if it involves falling a lot while on the kiddie slopes, then yep, that would be me shaming you on the snow."

"Not a skier?"

"I've been twice, last New Year's and the previous one. Both times I ended up spending most of my time just trying to stay upright. But third time's the charm, they say."

"Well, you do have my lucky bear blanket."

Smiling, she nodded. "There is that. Maybe I'll take a page from your book and wear it about my shoulders like a superhero cape and ski down the slopes with it flapping in the wind behind me."

He smiled at the image. "I wouldn't do that. Someone recently told me that capes were dangerous."

"Somebody was paying attention."

"Hard not to pay attention when it's you doing the talking, Julia."

Her gaze cut toward him. "Meaning I'm loud?"

"Meaning that when you say something, I'm all ears."

She snorted. "Nice recovery."

"The truth."

Taking a deep breath, she turned to look out into the darkness. "There's a lot you don't know about me."

"I look forward to discovering those things."

"You think that, but I've done things I wish I could change."

"That's true of most people."

"Even you?"

Did she think he was perfect? That he'd never made mistakes? That he hadn't been oblivious to the warning signs that his twin had started using again? That he hadn't failed to stop her from going down a path she hadn't been able to return from? He almost told Julia about Amy. Almost.

Instead, he just admitted, "Even me."

CHAPTER FIVE

THE FOLLOWING MORNING, clad in neon-green-and-pink ski pants and jacket she'd borrowed from Beth, Julia wondered if she should have brought her bear blanket as a good luck charm to keep her upright. She sure needed something as she was beginning to doubt that all the four-leaf clovers in the world would be enough to accomplish her staying vertical. At this point, she'd just like to get back onto her feet. Each time she tried, her skis went out from beneath her, preventing her from standing. She had a helmet for her head, but perhaps cushioning for her bottom would have been more useful.

"Hold your feet like this and dig the edges of your skis into the snow."

She glanced up through her also borrowed ski goggles. Boone was demonstrating his instructions. He wore a bright blue-and-yellow ski jacket and pants. His helmet and goggles matched. Someone should snap his photo because he looked like an advertisement for ski fashion. "You've already made it down the main slope? That has to be some kind of record."

"When I realized you hadn't gotten onto the chair lift with us, I asked Stephanie about you. She told me you had stayed behind, so I came back."

"You didn't need to do that." Sucking in a lungful of cold air, she sighed. "I may never be ready to go up. I think I mentioned that I wasn't very good at this."

He grinned. "Only because you've not had me to give you pointers."

"Ha. Last year the whole crew tried. I never left the practice area. In the meantime, I've forgotten how to stay upright and can't seem to get on my feet. Give a girl a hand?"

He shook his head. "No. It's time you learn." With that, he purposely fell over. "Watch how I do this, and then you do the same. I'm going to show you the simplest way to right yourself."

He talked her through how he positioned his legs and skis, then used his hands to walk himself into an upright position.

She wrinkled her nose at him. "You make that look easy."

"I had lots of practice when I was learning to ski."

"How long ago was that?" She emulated what

he'd done and was quite proud of herself when she managed to stand. Now if she could just stay that way.

"Honestly? I can't recall exactly. My grandfather was a big skier, and we took a few trips every year back when he was alive. He died my senior year of undergrad. Since then, I've gone with friends a few times, but we've not done any big family ski trips. It was a rough year."

"I'm sorry. I didn't mean to bring up painful memories."

"You didn't. Those trips are good memories of happy times. Losing my grandfather and the other things that happened that year don't change that." He dug his ski pole across the snow. "Now, let's practice duckwalking."

Disliking how his melancholy affected her and how strongly she wanted to put his smile back into place, she drew her brows together. "Perhaps you missed the part where I can't human walk with these things on my feet, much less duckwalk. However, lucky for you, I'm an expert duck talker." She pursed her lips. "Quack. Quack."

As she'd hoped, he laughed. "So many talents. Who knew? Now, let's see if you're as good a copycat as you are a quacker."

Deciding to go with whatever he showed her, Julia mimicked his walking movements.

"Relax your knees," he advised.

"Relax?" She fake-laughed. "You're kidding, right? Who can relax when they have long wooden sticks attached to their feet?"

"You're doing great, Julia. Just smile and have fun with it. If you fall, no big deal. It'll just be more practice of how to get up."

Which she could competently do now thanks to his earlier instruction. "Okay. Duckwalk while relaxed."

He grinned. "That a girl. You've got this."

Not really, but after following his instructions, she was staying upright. That was a start.

He patiently walked her through several more movements, demonstrating each one, then observing her attempts and giving pointers on ways to improve. Not once did he make her feel incompetent or hopeless. Before long, her smile was real. She didn't fool herself about just why she was enjoying herself. It had little to do with the skis and everything to do with the instructor.

"It's time for us to go down the beginner slope," he announced a few minutes later when she'd semi-successfully demonstrated each of the skills he'd taught her. "Just remember to relax and keep a smile on your face."

"You got it." She bared gritted teeth in a semblance of a smile, then blew out a cold puff of air.

He laughed.

With Boone patiently skiing near her, Julia made it down the beginner slope with no mishaps. After her second successful trip down the short slope, Boone convinced her to attempt a slightly more difficult slope. She wasn't sure that was a good idea, but he hadn't led her astray thus far. She'd just go slow and do her best to stay on her feet while he skied ahead. Only, when they reached the step-up slope, Boone continued to stay close, offering nonverbal tips and pointing out the beautiful mountains jutting up to meet the cloud-dotted blue sky.

A commotion ahead caught their attention. "Someone's down. They look hurt," he called. "Just keep doing what you're doing and meet me there. I'm going ahead to see if I can help."

Picking up his pace, he skied ahead over the powdery white snow, sliding to a stop near someone lying on the ground in front of several tall evergreens.

Julia maintained her slow and steady pace because if she'd sped up, she likely would have just fallen. When she got close, she saw actually two people were lying on the ground, with Boone knelt over one. She managed to slow as he'd taught her and came to a stop several yards away. She duckwalked to him.

"Julia, this is Craig and Sylvia. He seems the more seriously injured. If you don't mind, I'm going to use your scarf to make a tourniquet on his leg to slow his bleeding while you check Sylvia."

The man was pale except for his nose, which was red from the cold. Julia handed over her scarf.

"I've called for emergency services." Boone took her scarf. "They're on speaker now. Someone should be here to help within a few minutes."

Julia quickly unhooked her skis, then knelt next to the woman, who lay awkwardly in the snow with her hand to her head. Fortunately, she wore a helmet that had hopefully prevented a concussion. "Hi, Sylvia."

The woman gave a weak smile of acknowledgment, then closed her eyes again. "Hi."

"What hurts?" Julia asked.

"Everything, but at least I'm not bleeding like he is. I wanted to try to get up, but your husband said I shouldn't."

"Coworker," she corrected the woman, but her body instantly going clammy beneath her ski gear. "I'm an ICU nurse. Dr. Richards is the best doctor I know." A pulmonologist, but prior to declaring his specialty, he would have dealt with many different medical scenarios. She didn't doubt his ability to handle this accident. "Is it okay if I touch you to check you, Sylvia?"

Keeping her eyes closed, the woman made a sound of agreement.

Julia ran her hands over her arms, making sure the bones lined up, then proceeded to check the woman's legs. When she came to the woman's right ankle, she grimaced. Although the bones hadn't broken through the skin surface, both the tibia and fibula were broken and displaced just above where the woman's boot ended.

"That hurts." Sylvia opened her eyes and reached toward Julia to stop her.

"Sorry. I wasn't trying to hurt you. Unfortunately, your leg is broken. You aren't going to be crazy about this, but I'm going to pack snow around the area," she told the woman. "It'll help to keep the swelling down."

Once she had snow around the woman's leg, she ran through a quick neuro check. Fortunately, other than the ankle and being shaken up, Sylvia seemed okay and was in enough shock that her pain was only semi-registering.

"We collided. I was skiing, and the next thing I knew, I was on the ground," Sylvia explained, apparently deciding she no longer had to remain still as she propped herself up on her elbows so she could see what was going on.

"I'm sorry," Craig said from where he lay. "I couldn't slow down." He lifted his hand to his head. "Man, that hurts, and I feel as if my glasses are digging into my face."

Julia moved closer and pushed his ski glasses

onto his helmet to look into his eyes. His pupils were different sizes. He swiped at his nose. Blood streaked across his glove.

His frightened gaze went to Julia's. "That can't be good."

"You probably bumped it when you collided." Hopefully, that's all that it was, but his dilated pupils concerned her. Maybe something more had happened.

"He really doesn't look good, does he?" Sylvia's question only made Craig look worse.

"Why did she say that?" he asked. "What are you not telling me? Am I bleeding to death?"

"Blood scares some people," Boone assured him. He was further assessing the man's leg, trying to keep him calm. If he got excited, his heart would pump faster, and keeping his blood loss down would be more difficult. But the idea that he might be hurt worse than he'd thought had Craig struggling to sit up. Julia put her hand on his chest, staying him.

"Don't. Your leg is broken, and unlike Sylvia's, your fracture cut through your skin and you're actively bleeding. Plus, you may have further injuries. It's better to rest until the emergency workers arrive to help you off the mountain." When the man seemed uncertain, Julia waved her hand in front of his face. She'd have snapped her fingers if her gloves would let her. "Look at me," she ordered.

After a moment, he focused on her. "I'm going to have to go to the hospital, aren't I?"

"You need to see an orthopedic surgeon regarding your leg."

"Can't Doc there pop it back into place?"

"Not my specialty," Boone assured him. He was back on the phone with the EMS while continuing to slow the bleeding. "I'm a lung specialist."

"Too bad I didn't break a lung instead, eh?"

A punctured lung would have come with a whole different set of worries. "I'm glad you didn't," Boone assured him, then answered the operator's question.

Face pale, Craig closed his eyes.

"Craig?"

He didn't answer. He'd just been talking to them, but something about the laxity of his expression told her something more was going on. Had he passed out?

"Craig?" She knelt next to the man. Boone had already stopped what he was doing at the man's leg to move close to his upper body, as well.

While Julia pushed his high-necked shirt down so she could reach his carotid artery to check his pulse, Boone placed his hand on the man's shoulder. "Craig? Can you hear me?"

The man didn't respond.

"He has a pulse and is breathing," Julia assured Boone. "His pupils were off from some type of head injury."

"I noticed that, too." Boone gave her a worried look. "He likely just passed out, but keep a watch. He's bleeding too much, still. I'm going to see if I can get your scarf tied tighter around his leg." He gestured to one of the growing number of bystanders who'd joined them rather than continuing down the slope. "I want you to elevate his good leg. Gently."

He did as Boone instructed.

Julia kept a check on Craig's pulse and respirations, calling over to Sylvia repeatedly to make sure the woman was still okay. She was. When the rescue crew arrived, Julia sighed in relief. She and Boone helped get man and woman loaded into the back of an all-terrain vehicle.

When the rescuers were on their way with the injured duo, Boone glanced toward Julia. "Sorry about your scarf. I'll buy you a new one."

"It's not a big deal." At this point her adrenaline had her plenty warm. "I'm just glad you were able to get the bleeding slowed. With as much blood as there was, his fracture must have cut into an artery."

Boone glanced around. The spectators had dispersed with the emergency crew's departure with the couple. "You know that what happened with them was a freak accident, right? In all my years of skiing, I've never come across anything like that. Usually, any injuries are more along the lines of strains and sprains."

Pushing her glasses back into place, Julia nodded. She was quite proud of herself considering how she'd started.

"You made a lot of progress with your skiing today. I don't want you using this as an excuse to end your lesson."

"Hmm." She pretended to consider. "I hadn't thought of that, but you do have a point."

He stared directly into her eyes as if he could see beyond her glasses and into her very soul. "I won't let anything happen to you, Julia."

She'd been teasing, but his voice held such sincerity that she gulped back the emotions hitting her. "You're saying that had I been Sylvia, you could have saved me from an out-of-control skier?"

"Even if I'd had to throw myself into the line of fire to stop him."

Julia's heart swelled to the point that she wondered if the sound of it echoed around the mountains. Had there ever been anyone in her life who would truly sacrifice himself for her? She knew there hadn't. Not even her parents had ever put her needs first. She felt overwhelmed that, in this moment, she believed he would sacrifice his own good for hers. Panic had her desperate to lighten her thoughts. "My hero. I'll have to give you back the bear-blanket-slash-cape."

He grinned. "I like that."

"That I'm considering returning the blanket?"

"The blanket is yours. I meant you thinking I'm your hero."

There he went again, making her insides all fluttery and warm despite the brisk wind. "Everyone who just witnessed what happened knows you're a hero."

His look was intense as he said, "Just so long as you think so."

"I see what a hero you are at the hospital. No worries." She had been awed from the first time she'd caught him sitting next to a patient's bed, half-asleep, and realized that rather than going home, he'd spent the night at his patient's side. Since then, he'd only continued to break down every wall she had. Resisting his charms was impossible.

How would she ever stick to her Rules for Life Success? But she knew she'd only live to regret it if she didn't.

With the exception of the duo who'd been hurt on the ski slope earlier, Boone had had a fantastic day. Seeing Julia away from work, relaxing, laughing, and enjoying life, even teasing him at times, gave him a deep sense of satisfaction. Like all was right in the world.

Everyone hung out in the cabin's rustic decor living room, watching a Times Square special as they counted down until midnight and the changing of one year into the next. The fireplace crackled and had the room toasty warm. Hot-natured anyway, he'd shed his heavier layers for a T-shirt and jeans. Julia, on the other hand, wore a thick fuzzy maroon sweater and black stretchy pants.

"We are going to make such a mess," Julia mused, toying with the confetti popper she held.

"There's a vacuum in the closet. I'll help with cleanup," Boone offered, reaching out to straighten Julia's party hat. Stephanie had insisted they all wear them.

Julia arched a brow. "Like you men cleaned up after yourselves earlier?"

Boone grinned. "Hey, I wasn't going to argue when Stephanie said that the girls would clean since the guys had done the cooking."

Julia looked skeptical. "Not that I don't appreciate y'all toughing the cold, but is grilling really even cooking?"

It had mostly consisted of them standing around the grill while wearing their outdoor gear and shooting the breeze. "You have to admit that it tasted good."

She nodded. "I'm not much of a meat eater,

but I'll grant you that those vegetable skewers were amazing."

"Topped off by the desserts you ladies brought. Those no-bake cookies you made were my favorite. I'm a fan of anything that has peanut butter."

The fire's reflection added an extra sparkle to her eyes, giving them an almost golden look. "I'll remember that in case I ever need to get on your good side."

He could assure her that she already was, but just grinned. "I can send you a list of things that would work, if you'd like."

"Aw, you're always so helpful. I'm thinking food would be at the top of your list."

"Food is always good." Truth was, she would be at the top of his list. If he'd had any doubt, spending time with her this weekend had him convinced more than ever that Julia was different from anyone he'd ever known. That being around her made him different.

"Okay, everyone get together for a group picture." Stephanie glanced at her watch, then back to where she'd put her phone on a tripod. "I can't believe another year is almost gone."

Everyone piled onto the sofa or around it. Several of the women curled up in their guy's lap. Julia went to move to the floor, but Stephanie stopped her.

"No, you two sitting next to each other is

going to throw off the symmetry of the photo when we're otherwise all girls sitting in guys' laps." Stephanie looked directly at Julia. "Sit in Boone's lap."

Julia's eyes widened. "Um...no."

"It's only for long enough for me to get a group picture," Stephanie pleaded, the others joining in. "It's not a big deal. Come on. Hurry up so we can get back to the TV before the ball drops. We don't want to miss doing the countdown."

Boone winced at the peer pressure her friends were placing upon her and settled it by standing. "If anyone is sitting in someone else's lap, I'm sitting in Julia's."

Giving him a horrified look, Julia jumped up from her seat. "I don't think so."

"Party pooper," Stephanie accused, laughing. Then she motioned for one of the standing couples to take his place. "Fine. You two win, but only because the clock is ticking. Why don't y'all move to stand behind the sofa and just lean forward."

They did so, smiling when Stephanie said to smile and making funny faces when she said to make funny faces. Stephanie snapped photos by pushing the remote control's button. "Everyone, grab your horn and blow." They did so. "Now, grab your partner and get one last smooch for the year."

The look Julia shot her friend said it all. Boone would like to have had his *first* kiss for the year, but to try to ease what could be an awkward moment, he immediately held out his hand for a friendly shake. Glancing at his offering, Julia laughed.

"That's great," she said as she shook it. Boone got to hold her hand, and though it wasn't quite a kiss, the moment wasn't lost on him, either. Holding her hand, even briefly, was something to be cherished. Mostly, though, he was glad she was smiling.

Stephanie checked her phone attached to the tripod, then motioned for them to resume positions. "One more, guys. Then we'll get our drinks ready to toast the new year and all the wonderful things it will bring."

Everyone had champagne except Julia and Becky, whose glasses had sparkling cider instead.

"Oh, look, there's less than one minute to go!" Dawn motioned to the television where the Times Square ball would soon drop.

"Out with the old and in with the new," someone said. Several said cheers as they toasted each other.

"Ten, nine, eight..." they counted down, getting louder with each number. "One! Happy New Year!"

Several couples kissed. Julia's gaze met his, and she looked away almost immediately. She hadn't been quick enough, though, to keep him from seeing the desire in her eyes. Next year, he thought. No, not next year. This year, because they'd started a new year, the year Julia had agreed to go out with him in May.

"Happy New Year, Julia."

"You, too, Boone." Her gaze dropped to his mouth. Looking a little nervous, she moistened her lips, then took a sip of her cider. "I hope it's your best ever."

"It's off to a good start." He wanted to kiss her. To welcome in the year with the taste of her mouth on his lips. He knew better, of course. Five months. Then she'd go on a date with him. They might not kiss on that date, or even the next one, but they would kiss. Of that he had no doubt. She could stick to her no-dating-until-after-graduation rule, but he wasn't wrong about how she looked at him. He wasn't alone in whatever this was between them. For now, he'd be satisfied with spending as much time with her as she'd allow as friends anticipating whatever the future held.

"You're right. It is." Her smile was such a mixture of sweet temptation and guarded uncertainty that it was all he could do to keep from pulling her to him and assuring her she had no reason to doubt his attraction.

Instead, he reminded himself that patience was a virtue, and that Julia really was worth the wait.

Julia gulped back the lump that had formed in her throat. Boone was thinking about kissing her. He was looking at her mouth and…and she wanted him to take the initiative. She wanted his kiss. But she was glad that he had self-control. If he'd acted on his impulse, she'd have regretted it when they went back to their realities.

Maybe.

Because part of her wanted to know what kissing Boone felt like. She couldn't think of a single thing that would be a better start to her year than knowing what it felt like to lose herself in his arms.

"Cheers," Stephanie called again from where she was hugged up next to Derek, pulling Julia back from whatever fantasy world her mind had wandered off to. "I want to make a toast." Stephanie waited until everyone was looking her way. "To good friends and good times."

"Cheers," they all agreed, holding up their glasses, then taking a drink.

Soon thereafter, Kevin and Becky called it a night, as did Stephanie and Derek, saying they'd clean up in the morning. Dawn said she was headed upstairs, and Cliff offered to walk her up—not that anyone believed Dawn needed to be escorted to her room, but their PDA had been in full force all evening.

Not wanting to interrupt the couple's good-night, Julia knelt to pick up bits of colorful paper rather than going upstairs. Boone began gathering confetti, too.

"You don't need to help," Julia assured him, wondering if it was a good idea for them to be alone. Not that she thought he'd pressure her. She was more worried it might be the other way around. He'd been so kind and attentive all day, had made her laugh, opened doors, and been an absolute perfect gentleman. She'd felt self-conscious at times thanks to her friends' knowing looks, but the truth was, he'd made her feel cherished, as if she were a woman worth the effort. That scared her, because she didn't expect him to stick around. What if he did? What if she had to tell him about her past? Her fingers clenched around the paper she held. What if, like Clay, he never looked at her the same way?

"I like helping you, Julia. Besides, I figure our roommates are in the hallway saying good-night. We'll give them a few minutes of privacy."

When they went upstairs ten minutes later,

Julia and Dawn's door was shut. Boone and Cliff's door was open with no one in sight.

Realizing the couple were in her and Dawn's room and might be a while, Julia gave Boone an embarrassed look. "I'm going back downstairs for a while."

Because no way was she knocking on the bedroom door and interrupting whatever was going on in the room she shared with Dawn.

"Me, too." When she started to protest, Boone shook his head. "It isn't as if I'll be able to go to sleep with knowing you're downstairs killing time. If you even get to go to bed. Cliff might not reappear until morning."

Knowing he was right, she grimaced. "Regardless, you don't have to stay awake just because I can't go into my room. I can watch television. It'll be fine. Get some rest."

But he wasn't having it. "I'm not sleepy."

She wasn't sure she believed him but nodded. The living room was empty when they went back downstairs, and the house seemed eerily quiet. Rather than turn on the television, Julia gestured to an oversized woven game board on the coffee table. "Do you want to play checkers?"

"Sure. Why not?" Then he gave her a suspicious look. "Are you as good at checkers as you are at pool? Are you trying to shame me so I'll cry myself to sleep on the first night of the new year?"

Lips twitching, she shook her head. "Lucky for you, I'm not. I'd say I'm somewhere between my pool-playing skills and my ski skills."

His eyes twinkled. "Then what you're saying is that I have a fighting chance?"

She hesitated long enough that the silence stretched between them. Then her gaze met his. "Yes, Boone. I'd say you have a chance. A good chance."

But whether she meant checkers or something more was debatable.

CHAPTER SIX

"STILL CLOSED." Julia eyed her bedroom door more than an hour later. "I could knock and order him out of the room."

"Or you could just sleep in my bed," Boone offered. He stood next to her in the dimly lit hallway.

Her brows knit together in a deep vee. They'd had such a great time playing checkers. Laughing and each winning equally. As always, the sexual awareness was there, but not once had he made any untoward move. Until now. "Boone, I—"

"Hold up. That's not what I was implying," he assured her, his expression sincere. "You sleep in my room, lock the door, and I'll take the sofa. It's huge and has that extended side. I'll be fine."

Fatigue having caught up with her long ago, Julia considered his offer, but she doubted she was tired enough that she'd sleep if she was snuggled between Boone's covers. Would the quilts smell of his spicy male scent? Would she lie there imagining him, or would she drift off and dream he was there beside her?

Stop it, Julia. Do not let your mind go there.

She bit into her lower lip. "I'm not nearly as tall. It makes more sense for me to take the sofa."

"Except that it feels ungentlemanly to sleep in my bed while you're stuck on the sofa," he pointed out. "I wouldn't rest knowing I did that to you."

His mother would be proud of his manners. Boone was a gentleman through and through, and Julia appreciated that about him. However, on this, he wouldn't win. She wasn't sleeping in his room. Something about being in a bed he'd been in the night before felt too intimate, silly as it was.

"What if Cliff returns to his room during the night?"

"Doubtful, but like I said, just lock the door. Turnabout is fair play."

She shook her head. "I can't sleep in your room, Boone."

Appearing torn, he acquiesced. "At least let me give you my quilt and extra pillow."

"That would be great." Which meant she'd soon know if his covers smelled of him. How was she supposed to sleep if he filled her senses?

Going into his room, he got a blanket and pillow. "You're sure you won't let me take the sofa? Or how about if I took Cliff's bed and you slept in mine? You'd be completely safe. I wouldn't misbehave."

"I didn't think you would."

His grin was lethal. "Ah, I see. You're worried that you might misbehave."

"You've figured me out." She rolled her eyes as if she were teasing, but it might surprise him to know that there was a part of her that longed to sleep with his arms around her. She'd never been a cuddler, but there was something about Boone that made her long to know what it would feel like to snuggle next to him while she slept. All she had to do was say the word and he'd do just that. Sticking to her rules sure wasn't easy when it came to Boone, but veering from her plan would be a mistake. "It's me who is the problem."

Truer words had never been said.

"Hey, my intentions were pure." Eyes twinkling, he held out the bedding. "Can I help it if you have a dirty mind?"

Taking the pillow and blanket from him, she gave a dramatic eye roll. "Right. I should have known you had no ulterior motive."

"I wouldn't go that far. I'm not above trying to make a good impression, though."

Did he think he had to try? She wondered this

as she creaked her way down the wooden stairway. She must be doing a better job than she thought at suppressing how he affected her. No one had ever impressed her more than Boone. What would he have done if she'd said, yes, she'd share his room? Would he have backtracked or been just fine with their friends discovering she'd spent the night in his room and thinking they'd had sex?

Squeezing her eyes closed, she inhaled the faint scent of him on the quilt around her, allowing her mind the freedom to imagine that things were different, that she'd shared a kiss with Boone to ring in the new year, that she'd had the right to take him by the hand and lead him to a room they shared, and...

She gulped, knowing she had to get her mind under control. Even if she was willing, a dalliance with Boone could completely derail everything she'd worked so hard for. Even if he didn't hightail it the way Clay had and they got romantically involved, she had no delusions that it would last.

Clay's walking away had hurt, had almost led to a relapse to dull the ache of not feeling good enough to deserve to be loved. Boone affected her in ways Clay never had. How much more devastating would it be to fall for someone like Boone and then lose him? What if she wasn't strong enough to resist dulling her heartache? She couldn't imagine ever going back on that destructive path, but she also knew how easy it was to give in to a weak moment under the mistaken guise of diminishing one's pain. How many times had she witnessed someone relapse? Too many to count. The best way to stay clean was to not put herself into bad situations.

Protecting her new life, her hard-won success, was crucial. It was everything.

She'd be friends with Boone. He was a good man. But she couldn't allow things to go beyond that friendship. She just couldn't.

Come May, if he was still around, well, she'd figure that out then.

The following day, as Boone rolled his car to a halt at a stop sign, he snuck a glance at Julia in his passenger seat. "Stephanie was pretty obvious."

"You mean on foisting driving me back to Knoxville upon you?" Continuing to look out the window at the lightly snow-covered trees that lined the road, Julia sighed. "I'm sorry you got stuck with me."

"I'm not complaining. The company is nice." After glancing both ways, he turned the car onto the Gatlinburg Bypass. "How did you sleep?"

"Not too bad."

"But not as well as if you'd been in your bed?" he guessed, not surprised that she hadn't said one word of complaint about having her room taken over. Instead, she'd assured Cliff and an embarrassed Dawn that it was okay, she understood. Boone, on the other hand, had pulled their co-worker aside and had a talk with him.

"You should have taken my offer of my room," Boone told Julia. "I felt guilty being in my bed, knowing you were down on the sofa."

"It's really okay. Cliff apologized profusely. I guess a night on the sofa is a small price to pay for a friend to be nonstop smiles, eh? Honestly, I feel badly that he insisted on covering all of my stay."

"Only fair since you didn't get to sleep in your room last night." As he'd pointed out to the man that morning during their conversation. He didn't know Julia's financial situation, but judging from what he knew about her background and graduate school, he suspected funds were tight. She shouldn't have had to pay for a room she hadn't gotten to sleep in.

"I guess, but I didn't expect him to do that and tried to refuse." Glancing out the window, she added, "Even in the midst of winter, it's beautiful here, isn't it? The views of the mountains while we were driving down were breathtaking."

She was breathtaking. "We'll come back this

spring when everything turns green." Sensing her reaction to what he'd said, he revised, "We'll come back here this summer after you've graduated, and everything is green."

Julia sighed. "Boone, I...it would be better for you not to say things like that."

His gaze shifted toward her for a second, noting how she rubbed her finger across her inner left wrist. Sometimes he wondered if that tattoo caught fire to draw her attention to it. "Because you don't plan to spend time with me this summer?"

She tucked her right hand beneath the edges of her thigh. "This summer is months away. It's premature to make plans that far in advance when neither of us knows how we'll feel."

His gaze stayed on the road, but his grip tightened on the steering wheel. "You think our first date will go that badly?"

"If we even have a first date." She sounded as if she didn't belief they would. "You may meet someone between now and then, so taking me out wouldn't be feasible."

Frustration hit. Why was it so difficult for her to have faith in him?

"I'm not looking to meet someone, Julia." He'd already met someone. Her. More and more he wished Amy were there, that he could introduce Julia to his twin, and watch the two of them bond. Amy would have adored Julia, especially the fact that she didn't just give him his way. Sadness and anger seared through him. His sister would never meet Julia, and that was a crying shame.

"Isn't that when they say you're most likely to meet someone? When you're not trying to?" She'd kept her voice light, as if her comment was teasing, but it was obvious a world of hurt was buried deep behind her inability to trust that he would be waiting until she was ready to date. "Besides, you can't know how you're going to feel five months from now."

"I disagree."

"Okay, fine. You disagree." She twisted in her seat to face him. "Let me ask you this, then. Did you know five months ago that you and Dr. Cunningham would no longer be together?"

He kept his gaze on the curvy road, but Boone wanted to look into Julia's big brown eyes to let her see the truth in what he was about to say. "My answer may surprise you, but yes, deep down, I did know that Olivia and I wouldn't be together. We dated a long time, but maybe I've always known that we'd eventually go our separate ways."

"Did you tell her this?"

Guilt hit. "As soon as I acknowledged that truth, yes, I told Olivia. She's a wonderful woman and friend. I enjoyed her company. When we first started dating, neither of us was looking for a permanent relationship. But we got along well, had a lot in common, and our relationship was easy for the both of us. Now we want different things. Continuing our relationship would have been wrong knowing that. She deserves better."

Julia straightened in her seat and stared out the window. They rode in silence for a few minutes. Then, sliding her hand out from beneath her thigh to stroke her wrist, she said, "I find all this overwhelming, Boone. I'm flattered by your interest, but I need to focus on school and work and not have to take another person into account when making decisions. Having someone in my life gives that person power to pull emotional strings that I prefer being the sole controller of. That may sound selfish, but it's how I feel."

"Not so much selfish as lonely." Had what he'd admitted about his relationship with Olivia offended Julia? Maybe he'd been too frank if she was saying she'd rather stay hidden behind her walls than take a chance with him. Honesty was important. He wanted her to trust him.

"There are things far worse than loneliness." Her tone left no doubt that she spoke from experience.

"I take it you've had a bad relationship?"

"None in the past few years and none that

I want to talk about, but I doubt many get to twenty-seven without having fallen for the wrong person at least once. I'm no exception."

Julia had obviously cared deeply for someone who had hurt her. What kind of idiot had her affections and lost them?

"If you ever do want to talk, I'm a really good listener." An older-model Chevrolet catching his eyes, Boone changed the subject as he suspected if he didn't lighten the conversation, Julia would be completely clammed up prior to their reaching Pigeon Forge. "What's your favorite car?"

Seeming relieved, she shrugged. "I've never given it much thought. I guess I'd say the one that gets me back and forth and where I need to go without any hiccups. How about you?"

"A 1955 Corvette," he answered without hesitation. It wasn't the car that had caught his eye but had been his go-to favorite since he'd been a young teen.

"Obviously you've given it some thought." She twisted toward him as much as her seat belt allowed. "So why don't you have this dream car?"

"They're pretty rare. Only seven hundred were made, and even less than that are still in existence. Purchasing one isn't practical, but they're sharp."

Her gasp was overly dramatic. "I'm in shock over here. You don't get everything you want?"

He chuckled. "You of all people shouldn't have to ask me that question to know the answer."

After stopping in Sevierville to grab lunch prior to heading back onto I-40 West, they jumped from one topic to another that included a mildly heated debate about who the all-time greatest contestant was on their favorite singing competition for the remainder of the drive back to Knoxville.

When they arrived at her apartment, Boone popped the trunk and got out her bag. "I'll carry this up."

Surprisingly, she didn't argue, just smiled. "I'll give you this, Boone. You have impeccable manners."

He grinned. "My mother would be proud to hear you say that. I told her the same thing about you."

Julia's eyes widened. "You talked to your mother about me? When? Why would you do that?"

"I mentioned you when I was home at Christmas and several times since during phone conversations. She likes you." He followed Julia up the two flights of stairs to her apartment, then stood behind her while she unlocked her door.

"She doesn't even know me." Julia gave him a suspicious look. "You're coming in, aren't you?"

Boone hesitated. He had assumed he'd carry

her bag into her apartment, but he could see how that might make her uncomfortable. "Not if you don't want me to."

She grimaced, then sighed. "It would be rude not to invite you in after you carried up my bag."

"You are not obligated to invite me in. I can put your bag wherever you like and then leave, Julia."

"I...okay." She pushed the door open and stepped aside for him to enter. "Just place it by the door. I'll unpack it after you're gone."

He stepped into the apartment and glanced around the small but tidy studio. The walls were painted a pale yellow, and everything was trimmed in white. Her furniture was a hodge-podge of mismatched items that came together in a way that worked. Colorful throw pillows on the sofa and bed added vibrant splashes. "You live here alone?"

"Just me and Honey. My neighbor kept her while I was in Gatlinburg. She brought her home this morning before she headed out. Hello, Honey, I'm home," she called, then turned to him with an almost eagerness for him to meet the cat shining in her eyes. "She is a great cat, but just know that she doesn't take well to strangers."

How many strangers does Julia have at her apartment?

"She is a sweetie, but I'm convinced she believes this is her place and that she is just graciously allowing me to live here."

Honey didn't come when Julia called, and Boone arched a brow. "You know, if Honey was a dog, she'd be licking you like crazy right now."

"True, but I'm more of a cat person."

"Why's that?"

"I'm not sure. With a few exceptions at foster homes, I never had pets growing up. I can't say that I planned to have one as an adult. It wasn't something I'd given any thought to, but when this sweet kitten showed up scared and hungry in the hospital parking lot, well, I couldn't leave her."

It didn't surprise him that she'd not been able to leave the cat, but part of her answer shocked him. "Foster homes?"

Wincing, Julia was no doubt mentally kicking herself for her revelation. "My mother battled with a few demons. Occasionally, I'd be placed elsewhere while she got her act together."

"You didn't stay with your father?" He'd sensed she'd had a rough childhood but hadn't realized just how rough. Had her mother battled the same demons his sister had? Had that been how she'd died, too? No wonder Julia was such an advocate for their overdose patients getting appropriate post-hospital treatment.

"Sometimes. Sometimes not." She shrugged as if it were no big deal, but her voice was a little higher-pitched than normal when she called, "Honey? Where are you?"

He wanted to ask more about her childhood, to tell Julia about Amy and how he felt as if there were a hole inside him at losing his twin, but he didn't. They'd had too good a day to upset her. "So, where did the name Honey come from?"

"Not long after I brought her home, a television show was on while I was doing homework, and a character said, 'Honey, I'm home.' For whatever reason, the line resonated, and I started doing the same when I'd walk in the door. The name stuck." The previously sleeping cat rose up from beneath the pillows on Julia's bed. She'd been so nestled in them that he hadn't noticed her when he'd been scanning the room. "Here she is. Hello, Honey, I'm home." Julia picked up the cat. "How is my good kitty?"

Boone watched her love on the cat a moment and felt silly at the jealousy that hit him at how freely she bestowed her affections.

"Did you miss me? Hmm?" She rubbed her cheek against the cat's face. Honey meowed and nuzzled Julia. "I missed you, too. Do you want to meet my friend, Boone?"

Her friend, Boone.

Why did his heart skip at the description? He wasn't even sure if it was a positive or negative skip. Was he excited she considered him a friend or worried about the label when he wanted so much more? No way did he want to be permanently friend-zoned. Was that even a possibility with the chemistry between them? Sometimes when their eyes met, he'd swear the air sizzled.

Boone waited for Julia to indicate that he could pet the cat. Fortunately, the cat didn't hiss, scratch, or bite him when he gave her a gentle stroke. "Nice kitty."

"She likes you." Julia sounded surprised. "She usually doesn't like strangers, and particularly not males."

Like her owner. That Julia had taken in the cat and allowed the furry critter to steal her heart made Boone smile.

He had hope.

"Nice scrub top. Does that mean you have Valentine's Day plans for next week?"

At Stephanie's question, Julia glanced up from the electronic medical record she was reviewing. "Thanks. Candy conversation hearts are rather iconic, aren't they?" She recalled getting a few tiny boxes of them when in grammar school and meticulously going through them to read each little heart. The candies hadn't tasted very good, but she'd always been excited to read the messages each year, almost as if she'd expected some great love revelation. "I found the top last summer when we went to that thrift store, remember? And, yes, I have Valentine's Day plans."

Leaning over the desk that separated the area from the hall, Stephanie let loose with a squeal. "For real? You're going out with Boone? Yay! I knew it was only a matter of time. That's so wonderful."

Tucking a stray hair that had escaped her braid, Julia sighed. "That's not what you asked me. You asked if I had plans for Valentine's. I do. I'm working until the end of my shift. Then I'll be at home studying for a test later in the week."

Stephanie's disappointment was palpable as she scrunched her face. "Let me think, go on a date with a gorgeous doctor or study for an exam that we both know you're going to ace—girl, you have your priorities all wrong."

Julia's priorities were where they needed to be.

"I ace my tests because I study. And for the record, Boone hasn't mentioned Valentine's to me, nor should he. We aren't a couple," she reminded Stephanie for what felt like the millionth time since Gatlinburg. "We aren't dating. We are coworkers and friends. The sooner you accept that, the better."

"We had such a great time over New Year's, and you two got along beautifully. Don't bother denying it. If I hadn't seen you there, I've seen you here since. You both light up when the other one is around. Not that you didn't before our trip, just that it's now even more obvious."

"It's called friendship."

"I've never noticed you look like that when you see me," Stephanie teased, coming around the desk to sit next to Julia. "Please tell me you aren't seriously going to make that gorgeous man wait until you graduate before you go out with him."

Julia sighed and went back to typing her note into the computer.

Stephanie leaned forward and tapped her hand in a light smack. "I'm serious. What if he gets tired of waiting and starts dating someone else? He's too awesome to risk losing to someone who won't make him wait months and months."

"His dating someone else would be okay." The pinching sensation in her chest hinted she might be wrong. "Honestly, I expect him to."

Stephanie gave her an odd look. "Are you hoping he does, Julia? Is that why you refuse to budge on your no-dating-until-graduation rule?"

"No. Maybe. I—I don't know," she answered truthfully. There was a part of her that was terrified of getting closer to Boone. Perhaps even their friendship was too much. She had no doubt it was going to sting something fierce when he bored of her. "It would be for the best in the long run if he did start dating someone else."

Stephanie gave her a horrified look. "Why would you think that?"

"We've nothing in common."

"I didn't get that impression in Gatlinburg. Y'all seemed to get along fabulously."

"That was one weekend." They had, but a weekend getaway wasn't the real world.

"Y'all get along just fine here at the hospital, too."

The hospital was the real world, but in a very isolated environment.

Julia arched a brow. "He's a great doctor. Why wouldn't I get along with him?"

"Exactly. Why wouldn't any sane woman get along with a charming, fun, considerate, smart, successful man like Boone? I know your reasons for wanting to keep school as your priority. I even admire your determination to achieve success and am so proud of you, Julia. But one of life's greatest gifts is that as new and exciting things happen, we can adjust how we define success. Doing well in life and school isn't exclusive of dating. You're a smart lady. I've no doubt that you can do both without compromising your commitment to yourself." Stephanie looked her directly in the eyes. "You wrote your Rules for Life Success. You can update them."

"I—maybe." For so long, she'd kept her focus on graduation, not allowing room for any diversion from the course she'd set. She was so close to the goal that changing paths now seemed an unnecessary risk. Why chance getting distracted with Boone? Already, he held way too much power over her. If she let him in...she'd be hurt.

"Maybe just go to dinner with Boone as friends, if nothing else," Stephanie encouraged her. "Spending Valentine's with him sure beats having your nose buried in the computer for schoolwork."

Except one was what she had planned and would help her achieve her long-term goals, and the other...the other...she just didn't know. She couldn't deny that she'd enjoyed their Gatlinburg trip. Nor could she say that he'd been anything short of wonderful since they'd returned. He'd been friendly, but she never felt he was pressuring her. Too bad she couldn't say the same for her inner voice. Stephanie was just vocalizing what her inner voice already whispered over and over, tempting her to explore her feelings for Boone.

Sighing, she glanced toward her best friend. "I repeat, Boone hasn't asked me to dinner for Valentine's."

"Not because he didn't want to," Boone said from the opposite end of the nurse station, obviously standing in her friend's field of vision. How long had he been there, and why hadn't Stephanie given Julia some warning?

As she turned toward him, taking in how handsome he looked in his light blue scrubs, Julia's face heated.

"Sorry." His eyes searched hers. "I came to tell you that I saw Aaron West in clinic and to let you know he's doing well. I didn't start out meaning to eavesdrop, but I couldn't help but overhear."

"I'm glad to hear Aaron is still doing well. As for the other, that's why having such conversations at work is a really bad idea."

"Or a really good one," her friend countered, flashing a big smile, then standing. "Sorry to rush off, but I need to check on my patient."

"Which could be interpreted as 'I'm off to leave the two of you alone,'" Julia accused her, but Stephanie just waved her fingers at Boone, then disappeared down the hallway.

"Forgive her. She can't help herself." Julia made light of the embarrassing conversation. Why hadn't she realized he was there? Of all times for her Boone awareness tingles to fail her...

"I like her," Boone said.

"I used to," Julia admitted with a soft smile. "Truly, I'm sorry for what she was saying."

"Because you don't want to have Valentine's dinner with me?"

Because I want to so desperately that I can barely keep from averting my gaze from yours.

"It would be better if we didn't."

"Having dinner alone doesn't sound as if it would be better," he pointed out, the corner of his mouth hiking up.

"I'm not asking you to be alone that night, just not to ask me." If he did spend it with someone else, she'd rather not know. Or maybe it would be best if she did so she could squash down the crazy notions he put into her mind.

His brows veed. "You want me to spend Valentine's with someone else?"

No. "If you did, then you wouldn't be alone for dinner on Valentine's."

He came around the desk and leaned against her workstation. "I'm of the opinion that being alone is preferable to being with the wrong person."

Her breath caught at what she saw in his eyes. "I'm not the right person."

He studied her for a long moment. Julia could barely breathe. "Maybe not," he finally said. "I look forward to when we can figure that out. Until then, what's Valentine's dinner between friends? No strings attached."

Her mind reeled from how his blue eyes were drawing her in. She wanted nothing more than to drown in their warmth. "Bad idea. Valentine's Day is meant for spending with lovers rather than friends."

For one moment she thought he was going to pounce on her comment. "We can start a new tradition. I would enjoy taking you to a Friendslentine," his face twisted. "Friend-tine?" he tried again, then shook his head. "Val-friend-tine Day?"

He got an A for effort, but she shook her head. "Taking me to dinner on Valentine's sounds too much like a date."

"You could meet me at the restaurant and pay for your meal," he suggested as if that would resolve all her concerns.

She eyed him suspiciously. "You'd let me do that?"

"Not if I was on a date," he clarified. "But if that's the only way a friend would save me from a lonely evening—" he turned on the puppy-dog eyes "—then sure, why wouldn't I?"

The look he gave her was so over-the-top imploring that she couldn't hold in her laughter. "You should have gone into sales, Boone. Sorry, but I work on Valentine's."

"Me, too. But we both have to eat, so a late dinner works. I can book us reservations at—"

His excitement making her a little off balance, Julia interrupted. "Nowhere that requires reservations. That would be too date-like."

As if spending time on Valentine's with him wasn't going to feel that way already.

What had she done?

* * *

At around 3:00 p.m. on Valentine's Day, Julia blinked at her nurse director. "What do you mean I can go home?"

"Census is low. You know that with less patients admitted I have to send someone home, and today it's you." Patti waved her hands at Julia in a shooing motion. "Go. Before I change my mind."

Patti wasn't having it. "You always stay so someone else can go home or when we need someone to stay over. I'm not allowing it today. Quit arguing and get out of here."

"Do I even want to know why you chose today to insist I leave?" Was it possible that Stephanie had gotten to their boss? Not that her friend had control over the unit's census, but she wouldn't put it past Stephanie to have begged Patti to send Julia home early if the opportunity arose. Her friend had wanted to take her shopping for a new outfit and to have her hair done. Julia had declined, citing that she'd be spending her off-work day doing the studying she'd have otherwise done on Valentine's.

"Blame the census." Patti's grin said Julia should place blame on her, too. Did all her co-workers know she was having dinner with Boone? Although no one had directly asked, she'd gotten a lot of knowing smiles since New

Year's. Several of their work group at been there, had seen them, so it was no secret they'd spent time together there. Still…

The truth was, Julia would rather work late than go home early. Working late meant not obsessing about getting ready for a Valentine's dinner that wasn't a date, yet she had bees buzzing around in her belly. She'd refused Stephanie's offer, but that didn't mean she hadn't thought about what she would wear. She'd gone through her closet a dozen times, pulling out one outfit, then another. Everything seemed either too dressy or too casual.

After asking her about her food likes and dislikes, Boone had texted her an address for a mom-and-pop restaurant near downtown and promised they'd have a low-stress, no-pressure evening where they could relax—as friends. She settled on a bright red sweater, a pair of black jeans, boots, and silver hoop earrings and a bangle bracelet. She'd just finished brushing her hair when her phone rang. Seeing Boone's number, her heart thudded.

"There's been a change of plans."

Julia winced. He was canceling. She took a deep breath. This was for the best. She knew it was. "No problem. I have a ton to do anyway, and—"

"You think I'm canceling? That's not the

change of plans, Julia. The only thing that's changed is where you're driving to."

That she felt such relief at his words should have had her running.

"I think you'll enjoy this better than the restaurant I originally chose. I'll text you the address and see you in about fifteen minutes, if that works?"

Excitement laced his voice. Excitement that hinted she hadn't been alone in stressed anticipation of the evening. Excitement that had her curious. Just a dinner between friends…who was she kidding? Dinner with a friend had never had her feeling so…so…aware of every beat of her heart.

If she wasn't careful, it was the breaking of her heart that she was going to be so aware of.

CHAPTER SEVEN

HOPING HE HADN'T made a major miscalculation, Boone glanced around his kitchen for his and Julia's Valentine's plans. Going to a restaurant where they'd be surrounded by amorous couples had seemed more high-pressure, though. His hope was to keep tonight light and fun, and for Julia to relax the way she had in Gatlinburg. He got glimpses of that woman at the hospital, but whether it was her way of clinging to professionalism or just to keep space between them, she fought giving him those glimpses.

When she did, those smiles melted his insides and had him craving more. Which was the story of his relationship with Julia—him craving more.

His phone rang. Seeing her number, he answered, "You're not allowed to cancel."

"Ha. That's what I thought you were doing when you called earlier." He could hear her smile, and giddiness filled him. "But perhaps unfortunately for you, I'm not calling to cancel.

Although maybe I should. I'm confused. I'm sitting in the driveway of a fancy house in a fancy subdivision rather than in a restaurant parking lot." She paused. "Why is that?"

She was there.

"Have you ever heard of one of those places where you prepare your meal, then eat it?" he asked, heading toward the front door. "This is one of those."

"I'm cooking my meal at someone's house?"

"We're cooking our dinner together. It'll be fun." Worried that she might drive away, Boone opened his front door, smiling at the image of her sitting in the driver's seat of her small sedan. After a moment's hesitation, she got out of her car and headed toward him. She'd left her hair loose, and it spilled from beneath the stretchy red hat with a fuzzy ball on top that matched her gloves and scarf. Seeing her wearing the gifts he'd given her to replace the scarf he'd used at Ober, he smiled. Was she also wearing his necklace? He'd swear he caught glimpses of the chain from time to time, but she kept the pendant tucked beneath her clothes. Anticipation built in him with every step she took toward him. Tonight was going to be a good night. A great night. He'd keep things simple just as she'd asked. They'd have good food and relax with no one around except the two of them. No pressure.

When she joined him on the porch stoop, she arched a brow. "Why don't you have on shoes?"

Glancing down at his bare feet poking out from the bottom of his jeans, the cold of the porch registering for the first time, he shrugged. "It's a casual night between friends. I didn't think shoes were necessary. You're welcome to take off your shoes, too, but I recommend waiting until we're inside because you forgot your bear blanket to warm you up."

Looking as if she might take flight, she eyed him. "This is your house, isn't it?"

"Is that a problem?" He stepped aside for her to come in.

"It's not good." Rather than turn around and leave, she entered, glancing around his foyer in a way that had him doing the same, trying to see the interior-decorator-designed room through Julia's eyes. He liked the clean, crisp white lines of his home. It was functional and a place where he could relax.

"Sure it is. Just think, you don't have to worry about anyone seeing us and making false assumptions that we're anything more than friends."

"It's been too late for that ever since we got back from Gatlinburg. Perhaps even the Christmas party. I'm sure that's how I ended up being sent home early due to low census today." Julia played with the end of the red scarf wrapped around her neck. "My being at your house isn't a good idea, Boone. I should go."

"Please don't, Julia. I give you my word that I didn't invite you here for nefarious reasons. Tonight is dinner made together by friends and us relaxing without any outside pressure of being surrounded by couples prone to PDA because of the holiday. Please stay."

Looking torn, she took a deep breath, then another. Her chest rose and fell beneath her puffy black jacket. Then she sighed. "Why do I think I'm going to regret this?"

"This is good," Julia admitted later that night, taking another bite of the pizza she and Boone had made together. He'd had all their supplies out, giving her options to create whatever kind of pizza she wanted. He'd bought a couple of different premade crusts, and they'd rolled out the one she'd picked onto a round baking stone, then piled on various toppings. Once they had it baking in the oven, they'd made salads and ate them while the pizza filled his house with its delicious scent.

He grinned. "You doubted me when I told you it would be?"

"Not really," she admitted, taking another bite of the cheesy goodness. "Short of burning, it's difficult to mess up pizza."

"Our salad was pretty good, too," he reminded her. He sat catty-corner to her at the large black-granite-topped island in the pristine white kitchen. The kitchen was the nicest she'd ever been in. She'd felt awkward as if she hadn't belonged, but he'd been so relaxed having her there that it had been difficult to think of anything other than his smile and teasing as they prepared their meal.

"Salads are also difficult to mess up," she pointed out, holding up a half-eaten pizza slice. "The real test is whatever you have planned for dessert."

His lips twitched. "Who said anything about dessert?"

"No dessert?" She tsked, then tossed some pepperoni at him. "There went our friendship. Did you learn nothing about me in Gatlinburg? Dessert is my favorite part of a meal."

Eyes sparkling, he caught the pepperoni. "Seems like I did notice that you have a sweet tooth. I'll have to come up with something. Can't have our friendship ending over sweets." He popped the pepperoni into his mouth. "Let's finish our pizza, watch television while our food settles, and then we'll see about dessert."

"So, you do have something sweet planned?"

He grinned. "Was there ever any doubt?"

That he wouldn't provide the most perfect

evening? Not really. She suspected everything Boone set his mind to went off without a hitch. He was that kind of guy, and if this had been a dinner date, she'd admit, it would have been an absolutely perfect one.

Good thing it wasn't.

Boone glanced at Julia hugging a pillow to her. He'd agonized over what entertainment to have on tap for their evening, debating a romantic comedy versus an action thriller versus something else. What type of show said "we're just two friends watching a movie together"? What type of show said that without really sliding him into a just-friends zone? Because he didn't want to get stuck there.

He'd forgone movies altogether since Julia would have to drive herself home late. He'd chosen a family rivalry game show with a host sure to elicit laughter. Laughter was good. He wanted Julia to smile and laugh. Just as she was doing that very moment. Unlike when she'd first walked into his house, she'd relaxed and had even kicked off her shoes.

Sensing that he was watching her rather than the show, she cut her gaze toward him and brushed her fingers over her lips. "What? Do I have sauce on my face or something?"

"No sauce. I was just admiring that you're enjoying yourself."

"Top one hundred survey says…you're right. I am. Thank you for dinner, even if I had to help prepare it myself." Her smile said she hadn't minded. "I'm still curious about dessert."

At her mention of sweets again, he grinned. "We'll finish watching this episode to see if they win the money. Then we'll see what we can rustle up."

"I have to help cook that, too?" She gave an exaggerated sigh.

"You'll see." He started to tell her that someday, when they were dating, he'd cook for her. Tonight, he didn't want to risk ruining their evening by mentioning anything about the future. For now, having her here was enough. It had to be since she wasn't giving him a choice.

Watching the show, they each called out their answers as the host asked the questions, laughing when they gave three of five answers exactly the same.

"Great minds," he mused.

The episode ended with the family getting the necessary points to win the money.

"Yay! They won."

"Because they gave the same answers you did," he pointed out. "Four of five of your answers were the number one pick. You should apply to be on the show."

Her face flashed pale for the briefest second. Then she shook her head. "It's a family show, Boone. I don't have five family members."

Boone cringed. He'd made the comment without thought. He knew bits and pieces of her background and hadn't gotten the impression that she was close to her family, but he hadn't realized that was because there was no family. "No aunts or uncles? No cousins?"

She shook her head. "There's just me and my dad. It's possible he has more children, but none that he's ever mentioned. Last I spoke with him there was another stepmother as well, but I haven't talked with him for a while, so that may have changed."

"He doesn't live around here?"

She shrugged. "If he did, it wouldn't be for long. He's always on the move with one job or another. He works construction and goes wherever the next job is. We've never been close."

She was such a kind, big-hearted person that it was difficult to imagine her not being close to her one remaining relative. He would have guessed she'd have clung to that relationship. That she didn't said a lot about the man who'd played a role in her existence. The guy must be a real loser.

"What happened to your mother?"

"She died." For a moment he thought he'd messed up, that she was going to clam up and find a reason to leave. Instead, she took a deep breath. "My family doesn't make for great Valentine's dinner conversation. What about you? You've mentioned parents and a brother. You're a smart guy, so if they're anything like you, then maybe you should audition for the show."

There had been a sister, as well. A beautiful, brilliant twin sister who had gotten involved with the wrong crowd and ended up taking her life, whether by accident or intentionally, by overdosing on a mixture of too many pills and too much alcohol. His heart ached with the void left at her death. A part of him had died that day. He'd known before he'd gotten the call that something was wrong, that she was gone, and he'd tried to reach her to no avail. He'd... No, he couldn't let his thoughts go down that rabbit hole. He refocused on his conversation with Julia and shook his head.

"It would never work with my family. A feud would break out, for sure. We'd all want to be in charge."

Curiosity shone on her face. "Who would win?"

"My mother," he answered without hesitation, smiling as her face flashed through his mind.

He'd run his Valentine's dinner plan by her, and she'd given her approval. She'd also been curious about the woman who he kept talking about, but who was keeping him at arm's length. Part of him wouldn't have been surprised if she'd arrived in time for dinner so she could meet Julia. He loved that overall, she seemed to be doing well these days. For so long after Amy's death, she hadn't.

"I guess she had to be tough to be the only female in the house."

She hadn't been the only one. But just as Julia hadn't wanted to talk about her mother, he really didn't want to kill the vibe between them by telling her how his twin sister had chosen drugs over life. Amy was heavy conversation, just as he knew Julia's mother was. He suspected they had a lot in common in that regard. "Mom is definitely tough. Come on. Let's eat dessert. I won't even make you do the prep work."

She eyed him as if she knew there was something he hadn't said, but after a moment she smiled. "What? I don't have to work for dessert?"

"You'll be excited to hear that I did take note of your appreciation of sweeter things and stopped by that shop just down from the hospital. I may have gone a little overboard." He opened the pantry and pulled out the goodies he'd hidden away.

Her jaw dropped. "Oh, wow. We'll never eat all that."

"We can have fun trying," he suggested. "You get first pick."

She eyed the platter that held everything from chocolate-covered strawberries to cupcakes. "This is insane. I don't want to know what this cost."

"To see that light in your eyes, I consider every penny paid a bargain."

She frowned. "Stop it with the smarmy lines."

He could argue that he'd told her the truth, but instead put the platter onto the counter. "Which do you want to try first?"

"They all look good," she mused, studying the offering. "Let's share and sample several of them." She picked a white-chocolate-covered strawberry and took a bite, catching part of the candy coating that came loose. "Oh, this is heaven."

Watching her was heaven. Or maybe that other place, because he'd broken a sweat. Friends, he reminded himself. Tonight was just two friends having dinner. Friends to lovers, he thought. Because someday Julia would admit to the attraction between them. Until then he'd play by her rules because the end prize would be worth it. Despite his frustration, he admired her dedication to obtaining her degree and having a better life than the one she'd had.

"Taste?" she asked, holding the berry toward him.

Rather than taking the berry from her, he leaned in and, gaze locked with hers, bit into the candy-coated fruit she held. She was right. It was good. But not nearly as good as what he saw in her eyes. There was a promise there. A promise of things to come that was undeniable no matter how much she'd fought it.

She finished the berry, chose a truffle, then flashed a bright smile his way. "Best Val-friends-tine dessert ever. Thank you."

"You're welcome, *friend*."

She was his friend.

She was also so much more.

"I need a favor," Boone announced six weeks later.

Trying to tamp down her awareness tingles, Julia glanced up from the medicine cart. As always, her breath caught at the sight of him. Wearing navy scrubs embroidered with his name, his stethoscope poking out of his pocket, and a smile on his handsome face, he looked like he should star on a television show. She'd sure tune in each episode.

"I'll help if I can."

"Great. Go to Memphis with me next weekend."

"What?" She'd been expecting him to ask her to round on a patient with him or to help with a procedure, not go out of town with him. Things had been good between them since Valentine's Day. He'd been friendly, sought her company at work, but hadn't pushed to spend time with her outside of the hospital, for which she'd been grateful because of her school workload. He had to know she wouldn't agree to go out of town with him, especially not to his hometown. "That's a mighty big favor. Before I say no, do you want to tell me why you need me to go?"

"I'll tell you, but not so that you can say no." He looked straight into her eyes. "It's my birthday. My parents are throwing a party."

"Then I definitely shouldn't go with you." She couldn't believe he wanted her to go, but even if the timing was right, she knew his family was well-to-do, that they were very close, and that any woman, friend or otherwise, that he brought home would be under great scrutiny. No, thank you.

"There will be cake," he said as if that would tilt the scales in his favor. After the way they'd pigged out on Valentine's, she could see why he might think that, but there wasn't enough sugar on the planet to convince her to say yes. However, there was something in his eyes that called to her, a sadness that seemed at odds with his teasing comment.

"Tempting, but no." What was with his eyes? With her sense that there was something deeper to his request? She scratched at a stray piece of tape on the cart. "Going out of town right now doesn't work. My thesis is due in two weeks. I have just over a month before graduation."

"Knowing you, your thesis is done and you're just fine-tuning your wording, obsessing over making sure it's perfect before you turn it in. I could help with that, read over it for you, make suggestions, look for weak spots, point out how amazing it is." He put his hand on her arm, his thumb grazing over her tattoo and sending zings through her. "I know I'm asking a lot, but please go, Julia. This may sound crazy, but I need you there."

Breath catching, she glanced up, meeting his eyes again. Big mistake, because she'd swear he really did need her to be there with him, which was highly confusing as she knew he got along great with his family. Why would he need her there? Torn, she bit her lower lip and dropped her hand from the cart so his would naturally fall away. She couldn't think clearly with him touching her.

"On top of everything else, my brother's bringing his girlfriend's single and interested sister." He wrinkled his nose. "She's excited to meet me and wants to know if I have a favorite dinner-ware pattern."

Was he trying to convince her to run interference or to make her jealous? She'd be the first to tell him he should meet this woman. Well, maybe. Glancing away, she mumbled, "Lucky you."

"You think? If you don't go, I'll be avoiding matchmaking all weekend."

"She may be great."

"That doesn't matter when she's not you."

At his words, Julia's knees almost buckled, and she grabbed hold of the medicine cart to steady herself on the spinning tile floor. Did he have any idea how what he was saying sounded? How much their growing closeness scared her?

"It's not uncommon for someone to bring a friend to a birthday party," he continued.

"A friend who's the opposite sex?"

"I don't discriminate based upon gender." He gave her a hopeful look. "Going home alone for one's birthday is no fun, you know?"

She'd never gone home for her birthday, so she didn't know. What would have been the point? Birthdays had never been big deals even when her mother had been alive. Whether or not her mother would acknowledge the day was always a fifty-fifty toss-up.

"Friends don't let friends go home alone." His tone teased, but his eyes still held the hint of sorrow that had her insides knotting. "I'd owe you big time."

She should say no. She knew she should. No it was. Then she was walking away.

"Okay, I'll go." That's not what she'd meant to say. Traitorous tongue. "But only if Mrs. Smithfield can watch Honey."

"Thank you, Julia." A smile spread across his face. "You're not going to regret this."

Part of her already did. What was she doing? Going with Boone was nothing short of masochistic. Pure craziness.

The following weekend, sitting in the passenger seat of Boone's car, she was still telling herself the same thing. Her thesis truly had already been written. He'd read it the previous weekend and given her a few suggestions for tweaks, but that was it. She'd made the changes and read it to him during the first part of their drive.

"The changes are perfect," he assured her.

"I thought so, too. Thank you for suggesting them."

She pulled out study cards for her certification exam scheduled for after graduation.

Boone had her read the questions out loud,

give an answer, and then they'd discuss what the book had as the correct answer. Not a quick way to study, but she was unlikely to forget any of the items they touched on during their drive.

Keeping his gaze on the interstate, he asked, "How does it feel to know that you essentially have a month left of school?"

"Assuming that I don't opt to get my doctorate," she mused, pulling out a fresh stack of question cards from the book bag in the car's floorboard.

He briefly looked toward her. "You're smart enough that if it's something you want to do, then you should. You can do anything you set your mind to."

"Except say no to you?" The teasing question slipped out, but warmth spread through her chest at his words. She was able to do anything she set her mind to. No one had ever believed in her that way. That Boone truly did... Her eyes prickled with moisture that she refused to let escape.

He chuckled. "You're an expert at telling me no."

"Just not with sticking to it," she mumbled, glancing out the passenger window. The sun had started its descent and streaked the sky with orange hues, highlighting Nashville's skyline as they moved through the city marking their halfway point.

"Why does hearing you say that make me feel as if I'm a bad guy for convincing you to go with me this weekend? My goal is for you to want to say yes, Julia, not for you to feel you've conceded defeat when we spend time together."

"It's never been a matter of me not wanting to say yes to you, Boone," she admitted, clenching the note cards.

"It must be my birthday, because that's the nicest thing you've ever said to me."

Julia snorted. "Tomorrow is your birthday, and I'm always nice to you."

"True." Nodding, he tapped his fingers against the steering wheel to some beat only he heard as they'd had the radio off while reviewing her questions. "But I appreciate what you said, Julia. It gives me hope that you won't change your mind about celebrating your graduation with me."

She stared at him a bit in awe. He was serious. It was the end of March. He was still singing the same song, that he wanted to date her, that she was worth waiting for. Rather than changing his mind, he was concerned she was the one who wouldn't go. "I just don't understand you. Why are you doing this?"

His gaze flicked toward her, then quickly returned to the road. "This?"

"Waiting months for my graduation to take me on a date when you could be dating any number of women, Boone. I'm not oblivious to the fact that other women want you."

"That makes one of us, then, because I haven't noticed, other than my brother threatening me with Leslie's sister. But even if I had noticed, it doesn't matter what other women want. You're the woman in my life, as my friend until you're agreeable to something more."

She was the woman in his life. Whether she insisted upon calling it friendship until after a calendar date, he had been faithful to his claim that he'd wait. That he had boggled her mind.

"Did you have many girlfriends prior to Dr. Cunningham?"

He shrugged. "A few during high school and university. None that lasted as long as my relationship with Olivia, though."

"Do you still talk to her?" That wasn't jealousy coursing through her body. Maybe.

"Occasionally, but she hasn't forgiven me yet. She's gone out with one of her coworkers a few times and has realized what I already had—that she and I weren't in love."

Julia let what he said sink in. "You believe love exists?"

"Don't you?"

Did she? "It's not something I've had much experience with or even thought about much."

"No past boyfriends who stole your heart?"

"None worth talking about." Most of the men in her life had been the result of being intoxicated and not knowing or caring what she was doing. With Clay, she'd been clean, on track with her Rules for Life Success, and thought she'd found someone who saw beyond her past.

"Is it wrong for me to say that I'm glad?" He shot her a sheepish grin. "It's admittedly selfish of me, but I'd like to be the first."

Heat flooded through her. What was he saying?

"I'm not a virgin, Boone." She shoved the question cards back into their box and pushed them into the book bag. "If that's what you're referring to, then just get over yourself, because I doubt you are, either."

"Calm down. I wasn't referring to sex. Nor did I intend to make you so defensive. But my statement is still true." He paused, then said, "I meant that if you're going to fall in love, I'd like it to be with me."

She'd been nervously rummaging through her bag to pull out a study guide. Now her breath caught. She straightened and gawked at him. "That would be a horrible thing for me to do. You'd break my heart."

"I'm more concerned that you're going to break mine."

Heartbeat pounding in her ears, Julia glanced

down at the book in her lap. The words blurred until she couldn't read them. No matter. Her focus was completely shot, anyway.

It would be so easy to give in to the sweetness of Boone's words. But not in a million years did she believe he'd be the one left with a broken heart.

They drove in silence. Julia pretended to study as she absently toyed with the pendant he'd given her, the diamond a stark reminder of their economic differences. Who knew what Boone was thinking?

What had possessed her to say yes to going with him this weekend? She wouldn't fit into his world. She knew that. Had she needed to see proof? A visible reminder of why she needed to say no and stick to it?

She had less than a month until graduation.

Then what?

You have to tell him everything and let him decide if he wants to spend time with someone who was once very broken and sometimes still feels barely held together. And if he does, you have to be prepared that he'll change his mind and end up leaving, anyway.

CHAPTER EIGHT

EVEN BEFORE THEY arrived in Memphis, Boone sensed how uncomfortable Julia was, but from the moment they'd pulled through the gated entrance to his parents' home, she'd clammed up. Or maybe that had happened when he'd said things aloud that he shouldn't even be thinking, much less giving voice to. The words had just slipped out. Words that needed to slip out were to tell her about Amy. He missed her, but tomorrow would be harder than most days. How could it not when he'd spent most of his life sharing birthday celebrations with her?

They arrived around ten. Introductions had been made, polite but guarded on Julia's part, pleasantries exchanged. His father, an older version of Boone minus the blue eyes he'd inherited from his mother, wore a tie and slacks, and his mother looked elegant in a slim A-line dress that hinted they'd been out for dinner. They looked happy, which did Boone's heart good, because for a long time there hadn't been many smiles. He and Julia visited with them for about half an hour. Then his mother had shown Julia to a guest room. He'd texted her good-night, but she'd not responded until that morning, when she'd asked what time she needed to be downstairs.

He'd met her at the bottom of the stairs, admiring her brightly patterned top, relaxed jeans, and sandals. She'd left her hair long about her shoulders, but he noted the band around her wrist in case she opted to pull it back later in the day.

Rather than a more intimate family meal at the breakfast nook, his mother had pulled out all the stops. They were in the large formal dining room with their longtime housekeeper, Sue Ellen, serving the meal. Justin, his girlfriend Leslie, and her sister Jacqueline were there, along with his parents, one of his dad's two brothers and his wife, and two cousins and their significant others. Excited to finally meet the woman he'd been talking about for months, his mother was dressed to a tee in black slacks and a button-down blouse. She zeroed in on Julia, wanting to know as much about her as she could. Add in everyone else's curiosity and Julia was facing nonstop questions, and it wasn't even 8:00 a.m. yet. No wonder she kept rubbing her tattoo as if it gave her magical powers to face whatever his family tossed at her.

His mother smiled at Julia between sips of her

straight black coffee. "Have you visited Memphis before, Julia?"

Pausing with her fork midair, Julia shook her head. "No, ma'am. My parents moved a lot when I was small, so it's possible, but I don't think so."

"Your parents live in Knoxville now?"

Julia shook her head. "My mother passed when I was seventeen, and my father lives wherever his current construction job is located."

His mother reached for her toast, the light catching the large diamond on her finger that his father had given her for their thirtieth anniversary a few years back. "We look forward to meeting him. You'll have to let him know that he should reach out if his work brings him to Memphis. We could meet for lunch."

Julia's gaze bounced from his mother's ring to Boone. Regret in coming was etched in her brown eyes. He'd been so blinded by his desire to have her there, to not go home alone for a party he'd rather not have, that he hadn't considered just how much his parents would overwhelm her. He wanted her meeting his family to be positive, not an uptight torture session. That weekend probably wasn't the best choice.

She fielded more questions, politely, and always with a smile that he recognized as forced. He interjected frequently, asking his dad or brother about their work, asking his mom about the shipping business, but his mother repeatedly came back to Julia.

"Julia, Robert and I have a quick errand, but afterwards, you'll have to join me in making sure the last-minute details of Boone's birthday bash are perfect while the others play golf this morning."

Not that Julia couldn't hold her own, but Boone wasn't leaving her at his mother's mercy. "Sorry, Mom, but Julia can't visit Memphis without seeing Graceland."

His mother's brow arched. "You're not going with the others?"

"Not unless Julia prefers golf to my corny Elvis impressions." He turned to Julia, willed her to meet his gaze, and was relieved when she did. "What do you think? We can slip away for a few hours, see Graceland, have lunch on Mud Island or Beale Street, and still be back in plenty of time to get ready for the party."

Forever polite, Julia glanced toward his mother. "If there's something you need, I'd be happy to help."

For a moment Boone thought his mother was going to suggest Julia stay. His father must have too, because he spoke up. "If Boone wants to show you his hometown, then that's fine, isn't it, dear?" He gave his wife a look that said she should agree. "We wouldn't want to put our son's guest to work the first time she visits our home."

Although Boone knew she wasn't happy about having her time alone with Julia foiled, his mother, ever the perfect hostess, conceded. "Of course Julia should go with Boone. I never would have suggested she stay if I'd realized Boone hadn't planned to play golf." She reached over and patted Boone's hand. "I'd thought she and I would have girl time while the rest of you did your thing."

"Maybe some other time, but Julia's mine for the day."

After visiting with his family and finishing their meal, Boone whisked Julia from the house.

"Sorry about that," he said the moment they were outside the house. "Are you an Elvis fan?"

Following him to his car in the circle drive in front of the house, Julia shrugged. "I know some of his songs."

Which wasn't a glowing review of his suggestion. "We don't have to go if you don't want to. Mom is a huge Elvis fan, so it's what first popped into my mind."

"It's fine. I've never been. Sorry. I'm still processing everything from this morning."

Before the day was over, she'd have a lot more to process. His stomach clenched at the thought of telling her about his sister, but he needed to prior to the party tonight. Someone might mention Amy, and he didn't want Julia blindsided. Still, he'd wait until later in the day.

They toured Graceland. Julia finally relaxed about midway through the tour, laughing at his Elvis impersonations and reminding him not to quit his day job.

"Your family's home is more impressive," she pointed out as they ended at the site where Elvis and his parents were buried on the property. "You could sell tours."

"We don't have a room full of gold albums." He reached for her hand and was grateful when she didn't pull away. "Come on. We'll drive down by the Pyramid. Mud Island is right next to it and we'll have an early lunch there and walk along the river."

"Oh wow. It really is a pyramid," Julia said, staring out the window at the shiny structure.

"It really is. It was once called the Great American Pyramid and was an arena, but now it's owned by a sporting goods store that takes up the first few floors. Higher up is a hotel and at the top there's a bar with an observation deck. We can go there after lunch if you'd like."

"Maybe." But her gaze had gone to the Mississippi River.

"It's really muddy, isn't it?" she said of the brown water separating Tennessee from Arkansas.

"I've never seen it that it wasn't." He drove them to a trendy, low-key café with a river view.

"I can't believe I just ate all that after such a huge breakfast." Julia patted her belly. "If I don't slow down, I won't fit into my dress for tonight."

He ran his gaze over her, liking what he saw. A lot. "I'm glad you're enjoying yourself."

"It's hard not to enjoy oneself when something is as delicious as what we just ate." She glanced at her watch. "Do we still have time to walk? I'd love to stretch my legs."

Boone nodded. "Do you want to walk by the river or along the neighborhood here? There's several interesting stores in the area if you'd like to do some shopping."

"I may need to do both." Laughing, she patted her stomach again. "But by the river would be great."

They crossed the street to walk along the sidewalk than ran beside the Mississippi River with the Hernando de Soto Bridge to their backs. Boone reached for her hand and was filled with happiness when her fingers clasped his.

The breeze coming off the river whipped at her hair. "Thank you for my Memphis mini-tour and for lunch. It's been nice."

"You weren't expecting it to be?"

Glancing out toward a barge floating down the river, she shrugged. "I wasn't prepared for how big your parents' home was. I've never known anyone who lived on an estate."

Trying to make sure he chose his words wisely as he didn't want to make light or too big a deal of his family's success, he waited until a bicycler had ridden past.

"I lived there most of my life. It was my grandparents' home. Mom grew up there. When she and Dad married, she wanted to stay, so they did. I never thought much about us living with my grandparents. I didn't realize it wasn't common for families to do so until my early teenage years."

"It's big enough for several families. I've never known someone with a live-in housekeeper, either."

"Sue Ellen and her husband originally worked for my grandparents. As you said, it's a big place. Mom and Dad have busy lives. It made sense to keep them on after my grandfather passed. They're like extended family."

She gave him a get-serious look. "Extended family who serves you breakfast and cleans up after you?"

"It's what they are paid to do, just as my father is paid to provide medical care and Mom to run the shipping company. As with most families, different members carry different roles. My parents take very good care of them and vice versa. Does that bother you?"

Continuing to walk, she stared out toward the muddy river. "Not really. It's just yet another example of how different our lives are."

"Differences can complement each other," he reminded her.

"Or pull in opposite directions."

He gave her hand a gentle squeeze. "We have more in common than you think."

"What exactly is it that we have in common?"

"We'll start with the obvious things like that we both live in Knoxville, work at the same hospital, and want to take good care of our patients. We both enjoy dessert and have a thing for fuzzy bear blankets."

She snorted. "With all that, how could I have ever doubted our similarities?"

"I know, right?" He grinned. "Plus, there's this." He lifted their entwined hands and pressed a kiss to her fingers.

She turned to him, the breeze making her hair dance about her face. The sunlight gilded the brunette strands. "What's that exactly?"

"You don't feel that flutter in your stomach the way I do when we touch? Maybe I'm wrong, but I'd swear you do, Julia. Your heart races just as mine does, and that's why you came with me this weekend."

She swallowed. "I came because it's your birthday."

"And because you care about me," he pressed.

"Of course, I care about you. We're coworkers."

Boone had been patient for months, knew he needed to continue to be patient, that if he pushed too hard, Julia might forever shut him out. Perhaps it was because they were so far away from Knoxville, or that he was on his home turf, but rather than back down, he stared into her eyes and asked, "That's all I am to you? A coworker?"

Surprise darkened her eyes. "We agreed to be friends."

Which was a sharp reminder that he shouldn't be pressing.

"True. We did. Is that all you see us ever being?"

"What is it you want me to say, Boone? That I see us going from friends to lovers after I graduate? Is it that you want me to admit that my trying to keep us as just friends is a miserable failure?"

Even as he felt shame for pressing, Boone's chest puffed at what she'd admitted with her questions. "I've not tried to hide my feelings from you. You know what I want, Julia."

She sighed. "I just don't understand why me."

"Why you?" Unable to resist, he brushed a flyaway hair behind her ear, tucking it back. The touch wasn't enough, and he cupped her face. "Because you are a good person. You're kind, a fantastic nurse and friend. Your smile lights up any room, and the feel of your skin against mine makes me aware of every nerve ending in my body."

She took a sharp intake of breath but didn't pull away.

"You're beautiful on the inside and out," he continued. "When I'm with you, the world takes on a sharper edge, as if life is somehow more in focus, more vivid in color."

"You don't know what you're saying." Her eyes closed, but she didn't pull away. Instead, she nuzzled her cheek against where he held her.

"You're wrong, Julia. I know exactly what I'm saying, what I'm feeling. We can call it friendship for however long you insist, but what's happening between us is more."

"I don't like it," she admitted, squeezing her eyes more tightly. "It scares me. You scare me."

He bent and kissed the top of her head, inhaling the vanilla fragrance he would forever associate with her. "Don't be afraid, Julia. Not of me."

"You just don't know," she began, shaking her head, then looking up. When she did so, her face was so close to his that he could feel her breath as it mingled with his own and completely intoxicated his better judgment.

His gaze dropped to her mouth, and he longed for his lips to touch hers, softly, just for a quick taste. Only, a quick taste of her mouth wouldn't be enough. All he really wanted was to pull her to him, devour her mouth, devour her body, and lose himself with her until they could no longer tell where the one ended and the other started. He lifted his gaze to hers.

What he saw swirling in the brown depths of her eyes dissolved what little willpower remained. Because shining there was longing for all the same things.

Stunned, Julia stared up at the man who had just said the sweetest things to her. Never in her life had she been praised the way Boone did. But it was the sincerity with which he said them that unwound her best intentions. Boone meant what he was saying. Wonderful, brilliant Boone wanted her and thought she was amazing.

When his head lowered to close the short distance between their mouths, she didn't stop him, couldn't have if she'd wanted to, even though they were on a public sidewalk along the Mississippi. She hadn't wanted to. What she wanted was to feel Boone's lips against hers, to have him kiss her until she was breathless and too weak to resist. She wanted him.

But just as his lips would have claimed hers,

he turned his head, and rested his forehead against hers.

"One month, Julia. As much as I want to kiss you, I won't be the cause of you breaking the promise you made to yourself and have kept all this time. When we finally kiss—and make no mistake about it, we will—I don't want you to have regrets. If I kissed you now, you'd overflow with them." He brushed his fingertips across her cheek. "Just know, doing the right thing isn't easy."

Julia trembled at his gentle touch.

"Thank you," she managed, knowing he was right. As much as she longed to feel his lips against hers, she would beat herself up over her weakness where he was concerned. Not to mention there were people out enjoying the early spring sunshine and they'd have no privacy.

Not sure what else to say, she resumed their walk along the Mississippi. She'd never believed he'd stick around until her graduation. The thought of losing the way he looked at her, the way he touched her as if she was something exquisite, was enough to fill her with great sorrow. She should never have let herself get close to him.

She shouldn't have done a lot of things.

Falling for Boone Richards was at the top of the list.

* * *

Boone couldn't win for losing. He'd have regretted kissing her as he knew doing so prior to her graduation would bother her, yet he grieved what he could have had. In the moment, she'd not only been willing, she'd wanted his kiss.

After their almost-kiss, she suggested they head toward the shops, saying she should pick up a souvenir for Stephanie and, if anything, being overly bubbly to hide the underlying sexual tension that zapped between them.

"What do you think of this?" she asked, holding up an Elvis statue. "Does this scream Stephanie or what?"

Boone started to respond, but a fairy mixed in with the plethora of touristy items caught his eye. Someone had put the item on the wrong shelf as it didn't fit amidst the various iconic Memphis baubles. Barely able to breathe, he couldn't drag his eyes from the fairy.

Noticing, Julia asked, "You have a thing for fairies?"

"No, but Amy did."

Julia's expression softened. "You've mentioned her before, but not really told me who she was."

Boone picked up the fairy and traced over a wing. "Amy was my twin sister."

"Oh," Julia gasped. "I didn't realize…you had a twin?"

He nodded. "She overdosed my senior year of undergrad."

"I'm so sorry."

"Just something else we have in common." At Julia's pale face, he continued. "My sister and your mother died the same way."

"Oh. Yes. You're right." She seemed to struggle to get her thoughts together. "Today is her birthday, too, then?"

He nodded.

She gestured toward the fairy he held. "Maybe you should buy that for her."

"Huh?"

"You're looking at me as if I'm crazy. I... I just thought that since she liked fairies, maybe you could give her that as a birthday present." As he continued to stare at her, she grimaced. "I mean, if she's buried close by, that is."

Go to Amy's grave. He'd not been since the day he'd said his goodbyes. What was the point? She wasn't there. Not really. He went to put the fairy back on the shelf, but at the last moment, changed his mind.

"We could do that."

After Julia had paid for the Elvis and a T-shirt for Stephanie, he paid for the fairy, and they left the shop. Stepping outside the air-conditioned store and into the sunny day's heat had sweat popping out over his skin. That was the reason, and not the thought of going to the cemetery.

"Did Amy have a favorite flower?" Julia asked, gesturing to the florist next to the shop. "We could get some flowers to put on her grave."

Boone's throat tightened, but he managed to croak out, "Daisies. She liked daisies."

Heart aching, Julia clung to Boone's hand as they crossed the cemetery toward where his sister was buried. Amy had overdosed close to the time Julia herself had. She needed to tell him, but she'd never seen him distraught, and that was the only way she could describe him.

"I've never been back here," he said beside her, his palm clammy, as they reached the tombstone engraved with his sister's name. "I can't believe I'm here today, with you."

"I'm sorry if I shouldn't have suggested we come here."

Inhaling sharply, he shook his head. "I should have come years ago. Instead, I've just tried to forget. Just as the rest of my family avoids saying her name like she never existed because remembering is too painful."

Tears rolled down Julia's cheeks. "I'm sorry."

"Me, too. I should have been there for her. I didn't realize she'd started using again. I was in school, but how could I have missed that? She was my twin. We shared a special bond. I should have known."

"I'm sure she knew you loved her, Boone."

"It wasn't enough. I wasn't enough to keep her clean."

"You know addiction doesn't work that way."

Sighing, he stooped and placed the fairy and daisies on the grave, next to a huge arrangement that was a mixture of daisies and other spring flowers. "Mom and Dad must pay the grounds-keeper to tend to her grave."

"You don't think they were here? That this is the errand your mother mentioned?"

His face ashen, Boone's gaze cut to hers. "You think?"

Julia looked at the arrangement, at the care that had been taken, noting the slight impression on the grave as if someone had knelt there earlier. "I may be wrong, but that would be my guess."

To her surprise, and not letting go of her hand, Boone knelt in almost the same place that Julia suspected his parents had earlier in the day. She didn't comment on his tears, nor did he comment on hers.

When he stood and they walked back to his car, hand in hand, she'd never felt closer to another person.

Nor had she ever feared losing someone so much, because how in the world could she ever tell Boone she was an addict and had overdosed the same year his sister had? That she'd been clean for seven years, but the fear of relapse was never far away?

That evening at his party, the magnitude of Boone's parents' wealth continued to shock Julia. She recognized several of the people in attendance as political figures, and she'd swear one of the guests she'd seen talking with his brother earlier had a song on the current country music hits chart. Easily, there were a few hundred people inside the huge white event tent set up behind the home. White-cloth-covered tables with floral arrangements were surrounded by chairs, and there was a dance floor near a jazzy Memphis band playing.

Standing near the center of the tent, Boone greeted friends of his or of his parents one after another. Most of the evening, he'd had his hand on Julia's lower back, keeping her close. Even through her dress's fabric, his touch burned into her, making her wonder if he'd somehow short-circuited the logic centers in her brain. How could she be so aware of everything about him? Her nerve endings seemed to start right where his fingers began.

Earlier in the afternoon, when they'd gotten back to the estate and she'd been in the privacy of her room, she'd sobbed for his loss, for her own foibles, for how connected she felt to him when she knew his interest was fleeting. She showered and dressed in a bright blue dress she'd bought at her favorite consignment shop because she thought the color matched Boone's eyes. She'd been right.

Despite how awkward she felt, she smiled to the point that her face hurt. If she could have chosen, she'd have spent his birthday with him in a more relaxed private setting, something like what they'd done on Valentine's or a simple gathering with his family.

"My mother likes you," Boone whispered for her ears only. "She told me earlier after you'd gone upstairs to change."

Wondering what had prompted his unexpected comment, she glanced up. Wearing dress slacks and a tailored button-down, he looked handsome enough to steal her breath. "She was just being polite."

Because Julia's inner strength wasn't that admirable.

"She'd tell me if she didn't like you," he assured her. Then his expression tightened. "I told her that we went to the cemetery. You were right. She and Dad had been there."

"That's good."

He nodded. "Apparently, this isn't their first time. I should have gone sooner."

She put her hand on his shoulder, empathizing with the ache in his voice.

"Listen to me being all serious when we're at a party. Sorry."

"No worries. I'm glad you went earlier." And she was glad he'd trusted her enough to take her with him. Knowing he wanted a subject change, she glanced around the extravagantly decorated tent with its A-list attendees. "This isn't what I envisioned when you said your parents were throwing you a birthday party. You have a lot of friends."

"To be fair, the guest list includes family business associates and some of dad's and Justin's hospital colleagues who I don't know or barely know."

Still looking at the partygoers, her gaze collided with Leslie's. "Your mother may claim to like me, but I don't think your brother's girlfriend feels the same."

Boone didn't even glance toward the woman, just shrugged. "I did mention that she had me picked out as her sister's next boyfriend."

"Who was in the running for Miss Arkansas a few years ago." Boone hadn't looked nearly as impressed as Julia had been at the tidbit shared during breakfast that morning. "You should at least talk to Jacqueline to see if there's any chemistry."

"Quit trying to throw me at other women."

Flustered, she took a sip from her water glass. Was that what she was doing? She didn't want him to be with someone else. But she couldn't fathom him wanting to be with her when someone so beautiful was interested in him. Whether or not the woman was beautiful on the inside remained to be seen, but on the outside, she was stunning and belonged in Boone's world. "You should at least give her a chance."

Boone frowned. "She doesn't have a chance."

"You can't know that."

"I felt nothing when I met her, when I shook her hand, or heard her laughter." He stared directly into Julia's eyes. "There's no one I'd rather have spent today with than you, Julia. Not any part of today."

Heat flooded her cheeks, and she averted her gaze and searched for words to tell him that she felt the same, that there was nowhere she'd rather have been than by his side. But another couple came over to wish Boone a happy birthday, and she pasted on a smile as he greeted one of his former classmates. As he'd done all evening, he introduced her and included her in the conversation as much as possible when she had no history with any of the guests.

His mother stepped up and placed her hand onto Julia's upper arm. "Julia, dear, can I steal you away to introduce you to my cousin Martha? She's yet to meet you. We're as close as sisters, so she simply must meet the woman in my son's life."

"We're just friends," she reminded her, but Boone's mom just smiled and linked her arm with Julia's. As at the hospital, they weren't fooling anyone. Certainly, not even Julia's heart.

Boone excused himself from his friends, but his mother shook her head. "Stay. Catch up. We girls will be just fine for a few minutes. I promise to return her to you soon."

Hoping she didn't spill the water she held, Julia walked with Boone's mother across the tent to greet a stunning woman who appeared to be in her mid to late sixties.

"Julia, this is my cousin Martha, and Boone's godmother. She's been wanting to meet you all evening. I promised I'd steal you away from my son long enough for her to have a quick chat."

Julia blinked at Boone's mother.

The woman took Julia's free hand. "I was just telling Amelia that I had to meet the woman who'd stolen Boone away from Olivia. Such a sweet girl and from such a good family. We were all so surprised when they ended things, but meeting you brings it all into focus. He's quite smitten. Good for you for landing such a prize as my godson."

Julia started to correct the woman, to say that she and Boone were just friends, as she'd done with his mother moments before, and tell her that Boone had broken up with Olivia weeks prior to asking Julia out, but doing so felt a moot point. She sincerely doubted she and the woman would ever cross paths again as Memphis was on the opposite side of the state and she didn't expect her relationship with Boone to last. She certainly had no plans to come back to Memphis. Everyone was polite enough but mostly, she suspected they wondered what he was doing with the likes of her, rather than the beautiful Jacqueline or even Olivia.

"Nice to meet you." Rather than say more, she took another sip of her water. She wanted to escape back to Boone as quickly as possible, but his mother had other ideas and dragged her from the cousin over to meet another couple, a congressman and his wife.

Julia felt more and more out of place. She realized it was her own fault. Boone's mother wasn't trying to hide her in a corner since she was taking the time to introduce her and was genuinely pleasant. The problem was that Julia just didn't belong. She and Boone would leave the following morning, heading back to Knoxville and reality.

She glanced around the room, searching for him, and feeling both a nervousness and a peace when her gaze landed on him. He was standing with his brother, Leslie, and Jacqueline, laughing at something one of them had said. All gorgeous, they appeared to be straight from a glamour magazine. Smiling up at Boone, Jacqueline touched his arm. Julia's throat tightened. He belonged with someone like the beautiful woman who came from the right family and had the right background.

"She's wasting her time."

Julia's gaze cut to Boone's mother.

"Martha was right when she said my son is smitten. You're a lucky woman. I've never seen him so infatuated."

"Not even with Olivia?" she couldn't resist asking, then was completely mortified that she had done so.

Amelia shook her head. "Olivia is a wonderful woman, but she didn't put a light in my son's eyes the way you do."

"I—thank you." Guilt hit. "I don't know what he's told you, but we're not a couple. We're…it's complicated, but we're not a couple. Not really."

Amelia laughed. "He mentioned that you insisted upon being just friends until after your graduation in May. Prior to meeting you, I had my concerns that you were playing my son. I'll always worry about my boys, but he told me about going to the cemetery earlier, and I see how you look at my Boone. You'd never intentionally hurt him."

How did she look at Boone? As if he was the most wonderful thing to ever come into her life? In so many ways he was. He was also the most dangerous and might end up being the most devastating.

"I wouldn't, but I'm not sure we fit as anything more than friends."

"Why is that? You seem to get along well."

"We…we're just so different. My background is nothing like this." She gestured to their elaborate surroundings.

"Don't be deceived into thinking things make a person less human or hurt less. My son's heart is just as easily broken as any other man's who is in love with a woman. Treasure his affection for the gift it is."

Julia's eyes widened at Amelia's mistaken insinuation. "He isn't in love with me. Truly, we're not even dating."

Boone's mother's blue gaze pierced Julia. "But you are in love with him?"

"I— No— I mean—" Julia's head swam. She questioned if the room had started spinning. "I'm not in love with Boone." She wasn't. She couldn't be. Falling in love with Boone Richards would be foolish.

Amelia smiled rather smugly.

Averting her gaze from the woman's, she sought Boone's. He still stood with his brother and the two women. She wasn't in love with him. The thundering in her chest was nothing more than anxiety that she was such a fish out of water.

Only, looking at him, recalling when they'd been standing by the Mississippi, how she'd held onto his hand while he grieved at his sister's grave, she couldn't convince herself that there wasn't truth to what Amelia said.

Perhaps sensing that they were discussing him, Boone glanced up, met her eyes, and smiled in a way that left no doubt Julia was who he wanted. But lust wasn't the same as being in love with her. Swallowing the lump in her throat, Julia smiled back. For a short while, she got to have his attention focused on her in this fairy tale alter-universe.

His gaze not leaving hers, Boone excused himself from his brother, Leslie, and Jacqueline and headed toward Julia.

"You've had Julia long enough, Mom." He slid his arm around Julia's waist, his touch possessive enough that she wondered just how much she'd revealed when their eyes had met.

"You're right. I've stolen your lovely friend

much too long and must see to my other guests."
She smiled warmly, then kissed Boone's cheek.
"Happy birthday, dear. May all your wishes
come true."

They watched her walk away and be envel-
oped in a hug by a bear of a man who Julia had
been introduced to earlier as another cousin of
Boone's father.

"You're lucky to have her." Of all the things
she'd witnessed, his mother's love and protectiveness was the thing she envied. She'd known
from the way he spoke about her that they were
close. Meeting the woman and seeing how at
ease he was with her made it even more apparent. She had no doubt that Amelia Richards was
a killer businesswoman, but with Boone she was
melted butter.

"I am." He glanced around the tent, merry
with partygoers. "Let's get out of here for a few
minutes. You want to walk in the garden?"

"Your definition of a garden and mine are two
different things, but I'd love to get some fresh air
and escape from the crowd for a few minutes,
too." She paused. "Although it's your party, so
maybe we shouldn't?"

"It's fine. No one is going to miss me if we
duck out for a few minutes."

Julia doubted that but didn't press the point because she would like a few minutes away from

the others. Once outside the tent, Boone took her hand, and she didn't pull away, but instead marveled at how his touch could hold such strength and yet simultaneously be so gentle.

They walked around the immaculate garden for a while, hand in hand, talking, Boone pointing out his favorite play places as a child and Julia trying to imagine having grown up there. Come summer, flowers and fragrances would delight the senses, but Boone was what filled the night air. His handsome image was stamped permanently into her mind. His spicy male scent teased her nostrils. The amusement in his voice. The warm strength of his hand holding hers.

She loved him. Oh, God, she loved Boone.

"Tell me what you're thinking?"

Averting her gaze in case he could see her thoughts, Julia swallowed. "I—I left your present in my room."

"I can stop by later to get it."

She shook her head. "I don't think that's a good idea. I wouldn't want your mother to get the wrong idea."

"She doesn't think I'm a saint."

"I'm pretty sure you're wrong about that."

"Maybe. She's biased since she made me." He chuckled. "As far as the present, you didn't need to get me anything."

"I agree. I saw that big table of gifts. That's

insane." She glanced toward him. "What will you do with all that stuff?"

"Obviously, you didn't look close. The gifts are items to be donated to a local shelter that my mom sits on the board for."

Surprised, Julia stopped walking and turned toward him. "Your birthday presents aren't presents for you?"

Shaking his head, he pretended to pout. "It's terrible, isn't it?"

Stunned, she stared at him. "Is that something you suggested or just something your mother did?"

"More often than not there's a reason beyond what's on the surface when it comes to the parties my mother throws. My birthday was a great excuse for her to do a fundraiser for the shelter."

"She used you?"

He shook his head. "It's not like that. She's just a wise woman who knows how to take advantage of opportunities to do good. You surely don't believe I'd want all those gifts?"

Still taking in that Amelia had used the party for good, Julia shrugged. "I guess that depends upon what they are. I mean, if there was a set of keys to that old Corvette you want, then…"

He laughed. "You might be right." Sighing, he glanced toward the tent, noisy with music. "As much as I'd rather stay out here with you, we should go back."

Still hand in hand, they walked back and had barely made it inside the tent when his brother gestured for Boone to join him.

"Here is the birthday boy now," his brother announced. "Come on. I'm about to make a toast in your honor."

Boone glanced toward her, but Julia shook her head. She didn't want to be in the limelight of his toast, so she stepped back as he joined his brother near the band.

His brother made a big speech, causing several to laugh, including Julia.

"Now, if we could convince him to move back to Memphis," Justin continued.

Boone chuckled, listening as Justin recounted a story from their childhood. Would Boone eventually return to his hometown? It wouldn't surprise her. He probably had a contract with the hospital, and as soon as it ended, he'd relocate.

A woman coughed, causing Julia's gaze to shift that way. Next to her, Amelia's cousin Martha coughed again in an obvious attempt to clear her throat. Julia stepped closer.

"Are you okay?" she whispered, not wanting to draw attention to them during Justin's birthday toast to Boone.

Martha held up her hand, as if saying Julia

should hold on a minute, but whatever she'd been trying to clear with her cough must have shifted to block the woman's airway completely, because her hands went to her neck.

"Martha?" The woman's eyes watered, and her face reddened. "Is there something lodged in your throat? Are you choking?"

Martha gave a panicked nod, appearing more and more distressed.

"I'm going to do the Heimlich." Instinct kicking in, Julia moved behind the woman, wrapped her arms around her, placed her hands into the proper position, and gave a quick thrust. Nothing happened, so she gave another.

Still clutching at her throat, Martha sputtered. At this point, several nearby guests had realized that something was happening and had turned to observe what Julia was doing.

Ignoring them, she gave another hard chest thrust. Whatever had been stuck in Martha's airway shot forward. The woman gasped for air and simultaneously burst into tears. Relief swamped Julia so intensely that she fought doing the same. Helping the woman to a chair, she had her sit and knelt in front of her.

"It's okay. Just take deep, calming breaths," she encouraged, clasping Martha's hand.

Amelia rushed to them. "What's going on?"

"Martha got choked, and this woman saved her life," someone in the crowd said.

Glancing up, Julia saw they were surrounded by people. Justin had finished his speech, and most of the guests had lifted their glasses in cheers. Within seconds, though, Boone pushed through the crowd, as did his brother. Kneeling next to Julia in front of Martha, he began checking her. As Boone and Justin were both doctors, Julia started to move out of their way, but Boone stopped her. Justin had pulled out his phone and was calling for emergency services.

"Stay," he told Julia. Then he said to Martha, "I'm going to ask some questions. It's okay to just shake your head yes or no if you don't feel like verbally answering yet. Can you do that?"

The sobbing woman nodded.

"Can you take a deep breath?"

Martha did so, taking several.

"Do you feel as if anything is still hung in your throat, possibly blocking your airway?"

She started to shake her head, then looked uncertain. "I don't know."

Boone placed his ear against her chest, listening over multiple areas of her lungs. "I think whatever it was cleared, but you need to be checked to make sure your throat is okay. Sometimes dislodging a foreign object can cause trauma. Justin has called for an ambulance."

Still visibly shaken, Martha nodded. "I was so scared. I thought I was going to die."

"But you didn't, and everything is going to be okay." Boone placed his hand over where Julia clasped Martha's. "Thanks to Julia, you're going to be fine."

CHAPTER NINE

ALTHOUGH JUSTIN TRIED to convince Boone to let him go instead, Boone insisted upon riding in the ambulance to the hospital with Martha, saying he had a lot more experience with intubating someone if Martha's throat swelled. As a pediatrician, Justin conceded.

After the ambulance pulled away with Martha and Boone, Julia expected the partygoers to say their good-nights, but they didn't. All expressed their empathy for Martha, their appreciation of Julia's quick action, but then seemed to go back to enjoying the party as if nothing had happened.

Amelia gave Julia the biggest hug, thanking her, but even she had stepped back into the role of the perfect hostess. Julia supposed that since Martha should be fine, sending the guests home didn't make sense. But having played a direct role in the woman's life-threatening dilemma, she felt exhausted. As an hour turned into two with Boone still not back, she longed to go to her room. Deciding that no one would miss her if she slipped off for a bathroom break and a few minutes to just decompress, she headed into the house and toward the stairs that would lead to that section of the home.

"Wait," a young woman she'd met earlier called, chasing after Julia, drink in hand and sparkly designer bag bouncing at her side.

Saddened that her mini-escape had been interrupted, Julia pasted on a smile. She'd been introduced to so many different people that she had to rack her brain to recall the blonde's name. Patricia Brewer. Her family ran a popular restaurant chain. She'd batted her eyelash extensions at Boone so many times Julia suspected he might suffer from windburn.

"That was so cool what you did earlier." The woman's words slurred slightly, indicating she'd had a lot more to drink since their earlier interactions. "I could never have done that."

"With proper training, you could," Julia promised, looking at the woman more closely. Her pupils were constricted. Alcohol usually dilated one's pupils. What else had the woman taken, and how much, so that it counteracted the alcohol on her breath? "You should sign up for a CPR class. They teach the Heimlich and other lifesaving techniques. You don't have to be in the medical field."

"Oh, I'd be too nervous." The woman sipped

from her drink, raising Julia's concern for her safety. Drinks had flowed freely at the party, but she'd not noticed anyone grossly over-imbibing. This woman was intoxicated from something beyond what was in her glass.

"Are you okay? Will anyone be driving you home?" She wasn't sure what measure had been taken to prevent anyone from driving home who shouldn't, but Julia suspected someone as detail-oriented as Boone's mother had something in place. "It's Patricia, right?"

The woman blinked, causing another wind-storm with her long lashes. "I rode here with a friend and am fine."

Julia wasn't convinced. Since Patricia wasn't driving, she wasn't sure what more she could do other than keep an eye on her and maybe get her to drink some water to sober up a little. Re-gardless, the woman's droopy-eyed expression concerned her. "Mixing alcohol with other sub-stances can be dangerous."

"Quit being a party pooper." Patricia waved off Julia's concerns, sloshing some of her drink onto the gleaming hardwood floor in the process. Julia glanced around, but short of using her dress hem, there wasn't anything to clean the spill.

"I was heading upstairs to freshen up," she told the young heiress, planning to excuse her-self from the awkward situation. "I'll grab tissue to clean that on my way back down. Can I bring you a water?"

"Oh, girl, I could totally use a bathroom break, too. I know they have those bathroom trailers set up outside, but I'd much rather go in here, you know?" To Julia's surprise, the woman draped her arm over her shoulder as if they were the best of friends, then giggled. "I'm Patricia, by the way."

"Um…yes, we met earlier." Julia cut her gaze to the woman, who was an excellent reminder of yet another reason Julia appreciated her sobriety. Crazy to think this could have once been her, that she'd not cared about her behavior or whether she was in control of her actions, or even if she remembered them the following day.

"My family has been close with the Richards for a long time."

Julia wasn't sure about having the woman come to her guest room, but she would let her go to the bathroom and hopefully convince her to change over to water. Maybe after she'd returned the woman to the party and cleaned up the spilled drink, she could escape for that bit of a break.

When they reached her room, Julia sat on the bed and let the woman go first, then went herself. When she came out of the bathroom, the woman was closing the top to a pill bottle.

Sweat instantly coated Julia's skin. "What did you just take?"

Shrugging, Patricia dropped the bottle into her purse and pulled out a cigarette package, tapped a cigarette free, then stuck it unlit into her mouth. "Just something prescribed. It's not a big deal."

Cringing at the thought of the woman possibly lighting the cigarette where the fumes would be trapped into her guest room, Julia equally wanted to make sure the woman was okay and to get her out of her room. She suspected the Richards didn't allow smoking in the house, and she sure didn't want her room to have the lingering scent. "I don't know you, but I do know how dangerous mixing medications with alcohol can be."

"I'm fine." She eyed Julia from where she sat on the bed. "Lighten up and let a girl have a good time. Just because Amy overdosed doesn't mean it's going to happen to the rest of us."

Julia winced at the woman's crassness. Had she herself really ever been like this?

"I work in an ICU where we see way too many overdose victims. Many of the overdoses were accidental. Please understand that I worry when I see someone putting herself at risk." Julia swallowed as memories flooded her. Memories of so many mistakes she'd made. Memories that made her panicky inside. "I volunteer at a recovery home. I imagine there's similar places in Memphis where you could get help."

"You have me all wrong. I don't have a problem." Eyeing Julia, Patricia took a long drag off her unlit cigarette, then slowly blew out as if the cigarette truly had been burning. "Other than these things. They're what I'm trying to quit. Nasty habit, but just having it in my mouth helps, you know?"

Nothing she said was going to get through to the woman. "I hope you're right, that you truly don't have a problem. Let's head back outdoors to the party."

"You don't know what it's like." Patricia stood, then walked past Julia to toss her cigarette into the bathroom trash. "You just don't know.

"I know better than you think." Julia got her purse from the dresser and pulled out a business card with a number she knew by heart. "This is a twenty-four-hour hotline where you can get help. Maybe tonight is a one-off and you don't normally mix alcohol and medications. But the pill you just took wasn't your first one of the night. If you aren't able to stop on your own, call, get help, check yourself in somewhere," she implored. "Don't risk your life."

The woman took the card, glanced at it, then flicked it onto the floor. "Who are you to judge me?"

"No one." Once upon a time, she'd have acted the same way if someone had suggested she get sober. No one had. Not until Julia had lain in an

ICU and a compassionate nurse had made all the difference in the world. Julia strove to pay that kindness forward through her job and her volunteer work but recognized there was nothing anyone could do until a person was ready to make a change.

Sadly, sometimes they never got that opportunity.

Tossing his keys to one of the valets his mother had hired to keep parking from becoming chaos on the lawn and to call for transport for any intoxicated guests, Boone headed into the house. Cutting through was the quickest way to get back to the tent. He knew Julia understood that he'd needed to go with Martha, but he shouldn't have left her for so long at a party where she essentially didn't know anyone. As soon as he'd been sure Martha was stable with her husband and daughters by her side, he'd excused himself.

He didn't find Julia in the tent, and realized no one had seen her for a while. He texted but got no answer, so he headed into the house to go to her room.

"Julia? It's me." He knocked on her bedroom door. Was she inside? He pulled out his phone to try calling again.

The door swung open. Looking as if she'd just

awakened, she blinked. "You're back. You should have called. I'd have come down."

"I tried. Everything okay?"

"I came up to decompress a few minutes and dozed off." She yawned, then gave a guilty smile and tucked a stray strand of hair behind her ear. "Sorry. I can't believe I fell asleep. How's Martha?"

"They admitted her for observation, but her imaging didn't reveal any tears or significant trauma."

True relief showed on her face. "That's wonderful."

"Thank you for acting so quickly. You saved her life."

Her cheeks pinkened. "If I hadn't, someone else would have."

"Don't discount your actions. You saved her, and for that I am grateful." Feeling a little awkward at standing in her bedroom doorway, he asked, "Ready to go back down, or do you want to call it a night?"

"Going back to the party is fine. Just let me check that I don't have mascara smudges and look like a raccoon." She turned, then glanced back at him with excitement shining in her eyes. "Oh! I should give you your birthday present while you're here."

Glad that he wasn't having to bid her an early good-night, he grinned. "I admit I'm curious."

"It's just a little something that I thought would make you smile." Her own smile faded to a more hesitant expression. "But if you want to hurry back to the party, I can give it to you in the morning."

"I'm looking forward to opening your gift, Julia." Boone was in no rush to get back to the party. Everything that required his presence had ended long ago. He suspected the whole shebang would wind down within an hour as his mother would shut things down at midnight.

"You may be disappointed." She walked over to her bag and pulled out a small box. Her smile back, she held out the gift. "Happy birthday, Boone."

Having her here with him was the best gift. Boone opened the package. Inside was a toy version of his dream car. It was even the right color. He laughed. "This is great. Where did you find it?"

She looked pleased that he liked his gift. "Online."

He removed the car from the packaging, then spun one of the tiny wheels. "It's perfect." Just as she was. How fortunate was he to have met someone as kind, thoughtful, compassionate, talented, and smart as she was? Not to mention beautiful. Because with her smile brightening her face, no one could convince him that a more beautiful woman had ever lived.

"I'm not sure about perfect, but as close as my budget allows for." Happiness glittered in her eyes. He took her hand, giving it a gentle squeeze. "Thank you, Julia. For everything, especially for coming home with me this weekend and all the ways you've made this weekend special. I appreciate you going to the cemetery with me more than I know how to express. Other than what happened with Martha, it's been a wonderful birthday."

"You're welcome. Thank you for inviting me." To his complete shock, she stretched up on tiptoe and pressed a soft kiss to his cheek. When she pulled back, her cheeks pink, her gaze met his. "Happy birthday, Boone."

Explosions of color swirled through him, heating his insides until he wanted to burst from the intensity of her innocent kiss. There was little innocent about the way he wanted to pull her flush to him and kiss her until they were both breathless. Yet there was something so precious about the gesture that went way beyond the physical attraction he felt for her. He didn't know how to label those feelings, just that he'd never felt that way about anyone, and he longed to delve into exploring what was happening between them.

She'd graduate in May. He just had to be patient a little while longer. He just had to— His gaze landed on an oblong white tablet on the floor just at the edge of the bed.

Mind racing, he picked up the pill. Who had last stayed in the room, and how had the cleaners missed the tablet? His stomach knotted. What if someone with a child had been given the room? Julia looked at what he held, and he started to apologize that the cleaners had missed something that could have been treacherous if his parents had guests with a small child stay in the room. The guilt he saw on her face had sweat covering his skin.

He'd seen that look before on Amy's face.

Boone thought the pill was hers! Throat tightening, palms clammy, heart pounding, Julia shook her head in denial before he gave voice to what was clear on his face. "That's not mine. A woman was in my room earlier. Patricia Brewer. She wanted to use the bathroom. She must have dropped it while she was here."

Expression tight, Boone's jaw shifted. "There's bathrooms set up outside for guests. There was no reason for anyone to come to your room."

"Yes, I know, but—"

"Is that why you were asleep? Because you were doing drugs with Patricia? How could you do that, knowing what hell I went through with Amy's overdose?"

Julia took a step back. "I didn't do drugs with her, Boone. She had been drinking, but her eyes were constricted. I knew she'd taken something that had counteracted the effect of the alcohol, and I was concerned about her safety. She must have dropped the pill while I was in the bathroom."

Her words finally seemed to sink in.

"I'm sorry. I'm overreacting, aren't I? Going to Amy's grave today got to me more than I realized." He appeared gutted. "It caught me off guard to spot that pill on your floor, and then you looked— I don't know why my parents allow Patricia anywhere near this place. Mom believes she's recovered, but obviously she's not. Sometimes I think no one truly recovers from addiction." Boone raked his fingers through his hair. "You would never do drugs. I know that."

Did he really believe recovery wasn't possible? Julia's knees wobbled, and she sank onto the edge of the bed. Taking a deep breath, she knew what she had to do. What might destroy her world, but she had no choice. Not telling him beyond this moment would be unforgivable.

"About that… The truth is, Boone, that I would do drugs." Nausea rose up her throat as she forced herself to continue. "I would and I have."

Boone's face paled. "What are you saying?"

"I'm an addict."

"What do you mean, you're an addict?" Disbelief showed on his face along with a whole myriad of emotions that cut her to the quick. "You lied to me? You said this wasn't yours. Are you using drugs in my parents' home?"

"No. Sorry. I didn't word that well." Grateful she was sitting, she shook her head. "My thoughts aren't together. I hadn't planned to have this conversation tonight."

"You're an addict?" he repeated, his voice incredulous. "Telling me that is what you hadn't planned to do tonight? I'm so confused. What's going on, Julia? Are you trying to sabotage us again? Is that what this is?"

Embarrassed, and fighting devastation at the disillusionment she saw in his eyes, she lifted her shoulders. "I'm an addict, one who is seven years in recovery, but I don't fool myself that I'm not just one slipup from losing control. It's a battle I fight every day, and imagine I will for the rest of my life."

Boone grimaced as he held up the pill. "This isn't yours, but you'd have taken it if I hadn't found it?"

Would she have? She eyed the tablet in his hand. She knew exactly what it was and what milligram. She knew the way it would make her feel, the rush, knew the agony as it cleared from her system and her body craved more. She knew the risks.

"At one time, I would have. Pain medications were my drug of choice." Not for any physical pain she'd had, although she certainly hurt when coming off her high. Her pain had run much deeper than her body, to her very core. "But I took whatever I could get my hands on. I wasn't picky on how I numbed myself to the world."

Boone shook his head as if to dislodge her words. "I can't believe you're saying these things. You work in the ICU. You know what drugs can do to a person."

Knowing she had to tell him everything, she pressed on, wondering if the disgust would ever dim from his beautiful blue eyes, if he could ever look at her and see anything beyond her past. "I overdosed at twenty years old, Boone. I was in the hospital for weeks, then lived at a recovery house for several years, even after starting school. I've worked hard to stay clean since that time, sticking to the rules I wrote for myself to have a successful life."

"Yet you have a pill in your room."

"A pill that I told you wasn't mine." She tried not to flinch at the distrust in his expression. His face morphed into Clay's, and she heard the hateful words he'd once said to her, that he'd never be willing to tie himself to someone like her. Hadn't she always known Boone would feel the same? How foolish she'd been to let herself get caught up in his attention, to deep down want to believe that maybe, just maybe, Boone was different, that he could love all the parts of her, past, present, and future. She never should have allowed any of this to happen. The pain ripping through her chest was her own fault.

"It's not that I don't believe you. It's just—" Rather than finish whatever he was going to say, he paused, closed his eyes, and looked completely tortured. When he opened his eyes, sadness darkened them. "You know what happened with Amy, that she said she was clean, but then overdosed. You saw me today, how wrecked I am inside at losing her." His voice broke. "You should have told me months ago."

She should have told him. Yet her defenses were in full force and refused to lower. She'd worked hard to be a better person, and for what? To still never be good enough?

"I don't owe you a detailed history of my past, Boone. From the beginning, I told you that I didn't date, that you should move on to someone more suited. I never pursued you."

"So, I only have myself to blame for thinking you were different?"

She fought flinching. "If by different you

mean perfect and without flaws, then yes, you should blame yourself."

He did flinch, which pierced deep into her resolve. She could take no more. She just wanted to be home, to snuggle with Honey, and cry until there were no more tears to be shed.

Boone paced across the room, turning to look at her with red-rimmed eyes that continued the beating upon her heart. She'd caused this. Why had she ever thought that she might deserve happiness after the bad things she'd done?

"Stephanie mentioned your past a few times," he mumbled, perhaps to himself as much as to her. "I thought she meant your less than ideal childhood. I never dreamed she meant something like this."

Something like this. As if she were sullied and could never be good enough no matter how long she stayed clean. Clay had thought so. Apparently, Boone did, too. Maybe they were right.

She couldn't breathe. "Blame me. It's all my fault. I'm the one with the tainted past who is so far from perfect." She very seriously doubted he'd ever made such poor choices that he'd been homeless or so drugged out that he couldn't remember chunks of time. She knew better than to have let him behind her defenses. She'd subconsciously dared to dream when she should have strictly stuck to her rules. If she had, she'd be safe at home and not feeling as if her heart had been shredded. Fighting to keep from bursting into tears, she shrugged. "What does it matter at this point?"

"Because we'd never work anyway?" Hurt shone in his eyes.

"I've always known we wouldn't," she reminded him. "Now you understand. I'm sorry I didn't tell you everything sooner."

"You never gave us a chance, did you, Julia?" His expression tight, he walked over to the door, opened it, then paused. "You deceived me by omission and then crushed me with the truth. That's a lot for a man to take in. We'll talk tomorrow, but not until we've left here. I don't want my family hurt by this. Good night, Julia."

He closed the door behind him with a resounding click that echoed through Julia's heart.

If it was her heart breaking, why was it her eyes that leaked?

CHAPTER TEN

"WHERE DO YOU get off on leaving the way you did? Do you have any idea how upset I was when I realized you'd just left? How did you manage that, anyway?"

The following Monday morning, Julia glanced down the hospital hallway at several of her co-workers looking toward her, and she winced. She'd known she would eventually come face-to-face with Boone, that there was no avoiding it short of quitting her job—which she'd considered but decided against. She had run from her problems, her past, long enough. She'd known he'd be upset that she'd left, but no matter how many times she'd played the scenario over in her mind, she hadn't been prepared for the reality.

"I called for a hired car." She took a deep breath, then looked him directly in the eyes. Any affection he'd held for her was long gone, and only anger shone in the blue depths. Fine. Let him be angry. She was angry, too. Angry that he'd turned out to be no different from Clay, that he'd made her believe he cared for her. He'd only been caught up in the shiny package and not the depths of who she was.

"You taxied from Memphis to Knoxville?" he asked incredulously.

As many tears as she'd cried, she could have floated home.

"I taxied to a bus station and took a bus home, then called for another hired car to drive me from the station to my apartment." The drive had taken about nine hours to complete thanks to several stops along the way, but it felt as if it had been a hundred hours. But on that ride, she'd realized a lot of things about herself, who she was now, and who she was no longer going to be. Yes, she had a past. Who didn't? But she wasn't that person anymore. Rather than be ashamed of who she'd been, she was proud of the woman she'd become. If Boone, or any other man, couldn't see beyond her past, then they didn't deserve the woman she was today. "We're at work. This isn't the place to have this conversation."

"You should have thought of that when you repeatedly ignored my phone calls and text messages yesterday other than to message once to say that you were fine." His jaw worked back and forth, and then he blew out an exasperated breath. "*Fine*. Does anyone ever mean it when they use that word?"

He was right. She had set herself up for him to confront her at work. Although, truthfully, she'd thought he'd pretend she didn't exist rather than causing a scene. His ego must have taken a huge blow because she'd left Memphis on her own.

"I can't speak for others, but I am fine, Boone." If she knew nothing else about herself, it was that she was a survivor, and she would survive having fallen for him, too. She didn't need to check off all the items in a life success rule book to know she was a success. She got up every day and tried to make a difference in the world. Too bad if he couldn't see that. Maybe she even understood why he couldn't because of what had happened with Amy. Either way, she wouldn't let him or anyone else make her feel subpar ever again. She'd made mistakes, and she'd learned from them and become a better person. "If you'll excuse me, I need to check on my patient."

He rammed his hands into his scrub pockets, almost as if he had to do so to keep from reaching out. "That's it? You're just walking away from me?"

"Don't pretend that it's not what you were going to do to me."

His gaze narrowed. "I wouldn't have left you in Memphis."

"No, I didn't think you would, but I didn't want to be trapped in a car with you for six hours, either, when we both knew whatever this was between us was over."

He glanced toward their coworkers, then quickly looked away and pretended they weren't glued to what was happening. His gaze once again meeting hers, he stared at her for a long moment, then sighed. "Okay, have it your way. This isn't how I would have chosen things to be, but I could never put my family through the uncertainty of whether you'd relapse, anyway, so maybe it's for the best."

His words were echoes from Clay's lips and drove ice picks into her chest, piercing her heart. Surely it must be bleeding profusely. So much for her earlier bravado. No matter. As in the past, she'd rise out of the ashes. She rubbed her thumb across the tattoo on her wrist, then reached into her pocket to pull out a jeweler's box.

Barely able to continue to meet his eyes full of disillusionment, she called upon all her strength. "Lucky for you that you don't have to worry about that."

With her softly spoken words, she put the box into his hand, then walked away, head held high, and heart shattered.

Frustrated and watching Julia disappear into a patient's room, Boone closed his fingers around the jewelry box, knowing the diamond phoenix pendant was inside. How could she be so blasé about the fact that she'd left Memphis in the middle of the night without telling him? Her succinct text saying she was fine but wouldn't be riding back to Knoxville with him had completely gutted him.

He'd barely slept, thinking over the things he'd say to her while they drove back to Knoxville. He could make her understand why a relationship between them was impossible. After Amy's overdose, how could he risk that happening again? Instead, Julia had been gone, stunning him and his family, and he'd had six hours to stew.

Maybe she was right. Maybe it didn't matter, and at this point, the less said the better.

He slipped the jeweler's box into his pocket. He'd not wanted the pendant back. How could he when the phoenix belonged around her lovely neck? Had she taken great delight in shredding the calendar with his penciled-in dates?

"What did you just do?" Stephanie's question from behind him cut into his thoughts.

"It's not what I did that's the problem, is it?" Boone turned to meet Stephanie's accusing glare. "Rather than just saying that Julia had had a rough past, you could have gone into a little more detail and saved us both a lot of heartache."

"Really? That's what you think?" Stephanie's jaw dropped, and then her gaze narrowed. "If you can't see her for the beautiful person she is inside and out, then you don't deserve her."

Boone winced. "You don't understand."

He'd meant that they wouldn't have been in the situation that had happened Saturday night, that he'd have had all the facts. Then again, maybe if he'd told Stephanie about Amy, she would have revealed Julia's past. Or maybe she'd sensed there was a deeper problem, and that's why she hadn't told him.

"There is nothing you can say that will justify you hurting Julia," Stephanie spat at him. "Nothing. She's a better person than the both of us." Looking as if she'd like to say a lot more, scream a lot more, she took a deep breath instead. "To think I encouraged her to embrace what was happening with you because I thought you truly cared for her. Thanks for being as big a jerk as Clay."

"Who's Clay?"

"You'd have to ask Julia that, but I doubt she'd tell you, because you and he seem to have a thing for ripping the wings off of butterflies."

Was that how Stephanie saw him? How Julia saw him? As someone who had crushed a fragile being's spirit? Stephanie might see Julia as fragile, but her strength was one of the things Boone admired most. Still, what had this Clay done to her, and why did he want to punch the guy in the face for whatever it had been?

"How am I the bad guy here?" He'd been down this road with Amy. Knew how long someone could hide a problem until it was too late. How could he ever trust that Julia wouldn't relapse? His family had been devastated when Amy died. He couldn't risk putting them through that. Or maybe it was himself who he couldn't put through that again. "Julia didn't tell me the truth. Lying by omission is still lying. I'm not wrong to try to protect my family."

"Protect them from Julia?" Scoffing, Stephanie gave him an *are you crazy?* look. "Yeah, great job. She made herself vulnerable to you, and you stabbed her straight through the heart. You should be so proud."

"She's the one who walked away." His anger battled with so many other emotions. "She kept secrets, big secrets, and then she just left. Bash me if you want, but if anyone got crushed here, it's me."

Stephanie stared at him a moment. "Are you trying to convince me of that? Or yourself?"

Good question, and one that haunted Boone long after Stephanie had spun on her heel and walked away.

"Riley Sim," the dean announced over the loud-speaker at the University of Tennessee graduate school commencement ceremony the first Saturday in May.

Knowing she was next, Julia's knees shook. She didn't know how she was still upright. Her legs felt like jelly. Yet her head was held high. She'd done it. She'd turned her life around, gotten her bachelor's in science in nursing, held a respectable job she loved while attending graduate school to earn her master's degree, volunteered at a recovery home, and made a difference in the world. Check. Check. Check. Her Rules for Life Success book was full of check marks.

"Julia Lea Simmons."

An air horn blared from the audience section where a bunch of loud whoops and cries of "Julia!" sounded. Smiling at her friends' support, Julia crossed the stage, shook the dean's hand, accepted her diploma, and exited on the opposite side to make her way back to her seat. Inside, she was happy dancing. On the outside her smile had to be blinding people all the way to the top row of bleachers.

Hands trembling, she clutched the emblem of her hard work. Pride filled her.

After the ceremony, Stephanie, Derek, and the others who'd come to celebrate with her made their way through the crowded area where graduates, friends, and family were gathering for congratulations and photos.

Spotting them, warmth spread through her chest. She might not have blood family at the ceremony, but her tribe was there. Her people. She loved them and they loved her, even knowing all about her past and many flaws.

Swiping at happy tears, Julia nodded. "I'm so glad y'all came."

"Of course we came. I am so proud of you!" Stephanie squealed, wrapping her arms around her in a big hug as they jumped around together.

"We all are," Becky added as she and Dawn joined in on the hug and happy wiggling.

"Okay, guys, let's get in on this group hug," Cliff teased, spreading his arms around them, and causing them all to laugh as they pulled apart. "Seriously, Julia, you amaze me."

"Yeah, the only negative is that you've turned in your notice at the hospital." Stephanie poked her lip out in a big pout. "I am going to miss you so much."

There was that. Julia would miss the ICU crew terribly, too, but that a position had opened at the Knoxville House of Hope right as she'd graduated had been fortuitous. She'd considered staying at the hospital on an "as-needed" basis, working a couple of shifts per month, but ultimately, she'd decided that would only prolong the torture of being near Boone.

Boone. Oh, how her heart ached at his absence from her life the past month.

Part of her had hoped he'd be at her ceremony

and hear her valedictorian speech about rising from one's ashes and achieving anything one set their mind to, no matter their past. That he'd choose to be there along with their friends, celebrating this huge milestone. But his wasn't one of the smiling faces congratulating her. When they'd had to interact at the hospital, he'd been cordial, professional, but he'd been little more than that for weeks. For the most part, he'd avoided her and vice versa. No way would he have come today and risk giving her false illusions that he had any interest in her.

That was all right. She was okay and would continue to be okay. She didn't need Boone to have a happy life. She was happy. Mostly. Now she'd be able to make an even bigger difference in the hope that others would be able to overcome their addiction and achieve recovery, too. She'd serve as an example. If she could do it, anyone could.

Determined she was going to focus on the day's many positives despite the hole in her heart that only Boone could fill, she smiled, posed for photos, and embraced her friends and the love they showered on her. No matter what, she would soar.

"Um… Julia?"

Julia didn't need to turn to see what Stephanie was looking at. Who she was looking at. Julia's insides had gone into full Boone-is-near mode. Why was he there? Swallowing, she spun toward where her friend was staring.

There, holding the world's largest bouquet of red roses, stood Boone.

Boone had stood back, allowing Julia to enjoy her moment with their friends prior to making his presence known. He'd not sat with them, but they'd known he was there, known that he couldn't miss one of the most important days of Julia's life.

Wearing her cap and gown and the happiness that came with success, she'd never looked more beautiful. "Congratulations, Julia."

"Thank you." Her brown eyes studied him. "I wasn't expecting you to be here." Her gaze moved past him to the people he'd sat with during the ceremony. "Any of you." Confusion clouded her face. "But I don't understand why you're here."

"I couldn't keep them away," Boone began, thinking perhaps his family should have stayed in the background. "But they have orders to not say a word until I've gotten out the words I've spent the past four weeks trying to perfect."

He moved closer to her and handed her the flowers. "These are for you."

She glanced down at them, then back up at him. "Thank you. They're lovely."

"This is also for you." He reached into his pocket and pulled out the jeweler's box that held her pendant.

"I can't take that back."

"It belongs to you, Julia. It has from the moment I saw it. You are a bright and burning flame that lights up the world for all those lucky enough to be in your presence." He opened the box and removed the necklace. "Allow me?"

Looking hesitant, she finally nodded. He moved behind her and slipped the chain around her neck, then closed the clasp. "There," he said, coming face-to-face with her again. "It's back where it belongs."

"Thank you. I admit, I'd gotten used to wearing it as I hadn't taken it off until that night in Memphis." Her cheeks flushed from her memories. "I shouldn't have left like I did."

"I didn't deserve for you to stay," he admitted. Then, glancing around at all their friends and his family hanging upon his every word, he said what they'd come to hear. "I messed up, Julia. I could go into all the reasons I did so, but none of them stand up to the reality that I lost you in the process. Nothing is worth not having you in my life."

Her throat worked, catching his eye, and he continued. "You once agreed to allow me to take you out to celebrate your graduation. I'd like to hold you to that."

She blinked. "You want to take me to dinner? That's what this is? A date?" She grimaced. "Don't think me ungrateful for the flowers and for having my necklace back, but I've already been with a man who didn't see my worth, Boone. From the point I told him about my past, that's all he could see when he looked at me. I'm much more than that and won't live being treated that way. I deserve better."

"I don't see your past when I look at you, Julia." He took a deep breath and hoped his next words conveyed all the things in his heart. "It's my future I see."

"I don't understand."

"I'm in love with you, Julia. I think I have been from the moment you stripped me of my bear blanket." He smiled at the memory. "I don't deserve forgiveness for what happened in Memphis, but I'll spend the rest of my life making up for it if you'll give me the chance."

Stephanie and the girls let out a collective *aww*. Boone's mother clasped her hands together and the guys all stared at Julia, waiting for her response, but none so intently as Boone.

"You're in love with me?"

"I figured the roses would give me away."

"Because they're red?"

"They stand for love."

Glancing down at the flowers, she closed her eyes. When she opened them, she nodded. "You're right, they do." The moment the words were out of her mouth, she shoved the flowers back into his hands. "Here."

She'd given back his flowers. She didn't want his love. He'd blown any chance he had of winning her heart because of how he'd handled her sharing her darkest secret with him.

He shook his head. "No, I won't take them back, Julia. They're yours."

Her gaze met his, and what he saw had his breath catching. "Red roses are for love, Boone."

"You love me?"

"With all my heart."

Around them, their friends and family clapped and whistled, but Boone focused only on Julia. "I love you, Julia."

He pulled her to him and, handing her roses to an about to burst Stephanie, Julia willingly went, cupping his face between her hands. "No more secrets, Boone. I promise to always be honest with you, even when the truth may not be so easy to share."

"And I promise to always support you, Julia. In your career, in your school, in your sobriety, and in your moments of weakness. I'll be there to keep your fire burning so you can continue to shine."

And he did.

EPILOGUE

WITH HER BEAR blanket wrapped around her, Julia shook the Christmas package Boone had just handed her. The box was of a similar size as the previous year's gift, and the rattle inside was suspicious.

She glanced up at him and guessed, "Did you get me another calendar? I've really enjoyed checking off our dates on last year's."

"You'll have to open it to see."

"But Christmas isn't for two more days."

"True, but we leave for my parents' tomorrow morning, and I wanted to give you this before we go."

"I don't mind waiting until we're there. It'll give me something to open that morning."

"You think my mother isn't going to lavish you with gifts? According to Justin, half the gifts beneath my parents' tree have your name on them. He's even lodged his complaint that Honey has more gifts than the rest of us."

"Your mother and my cat have definitely bonded," Julia mused, smiling as she shook the box again. "Okay, if you're sure you want me to open it early, then I will."

"Glad I could twist your arm that way," he teased.

"Hey, I'm not opposed to waiting," she shot back.

Taking his phone out to snap photos while she opened her gift, he motioned for her to proceed. Julia tore into the paper, laughing when, saving the smaller box for last, she pulled out a calendar for the upcoming year. Rather than corny doctor jokes, this one had corny nurse jokes.

Opening it to the first the page, she read, "'Ski with Boone at Friends-mas.'" On January first.

Flipping the page, she laughed when she read, "'Break Val-friend-tine tradition by making out with Boone.'"

In March, he'd written, "Go green with Boone" on the seventeenth and "Give Boone birthday kiss" at the end of March.

But when she read April's message, she glanced up to see he'd propped his phone so it recorded her hands-free, and he'd moved next to the sofa.

"'April showers...'" She turned to the following month. "'...bring May...'" She looked at him in question. "Did you forget to write *flowers*?

Because that's what April showers bring. And if you didn't pencil in any dates for us in April or May, should I be worried?"

Grinning, he knelt next to her and gestured to the smaller package that had been inside the larger box along with the calendar. "You better open your other package before you look at the rest of your year."

Curious, she reached for the smaller package that was of similar size to the previous year's jeweler's box. "Did you get me earrings to go with my necklace?"

The necklace she'd not taken off since he'd put it around her neck on her graduation day.

"Open and see."

She opened the lid and gasped. "Boone?"

His eyes full of everything she could possibly have hoped for, he gestured to her calendar. "Turn the page, Julia."

"My hands may be too shaky," she warned, not quite believing what was happening. She'd known Boone loved her. He showed it to her every day in all he did, but she hadn't dared to let herself dream of what was happening. Or at least, what she thought was happening. Holding her breath, she exchanged May for June. Her vision blurred with tears, but she read, "'Julia marries Boone.'" On the following day, he'd written, "'Julia and Boone live happily ever after.'" And he'd drawn a line indicating it included the rest of the month, then the following, and so on through the end of the calendar.

"I...um...think you're going to have to return this," she managed, staring up into the most beautiful blue eyes she'd ever seen. "Someone's scribbled in it."

"You know how doctors' handwriting can be," he quipped, as he'd done the previous year, then knelt beside her and took her hand. "Will you, Julia?"

"You're sure that's what you want?"

"I'm sure you're what I want, who I want, now and forever. I want the world to know you're mine."

"Hmm, and all this time, I thought it was the other way around, that you were mine," she teased.

Lifting her hand to his lips, he kissed it, then took the ring from the jeweler's box. "Marry me, Julia. Pick whatever day you want. Just pencil me in for every day for the rest of your life."

"Yes." Tears of joy ran down her face. "You know my answer is yes. I adore you and can't imagine life without you."

"Then don't ever," he ordered, sliding the diamond ring onto the fourth finger of her left hand. "Just put me at the top of every page of your Rules for Life Success."

"The way you've put yourself on every page of my calendar?"

His gaze met hers, and he gave her a sheepish grin. "You have to admit it worked out pretty well for me this past year."

"For both of us." She stared at the ring. "I promised to always be honest with you, though, so I have to tell you that I tossed my rule book. I don't need to check items off a list to know I have a successful life, not anymore. As long as I'm clean, helping others, and you keep penciling yourself into my calendar, I know I'm doing something right, and that's all the affirmation I need."

He laced his fingers with hers. "Just wait until you see what I have in mind for next year. Good thing I have a year to figure out if I want to use blue or pink ink."

Filled with a giddiness that surpassed any high she'd ever known, Julia wrapped her arms around his neck. "Why not both? After all, you're a twin, so it's possible."

Not only possible, but Julia and Boone's reality, nine months after they said, "I do." A boy and a girl and their very own happy-ever-after.

* * * * *

MEDICAL

Life and love in the world of modern medicine.

Available Next Month

All titles available in Larger Print

One Month To Tame The Surgeon Carol Marinelli
An American Doctor In Ireland Karin Baine

....

Healing The Baby Doc's Heart Fiona McArthur
Resisting The Off-Limits Paediatrician Kate MacGuire

....

Tempted By The Single Dad Next Door Amy Ruttan
Accidentally Dating His Boss Kristine Lynn

MEDICAL

Life and love in the world
of modern medicine.

MILLS & BOON

Keep reading for an excerpt of a new title
from the Western Romance series,
THE COWGIRL'S HOMECOMING by Jeannie Watt

CHAPTER ONE

"Do you believe bad things happen in threes?" Whitney Fox pulled a rose-pink satin bridesmaid dress out of its packing material and shook out the folds as she spoke. If things did happen in threes, she was afraid of what might happen next.

"Me? Oh, come on." Maddie Kincaid, one of Whit's best friends and the owner of Spurs and Veils Western Bridal Boutique, made a face as she took the dress from Whit and slipped it onto a hanger for steaming. It was mid-May, and the bridal season was ramping up, one reason that Whit had volunteered to help. The other was that she needed to talk to someone other than her dad and job recruiters.

"Thinking that way sets you up for the next bad thing to happen," Maddie added as Whit opened another giant cardboard box, this time to reveal pale blue dresses.

"Fine." Whit started pushing aside thin plastic. "I'm on the cusp of something good. A new beginning."

An unexpected, scary new beginning. One door had slammed shut and now she had to pry another one open. Which door would it be? And how long would it take to find it? Her stomach tightened at the silent questions.

"That's better." Maddie tended to look on the bright side and right now that was exactly what Whit needed. Someone to tell her things would work out, because for the first time since the trauma of losing her mom nine years ago, Whit was floundering.

She needed to come up with Life Plan Number 3, and so far, she had nothing.

Life Plan Number 1, developed during middle school, had been to become independently wealthy, buy the ritzy Hayes Ranch next door to her family ranch, and raise and train champion Quarter Horses there.

That plan had not panned out.

Life Plan Number 2, formulated during high school while her mother had been ill, had been to get a sensible college degree, save money in a sensible manner and work her way into a lucrative, sensible corporate position. Her dream of becoming a horse trainer had been pushed so far aside that she knew it was never going to happen, although she'd never officially broken the news to her friends Kat and Maddie. The three of them had formed their middle school dream pact together, and Kat and Maddie had achieved their dreams. Kat now owned a small farm and Maddie had her bridal shop. Whit did not have her ritzy ranch and horse training facility. Nor did she want it.

The final few years of her mom's life had taught Whit a hard lesson about ranch economics. Medical bills had sapped them during a time of drought and low cattle prices, and while her dad had been able to pull the ranch out of the red eventually, those nip-and-tuck years had convinced Whit that she needed security. Maybe even some luxury. She needed to become a city girl.

Which she had done. Missoula wasn't exactly a megacity, but it was more urban than Larkspur, and she'd landed a well-paying job there, managing regulations and permitting for a renewable energy company. She'd worked long hours and some months spent more time on the road than she did in the office, but the rewards had been worth it—job security, stellar benefits and a healthy paycheck.

Then the axe fell.

Corporate buyouts were rarely good for the employees of the purchased company. Whit's case had been particularly painful—she'd worked her butt off to get the promotion that (a) allowed her to splurge and pay cash for a luxury car—the symbol of her success, and (b) put her in the direct path of the axe. Her job had been meshed with another position that an employee from the purchasing company now filled. The one bright spot was that the yearly lease on her property was close to renewal, thus allowing Whit to move from Missoula back to the home ranch without paying penalties. It was a pretty dim bright spot, but the only one she had.

"You know," Maddie said, as she began running the steamer over the dress, "you can fill in here until you find something."

"Probably best if I don't," Whit replied before pulling a dress out of the box and removing the protective tissue and plastic. "At least not in the front part of the store."

Maddie murmured something that sounded a lot like, "You make a good point," and Whit laughed as she stripped off the last of the tissue from a blue silk slip dress. Maddie was a master at gently directing people to flattering fits and colors. Whit, not so much.

"I'm going to sell my car." She tried to sound matter-of-fact, but it was hard to keep regret from coloring her voice.

"Sorry." Maddie knew how much Whit loved her first major splurge.

Whit and the Audi TT had seen three thousand miles together before she'd received the layoff notification. They'd been good miles, too, but Whit needed to recoup as much money as possible to provide herself with a cushion until Life Plan Number 3 came to fruition. She'd sunk her entire promotion bonus plus a chunk of her savings into the car. It hadn't seemed risky at the time, but now Whit would dearly love to have a do over. She and her coworkers had not seen the buyout coming or she wouldn't have made her splurge. One day, security. The next day, pink slip.

"After you sell the car, then what?"

"I don't know." A difficult admission, but an honest one. Whit felt like next steps should be obvious, as in, get a new job in her field ASAP, but other factors were coming into play. Like a sense of inertia. She felt freaking paralyzed. Why?

Maddie lowered the steamer head and it spit hot water at the floor before she brought it back up to horizontal. "So your entire plan is to sell the car?"

"Sad, huh?" Whit was determined to put on a brave face while she sorted things out. She hated when people worried about her, having had enough of that after her mother died.

"You need time to regroup," Maddie said sympathetically. "Anyone would, given the circumstances. Maybe you can get something temporary here until you find your next real job."

Whit searched her brain. "I can't imagine what that would be, although—" she made a face "—I can play the banjo."

"Not that well."

Whit tossed a wad of plastic at Maddie. "I'm a great banjo player." Her expression sobered. "I'll figure something out."

"I know you will. Just please—no 'Foggy Mountain Breakdown.'"

"But it is foggy in here." Whit, thankful for the change of subject, fanned the moist air, wondering why the old hardwood floorboards weren't warped, considering the amount of steaming that went on over the years as garments were unpacked and hung.

Maddie turned the dress to tackle the back while Whit

unpacked the rest of the shipment. After pulling the last gown out of the box, she smoothed a hand over her hair. The long blond strands that usually behaved nicely were starting to frizz.

"Have you ever watched *The Fog*?" Maddie shot her a frowning look and Whit shrugged. "Just wondering if anything sinister ever appeared out of the swirling mist back here."

"Nothing sinister, unless you count my former business partner." Who'd secretly hooked up with Maddie's now-ex-fiancé. "Steam is great for the skin."

"So that's your secret," Whitney murmured as she retrieved the plastic wad and tossed it into the trash. Maddie did have beautiful skin.

"Lots of steam and the love of a cranky cowboy."

Whit grinned. "I don't find Sean cranky."

"He tries, but yeah, he's missing the mark more and more." Maddie's lips curved into a gentle smile that made Whit want to smile in return. After breaking up with her cheating fiancé, Maddie had found a guy who truly loved her for who she was, and vice versa. Heartwarming, but not what Whit was looking for.

What are you looking for?

Not a man. She was doing fine on her own, thank you very much. But other than that parameter, she felt uncharacteristically lost and she hated it.

Whit busied herself gathering packing materials and stuffing them into the box for recycling while Maddie emptied the steamer tank. She returned to the room and stood a few feet away from the rack, admiring the shiny, smooth rose-pink satin dresses hanging next to pale blue silk gowns. A few bars of the wedding march played in the main part of the shop, indicating that a customer had entered the store, and a familiar voice called, "Where are you guys?"

"Back here," Maddie replied.

A few seconds later Kat, the third member of their decades-long friendship triad, came into the room carrying a box that made suspicious scratching noises.

"Kittens," she said. "They were giving them away at the grocery store, so I took them all."

"As one does," Maddie said.

"I had to. They're very young, and I'm of the opinion that you can't have enough kitties." Kat set down the box and opened the lid. Maddie and Whit both made an automatic "aw" sound as the three little black-and-white kitties inched their way along the cardboard on their bellies.

"I think they need to be bottle-fed for a while," Kat said. "I guess the mama just disappeared."

"I'd take one off your hands, but I don't know what my situation looks like yet," Whit said as Maddie reached in the box to pull out a kitten. Whit did the same, tucking the squirming baby against the warmth of her neck.

"But you have a plan, right?" Kat replied, stroking her kitten's head with a single finger as it lay in her palm.

Whit's stomach tightened again, but thankfully Kat's phone chimed before Whit had to confess that she had no plan at all. "Oops," Kat said while reading the screen. "Troy is ahead of schedule and waiting in the back lot, so I guess I'd better collect my kitties and go."

"What kitties?" Maddie asked innocently, pulling the collar of her blouse over the kitty she held.

"Livia's kitties," Kat replied, Livia being the one-year-old daughter of Troy, Kat's fiancé.

"I will not deprive her," Maddie said with a sigh. She set the kitten back in the box alongside the other two and Kat gently closed the lid.

"I'll be in touch," she said as she lifted the box, holding it in front of her with both hands. "Good luck with the job hunt," she said to Whit. "Keep me posted."

At a tick after six o'clock, Whit and Maddie stepped out of the shop and into the crisp late-spring air. It appeared that everyone from shop employees to the patrons of the nearby bar whose happy hour had just ended were headed to their vehicles at the same time. Doors slammed; engines started.

Whit led the way across the lot to her car. She'd parked the luxurious dark gray vehicle in a far corner to protect it from parking lot dings and dents. She felt a little pang as she beeped the lock open, then gestured to Maddie to climb inside the plush interior.

"It's beautiful," Maddie said, running her hand over the leather console that separated the bucket seats.

"Nicest vehicle I ever owned." Whit buckled in, then pressed the start button and the engine turned over, purring so gently that it was hard to tell that it was running. Soon she'd be driving the Corolla again, a car so old that she'd parked it on the ranch rather than trade it in for the negligible amount it would have brought.

Thank goodness she had.

A line of vehicles had formed at the parking lot exit and Whit nosed her car in behind a Corolla similar to the one she'd be driving in the future, moving forward a few feet at a time as the vehicles ahead of her waited for breaks in the traffic. When her turn came, a long open stretch appeared and she swung out into her lane, glad to have made a quick escape. She glanced in her rearview mirror and saw a big truck follow her out, its grill just a little too close for comfort.

"Look out!" Maddie cried, and Whit jammed on the brakes, barely missing the dog that had darted in front of her. Less than a second later a crash from the rear snapped her head forward and then back, rattling her brain, but thankfully not deploying the airbag.

She shot a dazed look at Maddie, and then they twisted in their seats to stare out the back window.

"Son of a—" Whit wrenched her door open and stepped onto the pavement. She ignored the passersby approaching from various directions as she strode to the rear of her car. Her bumper and one taillight had been smashed, and there was a big crease in the trunk.

"No, no, no," she muttered, taking in the damage and trying to calculate the impact this would have on her already limited plan. Of course the truck had a deer guard on the front, and the damage to it was negligible.

"Why did you stop so fast?" a deep voice growled from behind her.

She turned to find a tall guy in a cowboy hat staring at her with an outraged look on his face. She was having none of it. She drew in a breath and fired back.

"What were you thinking riding my bumper like that?" The words were barely out of her mouth when recognition struck.

Tanner Hayes. It'd been years since she'd seen the man, but there was no mistaking those chiseled features when he tipped his hat back. He, in turn, gave her the once-over, looking like he couldn't quite place her.

"Whitney Fox," she said drily. "Your neighbor."

"I know who you are."

Maddie cleared her throat and they both turned to look at her. "I'll see if anyone saw anything." She spoke to Whit, pointedly ignoring Tanner.

"Please do," Whit said in a grim voice. She turned back to the man, thinking that her one saving grace was that the Hayes family was swimming in money, so he should have no problem handling the repairs.

But repairs took time and would bring down the resale value of her car. The only concrete part of her plan had just taken a massive blow.

"This is your fault." They needed to get that much straight here and now. Whit gestured at the damage. "You hit me."

"You stopped dead in the middle of a turn." His voice was low and not one bit apologetic.

"Because I didn't want to hurt a dog."

"I didn't see a dog," Tanner said stubbornly.

"Well, a dog ran out in the road in front of me. Anyway, it doesn't matter," Whit replied. "You rear-ended me. The law is on my side."

"Not necessarily."

Whit propped her hands on her hips, noting that a crowd was edging in. Fine. Maybe public shame would do some good.

"Right. Because if you're the guy with the money, then the law tends to be on your side."

"Now wait a minute."

"All I'm saying—" she poked a finger at his chest "—is that you're not buying your way out of this like your dad bought his way out of everything."

His expression went stony, which meant that she'd struck a nerve. Good. She wanted to strike more than a nerve but had to make do with what was legal and available.

"Don't bring my father into this."

Whit felt a small wave of shame. Tanner's father had recently passed away, but the man had never been close to anyone, not even his two sons, who'd left home before

Whit was out of high school. But, yeah, she shouldn't have brought his dead father into this.

She lifted her chin, but didn't mutter the apology that teetered on her lips. Something told her not to and she listened. "All I'm saying is that, often, in cases like this, money talks."

Her head came up as the deputy sheriff's vehicle turned onto the street and parked opposite. Bill Monroe got out of the cruiser and crossed the street. He looked over the damage as he approached, giving a low whistle, then he tilted his hat back as he recognized Tanner.

"Hey, Tanner. It's been some time. Some homecoming."

"It was his fault," Whit said stonily.

"That remains to be seen," Tanner said.

The deputy propped his hands on his hips. "That's for me to decide."

Whit rolled her eyes. Bill and Tanner were old high school buddies, but she knew she was in the right here. "I stopped to avoid a dog. He—" she pointed at Tanner "—was following too closely and smacked me from the rear, and I want that in your report."

Maddie appeared out of nowhere to touch her arm and Whit gave her friend a quick look. Fine. She would allow law enforcement to do their job.

She stepped back and watched as Bill commenced taking measurements and speaking to people who'd witnessed the accident. She gritted her teeth as Bill noted various conflicting eyewitness accounts in his book.

Yes, there had been a dog...

No, Tanner hadn't been following too closely. She'd stopped too abruptly...

Yes, he was too close. She'd done the only thing she could...

They were both at fault...

Neither was at fault...

And all the while this was going on, Tanner stood silently watching the proceedings like the heir to a throne would do—the throne being a sprawling ranch in this case—confident that things would work out in his favor.

And they probably would.

Once Bill had gathered his information and allowed them to move their vehicles, Tanner jerked his head to the side of the street, as if he expected Whit to follow. She frowned at him, and he exhaled and decided to speak where he stood.

"This was unfortunate, but insurance will cover it, and your car will be as good as new—regardless of whose fault it is."

"No," she said grimly. "It won't be as good as new. Its value has now decreased. Some of us don't have the ability to buy a new car on a whim."

"And you think I do?"

Whit sensed Maddie moving beside her, as if trying to signal to her that it was time to drop the matter and leave. Normally, Whit would have done that. She would have taken the hit in stride and moved on. But these weren't normal circumstances. Her vehicle was now worth less than it had been a few minutes ago, through no fault of her own. And the Hayes family had always rubbed her—and most of the community—the wrong way. But money talked and the townspeople listened, regardless of their feelings.

Tanner was watching her, waiting for a reply to his question, which Whit had no intention of giving. It appeared that he had no intention of speaking, either. In the end, Whit was the first to blink.

"I think that when you grow up wanting for nothing, it twists your sense of reality," she said tightly. His mouth went even flatter than it had been before. The crowd that had gathered on the sidewalk was still good-sized, probably because most were patrons from the nearby pub who'd come out to see what the ruckus was about.

And who didn't want to watch a fiery verbal face-off between two people who'd just been involved in a collision?

Maddie gave Whit's arm a yank, and as she gave in and allowed her friend to steer her to the car, she was surprised to find herself guided to the passenger side.

"I'm driving," Maddie said in a no-nonsense voice. "You've had a shock. You can take over after you drop me at my place."

"Fine," Whit muttered, opening the door and getting in without a backward glance—although that part was hard.

Maddie adjusted the mirror and then pulled away before Tanner did. Whit sat back in the ridiculously comfortable seat. "Guess it'll be a minute before I sell my car."

"But you will."

Spoken like the positive-thinking soul her friend was.

"Whose fault was it, Maddie?" Bill had taken witness statements, but so had Maddie in an informal way.

"He was too close behind, but you stopped abruptly. He probably would have hit you even if he'd been farther behind." Maddie stopped at the light. "It was the dog's fault, actually. And whoever allowed him to run."

Whit leaned her head against the window. Her friend was right. It was done, and now it was a matter of mitigating damages, not flinging blame. The blame-flinging had made her feel good in the moment, but it wasn't going to fix her car. It was annoying that she was going to struggle after this, and Tanner Hayes would throw money at the problem and it would, no doubt, go away.

OUT NEXT MONTH!

No.1 *New York Times* bestselling author Linda Lael Miller
welcomes you back to Mustang Creek, Wyoming,
home of hot cowboys and the smart, beautiful women
who love them.

Book three in The Carsons Of Mustang Creek series.

'Linda Lael Miller creates vibrant characters and
stories I defy you to forget.' — Debbie Macomber,
No.1 *New York Times* bestselling author

In-store and online February 2024.

MILLS & BOON

Want to know more about your favourite series or discover a new one?

Experience the variety of romance that Mills & Boon has to offer at our website:

millsandboon.com.au

Shop all of our categories and discover the one that's right for you.

MODERN

DESIRE

MEDICAL

INTRIGUE

ROMANTIC SUSPENSE

WESTERN

HISTORICAL

FOREVER
EBOOK ONLY

HEART
EBOOK ONLY

f @millsandboonaustralia **𝕏** **◎** @millsandboonaus